GIRL IN TROUBLE

AN ALEX MERCER THRILLER

Stacy Claflin

www.stacyclaflin.com

Down

One Year Ago

THE RICKETY WOODEN BOAT swayed slightly as the tall man sat, clutching the edge. He watched as the girl's body sank lower and lower until it was completely underwater and out of sight.

She hadn't been the one.

He'd been sure she was, but once again, he'd been proven wrong.

He waited until the bubbles stopped.

It was over.

Until next year.

Then it would be time to find the next girl. Would *she* finally be the one?

He grew tired. Exhausted, really. Not enough to stop his search, though. He *needed* to right the wrong from so many years ago.

Next year would be thirty years.

Thirty.

That was a big anniversary.

Perhaps next year's girl would be the one he'd waited so long for. Year thirty could be when he finally received his big payoff. He was starting to get too old for this. His shoulder ached.

Everything would be made right.

Next year *would* be his year.

All he needed was just a little patience.

He had a full year to plan everything out.

The tall man glanced back out at the still lake.

Another lake, another girl, another year.

When would all this finally end? Would everything finally be as it should?

Next year. It had to be next year. No, it *would* be.

He grabbed the oars and rowed back to the shore, already making plans for next Halloween.

Bar

~

Current Day

A LEX MERCER GLANCED around the bar.

His head pounded—not from drinks, but from another tedious day of futility. He tried to convince himself he was doing some good by fixing people's roofs, but inside he knew his life was going nowhere.

"Want more?"

Alex pushed the glass toward Cole with a grunt, wondering what made him more of a loser—his dead-end job or the bartender being his only friend?

Cole filled the glass and leaned against the counter. "I was thinking about decorating for Halloween. Think I should bother? It's less than a week away."

Blood drained from Alex's body.

Halloween.

He licked his lips and found his voice. "Less than a week away?"

Cole glanced at his phone. "Yeah. You okay, Alex?"

Alex ran his hands through his short hair, loose dirt falling to the bar top in front of him.

He hadn't missed the most important day of the month, had he?

Alex swore under his breath. "It's tonight. Tonight, and I

almost forgot."

"You got a date?" Cole arched an eyebrow.

"Me? You know I swore off women."

"Yeah, but that can't last long." Cole greeted another customer then turned back to Alex. "What's tonight?"

Alex's body pulsed and his head pounded.

"My daughter's Halloween party. It's more important to her than Christmas or her birthday combined." He finished his drink with a swallow and scattered some bills on the counter. "I gotta go. I'm barely gonna make it with rush hour traffic."

Cole's mouth gaped.

"What?" Alex jumped from the stool, nearly knocking it over.

"You have a *daughter*?"

"It's a long story, and I don't have time. But I can't show up like this." He glanced down at his filthy clothes, nose curling from the stench of alcohol.

Ariana was lucky Alex had given her up for adoption the day she was born. Giving the girl a decent chance at a good life was probably the only virtuous thing he'd ever done.

Cole shook his head. "I can't believe you're a dad."

"Barely." He only made a few appearances a year.

"Tell me more."

Even clipped it could take all day. "Sure. Later."

"How old is she?"

Alex's blushing cheeks were buried behind his shaggy beard. "Eleven."

Cole choked. "Aren't you only twenty-five?"

"Yeah. Like I said, long story." Alex grabbed his coat from a hook, hurried outside before his friend could ask any more unwanted questions, and tripped over a homeless man staining the outside stoop.

"Got any cash?" The old man was caked in dirt and what was probably dried blood. He had at least four missing teeth.

Alex opened his mouth, paused, then dug into his pocket and handed the man a ten.

He snatched the bill, his face turning bright. "Thanks."

"No problem." Alex jogged over to his beat-up, ancient gold Tercel and raced home to his tiny one-bedroom apartment and the stench of something rotten.

He sniffed, not quite placing the smell. Maybe he'd forgotten to take the trash out again. It didn't matter. He needed to clean up and pull something together for Ariana's party. He stepped into the living room and tripped over his coil nailer.

"That's where my nail gun went," he muttered. He'd been looking for that when installing the roof at his job site.

Alex peeled off his work clothes and left them in a pile on the floor, then he jumped in the shower and quickly trimmed his beard. Zoey would probably still criticize it, but he didn't care. He wasn't there to impress her. This was all about Ariana and the fact that she'd be crushed if he didn't show. She was the one person who actually held him in high regard—for however long that would last. Eventually, she too would see what a screw-up he really was.

With a towel around his waist, he dug through his closet, looking for something that would work as a costume. Finally, he settled on tattered black jeans—those were easy enough to come by—along with a white shirt and a red bandanna to wrap around his head. Now he was a pirate. Sort of. He found a vest and pulled on some brown work boots. That would have to do.

He checked the time. With traffic, he'd be a little late, but at least he'd be there.

As he got back into his beater, his phone buzzed with a new text.

It was from Zoey.

You're coming, right?

Alex groaned. "Thanks for the vote of confidence." He could always count on his ex-girlfriend to boost his morale.

Wouldn't miss it.

Good.

Alex held back an eye roll and didn't respond to her last text. He started the car and braced himself for the traffic. It was usually an hour drive, but it might take two—and he would definitely be late. Maybe he could slip in, unnoticed. Ariana's parties seemed to get bigger each year.

He coasted along the I-5 corridor at twenty miles an hour heading south toward Seattle, though he'd have to drive farther. His mind wandered to everyone he would see at the party. Zoey, of course. Her parents were raising his and Zoey's daughter as their own, though Ariana knew and understood they were actually her grandparents.

His parents would be there. They still lived next door to Zoey's parents. Ariana had always visited them regularly, and they were always first choice as babysitters.

Alex's heart constricted. Part of him wished he could be more of a part in her life, but it was better this way. He really had nothing to offer to her. He just worked, went to the bar, and slept. Rinse and repeat every single day, except Sundays when he slept all morning and watched sports in the afternoon.

He turned up the music and sang along with the song so he wouldn't have to think.

Finally, he pulled into the neighborhood he grew up in. His old street was filled with cars and nearly every house had spooky decorations.

Alex pulled into his parents' driveway and stared at the tri-level he'd grown up in.

His stomach twisted into tight knots.

Party

~

ALEX GOT OUT of the car and looked next door at Zoey's parents' house. It was the most decorated home in the neighborhood. He could hear festive music playing from speakers in a tree.

Clementine, his parents' orange tabby, walked up to him and rubbed against him. Alex kneeled and ran his hand along the cat's back and relaxed somewhat.

He rose and cut through his yard to the house that had been his second home growing up. He tried to distract himself with the yard decorations. Playful skeletons pulled at each other in a wagon. Ghosts danced around a tree. Smiling pumpkins lined the walkway. Giant bats and spiders hung from the house.

It was all cute, and he could see Ariana's touch behind it all. The girl spent the entire year planning her Halloween party, and she always made sure to turn it into the event of the year, with each celebration outdoing the last.

Alex stopped in front of the door, pausing for a moment. For so many years, running in uninvited had been the natural thing to do. He and Zoey had continued dating for years after Ariana's birth. But that had been so long ago.

He took a deep breath and knocked. Playful Halloween music played inside over the sounds of kids giggling and shrieking.

The door opened. Ariana stood there, wearing a costume that looked like a cross between a witch and fairy. Ari's dark brown hair now went halfway down her back, and she'd grown at least a few inches—she already looked like she could be thirteen. How could she have grown up so much in the last few months since her birthday party?

Her gorgeous brown eyes widened and her entire face lit up. "Dad!" She wrapped her arms around him, squeezing him so tightly that he couldn't breathe.

He flinched as he always did at the word 'dad' and awkwardly put his arms around her, patting her back.

Ariana stepped back and looked him over. "I love your pirate costume! I almost went with pirate this year, but I think I'm going to do that next year. Do you like my outfit?" She spun around.

Alex's breath caught. She was so beautiful. "I love it."

She stopped and smiled, her eyes shining with excitement. "Do you know what I am?"

"Either a witch or a fairy?" he guessed.

Ariana squealed. "You figured it out! I'm a fairy-witch." She grabbed his hand and pulled him inside. "Mimi! Papi! Dad is here!" Ariana called her grandparents 'Mimi and Papi' and she called Zoey and Alex 'Mom and Dad.' It was how she'd always differentiated her adoptive parents from her birth parents.

Alex took in the scene before him. Aside from the loud, spooky music and kids running around, fake cobwebs hung from everything, even the furniture. More bats and spiders decorated the walls, and every portrait now had a witch hat added. The tables all had black coverings with skeleton decorations. Festive treats lay everywhere for the taking.

Valerie and Kenji Nakano, Zoey's parents, came over to them. Kenji was dressed as a baseball player—hardly a costume since he'd been a professional in Japan when Zoey was growing up. Valerie wore a wedding dress covered in fake blood.

Kenji greeted Alex with a wide smile and a firm handshake. Valerie barely nodded an acknowledgment. She hadn't liked him since he and Zoey had broken up. Mother and daughter despised him equally.

But the joke was on them. No one could hate Alex more for what he'd done than he hated himself. Not that he would admit that to anyone else. The regret followed him around like a shadow, choking him when he gave it too much thought.

Ariana dragged Alex away, showing him off to all her friends. She introduced him to the ones he'd never met. Then she stopped for a skeleton cookie and handed a bat-shaped one to him. "Want to see my room?"

"I've seen it." He bit into the cookie, glancing around for Zoey. She had to be avoiding him.

"No, I'm in Mom's old room now. We totally redecorated it after my birthday. Please. I want to show you." Ariana's eyes grew wide and she folded her hands together. "Please."

How could he say no to that?

He smiled. "Let's see it."

She squealed and her grip around his hand tightened. "Come on."

Alex followed her up the familiar stairs and into Zoey's old room. His heart pounded against his chest as a flood of long-gone happy memories flooded his mind.

"What do you think?"

Ariana's voice broke through his thoughts. Alex blinked a few times and focused on the very pink room. Pale blush walls matched the bedding and upholstered furniture. Dark rose pillows accentuated the light shades of paint and fabric. It seemed so much more mature than her old room filled with cartoon characters.

"So grownup," he whispered.

"I know! Oh, and look at this." Ariana let go of his hand and ran over to the bed. She picked up a framed picture from the nightstand and showed him.

It was a picture of him and Zoey from the night of Zoey's

senior prom. She wore a beautiful teal dress, and Alex had on a tux. They looked so happy. They *had* been so happy.

Ariana held the frame close and closed her eyes. "I love this picture so much. I even remember that night, but Mimi says that's impossible. You came over and gave Mom the flower on her dress. Nobody told me that. I *remember.*"

"I believe you."

Her grin widened big enough to light up the room. She twirled a strand of her rich, dark brown hair around a finger. "You do?"

Alex gave a slight nod. "You were wearing pink pajamas with kittens dancing in the snow. You said we looked like a prince and princess going to a royal ball."

Ariana's mouth gaped.

He tapped her button nose. "I think you really believed we were."

She set the frame on her bed and squeezed his middle again. "I wish you lived closer."

"Me, too." And he actually meant that—for the moment, at least.

"Ariana? Are you up here?" came Zoey's voice from the hallway.

Before he had time to react, Zoey came into the room. She was dressed as a pirate also, but she had gone all-out with hers. Compared to Zoey, his felt especially thrown together.

Their gazes locked. He studied her dark eyes. They were the same as they'd been for as long as he'd known her—as far as he could remember. Having messed up with the two people in this room was his biggest regret.

Ariana released her hold on Alex. "I was showing Dad my new room!"

Zoey's expression stiffened. "It's hardly new. You moved in here on your birthday." She threw a glare at Alex.

He turned away, unable to take the guilt and regret.

"Well, it's new to him." Ariana bounced toward the door. "Let's go downstairs. Time to bob for apples! Wanna go first, Dad?" She batted her eyes at him.

"Yeah." Zoey's brows came together. "Want to go first?" Though her expression seethed anger, he knew her well enough to see the hurt beneath it all.

He turned to Ariana. "If you want me to."

"Yay!" She spun around and bounded down the stairs, skipping every other step.

"Nice of you to show up," Zoey muttered.

"I know what it means to her."

"At least you care about *someone* other than yourself."

Alex bit back a retort and recovered quickly. "How's your boyfriend?"

Zoey held up her left hand and showed him an engagement ring with a diamond the size of an iceberg. "Kellen proposed."

He nearly choked. "You're getting married?"

"Next summer." She stared at him, her glare icier than ever.

The room spun around him.

It was official now. He'd lost Zoey forever.

Games

A LEX STOOD IN front of the bucket of apples floating in water. Kids chanted for him to bob for one. His parents and sister clapped, urging him on. Zoey glared at him, leaning against her blond-haired, blue-eyed, golden boy fiancé.

He focused on Ariana, who was jumping up and down. "Do it, Dad!"

Only for her. Alex took a deep breath and bent down. He tried to bite into an apple without getting his face wet, but it didn't work. He tried again, just as unsuccessfully. The story of his life.

The shrieks of the kids all around grew louder. Children pressed against him, calling out his name.

Alex shoved his face into the water and pressed an apple against the wall of the bucket. Water stung his nose as he breathed in. He grimaced, but managed to dig his teeth into the fruit. Once he had a solid hold on it, he stood up straight. Water dripped down his face onto his shirt and vest.

Kids and adults alike cheered for him. Ariana threw her arms around him and stared at him like he was a hero. "I knew you could do it."

He pulled the apple from his mouth and put his arm around her shoulders. "Thanks, kiddo. I think you can, too."

She laughed and bent over, getting an apple on the first try. She'd probably spent all year practicing. She stood tall and bowed dramatically a couple times. Everyone clapped and cheered for her.

Ariana took the apple from her mouth and tapped one of her friends. "You're next, Em."

Alex stepped back and found he enjoyed watching Ariana with her friends as they played the game.

Someone cleared her throat next to him. Alex turned to see Zoey. She rubbed her finger just beneath her nose. He arched a brow. She rubbed her finger again.

He ran his finger under his nose and felt something wet. Some snot had fallen onto his face after getting water up his nose.

"Thanks." He grabbed a napkin and wiped it off.

Zoey shrugged. "Thought you'd want to know."

A hand rested on his shoulder. Alex turned to see Macy. He and his sister had grown so close in their teen years after she'd been kidnapped, but now they hardly talked.

She smiled, her eyes kind and concerned. "How are you, Alex?"

Guilt ravaged him. He shouldn't have pulled away from her. Not after everything she'd been through. He shrugged. "Gettin' by. How are you and Luke?"

The skin around her eyes crinkled as she broke into a grin. "I got a job at a clinic. I'm finally going to be a child psychologist."

He looked away and studied a jack-o-lantern. "Sorry I missed your graduation. I…" There was no excuse for it. He'd been drunk and forgotten. "I'm a jerk."

"You're busy, I know. It's okay."

Alex turned to her. "No, it's not. I should've been there."

"Don't worry about it. You'll make our baby shower, right?"

His eyes nearly popped out of his head. "What? You're pregnant?"

She laughed and ran her hands through her shoulder-length brown hair. "Not yet, but we're going to try soon. I just wanted to give you some notice," she teased.

Luke came over to them and gave Alex a fist bump. His hair

was almost as long as Macy's.

They made small talk until the game of bobbing for apples was over. Ariana led the kids over to another wall for a round of pin the head on the skeleton.

Alex snuck away from his sister and brother-in-law and headed for the main snack table. He grabbed a sandwich that looked like a mummy and poured some punch.

"That's non-alcoholic, you know." Zoey took a zombie-shaped cookie and smirked. Her unspoken words rang louder than the ones she actually said. *Unlike him.*

He shrugged and turned his attention to Ariana, who was posing for pictures with her friends.

"When are you going to pull yourself together?"

Alex ignored the question. He hated that she thought so poorly of him.

"You're twenty-five. It's time to start acting like an adult."

He turned to her and narrowed his eyes. "Stop."

She flinched.

"I can't change the past, but you can stop with the holier-than-thou routine. Maybe it's time we both grew up."

Zoey's mouth dropped. "I—"

"Don't. Ariana pretends not to notice your cutting remarks, but how do you think it makes her feel?"

Her mouth formed a straight line. "I'd know better than you. I have plenty of experience with an absent father. She and I have far more in common than you'd think."

"Except that she doesn't resent me like you did Kenji."

"Maybe she should."

Alex took a deep breath and exhaled slowly, counting to ten forwards and then backwards. "Congratulations on your engagement, Zo. I hope you're very happy." He spun around and wove his way through the room to get as far from her as possible.

The kids were now all barefoot and playing a game that looked like spin the bottle with nail polish. A girl dressed as a zombie spun the bottle. It stopped and pointed to bright pink nail polish. She squealed, grabbed it, and painted a nail. Another girl spun the bottle, her eyes wide with anticipation.

"Alex."

He stopped and turned around. "Mom."

She pulled some long, now-auburn hair behind an ear and smiled. "It's so good to see you. I thought you were avoiding me."

More guilt. He scuffed his shoe along the floor and played with his bandanna. "It's not like that. I'm just so busy with work and then I'm exhausted when I get home. These bags under my eyes—they're not Halloween makeup."

His mom frowned. "Why don't you stay with us, hon? You could get a job with better hours, and you know your room is always here for you, right?"

Alex sighed. "I know, but I don't wanna bum off you guys. You and Dad raised me to be independent and take care of myself. That's what I'm doing."

"We don't mind helping you out, either."

Great, pity.

"You heard that Dad's book hit the New York Times bestseller list, didn't you?"

He gave her a double-take. "It did?"

Mom nodded, beaming. "Several weeks in a row. It hit some other big lists, too. You wouldn't believe how much it's bringing in. He's worked so hard, and now it's all paying off."

"That's amazing—it really is. I mean, it all started with his little blog that we all thought was more important than us."

She nodded. "Oh, I know it."

"And what about you?"

"I'm having a blast with my little hair studio. I take clients a few days a week, and the other days, I either help Dad with his stuff or we relax together. Macy and Luke stop by a couple times a week for dinner. It'd be great if you did, too. The door's always open. I know Ari would love to see you more, as well."

No one could quite do guilt trips like his mom. "I'll see what I can do."

He glanced at the clock, eager to get back to his crappy life.

Hope

~

ARIANA NAKANO PUT the last of the purple nail polish on her pinky toe and glanced around. The party had gone perfectly—just as she'd imagined and planned. The notebook she'd been filling in all year had been so worth it. Everything was just like she'd hoped.

The best part was that her dad had come. She only got to see him a few times a year, and she'd really been hoping he would make it tonight. She sighed happily and twisted the lid back on the nail polish.

Her friends' parents were already arriving to pick them up. She couldn't wait until they all got a little older and her parties could go later. They'd be teenagers in two years. Her parents always said a couple years would go by fast, but to Ari, it may as well have been a hundred years. It felt so far away.

Emily ran over to Ariana. "Another great party, girly! I gotta go. Mom's whining that my brother needs to get to bed."

Ari hugged her friend. "We'll do a sleepover soon."

"Oh-em-gee. Totally!"

The two girls squealed and hugged again.

"Come on, Em," called Emily's mom.

Emily groaned. "I'll text you later."

"Can't wait." Ari leaned closer and whispered, "Can you believe Joshua came?"

"What do you think I want to text you about?"

They both giggled and Emily's mom called for her again.

Ariana turned to some other friends to say goodbye. She was thrilled the party had been so much fun, but bummed about it having to end. Maybe next year, she'd have to turn it into a sleepover. It would take a lot of convincing, so she'd have to start working on her begging speech to her parents the next day. Maybe later after texting with Emily.

She glanced around the room, trying to figure out who was leaving next.

Dad was putting on his coat.

Her heart sank and crashed onto the floor.

Ariana had hardly gotten to spend any time with him. She would have to think fast to find a way to talk him into staying longer—especially with the way Mom kept arguing with him.

Ari ran over to Dad and grabbed his hand. "Let me show you the rest of my room."

He smiled at her—oh, how she adored that grin—and patted her head. "You already showed me, remember?" He glanced over at Mom. Obviously, he was worried about her harping on him. She was good at that.

Ariana frowned. She'd need a new plan, and fast. "I can show you some of the decorations you didn't see yet. Did you see the bathroom?"

Dad's grin widened. "I did. How'd you make the ghost jump out like that?"

"I'll show you. It took forever! I found this really cool trick online."

He gave her a sad look. "I really should get going. Work in the morning."

Tears threatened. Ariana blinked them back and swallowed. "Please, Dad. Please just stay a little longer." She gave him her most pitiful expression—the one that even worked on Mimi if used at the right time.

Dad flinched. "Oh, Ari."

Excitement ran through her. She was making progress.

"I *never* get to see you. Can't you stay a little longer? I don't want to wait for Christmas."

He opened his mouth, but didn't say anything.

"Please." She squeezed his hand with both of hers and stared into his eyes.

Mom came over. "Don't bother him, Ari. I'll help you and Mimi clean things up."

Ariana refused to take her gaze from Dad. She shook her head.

"I do have a long drive," Dad said.

She glared at Mom. Why did she have to interfere?

"Don't look at me like that."

Ari turned back to Dad. It was Mom that he wanted to get away from. "Let's go somewhere, Dad. Just you and me. It'll be fun."

"But the party cleanup," Mom said.

"I have all weekend." Ariana squeezed Dad's hand all the more. "Come on, Dad. Please. I know the perfect place."

He arched a brow. "Where?"

"The Ball Palace."

"Never heard of it."

He hadn't? She jumped up and down, still clinging to him. "You'll love it. They turned a huge building into a big ball pit. It has tons and tons of slides—giant ones—and you can joust and play all kinds of games. I've been begging to go there, but never have."

"I... Don't you have to be in bed soon?"

"No! It's Friday. *Please.*" She let go of his hand and wrapped her arms around him. "You'll have fun. I promise. All my friends' dads love it. I swear."

"Oh, all right. If it gets too late, I can use one of my sick days tomorrow."

Ari's mouth dropped. Yes? He'd actually said yes? She jumped up and down. "Let's go!"

Mom stepped back with her arms folded. She had a disapproving look on her face.

Nothing was going to sour Ari's mood. She and Dad were going to the ball place together. She scrambled for the coat closet and pulled out her favorite jacket.

"Maybe you should change first," Dad said.

Ariana glanced down at her fairy witch costume. If she ran to her room for regular clothes, that would only give him time to think up a reason not to go. "I don't care."

"Nobody else will be dressed for Halloween. I'm going to take off my bandanna and vest, too."

"You'll wait while I change?"

"I won't move from this spot." His expression told her he meant it.

Ariana scrambled up the stairs, pulling off her wings as she ran. In her room, she threw off the wings and grabbed the clothes she'd worn to school that day. No, she didn't want to wear them. She just put some leggings under the dress since they'd be running around. There was no time to think. She had to get downstairs before Dad changed his mind.

She glanced in the mirror. Her face was still covered in makeup and her hair was full of glitter. Not that she cared. She and Dad were going to the Ball Palace!

When she got downstairs, Dad was talking with Uncle Luke.

Dad tilted his head. "Don't want to wash your face?"

"Nope." Ari slid on her jacket. "Kids go there with their faces painted all the time. Let's go."

"Have fun, kiddo." Uncle Luke patted her shoulder.

She glanced up at Dad and beamed. "I will."

Mimi came over and looked at Alex. "Do you know when you'll bring her back?"

He glanced at Ari. "I was going to leave that up to her."

Ari's mouth gaped. She'd stay there with him all weekend if he'd let her.

"Just give us a call if it gets late." Mimi hugged Ariana.

She returned the embrace. "Bye!"

Dad ruffled her hair. "You ready?"

"Am I ever!" She grabbed his hand just to make sure it was really happening.

Palace

~

ARIANA'S HEART THUNDERED against her chest as she and Dad walked up to the Ball Palace. Shouts and music sounded from the wide-open front doors. Bright lights lit up the path, almost making it feel like daytime.

"It definitely sounds like people are having fun in there," Dad said.

"Wait until you see the inside."

He arched a brow. "I thought you hadn't been in there before."

"I haven't, but I've seen a ton of pictures, so I know it's the most amazing thing in the whole town."

They walked in through the huge double doors. Video games sounded from an arcade just on their right. Just behind that, lights flashed from a room filled with games Ariana had seen at the county fair. The enormous ball area lay on their left. From her view, it looked bigger than her entire school. Twisty, bumpy slides ran as far as the eye could see.

She grabbed Dad's hand, determined never to let go. At least not until she picked up a jousting stick.

He led her to the line. When they reached the front, the man behind the counter flicked a nod at Ariana. "How old is she?"

"Eleven," Ariana said, grinning. She loved being a pre-teen now.

The guy looked at dad. "Twenty-five bucks for you two. You

can buy tokens for the games by the concession stand."

"Okay." Dad pulled out his wallet and handed the man some cash.

They walked past the counter and looked around.

"What do you want to do first?" Dad asked.

"The balls!" She grabbed his arm and pulled him into the giant room. Kids ran around and shrieked with laughter. Ariana recognized some kids from school, mostly older kids at this hour. A boy ran by them, carrying an armload of tickets.

Dad gave him a double-take. "He must have been playing all night to get those."

"Guess we'll have to find out." Ariana grinned.

"I'd like that." He smiled, seeming more relaxed than he'd been at the party. "Wow, there's so much to do. I can't wait to try that long, twisty slide."

"I know! Oh, wait." She pulled her phone out from her inner coat pocket.

"Need to call the president?" Dad teased.

She laughed. "No, it's my game. Have you heard of Halloween Catch?"

He shook his head.

"Oh, it's so much fun. All month long, you can capture Halloween items. There are different ones in different places. Fun places like this sometimes have rare items." She slid her finger around the screen and held the phone up, scanning the room. The screen showed the ball pit, but also some digitized Halloween items.

She tapped one on the screen. "Got a bat with red eyes! That's new. Oh, and there's a zombie leg."

Dad chuckled, seeming amused. "Is this why you really brought me here?"

Ari's eyes widened. "No." She captured a goblin and then put her phone away. "I just remembered. Let's play tag." She tapped his shoulder. "You're it!" She ran toward a long, twisty tube slide. Her feet sank down into the balls. They went to her knees—it was seriously the best place ever.

He caught up easily, having much longer legs. Dad reached for her, but missed—probably on purpose. Adults always did that.

She wasn't going to argue this time. It only took a minute to adjust to running in the ball pit. The slide she had her focus on was almost within reach. She laughed as it neared. Then she jumped onto the wooden platform and threw herself down, head first. She screamed—the slide took her down and around at a higher speed than expected. Without warning, she was thrown into a huge ball pit. She landed on her butt, and the balls went up to her chin.

Dad flew out of the slide, flying past her and spraying balls all around her.

Laughing, Ariana rushed to her feet and jumped away from him. He reached for her again, but missed. She was sure that wasn't a pity miss that time. He struggled to his feet, but she was already running.

Ari headed for some foam pads and climbed up. She had to balance on a beam about five feet above the balls below. Dad was already climbing up, not far behind. She stretched her arms out and hurried, knowing he was probably better at balancing since he spent his time on roofs. He was probably the best balancer in the world.

She was almost to the end. Then she would just have to climb up another platform and she would have her choice of slides. They all went in different directions. If she could trick Dad into thinking she went into a different one, she would gain a better lead.

"I'm almost to you," Dad called from behind.

Ari didn't doubt that. She glanced back, and sure enough, he was almost close enough to tag her. She hurried, but her right foot caught on her ankle.

"Whoa!" She overcompensated and tumbled down toward the balls, landing easily. Plastic balls shot out in every direction and then rained down on her.

Laughing, she tried to find the ground, but couldn't. She was going to have to 'swim' through them to reach the platform.

"Ready or not, here I come!" Dad squatted and then jumped.

Ariana squealed and tried unsuccessfully to run. Dad landed near her, sending a geyser of balls flying out everywhere. Laughing, he threw himself down right next to her.

She gasped for breath and landed next to him, putting an arm around him. He wrapped both arms around her and squeezed. "You know, I honestly don't think I've ever had more fun in my life."

Her heart nearly exploded in her chest. "Really?"

"I mean it."

Ari leaned her head against his shoulder. "Me, too."

Dad stroked her hair for a moment.

Her whole life was completely perfect. She had Dad to herself, she was finally at the Ball Palace, and her party had been awesome. The only thing she could possibly ask for would be for him to live closer so she could see him more. But she had this perfect moment, and she wasn't going to let anything ruin it.

He gasped for air. "Are you as tired as me?"

"Nope." She giggled.

Dad kissed the top of her head. "That's good. Do you know why?"

"Why?"

"Because I still have to tag you."

She shrieked and scrambled away. He laughed and chased after her, having the advantage of being able to touch the floor. She barely made it to the platform before he could tag her. Ari climbed up, her eyes focused on a wobbly bridge up ahead. At least it had rails so she wouldn't have to worry about falling—just remaining steady.

Dad teased and taunted her, nearly tagging her. Finally, she reached the bridge. She clung to the sides and ran, barely able to stand up as the bridge swayed back and forth while twisting.

Luckily, he seemed to have just as hard of a time with it as she did. Finally, she made it to the end. The high platform went in four different directions. She headed to the right and found herself at the top of a line of five tall, steep slides that had big bumps going all the way down.

Just as she sat down at the top of one of the middle ones, Dad plopped himself next to her and winked. She pushed herself and went flying down. Dad caught up in just a moment, and they went down together. He could have easily reached over and tagged her, but he didn't.

They landed in another pool of plastic balls. He reached down and pulled a bunch into his arms. "Maybe we should play tag with balls. If I hit you, you're it."

Ariana gasped in protest. "You can't!"

"Why not?"

She scrunched her face, thinking. "Because it's cheating."

"Are you sure?" He aimed a red ball at her.

"Yes!" But she ran, anyway. A ball bounced against her back. She spun around to find Dad laughing.

"Gotcha!"

Ariana scooped up as many balls as she could, chucking them at him in rapid-fire succession. He laughed and threw just as many balls her way. It was impossible to tell who tagged who with balls bouncing off each other left and right.

Finally, Dad dropped his pile and held his arms in the air. "I give up. You win—I don't stand a chance."

"If that's the case…" Ari aimed for him and threw a ball, hitting him square in the forehead.

His eyes widened and he brought his hands to his chest. "You got me!" He fell backward with his arms outstretched.

"Funny." Ariana waited for him to get up.

He didn't.

"Dad."

No movement.

"Dad?" Ariana crept over toward him until she was right next to him.

He didn't budge. In fact, he didn't even appear to be breathing.

She opened her mouth to speak, but before she could make a sound, he reached out and grabbed her wrists. Ariana fell over, laughing.

"Gotcha." Dad grinned, his eyes shining.

Ari gasped for air. "I'm usually really hard to scare, you know."

"Then I must be the master."

"I think so."

They held each other's gazes for a moment before bursting into laughter. Dad put his arm around Ari. "You know what? It's getting late—"

"Oh." Ari's heart sank.

"So, maybe I should stay in my old room. Then tomorrow we can spend the day together."

Excitement ran through her. "Really?" Not just tonight, but the next day, too?

He nodded. "If I'm going to use a sick day, I may as well make the most of it."

Ariana beamed. "Does that mean we can stay here longer?"

"As long as you want."

"I heard it stays open until midnight."

His face turned serious. "I think both your moms would have my throat if I kept you out that late."

She couldn't disagree. "Let's go try the jousting."

"Let me just text my boss before I forget."

"Okay."

He pulled out his phone and Ari looked around. They were at the other end of the building, maybe there were some new characters or items she could find for her game. She grabbed her phone, too, and went to the app, holding the screen up to look.

Her heart skipped a beat. Near an emergency exit stood a zombie bride. She'd only heard rumors about them. Nobody she knew had actually seen or captured one. Yet there it was, and nobody was close enough to get it.

"I'm gonna run over there," she said. "I have to get that zombie bride."

Dad nodded, not looking away from the screen.

"I can go?"

He nodded again.

"Yes!" She threw her fist into the air and scrambled for the exit. Nobody else had grabbed it yet, and she also couldn't see anyone headed that way.

Ari's heart felt like it would explode as she made her way over. She watched as the zombie bride paced by the door, flesh dripping onto the ground. It was completely gross—and totally cool.

Finally, she got close enough to capture it. Ari tapped the screen, and a moment later, the zombie bride was hers! Her screen flashed and played music, congratulating her on such a rare find.

She couldn't wait to get to school on Monday and show everyone.

"Oh, darn," came a male voice from behind. "I missed the zombie bride. Did you get it?"

Ari turned around.

The voice belonged to a tall, skinny man about the age of Papi. He was tan with thin, balding hair. The man smiled, exuding friendliness. "Did you get it?"

She nodded. "Yeah. I didn't even know it was real. Do you

play?"

"Who doesn't?" He arched a dark, bushy brow. His eyes shone with excitement. "Can I see the bride?"

"Sure." She held out her screen.

He leaned closer, studying it. "You're so lucky. Did you hear that someone saw a pumpkin king out in the parking lot?"

Ariana's mouth dropped. "For real?" The king was even rarer than the bride.

"That's what people are saying, but the king is fast. Nobody who has seen it could nab it."

Ari's mind rushed. What if she could get it?

"Want me to show you where it's supposed to be?"

She studied the man. He seemed super nice, but she knew all the stranger safety rules. She'd be stupid to go out with him... even if he did know where a pumpkin king was.

"I should get back to my dad."

He nodded. "Of course. Well, if you change your mind, let me know. You can even bring your dad. Maybe between the three of us, we can get that king for you."

She hesitated. If he was bad, he wouldn't tell her to bring her dad to meet him. She glanced over at him. He was still texting. A kidnapper would just grab her and run, right?

Maybe it wouldn't be so bad just to go outside—not way out into the parking lot. Just out the door to look. If she could catch the king, it really would be the perfect ending to the most amazing day.

"Do you want to check?" asked the man.

Ariana glanced back and forth between her dad and the exit. Part of her was telling her not to go. Lectures from her parents ran through her head, but she really wanted the king. It would only be a minute, then she could run back inside.

Text

~

ALEX HIT SEND and took a deep breath. Darren had really given him a hard time about one sick day. It had been well over six months since Alex had used a sick day. His boss could've been more understanding, but all he cared about was getting the job done.

His boss needed to get used to this because Alex was going to start taking more Saturdays off to spend with Ariana.

He jammed his phone back into his pocket and glanced around.

Where was Ariana? Had she decided to play hide and seek? She'd said something to Alex while he had been text-arguing with his greedy boss.

What had she said? Something about…? He couldn't remember. He'd been too focused on his idiot boss.

He glanced around again. With all the kids and teens running around, shouting, it was hard to think.

Why hadn't he stopped texting for a moment when she was talking to him?

Alex scratched his head, squinted, and looked around again, this time paying closer attention.

Some kids shouted on his left, breaking his concentration. Reflexively, he turned in that direction.

A girl who looked just like Ari from behind was leaving with a balding man in a jean jacket. The girl had the same blueish-green colored jacket as Ariana. The same ponytail, too.

His heart sank and his eyes widened.

It *was* Ariana.

"No!" He burst into a run, terror seizing him. The stupid plastic balls made it hard for him to find his footing.

What was Ari doing? Hadn't anyone taught her to stay away from strangers?

He had to get to her. They seemed to be walking in slow motion, yet he couldn't move any faster than they were.

Finally, he broke free of the ball pit.

"Ariana! Stop!"

The man and his daughter turned a corner up ahead. It may as well have been miles away.

"Stop them!"

No one noticed him. Or the man walking away with Ariana.

His throat closed up. He forced his legs to move faster. Everything moved too slowly, except for that man and Ariana.

"Stop them!" His voice was high and squeaky.

Alex's pulse raced, making it hard to breathe. He rounded the same corner they had, but now they were out of sight.

They could have gone anywhere—the arcade, the food court, or even outside.

His stomach twisted in tight knots. Beads of sweat broke out on his forehead.

He released a string of profanities and ran over to the man selling tickets. "Have you seen my daughter?"

"What does she look like?"

"You just sold us tickets to get inside! You don't remember?"

The dude shrugged. "Do you know how many people come and go around here?"

Alex swore again. "Did you see a little girl about this high,"— he held his hand to his side, just below his chest—"with dark brown hair full of sparkles?"

"Maybe." He played with his goatee. "Not sure."

"You're useless!" Alex ran to the arcade and glanced around. No little girls.

He ran to the exit.

"You're going to have to pay to get in again, you know."

Alex would have it out with that little punk later. He ran outside. Thankfully the bright overhead lights made it easy enough to scan the parking lot.

He saw them.

At the far end of the parking lot, Ariana held up her phone as if showing him something on the screen.

"Ari!" he screamed, his voice shrill and cutting his throat. "Ariana!"

Neither seemed to hear him.

He burst into a run, his heart pounding against his ribcage. Alex had to dart around parked cars, but finally he neared them. He could see Ari's profile—it was definitely her.

Alex studied the man's face. He was just a tanned, skinny balding guy who looked like he'd been through a lot because of the deep lines around his eyes and mouth. His cheeks were a bit sunken, but otherwise there was nothing striking about the man.

"Ariana!" He was so close, yet so far. He continued running.

That time, she turned. The man wrapped an arm around her.

"Dad!" Ari called, fear in her eyes.

The man covered her mouth, hoisted her up, and ran.

Alex's blood turned cold. "Stop!"

He didn't. In fact, he ran around the corner of the warehouse.

Alex caught up just in time to see the man stuff Ariana into an already-running black SUV. The man jumped inside and slammed the door shut.

Pulse drumming in his ears, Alex ran faster. He got closer to the vehicle, and closer still.

He reached for the door.

The SUV squealed away just as his hand grasped air rather than clasping the handle.

"No!" Alex tried to make out the license plate, but it was caked in mud. Not one number or letter showed. Even the make and model of the car had been hidden by dirt and grime.

He ran after it, managing to keep up until it tore out of the parking lot. The tires squealed again as they turned the corner.

Alex continued running, but the SUV had to be going at least twice the legal speed. It turned onto a main street, going out of sight.

Determined, he continued running, gasping for air and crying out for Ariana. By the time he reached the main road, the vehicle was out of sight.

He ran his hands through his hair and looked up and down the street for any clues.

There was no point.

She was gone.

Searching

~

A LEX WAVED HIS ARMS like a maniac, trying to flag someone down. He needed to get into a car and chase down that bastard. Not even a single car slowed to help him.

He stopped, rubbed the back of his neck, and pulled at his shirt's collar.

What was he supposed to do now? If he went back to the ball place, he would be going *away* from her. But he didn't know where she was. On the other hand, he could get into his car and try to find the jerk. He knew what the kidnapper looked like and he could easily spot that dirty SUV.

Alex turned around and ran back to the parking lot. His mind raced out of control. He needed to think clearly.

The police. He needed to call them. They could put every last one of their men on this.

He stopped and took deep breaths as he pulled out the phone and dialed 911.

"Nine-one-one," said a bored-sounding lady. "What's your emergency?"

"My daughter…" Alex gasped for air. "She's been kidnapped."

"What? Where are you, sir?"

What was the name of that place? He checked the sign on the warehouse. "The Ball Palace." It was too dark to make out any road signs.

"Over near Wilson Avenue?"

"Yeah." That sounded right.

"Stay where you are. I'm sending officers over right now. Are you inside or outside the building?"

"Outside." Alex started walking again and headed for the entrance.

The operator asked him a series of questions and Alex described what Ariana looked like, what the kidnapper looked like, and what he could tell her about the SUV.

By the time he reached the warehouse, he could already hear sirens in the distance. He leaned against a pole, rubbed his arm, and glanced all around.

This couldn't be happening. But it was. Ariana had been snatched on his watch—right before his eyes—and he'd been unable to stop it. And to think he'd thought he was a bad father before. Now he took the award.

"The officers are there," said the operator. "I'm going to hang up now."

"Sure." Alex ended the call.

The sirens grew louder and flashing lights brighter as the police cars turned into the parking lot and all stopped around him. There were at least four or five of them.

Alex ran over to the first officer out of a cruiser. "They went that way." He pointed toward the main street. "He took her in a black SUV. It was caked in dirt and mud. The man—"

He pulled out a tablet and slid his finger around the screen. "Slow down. What's your name? Her name? We need a description and a picture. Do you—?"

"She went that way!" He pointed again, this time with more flair. "Someone needs to go after them!"

"Sir, you need to calm down."

"Calm down?" Alex shouted. "My daughter has been kidnapped! He could be hurting her right now."

A female officer came over and put a hand on his arm. "We

need to know this information, sir. It'll give us the best chance at finding your daughter."

"No, chasing down that SUV is the best way to get her back!"

Why had he bothered calling the cops? They hadn't helped much when his sister had been kidnapped. What made him think anything would be different now?

"Sir?" asked the female officer. "What's your name?"

Alex threw his head back, hitting the pole. "Alex Mercer."

Her eyes widened. "Alex Mercer? You mean the brother of Macy Mercer?"

"Yes! I'm the brother of the kidnapped girl from twelve years ago. Now, can you get my daughter?"

A murmur of whispers surrounded Alex as the police officers realized the connection. The only two kidnappings in their small town were both within the same family.

"Just find her," he pleaded.

Discussion

ZOEY CARTER PUT the last of the leftover sandwiches into her parents' fridge. At least all the messes were cleaned and the food was now put away. It had been another great party—the only thing that would have made it better would have been if Alex hadn't shown up. But Ariana had wanted him there so badly, it would have ruined it for her.

At least she had the memory of the look on his face when she'd shown him her new engagement ring. The shock, the hurt. Now maybe he felt a little bit of what he'd done to her.

Kellen came in and wrapped an arm around her. "Are we leaving the decorations up, sweetie?"

She gave him a quick kiss. "Yeah. Ari adores them. She'll probably want to keep them up until Thanksgiving."

He smiled and rubbed her shoulders. "That's so cute. You ready to go? I'm exhausted."

"Me, too, but you can keep doing that." Zoey closed her eyes and relaxed her head as he continued massaging.

"There you two are." Kenji—otherwise known as her dad—came into the room and smiled at the couple. "Another great party, wouldn't you say?"

"The best." Kellen stepped back. "Need any help with anything else? I can take out the garbage."

Kenji glanced at Zoey. "This one's definitely a keeper."

Zoey gave him a tired smile. "He sure is."

Kellen grabbed a trash bag and headed out the back door.

Kenji opened the cabinet. "We're out of plastic bags. Must've used them all for the party. I'll head out to the store." He grabbed his coat.

Kellen came in. "Where are you going?"

"We're out of trash bags. I'm running to the store."

"Nonsense." Kellen shook his head. "You guys have been working tirelessly on this party. I'll just run down to the gas station. It'll only take a minute." He ran out the door before anyone could respond.

"Have you two set a date yet?" Kenji asked Zoey.

"No, we still need to reserve the venue. Once that's set, we can plan everything else."

Zoey's mom came in and gave Kenji a kiss. "Thanks for all your help."

"My pleasure. *Koishiteru.*"

"I love you, too." Mom beamed and then turned to Zoey. "You don't have to stay and clean everything up. We'll get the rest tomorrow."

Zoey shrugged. "I was hoping to stay until Ari got back. I want to say goodnight to her."

"Don't trust Alex, do you?" Kenji asked.

Zoey didn't reply.

"He's always been a good kid."

"Alex isn't a kid," Zoey snapped. "He's twenty-five and lives like a college frat boy. It's ridiculous. His life is going nowhere and yet Ariana thinks he's some kind of superhero."

Mom and Kenji exchanged a knowing look.

Zoey shook her head. "I don't want to hear it."

"There *was* a time you looked at him like that, too." Kenji arched a brow.

"And there's a reason I don't anymore."

Zoey excused herself and went to the bathroom to get a moment alone.

When she returned to the kitchen, Kellen had already returned and replaced the garbage bag.

"Thanks so much for all your help, you two," Mom said. "It's late. You guys should get going."

Zoey checked her phone. "Has anyone heard from Alex or Ari?"

"They're fine," Kenji said.

"Since we're all here without Ari, there's something I want to talk about." Zoey sat at the table and pushed aside some Halloween plates.

"Now?" Mom yawned.

Zoey's heart picked up speed. This wasn't a conversation she was looking forward to, but it was best to get it out of the way. "Yes."

Everyone took a seat. Kellen took Zoey's hand. "What's going on, Zo?"

She took a deep breath and then made eye contact with everyone around the table. "Now that I have a solid career and am getting married…" Her voice trailed as she considered her words. She'd already practiced the speech in front of her mirror several dozen times, but that hadn't been the same. Suddenly, she sat upright. "I want split custody of Ariana."

"What?" Her mom gasped.

"Are you serious?" Kenji asked.

Kellen stared at her, his shock equal to her parents'.

"She is my daughter, and I want her to be an active part in my family."

Mom and Kenji exchanged a worried expression.

"What exactly do you have in mind?" Kenji asked.

"I think fifty-fifty is fair."

"Fair?" Mom exclaimed. "For whom?"

"Everyone." Zoey cleared her throat. "Ari's used to living here, but at the same time, I'm her mom and she needs me. So, fifty-fifty is a good split."

"It sounds like you've put a lot of thought into this," Kenji said.

"Yeah, it does," Kellen muttered.

Mom slammed her hand on the table. "This isn't what we agreed to."

"When I was sixteen? Things have changed, Mom."

"You said you wanted us to raise her. That we would give her the best chance at a good life. To give your dad a chance to raise a child."

Resentment bubbled over the surface. "It's not my fault he chose not to raise me." She glared at Kenji.

"We adopted her," Mom said. "You signed over your rights."

"I gave birth to her. No court would deny me custody—especially with the home I could provide her."

Tears filled her mom's eyes. "Court? You want to sue us?"

"No. It's not like that. I was just making a point. I'd rather us come to a verbal agreement and carry on."

Kenji leaned over the table. "Going from living here full-time to half-time will be a big adjustment for Ariana. Think about her."

"We can start small," Zoey agreed. "Start with every other weekend and add time until it's every other week by the wedding. That should give us at least a year."

Tears ran down her mom's face. "I can't believe you're doing this." She shook her head. "I never thought I'd see the day. Don't you and Kellen want to start your own family?"

Zoey squeezed her fiancé's hand. "Of course, but we can't deny that Ariana's part of that. Right?"

Kellen nodded, but didn't say anything.

Zoey's phone rang. She pulled it out and glanced at the screen. "Oh, thank God. It's Alex. Hopefully they're on their way home. I can't wait to tell Ariana the good news."

Desperate

~

ZOEY PRESSED THE paper bag to her mouth, but it didn't help her breathing. She couldn't get it under control. Not that it mattered. The only thing that mattered was that someone had stolen Ariana—that Alex had let it happen.

She would kill him. *Kill* him. How dare he be so irresponsible?

Kellen rubbed Zoey's shoulders. "Try to relax. Ariana needs you calm."

Zoey pulled the bag away. "Nobody knows where she is! It doesn't matter to her how upset I am. Actually, I think she'd be glad to know I'm freaking out. How do you think she'd feel if I acted like I didn't care that some man threw her into a van?"

He pulled his hands away. "If you say so."

"I do." She glanced up at Kenji. "Can't you drive any faster?"

"Not unless you want me to get pulled over."

"All the cops are at that ball place, looking for Ari."

"I'm sure not all of them."

"They should be! Look, if someone pulls you over, we can chew him out about not doing his job. What could be more important than looking for a lost child?"

"We're almost there," Mom said.

"I don't know how you can all be so chill."

"Chill?" Valerie exclaimed. "I've never been more upset in my life. I'm just trying to hold myself together. Now isn't the time to fall apart."

"Seems like a good time to me," Zoey snapped. "I can't think of a better time, actually."

"The police are going to question us."

"Us?" Zoey shook her head. "We weren't even there. I just want to get out there and look for Ari."

"Don't you remember when Macy was kidnapped? They questioned everyone she knew, even you."

"Especially me." Zoey didn't want to think about her best friend's abduction. Not now. The whole thing was too painful, and it looked like she might have to relive it through Ari, thanks to Alex—the selfish, irresponsible loser.

"We knew her best. She was like a second daughter to me because of how much time you two spent together."

Zoey didn't respond.

Finally, Kenji pulled into the parking lot. Lights flashed all around and people milled everywhere. Yellow police tape blocked off part of the warehouse.

Terror shot through Zoey. What was the tape for? Had they found something to indicate foul play? She took the seat belt off and ran outside without a word. She saw Alex's parents huddled together and headed for them.

As she neared the building, an officer put his arm out and stopped her. "You need to stay back."

"I'm her mother! The missing girl! Let me get by."

The officer's brows came together. "What's your name?"

"Zoey Carter."

He slid his finger around the screen of a tablet. "Can you tell me the girl's full name?"

"Ariana *Zoey* Nakano."

"Why the different last name?"

"That's not relevant! Let me by."

Alex ran over. "She's the mom."

Zoey almost thanked him, but then remembered the whole

thing was his fault.

Kellen, her mom, and Kenji caught up.

"Those are my parents and fiancé," Zoey told the cop. The last thing she felt like doing right then was explaining that Ariana had two sets of parents.

He looked at them. "You'll need to stay back. Immediate family only."

"We're Ariana's legal parents. We adopted her the day she was born."

The cop turned to Zoey. "Is this true?"

She threw her head back. "Does any of this really matter? We're all her parents, okay? Now help us get her back!"

The officer turned back to Alex like he was the authority on the matter. "Is all this true?"

"Yes." He turned to Zoey. "Come over here."

She followed him. "What the hell happened?"

"It's like I said on the phone, a guy grabbed her and ran off with her in an SUV. I tried to catch up, but it was too late. The car was already running. He had the whole thing planned."

"I hate you, you know that? I've never loathed anyone so much in my entire life."

Alex stopped and spun around, causing Zoey to nearly crash into him. He glared at her. "All I care about is getting Ariana back. Blame me if you want, but that isn't going to help Ari."

"You sure didn't."

His face tensed. "I did my best."

She snorted. "Right."

"Do you want my help or not? That cop didn't look like he was going to let you in. The main investigators are over here."

"Just take me to them. What's that yellow tape for? Did they find her blood or did they find something from the kidnapper?"

"The entire place is a crime scene, Zoey. That's it."

"Do they know anything? Where he took her? Who he is?"

"Only what the SUV looks like and what direction it went."

Alex stopped walking again. "You know what? Go introduce yourself to the investigators." He pointed to a group of cops. "Those are the ones."

Zoey stood taller. "Fine." She adjusted her shoulder strap and marched over to the group. "I'm Zoey Carter, Ariana's mom."

One of the officers took her aside and asked a rapid-fire round of questions. All stuff that Alex probably hadn't been able to tell them—where she went to school, who her friends, babysitters, and teachers were, who might have reason to take her.

Alex may have been the cool dad who took her to the ball pit, there was no way he knew any of that since he wasn't *really* involved. He showed up just enough to be elusive and mysterious—a real superhero to Ariana, who wasn't old enough to know better yet.

Then the questions turned personal. "What's your relationship like with your daughter?"

"What do you mean? We love each other."

"Would you say you're close?"

"Of course."

"Does she confide in you?"

"Yes. I know all about the boy in her class that she thinks is cute."

The officer glanced up from taking notes. "Would he have motive?"

"He's *ten*, and from the sounds of it, thinks girls have cooties."

"What's his name?"

Zoey paused. Had Ari even told her? She couldn't remember. "I don't know. It's hard to think when my daughter is *missing*."

"It's okay. I understand. If you do remember, let us know."

He understood? Right. Doubtful his kid had been abducted. "Yes, of course. Is anyone out there looking for her?"

"Patrols are on it now. There's also an APB out on the vehicle."

Zoey sighed in relief. At least someone was doing something.

"Speaking of that," the officer said. "Did you bring any article of hers?"

"An article? What do you mean?"

"K-9 units are en route, and we need to give them something with her scent."

Zoey's stomach lurched. Did they think she was dead?

"Do you have anything of hers on you?"

Her mind raced. "No, I don't think so."

"In your car?"

"Maybe. I'm not sure." Everything seemed to spin around.

"We'll need to send a K-9 over to your home, then. Her bedroom is probably the best place for him to go, anyway. The scent will be strongest there."

Zoey took a couple steps back and leaned against the nearest car. It was all too much. The only thing she wanted was to wrap her arms around Ariana and never let go.

Would she ever be able to do that again?

"Ma'am?"

She glanced up at the cop. "Yeah, her room. That's a good idea."

"What's your address?"

Zoey brought her hands to her face. Ariana didn't have a room at her condo yet. She needed to convert her exercise room into a girl's bedroom, but hadn't started yet. The plan had been to wait until after she spoke with her parents about splitting custody.

"Ma'am?"

"You'd better speak with my parents." It felt like admitting defeat. She'd failed as a mom by not raising her daughter.

Why had she ever agreed to the adoption in the first place? Maybe none of this would have even happened if she hadn't. She'd have had a hard time raising Ariana in high school and college, but at least she'd have her with her now.

She broke down into a fit of sobs.

Sleepless

❧

ALEX THREW HIMSELF into his childhood bed, exhausted, but certain he wouldn't be able to fall asleep. His parents had practically dragged him home—they'd literally followed him in their car, making sure he made it safely.

He couldn't think straight. The cops had assured him they were doing everything they could, but Alex wasn't convinced that it was enough. The same police department had been next to useless when his sister had been taken. At least that was how he remembered it. He'd only been thirteen at the time, and those twelve years may as well have been a hundred because it felt like a lifetime ago.

Alex had done everything he could to not think about his sister during that time. He'd been a social smoker before that, but it had quickly turned into a habit—one that had taken him years to be able to drop. He'd even gotten Zoey hooked before knocking her up.

Now the cycle had completed itself. Their daughter, conceived during an abduction, had now been kidnapped herself.

Both were Alex's fault, at least in part. Nobody else ever blamed him for any part in Macy's disappearance, but that didn't stop him from thinking he could have done something to prevent it.

He sighed and rolled over, pulling the pillow over his face. Wallowing in guilt wasn't going to get him anywhere. Focusing on finding Ariana would. Macy had made it back home, and Ariana had the same Mercer blood flowing through her veins. She would be a survivor, too.

Alex tried to shut off his brain, but he couldn't. It raced, running off in every direction imaginable. He blamed himself—if he hadn't been so distracted by his greedy boss, he could have prevented the whole thing. He blamed his boss for being the greedy jerk that he was. He even blamed Zoey and her parents—why hadn't they taught Ariana about stranger danger?

The blankets twisted all around him as he tossed and turned. It was pointless.

It was also getting light outside.

Swearing, he sat up and untangled himself from the covers. He went over to the window and glanced outside. A police cruiser drove by, slowing in front of his house and then the Nakano's. Were they protecting them or considering them as suspects?

Alex tugged on his hair.

Would they get Ari back? Could he forgive himself, whichever way the outcome went?

He moved from the window and paced. The room didn't feel quite right so neat and tidy. Whenever he paced in the past, there had always been an obstacle course of things to step over and around.

A sharp pain stabbed him in the right temple. It radiated out, moving around his skull.

Alex went into the bathroom and found some painkillers. He took twice the recommended amount and then went back to bed. Clementine followed him and snuggled against his chest, purring. Alex stroked the cat, finally starting to relax a little. Eventually, his head started to feel better, but he still couldn't sleep.

Would he ever?

How had his parents lived through their ordeal? The pain in his chest felt like it would rip him apart.

Maybe what he needed to do was to get outside and start looking for that SUV. He could probably think of places the cops hadn't. All he'd need was some coffee, and plenty of stands would be open at this hour.

He picked up his phone from the dresser and pushed the button to turn on the screen. It was almost six o'clock and he had over a dozen new texts. He rarely had more than a few a day.

Alex tapped his code to unlock the phone and read through the messages. They were all from people asking about Ariana. Apparently the news was all over social media.

Dread washed through him. What were people saying? He knew firsthand how cruel people could be online.

Did he dare look?

He had no other choice. He needed to be prepared for when he ran into people at the store or wherever he went.

Alex's finger hovered over the app to his favorite social media site. He took a deep breath and then pushed it. He had a flood of notifications. Over a dozen new messages, a bunch of friend requests, and almost a hundred general notifications.

His head ached, despite all the painkillers.

He checked the messages first. They were no different from his texts—friends and coworkers demanding to know what the hell had happened. The friend requests were all strangers—jerks who just wanted to find out more about him because his family was a trending topic.

He braced himself and click on the trending topic, *Macy Mercer's Niece Kidnapped.*

His stomach twisted in knots as the flood of posts loaded.

The titles of the links to news stories and blog posts were enough to feel like a solid punch in the gut.

Oh, The Irony

Don't the Mercers ever Learn?

Another Mercer Kidnapping

It's a Decade After Being Abducted, and You'll Never Believe what Happened Now

Deadbeat Dad lets Daughter Get Kidnapped

Alex threw the phone onto his pillow. Clementine jumped from the bed and scurried out of the room. It was already too much, and Alex hadn't even read any of the comments yet. They were bound to be much worse.

He paced the room again, and finally glared at his reflection in the mirror above his old dresser. It had only been six years since he'd last lived in this room, but he looked like it had been at least twice that long. The bags under his eyes and the creases around his mouth gave him the illusion of being older than he really was. He felt like he'd aged five years since the previous morning.

Exhaustion squeezed him. He needed to either sleep or get out there and help find Ariana. Pacing and looking in the mirror were such a waste of time.

Alex grabbed his phone, climbed under the messed up covers, and set the alarm to go off in a few hours. His mind raced, so he opened an ebook. But that didn't work—he couldn't focus on a single sentence, much less the story. He turned back to social media, hoping that might somehow help.

Even more notifications. There were all kinds of posts on his profile. Skimming them, they mostly expressed condolences, but he couldn't take the time to read those. He was too raw.

He went to his feed, but that proved to be a mistake. It was full of articles about Ariana's disappearance, and all of them had more than a handful of comments.

Sighing, he clicked on one. That was an even bigger mistake.

How could he let that happen? What a jerk.

I know, right? How stupid do you get? A text isn't more important than your kid.

I'd never take my eyes off my girls in a place like that. You're just asking for them to get snatched away.

Alex Mercer is the worst father.

I feel so bad for that girl. Even if she does come back alive, she has to deal with that scumbag as her dad.

He felt like he'd been punched in the gut. It was one thing to read comments like those about other news articles, but it was something else entirely having them directed at him. And yet he couldn't stop reading them.

Some people are too stupid to live.

He needs to die.

If I ever see him in person, Alex better watch out. I'll do to him what the kidnapper is probably doing to Ariana.

Alex closed the app and threw his phone across the room. He'd read too much. Stupid jerks spouting off empty threats.

He pulled the pillow over his head, but the comments all ran through his head, practically shouting at him. He sat up and threw the pillow. This was getting him nowhere. If he couldn't sleep, he may as well get out there and do something useful.

Station

ALEX FLUNG OPEN the door of the police station. A flurry of memories rushed at him from a kidnapping long ago. He and his parents had been dragged down there more times than he could count when Macy was gone.

He cleared his throat and walked up to the main desk. "I need to talk with someone."

The tired-looking lady pulled some hair behind her ears and glanced up at him. "About?"

"Ariana Nakano."

"You are?"

"Alex Mercer. Her dad."

She glanced down at a paper. "That's not the name I have for her dad."

"I'm her birth dad. She was adopted. I need—"

"I can help," came a deep male voice behind the desk. A tall man with dark hair and big muscles stepped into view.

"Detective Fleshman?" Alex asked. "You still work here?"

"Yes, and I'm captain now. Come on back to my office." He waved Alex down the hall and led him past the interrogation rooms.

It was a relief to not be going back into those. Seeing them made it feel like he'd sat in them just the other day.

Fleshman stopped in front of a door with his name on it and motioned for Alex to go in first. Once they were inside, Alex sat in a plush chair across from the desk and Fleshman sat behind the desk and shuffled some papers. "I'd say it's good to see you again, Alex, but when people come in here, it's usually the worst day of their life."

Alex nodded and raked his fingers through his hair. "Have you guys found anything?"

Fleshman frowned and shook his head. "We have all our manpower on it and someone is scrubbing local security camera footage and traffic cams to try and find the vehicle. I've put officers on the case around the clock and clearly, I'm here late. We—"

"Someone should also be looking at the Ball Palace cameras, to see if they can get the guy's face in a shot. They have to have cameras there."

"We're on that, too. There's more going on than I can list for you at the moment. Everyone has their job, and all the bases are covered."

"There has to be more we can do," Alex said. "But what?"

"We're doing everything we can." Fleshman held his gaze. "These first forty-eight hours are crucial. Statistically speaking, they're the most important hours of the case. I've contacted the FBI, and their agents should be here,"—he glanced at the clock—"in a few hours."

"You're going to let them take over the case?"

Fleshman shook his head. "This isn't TV. They're here to work *with* us and give us resources we don't have access to as a small town department."

"I need to do something." Alex buried his face into his palms.

"You look like you could use some sleep."

"It's not happening." Alex glanced up, his mind spinning. "Can I talk to a sketch artist? That would be better than the description I already gave. Or I could try to think of something about the SUV that I didn't before?"

Fleshman gave him a sad but reassuring expression. "I'll make sure the sketch artist has your number. Officers all over the state are on the lookout for them. We've issued an AMBER Alert, and your daughter's picture is all over the news and social media."

"It doesn't feel like enough. I need to be *doing* something."

"I can only imagine. If it was one of my kids, I'd be coming unglued."

They stared at each other for a moment. Alex believed him, but he couldn't just go home and sleep.

"You know, I never forgot about Macy's case. It's stuck with me all these years, and I never forgot about you or your family. I've wondered many times how you're doing. The others, I usually see around town."

Alex frowned. Maybe he really was a rotten dad. "I'm busy with work."

A look of regret covered Fleshman's face. "I know how that goes." He cleared his throat. "Anyway, while everyone else is focused on other aspects of the case, I'm looking into other kidnappings around the country for similarities."

Alex sat up. "Have you found anything?"

"It's too early to say just yet, but I'm not going to stop until I find something."

"Too early?" Alex exclaimed. "Isn't the first two days the most crucial? That's what you said."

"That's why I'm here. My shift ended hours ago."

Alex stared at him. "It did?"

Fleshman nodded. "Like you, I have a nine-to-five job, but as soon as I heard about this, I dropped everything and came in. Yes, it's an all-hands-on-deck thing, but we're still not required to work outside of our typical hours."

"Then why are you?"

"Like I said, I never forgot you or your family. I'd just had my first child when Macy went missing, and it hit me hard. I couldn't imagine anything happening to my Ava. I've always remembered you. In a way, your family has kept me going in this job—it's rough at times. But I know I'm making a difference."

Alex gave a slight nod, not sure what to say. It was strange to have the tough cop level with him like that.

"I'm doing everything I can, and I'll stay here all weekend if I need to. These hours really are crucial."

"What about your family?"

Fleshman shifted some papers around on his desk. "My kids live with their mom. I'm free to focus all my efforts here."

Alex gave him a double-take. They had more in common than he'd thought—they were both separated from their children's mother, and Fleshman probably didn't see his kids as much as he should, either. Alex felt overwhelmed with gratitude for the captain's concern. In fact, he had to blink back tears he didn't want the other man to see. "Is there anything I can do?"

"I wouldn't mind some real coffee. The stuff here is pretty stale."

He was working outside his normal hours to find Ariana and all he wanted was coffee? Alex fumbled out of the chair. "What do you want? Mocha? Latte? What else is there?"

"I usually just get a drip coffee, black, but a mocha sounds great right now."

"Sure thing."

"Hey, thanks. And when you get back here, just tell them I'm expecting you."

Alex nodded and hurried out of the station with renewed hope. It wasn't much, but it was something. He climbed into his car and made his way to the nearest coffee shop.

It was, and even better, almost nobody was there. He wasn't sure he could handle seeing anyone. Some of those people could have been the ones writing horrible comments about him online—there had been so many more that he hadn't read. He just hadn't been able to stomach it. He wasn't sure he ever could.

Alex reached into his backseat and found a baseball cap. He wasn't going to make it easy for anyone to recognize him, and around here, everyone already knew him. He'd been forever branded as the brother of the kidnapped girl years ago. Now his daughter…

He sighed and went inside, ordering two mochas without making eye contact with the barista. He even gave her a twenty and told her to keep the change.

While he stood waiting for the coffees, a group of ladies came and whispered.

"That's him."

"No, it's not."

"Yeah, it is. My friend had a crush on him in high school. That's definitely Alex."

"What's that lowlife doing here? His daughter's missing and he's getting a latte?"

Alex gritted his teeth and pulled out his phone, pretending to text. It was just gossip. People would move onto something more interesting soon enough. No, it wouldn't be soon enough.

"Do you think he really had something to do with it?"

"I don't know. He doesn't look like he got any sleep. Poor guy."

"Poor guy? Are you kidding? If it weren't for that loser, little Ariana would be sleeping in her bed now."

Alex's anger nearly bubbled to the surface. It took all of his self-control not to turn around and tell those two cows off.

A barista called his name and put the two mochas on the counter.

One of the whisperer's gasped. "It *is* him."

"Told you."

Alex grabbed the mochas and glared at the two women, making eye contact with each of them. "Would you grow up? Yes, I'm dad of the missing girl. No, it wasn't my fault—a man grabbed her and put her into his car. I couldn't stop him. This coffee,"—he held up one of the cups—"is for a cop working the case. If you have any more questions, next time, ask them to my face!" He stared down one and then the other.

Both looked away and moved from him, hiding behind a shelf of seasonal coffee mugs for sale.

Alex swore loud enough for them to hear and stormed out of the coffee shop.

Rest

~

KELLEN MCKAY SANK into the white leather couch and rubbed his fiancée's back. "Get some sleep, Zo."

Zoey spun around and glared at him. "Sleep? Ariana's missing!"

He kissed her temple, reminding himself to stay patient. He focused on a framed poster of Paris at sunset. "I know, but you have to rest."

"For what?" She grabbed a silver throw pillow and squeezed it.

He took a deep breath and silently counted to ten. "Someone said something about a press conference tomorrow. You'll have an easier time fending off the questions if you're not exhausted." He massaged her shoulders.

"I think people would understand if I'm not at the top of my game." She rose from the couch and paced the room, stopping only to pick up a picture of Ariana.

Kellen stifled a yawn. He would pass out if he didn't get some sleep soon. It had been a horribly long night, and neither of them would do any good in the state they were in.

He got up and put his arm around her, not saying anything for a few moments. Obviously, there was nothing he could say to make the situation better. He didn't want to give her false hope and say they would find Ariana. Who knew what the outcome would be?

"She knows how much you love her," Kellen finally said.

Zoey leaned her head against his shoulder and sobbed. He led her to the bedroom and helped her onto the bed without a word. She whimpered, her only protest to lying down, then rolled onto her side and trembled.

Kellen's heart broke for her. He slid off his shoes and wrapped an arm around her, lying down, also. He could feel the picture frame still in her hands. He moved her long, thick hair away from his face before rubbing her shoulders. He fought to keep his eyes open until Zoey's breathing turned into the soft, rhythmic breathing of sleep.

He lightened his touch as he continued rubbing until he could stop without waking her. Her breathing grew deeper, and finally, he relaxed. Kellen rested his arm over her waist and closed his eyes.

Sleep didn't overtake him as he'd hoped. His mind spun out of control over the events of the long night. He still felt the sting of shock from Zoey announcing that she wanted custody of Ariana. He'd been stunned speechless at her parents' table. They were getting married, but she hadn't even bothered to talk with him about that before bringing it up with her parents—who had been equally surprised by the news.

Zoey had always told him that her parents would always be solely responsible for Ariana. That had been their deal, and it was also what Kellen expected going into marriage. He knew Ariana would be part of their lives, but he was not ready for becoming an instant parent. He knew that much about himself.

Kellen had had no time to digest the news when they heard about Ariana's abduction, which was by far a worse slap. He was worried sick—he'd really grown close to the girl over the time he'd spent with Zoey. Ariana was sweet and charming, almost to a fault. She'd managed to win him over quickly, and Kellen had never had any interest in kids. Not even with his own nieces and nephews. He'd always felt awkward around kids until Ariana.

Guilt stung at him for having been so upset over Zoey's announcement now that Ariana was missing. He felt like the world's biggest jerk. He would do whatever he could to help find her.

He'd already spoken with his parents who had promised to spring for the best attorneys money could buy. It was a mystery how lawyers could help find a missing child, but he wasn't going to turn down their help.

Kellen's thoughts grew fuzzy and slow, and finally, his mind tumbled into a restless sleep.

He woke to an empty bed and the sounds of a shower. Zoey had covered him with a blanket. He rubbed his eyes and stretched.

The sun shone brightly through the blinds and he felt rested— well, more rested than before falling asleep. He still felt like he'd been hit by a semi-truck. His stomach tightened as he thought about Ariana. Ugly, bloody images flashed before his mind. As a teenager, he'd been obsessed with horror movies, and now they haunted him.

Kellen got up and tried to shake the thoughts away, but they wouldn't leave. Bloody knives, ropes, and bodies were all he could see. Along with that sweet face and big brown eyes.

He tightened one hand into a fist and clenched it. He punched his other palm as hard as he could. That little girl was the last person on earth who deserved anything bad.

Zoey came into the bedroom, wearing a thick bathrobe and a towel wrapped around her hair. "Are you okay?"

Kellen clenched his jaw. "Just thinking about what I'd like to do to the kidnapper."

She frowned and nodded. "I don't have any messages from the police. I guess that means they haven't found anything new."

"I'm going to check my phone and see if any of the attorneys called."

"On a Saturday?"

"They jump when my parents call."

"I need to do something." She leaned over and rubbed the

towel over her hair. "We passed out fliers when Macy was missing. I think I need to make some."

At least that would keep her busy. "You do that, and I'll make some calls." Kellen went out to the living room and found his phone on the coffee table. He had a couple missed calls from the attorney's office.

They'd never steered his parents or siblings wrong. Hopefully, he would be able to say the same for himself.

He returned one of the calls, and went straight through to the lawyer's office.

"Kellen," he answered. "I hear you've had a terrible night."

"The worst." Kellen flung himself onto the sofa and played with the fringe of a decorative pillow.

"I'm afraid it's going to get worse."

He sat upright. "What do you mean?"

"I've got the inside track that they're looking at you as a suspect."

"Me? What?" His pulse raced through him like an out-of-control locomotive.

"The police say nobody saw you at the time of the abduction. Where were you?"

Kellen's mouth dropped. He'd gone home for more trash bags because Zoey's parents had run out.

"Kellen?"

The room spun around him. "I went home. They needed garbage bags."

"Did anyone see you?"

"I... I... No."

"You'd better get down here. Now. And you need to tell me everything."

Home

～

ARIANA WOKE WITH a start. Everything was black, and her arms were pinned back behind her. She tried to move them, but her wrists were tied together. The more she struggled, the more everything hurt. Her ankles were also bound.

Wherever she was, it had a funny smell. Like a strange mixture of sweet perfume and old stuff.

She continued struggling against her restraints. The mattress beneath her creaked and groaned.

Where was she? Ariana couldn't remember anything after being shoved into the car. There had been a bad smelling cloth and then... what?

A door squeaked and made the noise of opening on top of carpet.

Ariana held still.

What was going to happen next?

Her heart beat so hard she was afraid it would break out of her chest. Surely the person opening the door could hear it. It had never been louder.

"You're awake," said the familiar masculine voice. It was the man who had said he'd found the pumpkin king.

He hadn't.

"How do you feel?"

Ariana didn't reply. Maybe if she stayed perfectly still, he would think she was still asleep and leave her alone. But then her stomach rumbled, giving her away.

"You're hungry. I'll make bacon and eggs—your favorite breakfast."

Ariana flinched. How did he know?

"First, let's get this stuff off you." He tugged around her ears and pulled off a blindfold.

Bright light assaulted Ari's eyes. She closed them and tried to cover them, but sharp pain shot through her shoulders, reminding her that her arms were still behind her back.

"Do you still like your eggs sunny side up?"

Ariana opened her eyes and blinked quickly, trying to adjust to the light.

"And your bacon, crispy and almost burnt?"

She stared at the man, confused. He looked the same as he had the night before, only now he wore green and blue plaid pajama pants with a matching button up shirt and a stocking cap like she had seen in old Christmas movies.

"What's the matter, Jan?"

"Jan?"

He smiled at her. "You really need some breakfast. Will you stay in the bedroom if I remove the tape from your wrists and ankles?"

Wide-eyed, Ariana nodded. "I promise." Between the aches and sharp pains, she wasn't sure how much longer she could handle staying in that position.

"I'm so happy to hear that." He kissed her forehead and pulled out a pocket knife. "You don't know how long I've been waiting to take care of you."

Her eyes widened even more. What was he talking about?

A rip sounded as he cut the tape along her wrists. Her arms sprung forward when both sides had been cut. She brought them in front of her and pulled off the silver tape, ignoring the pain in her shoulders.

The man moved to her ankles and cut off that tape, also.

She stretched her legs, staring at him. Her heart still beat wildly out of control.

He ran the back of his fingers along her cheeks. "You're so beautiful, Jan. You haven't changed a bit."

"M-my name's Ariana."

"Don't be silly, Jan. You and your games. Why don't you change out of your costume while I get breakfast ready?"

Tears stung her eyes. "I want to go home."

"You are home. Don't you recognize your room? I know it's been a while, but I've kept it exactly as you left it."

Ari's lips quivered. "Please."

"With a cherry on top?" He twirled a strand of her hair between his fingers. "You're just as sweet as you've always been. You'll find all your clothes in the drawers—just where you left them."

"I just want to go home. My dad—"

"Jan, this is your home." His face clouded over. "And about Dad… He's not with us any longer."

Ari's mouth dropped. "What did you do to him?"

"You know how he never liked me?"

She gave him a double-take. "What?"

He sighed and clenched his fists. "This isn't how I pictured our reunion. Just get the costume off, put on your favorite outfit, and then we'll have a pleasant breakfast together. It's been too long. Hurry up now, Jan. Okay?"

Ariana swallowed and nodded. She wanted to go home, but she *was* hungry and at least the man didn't seem like he was going to hurt her.

"Good. Then you can tell me what you've been doing while you were away." He gave her a sweet smile and left the room. Something clicked, like he was locking it from the outside.

Tears welled up in her eyes and finally spilled out. Ariana sat up and pressed her palms on the stiff bed, looking around the room. The walls were a deep pink, almost purple. The ugly flowers on the bumpy bed coverings were the same shade. The canopy of the bed had the same patterns and colors.

Knock, knock.

"Are you getting dressed?"

Ariana slid off the bed, making it creak as it adjusted to her lack of weight on it. "Yes."

"Good. I've got the food cooking."

Without a word, she padded to the dark brown, wooden dresser. It had four long drawers and a couple smaller ones above them. Creepy dolls and stuffed hippos sat on top, seeming to watch her. She pulled open the top long drawer. Shirts in bright tones of yellow, red, orange, and brown sat folded neatly. Some were polka-dotted, flowered, or striped, but they were all ugly. The pants and skirts were no better.

Not that it mattered. She had to focus on finding a way out.

Ariana left the drawers open and went over to the window near the bed. It was nailed shut, and they were on the second level, anyway. It was too far to jump—it looked miles down to the pavement below.

The lock clicked. Ariana jumped over to the dresser and grabbed a shirt.

"You're still in your costume?" The man looked disappointed. "What's wrong, Jan?"

"I... I can't remember what my favorite is." She had to play along with his game if she was going to get out of there.

"Has it been that long?" He came over and looked at the bright yellow shirt in her hands. "No, not that one. Grandma got that for you, and you detested it, remember?"

Ariana nodded.

"You only ever wore it when she came to visit."

"Oh, yeah. I forgot."

He took the shirt from her and folded it neatly before setting it back in the drawer. "You loved this one." He pulled out a button-up shirt with flowers of every color and a long, pointed collar.

"Right. I guess I didn't see that in there."

"Hurry up. The food's almost done."

Ariana nodded.

The man's face lit up. "I'm so excited we finally get to be together again."

She forced a smile.

He cupped her chin and held her gaze. "You're going to have to tell Lloyd everything you've done while away. I haven't been able to stop thinking about you."

"M-me, too."

Lloyd left without a word, locking the door behind him.

Ariana slid out of her fairy-witch dress—the wings had disappeared. No, wait. She'd taken them off in her *real* room.

Hopefully she'd get to see it soon.

Breakfast

~

THE LOCK SOUNDED again. Ariana pulled on the stiff, uncomfortable clothes as quickly as she could. The door opened slowly, giving her just enough time to zip the high-waisted, scratchy pants.

Lloyd came in. His face softened and his head tilted. "You look exactly as I remember you, Jan."

Ariana bit her lower lip. "So do you."

His eyes widened. "Really? You've never said that before."

She nodded.

Lloyd pulled her into an embrace, holding on tightly and restricting her breathing. She turned her head so her face wasn't pressed against his flannel shirt. He smelled like bacon, eggs, and coffee.

"You don't know how happy that makes me." He released his hold on her. "Come and eat."

Ari's heart thundered. Maybe she could find a way of escape once out of the room, but she'd have to be careful because she didn't want to end up tied again.

He took her hand and led her out of the room, down a short hall with fuzzy green carpeting, and into the bright kitchen with a lot of yellows and greens. It made her eyes hurt. A small white and gold table sat to the side with two plates full of food.

"Sit, Jan. Do you still like orange juice?"

Ariana didn't, but she nodded anyway to keep him happy. She

sat at the seat with an empty glass. The other had a steaming cup of coffee.

Lloyd went into the fridge and pulled out a glass jar of OJ. "Freshly squeezed, just for you."

She smiled weakly, trying to figure out why he had her confused with whoever Jan was.

Her stomach rumbled at the sight of the food.

Lloyd poured her juice. "What are you waiting for?" He set the pitcher in the middle of the table and sat across from her, gazing at her.

Ariana squirmed. Could the food be safe? What if he wanted to poison her?

He ate the food on his plate. Maybe it was okay. She was too hungry to refuse the food in front of her. Ariana grabbed the fork and dug into a fried egg. Yolk spilled over the egg white, nearly covering the entire thing. She took a bite, and found it surprisingly tasty. Before she knew it, she'd emptied her plate. The only clue that any food had been there was the dried yolk on one side.

"I should've made more. Are you still hungry?"

She was, but didn't want to upset him. "I'm fine."

"Did you like it?"

"It was delicious."

He beamed. "Sure you don't want some cereal? You have to be hungry given the way you scarfed that down."

Ariana shrugged.

Lloyd set his coffee mug down and went to the cupboards. She took advantage of the moment to look for a possible escape. The window over the sink was probably too small to climb out of, and even if it weren't, she didn't know what was below. A deck or more concrete way down on the first level?

One doorway led into the cramped hall and the other? Hopefully she would find out. Maybe she could ask to use the bathroom and then look around when she was done.

He came over with two boxes of cereal. "Which one?"

"I dunno." She wasn't usually allowed to eat sugary cereals.

"This used to be your favorite." He opened the white box and poured colorful food into a bowl and filled it with milk and added a spoon.

The sweetness nearly exploded in her mouth. It was like eating candy for breakfast. She ended up eating two bowls before getting full.

Lloyd sipped his coffee, seeming to never take his gaze away from her.

She fidgeted with a nail under the table. It seemed like she should say something, but nothing came to mind. She knew better than to ask the questions she really wanted to—Why was she there? Would she ever get to go back home? What was he planning on doing with her? Was her family worried? They had to be worried sick. Once, she'd lost track of time playing in the neighborhood and come home late. Mimi had been in tears, scared that something had happened to Ariana.

Now something had happened to her, and she'd been gone far more than a half an hour.

"What have I missed?" Ariana finally asked. She had to think of this like her class play. She needed to stay in the character of Jan.

Lloyd sighed and set his cup down. "Do you really want to know?"

"Yeah."

He rubbed his eyebrows and took a deep breath. "Things have changed a lot. I'm sure you've noticed it's just me and you now."

"Uh huh."

Lloyd stared into her eyes. "Mom's not coming back."

Ariana's eyes widened, but she didn't say anything.

"Do you want to know what happened to her?"

"What?"

He pulled off his stocking cap and wrung it tightly, focused on that for a moment before turning his focus back to Ariana. "She took your death really hard. *Really* hard. She blamed me."

Ariana gasped. Had he killed a girl?

"But you know it's not my fault, right, Jan?" He stared at her with an intensity that nearly suffocated her.

Holding her breath, she nodded.

"Dad had her institutionalized, but…"

"What?" Ariana's stomach twisted.

"She hung herself."

Ariana's mouth dropped.

"I'm sorry," Lloyd said. "I hate being the one to tell you."

She just stared at him.

"You're in shock. I shouldn't have said anything." He smacked his own forehead. "Stupid!"

Ariana swallowed, afraid to move or say anything.

Lloyd smacked himself again and then turned to Ariana. "Dad got mean after that. Took to the drink and blamed me for everything. You, Mom. Everything. Even Barky."

"Barky?"

"It's best you don't know what happened to him."

"Did he—?"

"I said it's best to leave it alone!" He rubbed his temples. "It couldn't be helped."

She slunk down in the stiff chair. "Sorry."

He took a deep breath. "I know it's a lot to take in, but I am trying to find Mom, too. If she's forgiven me—and why wouldn't she? You're back safe and sound—she can take care of both of us. But don't worry, I'll take good care of you while we wait."

Ariana had no idea what he meant about the mom, so she just held his gaze.

"I'll be the best big brother there ever was," Lloyd said. "I swear it won't go like last time. This time, we'll grow up together happy."

She studied the man, at least as old as Mimi and Papi. He wanted to *grow up* with her?

"We finally have our do-over button, Jan. Everything went so wrong the first time around, but not this time. We've learned, right?"

"Um, right."

"And you know better now, don't you?"

"I think so."

"The water! You know how dangerous it is."

Ariana nodded. "It is."

He breathed a sigh of relief. "Good. This time we can turn everything around."

"Okay."

Lloyd picked up the empty plates and took them to the sink. Ariana picked up the glasses and set them on the counter next to him.

He turned to her. "I don't want you doing anything. Today, you're a princess."

What about tomorrow? She forced a smile and sat back at her spot, studying the kitchen while he hand-washed the dishes, humming.

What did he mean that he was going to try to find his Mom? If she'd hung herself... But then again, the real Jan sounded dead, too. Was he going to kidnap some lady to be their mom? Would he try to replace the dad and the dog, also?

Lloyd would be outnumbered. Maybe that would be a good thing.

He put the last plate on the dish rack and turned to Ariana, wiping his hands on his flannel pants. "Back to your room."

Disappointment washed through her. When would she get to see the rest of the house?

"But I have to go to the bathroom."

"We'll stop off there first." He waved her over.

She got up and went to him, dragging her feet.

He took her hand and led her down the hall again, stopping in front of a door. "Let's hurry."

Ariana let go of his grip and went in, locking the door. At least she could control *that* lock. She sat on the toilet and looked around the orange and green bathroom. It had no window, only a tiny vent in the ceiling.

"Are you done in there?"

She got up, pulled on the scratchy pants, and flushed. That was her answer. She washed her hands, trying to think of a way to escape. Maybe she could convince him to take her outside.

Ariana opened the door.

He came in and ran his hands through her hair. "I don't know why you cut your beautiful hair, but we need to grow it out again."

She nodded, but had no intention of staying that long—or growing out her hair. It was so thick that it became a tangled mess, nearly impossible to brush through.

Almost as though reading her mind, he pulled a brush out from a drawer and ran it through her hair. The brush stopped before he reached her ear. It was already snarled from not having been taken care of since before the party last night.

"We can't have this." He turned on the water and ran the brush under the sink before brushing again. He stopped and worked his way through each of her knots until finally he was able to brush through all of it with ease. Then he put the brush away and ran his fingers through her hair. "Much better. Back to your room, now."

Hand-in-hand, they went back to the very pink room. Ariana liked pink—her own room was in pale pinks and white—but this place was like a pink monster had thrown up from a time warp.

Once inside, Lloyd released her hand. "I fixed your dollhouse. Why don't you play with that while I'm gone?"

"You're leaving?"

"I wasn't expecting to find you last night. I need to go grocery shopping. This place has been a bachelor pad for a while—that's no place for my sweet little sister."

"Oh." Ariana played with the pointy collar on her shirt.

"Just get yourself reacquainted with your room, and you'll hardly notice I'm gone."

"Okay."

He kissed her forehead and held her gaze. "I'm so glad to have found you. You're back where you belong at long last."

Determined

ALEX'S EYES GREW heavier by the moment as he continued driving through town. He'd seen plenty of black SUVs, but not a single one matched the one he'd seen Ariana thrown into. He'd already downed three mochas, but now his heart raced and he was no less sleepy.

He would have to surrender and climb back into his old bed soon. But first, he wanted to drive down a couple more blocks. Maybe one of those would be the one. Then he could bust into a house and save Ariana. He'd be a hero, at least to her. The rest of the world could continue thinking of him as public enemy number one, but as long as his daughter was in his arms, nothing else would matter.

Alex turned down a residential road, slowing to study each vehicle. As with the other neighborhoods, the majority of the cars were white minivans, many sporting stickers of stick-figure families.

His stomach rumbled, begging for something other than caffeine, and his hands shook.

A little brown dog ran out into the street in front of him. Alex slammed on his breaks, barely missing the animal. A woman ran out from a house. She shook her fist at Alex and scooped up the ball of fluff. He waited for her to get back to her yard before driving away. Once he made it out of the neighborhood, he searched for the vehicle.

After a few minutes, he came to a store. A black SUV sat parked near the side. Alex's heart raced. It looked just like the one Ariana had been pulled into. He parked on the other end of the lot and walked as nonchalantly as possible to the vehicle.

He circled the SUV, listening and looking. It was sparkling clean, as though it had recently been washed. The windows in the back were tinted so dark, he couldn't see inside. Around front, the windows were also tinted. The front one, less so, but a curtain hung behind the driver's and passenger's seats.

If that wasn't suspicious, nothing was.

Alex walked around the vehicle again. "Ariana?"

Nothing.

"Are you in there?"

Silence.

He glanced around and then shook the SUV, fully expecting the alarm to wail. It didn't.

"Ariana!"

Nothing.

He pounded on the side of the vehicle.

Silence.

Alex pressed his face against the window, trying to get a better view. More curtains.

He swore.

Wait. If the abductor had gone inside, would he have been so stupid to take Ariana in there with him?

Alex snapped pictures of the SUV from all angles and then went inside, pretending to be unsure what to get. The smell of fried chicken wafted his way. He followed the aroma to the back, where he found a deli. He ordered twice as much as he should have and made his way to the registers, glancing down every aisle.

He froze mid-step in the pasta aisle. At the very end, stood a man who looked just like Ariana's abductor. No, it was him. Ari was nowhere in sight, though.

His pulse drummed in his ears. The man picked up a bag of pasta and put it into his short cart.

Alex's mind raced. Did he confront the man? Walk up and punch his ugly face? Call Fleshman?

The man turned to leave the aisle.

"Stop!" Alex dropped the chicken and ran after him. The man didn't seem to notice him. He simply pushed his cart out of the aisle and turned left.

Fury burned through Alex. His feet seemed to take off on their own. His boots weren't made for running and slid on the sleek floor. He steadied himself and took off after the kidnapper, skidding as he exited the aisle and turned left.

The jerk turned down the bread aisle.

"I said stop!"

The dude either didn't hear him or was pretending Alex was talking to someone else. Oh, how he wanted to beat the crap out of him.

Alex ran down the bread aisle, nearly crashing into a lady examining two bags of bagels. She glared at him and turned back to the bags.

He didn't bother muttering an apology. The man was already at the end of the aisle. There was no time to waste. "Stop!"

The jerk continued ignoring him and went to the frozen food section.

Alex caught up with him. It was definitely the same guy. Tall, balding, and that same big, ugly nose. "Hey!"

He turned to Alex, with a surprised expression. "Are you talking to me?"

"Yes! What'd you do with my daughter?"

"Pardon me?" He stared at Alex and then glanced around. "I've never seen you before, and I have no idea who your daughter is."

Several people stopped and stared.

"Really?" Alex scoffed. "I saw you throw her into an SUV."

The man shook his head. "You must have me mistaken for someone else."

"It was you!" Alex grabbed his collar. "Admit it."

He shoved Alex and stepped back. "I'm telling you, I have no idea what you're talking about. Leave me alone, or I'll press charges."

"Where's Ariana?" Alex demanded.

A lady in a suit stepped between them. "I'm the store manager. Is there a problem?"

"Yes," said the abductor. "This man is harassing me."

"He kidnapped my daughter!"

She turned to him. "Did you?"

"Of course not."

The manager turned to Alex. "I'm going to have to ask you to leave."

"Are you kidding me? He's a criminal!"

She put a hand on Alex's shoulder. "Sir, I'm not going to ask again. He is a regular around here. I've never met a more upstanding citizen. Security has already been called." She turned to the kidnapper. "Do you want to press charges?"

He shook his head and turned to Alex. "I really do hope you find your girl."

Anger tore through him. Alex pointed to the kidnapper. "You have my daughter!" He looked at the manager. "Now you're just as responsible for anything that happens to her as he is." Alex balled his fist and aimed for the man's face. He moved to the side and Alex only hit his shoulder. "You haven't heard the last of me." He glared at that manager. "Neither have you."

Two burly men in mall-cop uniforms sauntered over. One reached for Alex, but he moved out of the way. "I'm leaving."

He stormed out of the store, muttering under his breath. He bumped into a guy about his height with a baseball cap pulled low.

"Sorry," Alex muttered.

"It's fine." The man turned his back to Alex and walked away.

Once outside, Alex stood behind a pop machine. At the very least, he would follow the man to his SUV. Or maybe he should follow him. Then he might be able to find where Ariana.

Alex glanced around the parking lot. Clenching his car keys, Alex waited with baited breath.

Finally, the abductor exited the store. He pushed the short cart to a silver Volvo.

A Volvo?

He filled the trunk with paper bags and returned the cart to the store. If Alex didn't know any better, he'd almost believe the man was a decent, responsible human.

Snorting, he headed for his car. As he passed the silver sedan, he snapped as many pictures as he could with his phone. Not that it would help if it was stolen. The abductor would probably abandon it as soon as he got his food home.

Alex hurried into his beater, started the car, and sat low. The kidnapper returned to the Volvo and started it. Alex pulled out of his spot and followed from a distance, even though what he wanted to do was to ram into the car until the driver surrendered and pleaded for mercy.

The Volvo turned right out of the parking lot. By the time Alex pulled up, a large delivery truck moseyed down the road, blocking his vision of the car. Alex squealed out of the lot and tried to get around the truck, but there was too much oncoming traffic to get around. He tailgated, trying to convince the driver to either speed up or move aside so he could pass. He did neither.

"Come on!" Alex hit the horn.

The truck slowed to a stop at an unmarked intersection, his left blinker on.

Alex ran his hands through his hair. He should have just beat the crap out of the kidnapper at the store. He'd be on his way to jail, but at least the abductor wouldn't be getting away—again. He'd probably be more careful in the future now that he knew Alex was onto him.

He'd probably only made things worse.

Finally, the delivery truck turned. The Volvo was out of sight. Alex peeled forward, still not seeing the car anywhere. He glanced down side streets. Still nothing.

He needed to get the pictures to Fleshman.

Clue

~

A LEX BURST INTO the police station and hurried past the desk clerk.

"Hey, you have to check in!"

Muttering, Alex spun around. "I'm here to see Fleshman. He's expecting me."

"Really?" The clerk lowered her glasses and arched a brow.

"Yeah." Alex stood taller.

"Then I suppose you know he's home, sleeping."

Of course he was. Just like Alex had been planning to do before running into Ariana's kidnapper. "That's fine. I'll call him there." Alex held out Fleshman's card, which had his personal number scribbled on the back. "He told me to call anytime."

"Whatever." The clerk popped her gum, turned back to her computer, and started typing.

Alex headed back to his car, debating on whether or not to call and wake Fleshman. This was important enough. He'd found the kidnapper! There was no time to lose.

He started the car and called him.

The third ring cut off, followed by scratching noise and a groggy, "Hello?"

"I found him," Alex said. "The kidnapper."

"What? Where?"

"At the Giant Pear grocery store over on third."

"He's there now?" Fleshman asked, starting to sound more

awake.

"No, he left but I got his license plate. He's driving a Volvo now."

"This is Alex, right?"

"Yeah, and I know it's him."

"Okay. Give me a few minutes. Meet me at the station."

"Already here."

"You are? Okay, go in and talk to Head Detective Anderson. Tell him everything, then wait for me."

"Anderson. Got it." Alex repeated the name in his mind so he wouldn't forget.

"I hope you're right."

"I am."

"See you soon." The call ended.

Alex cut the engine and stepped back into the chilly air. There were some pumpkins by the entrance he hadn't noticed before. Everything about the upcoming holiday was a reminder of Ariana. She couldn't get enough of any of it.

He hoped she'd be back in time to enjoy a night of trick or treating.

She will. Alex clenched his fists. She had to be, or he'd hunt down the abductor and make sure he never saw another Halloween.

He held his head high and marched back into the station like he owned the place.

The clerk shot him an annoyed glance. "You again? Fleshman's still out."

"I know that. I need to speak with Head Detective Anderson."

She grumbled. "I'll get him. Have a seat. What's your name?"

"Alex." He glanced around the waiting room. Three others sat, all appearing strung out and agitated. He stood by the door to wait and mentally went over every detail of his interaction with the kidnapper. They couldn't afford to miss anything.

"Alex?" A male voice broke through his thoughts.

A familiar man with graying brown hair and bright eyes stood in front of him, wearing a suit and a badge on his belt. Alex thought he'd worked on his sister's case. He nodded. "I'm Alex."

"I'm Head Detective Anderson. Come on back."

Alex followed him into one of the interrogation rooms. He shuddered, remembering the times spent there being questioned as a kid.

"Do you have new information?" Anderson shut the door.

Alex glanced over at the two-way mirror, but ignored it. The more people who heard what he had to say, the better. "I saw the kidnapper."

"You did? Where?"

He told Anderson everything he'd told Fleshman over the phone.

Anderson scribbled notes onto a tablet as he spoke. "You say this all just happened?"

"Right before I came here."

"I need to find out if they called here to report the incident. If not, I'm going to need to get their statement." He rose from his seat.

"Fleshman is on his way," Alex said. "He wants to talk with me, too. Can I wait for him in his office?"

Anderson shook his head. "Just relax here. I'll make sure he knows where you are. Need some coffee?"

That was the last thing he needed at this point. Alex shook his head.

"Just hold tight." Anderson left the little room.

Alex glanced around and rubbed his eyes. His body ached with exhaustion, but between all the caffeine and his nerves, he could hardly sit still. He ran his hands through his hair and then over his beard.

Did all the fidgeting make him look nervous? Someone was

definitely behind that mirror watching him. The cops wouldn't give up the opportunity to watch the dad of the kidnapped girl when he was alone—especially when Alex had been the only witness to the crime.

He sat up straight in his chair and forced himself to sit still. It was tempting to get up and pace. Instead, he grabbed a pad of paper and a pen that sat at the other end of the table and started drawing a picture of the kidnapper as best as he could. Sure, the store should have cameras, but he had to do something with his hands and at least this might help the case.

Alex was adding the final touches when the door finally opened again. Fleshman walked in, looking no more rested than Alex felt. "Come with me to my office."

He ripped off his drawing and followed the captain.

Fleshman slammed his door and turned to Alex. "You assaulted the suspect?"

Apparently he'd caught up on everything. "He denied the whole thing and the store manager was going to kick *me* out."

"Sit," Fleshman ordered.

Alex sat.

"Don't do that again. It just makes you look bad. And besides, you're lucky he or the store didn't press charges."

"What about *him?*" Alex exploded. "He kidnapped Ariana! I saw him do it!"

Shaking his head, Fleshman sat in his chair behind the desk. "Next time you want to hit someone, call me. This crap just makes it a whole lot harder for me to do my job. I want to focus on catching the bastard, not cleaning your messes."

Alex nodded. "I wasn't thinking."

"Clearly. What's that?" Fleshman nodded toward Alex's drawing.

"The kidnapper." Alex handed the sketch to him.

Fleshman studied it. "That's actually pretty good. Looks a lot like the security footage."

"So, you saw him? Why aren't you out there, busting down his door?"

"Because this isn't TV. You say you got his license plate?"

Alex went to his pictures and handed the phone to Fleshman.

"I'll look into it. Chances are, it's stolen and won't lead us anywhere. Let me just text these to myself." He slid his finger around Alex's screen.

"But you'll look into it?"

"Of course. First, tell me everything about your run-in with the suspect."

"It sounds like you already know everything."

"Not from your perspective. Don't leave out a single detail. Something small could be a case-breaking clue."

Alex took a deep breath and told Fleshman everything, not even leaving out details that made Alex look bad. Maybe he'd left a mark on the jerk that would somehow help prove it was him if he tried to disguise himself.

"That's everything?" Fleshman asked when Alex was done.

"Yeah." He slunk down in the chair, nearly overcome with the need to sleep.

"Something doesn't make sense, though."

Alex's stomach twisted. "What?"

"Why would there be two vehicles? The SUV is what caught your attention, but we have the guy leaving in a Volvo."

"I don't know! Maybe he ditched the SUV in the parking lot. He could've stolen the Volvo. If you look into it, I'm sure you'll figure it out."

Fleshman nodded. "You didn't forget anything? No seemingly insignificant detail?"

"Wait!" Alex sat upright.

"Yes?"

"There was a guy at the grocery store. I didn't pay attention at the time, but when I was leaving, he was in my way. He was covering his face with a hat. Maybe he's got something to do with it! He could be working with the kidnapper."

"What did he look like?" Fleshman asked.

"His hat was covering his face."

"That's not a lot to go on."

"He was about my height."

The captain sighed. "Okay. I have to look at the store's security footage, anyway. I'll look for that guy as well. Can you think of anything else?"

"No, but if I remember something, I'll let you know."

"Okay, I'll go over all this with the team before I go back home for some sleep." He leaned over his desk. "I've also been looking for similar cases, and I found something."

Alex bolted upright. "What?"

Fleshman leaned even closer. "It's a long shot."

"What is it?"

He seemed to be debating whether to tell Alex.

"You can't leave me hanging like this."

"I've discovered a possible pattern. It could be a long shot. For about a decade, each year in late October, a girl goes missing in Washington. They all basically match Ariana's description—similar height and coloring. The locations vary a lot, and there are some other discrepancies, but there are too many similarities for me to let this go."

Alex stared at him, unable to blink or speak.

"I don't believe in coincidences. Something's going on." Fleshman's expression grew more intense.

"So, the same thing? Every year?"

"The cases have never been linked together, mostly because they're all over the state."

"Don't kids go missing every day? What makes these abductions unique? How did you figure out they're connected?" Alex's brows came together.

Fleshman's expression tightened. "In each of these cases, the girls were all found dead in or close to various lakes. All the deaths were determined to be right around Halloween. They all were drowned on or close to the holiday."

Alex's mouth dropped. "You... how... you think that could be Ariana's kidnapper? The person who *killed* those other girls?"

"It's a possibility. A lot of them were taken from a park, and the Ball Palace is basically just an indoor park, wouldn't you say?"

It took Alex a moment to find his voice. "And the other girls, they look like Ari?"

"Most have a little longer hair, but yeah. Most have the same color hair, skin tone, and big brown eyes. The only thing is that they're a little older, but Ariana's tall, so he may have thought she was older."

The office spun around Alex. "Most? Not all the girls? Maybe this isn't our guy."

"One girl had bright red hair, but it turns out she was wearing a brown wig with her costume when she was taken. Another girl was Mexican, but otherwise fits the bill."

His stomach lurched. The guy he'd punched in the store was old enough to have been doing this for that many years. "What do the other cops think?"

"I haven't brought it up yet. It's only a speculation, and I don't want it to get shot down before I can build my case. The girls have been taken from all over the state, from Vancouver to Yakima to Spokane and even here, not far from Seattle."

"We have to find him *now*. There are so many lakes in the area." Alex's breathing became labored.

"I don't want this theory to get blown out of the water for lack of evidence, so I'm going to keep digging. Once I have something compelling, I'm going to tell the team."

"Sounds compelling to me."

"That's why I'm telling you. If you want to search online, I can't stop you."

Alex nodded. "Okay, but don't you have better resources? Especially with the FBI helping?"

"Yes, but my time is limited. After I get some sleep, I'm going to be busy with the investigation team. I can't be off chasing theories like this, as likely as I feel it might be. I need to interview our newest suspect, and if the license plate pans out, that could be sooner rather than later. But I'm already up to my eyeballs with things to do."

Alex got up. "I'll see what I can find. Thanks, Captain."

"Call me Nick."

"Really?"

"Yeah. Let's talk tonight. Hopefully we'll both have something to share. I don't know about you, but I need some sleep. I'm going to put Anderson on finding the guy. If possible, one of us will have interviewed him by the time I talk to you."

"Hopefully put him in jail, too."

"We'll see."

Fleshman—Nick—handed him a folded piece of paper. "This is what I have on the other kidnappings. Start there."

Stuck

~

ARIANA JUMPED, STARTLED by the sound of a car door slamming outside. She shoved the nightstand back to it's original spot, making sure the legs went in the exact places the carpet was indented. Then she returned the lamp and decorative toys back to where they'd been.

The entire time Lloyd had been at the store, she'd been trying to escape the ugly room. She hadn't even found a loose floorboard. He'd been careful to make sure there was no way out.

Footsteps sounded and stairs creaked.

She ran over to the dollhouse and pulled out some of the dolls onto the floor. He'd said something about Jan liking those. She needed to get into character.

Thuds sounded out toward the kitchen as he put the groceries away. Ari was glad he was going to keep feeding her, but she didn't know why he wanted her there.

Did he really think she was his sister? He had to have known that she wasn't. That was why he had taken her, right? He'd been smart enough to lure her away with the game, so he couldn't be stupid enough to really think she was Jan?

If only she could figure him out, she might be able to find a way to get him to let her go. The first thing she needed to try was to get him to take her into the backyard. She'd seen swings when looking out the tiny window in the kitchen. Maybe if *Jan* begged him to go out there, he would give in.

The lock clicked.

Ariana grabbed two dolls and held them up, facing each other to make it look like they were having a conversation.

Slowly, the door opened. Lloyd came in. His face was red and the lines on his forehead seemed deeper.

"Th-thanks for fixing the dollhouse," Ariana said. "I love what you did to it."

His expression softened somewhat. "I'm really glad." His eyes darted back and forth across the room, lingering slightly on the window. "I really wanted to make your favorite lunch, but something came up. Someone—never mind. Are you going to be okay if you don't eat for a little longer?"

"Sure." If she was agreeable now, maybe he'd be more likely to take her out back later. Later might even be better. At dusk, it would be easier for her to try to find a way out. It was so bright out now, it would be hard to be sneaky.

"Thanks, and I'll make it up to you." His wide eyes made him seem truly sorry.

Ariana forced her sweetest smile—the one that usually got Papi to give her whatever she asked for. "It's okay."

Lloyd's shoulders relaxed. "You haven't changed a bit. I'll be as quick as I can." He left the room, locking the door.

She sighed and leaned against the bed. As anxious as she was, she wasn't really hungry, anyway. The only thing she wanted was to get out of the room and into her own clothes. She scratched her shoulder and then her side, hating the feel of the clothes. She always picked out soft fabrics for herself.

Ariana dropped the dolls on top of the others and went over to the window. Down below, Lloyd pulled out of the driveway in a silver car and down the rocky drive between the thick covering of trees. She squinted, trying to find another house through the woods.

Nothing. They could be miles and miles away from the nearest people for all she knew. Given how long Lloyd had been gone to get groceries, that was probably the case.

Interview

CAPTAIN NICK FLESHMAN poured himself a cup of coffee. It was stale as usual, but if he was going to stay awake, he would need it. He added sugar and cream, not that it helped any.

Anderson stopped and poured himself a cup, too. "Hey, Nick. What do you make of Mercer?"

"He just wants to find his daughter." He gulped down the drink, trying to ignore the taste.

"He's not the same kid he was back then, you know." Anderson leaned against the wall. "He's got a temper. We have to keep an eye on him."

"If you were face to face with the person you thought abducted your son, you'd punch him."

Anderson shook his head. "No, I'd *want* to hit him. I wouldn't do it."

"Because you know the law, and also how bad it'd make you look in the middle of a case."

"Obviously."

Nick crinkled his cup and tossed it into the garbage. "So, do you want to go with me to question the suspect?"

"He's going to love that. You think he's the guy?"

"Mercer is pretty sure."

"I know that. What do you think?" Anderson dropped his cup into the trash.

"We'll find out."

"Let me grab my tablet and a coat. Then we'll head over."

Nick nodded. "Meet you in the room." *The room* was where they kept everything for the big cases like this one. Every bit of evidence was laid out in order and white boards were filled with information on suspects, locations, and anything else pertinent. He headed over with Alex's drawing.

He glanced around the room, checking out what had been added to the list of suspects and timelines. Nick grabbed a magnet and added the sketch to the suspect list.

"What's this?" Special Agent Jones asked. She adjusted her brown glasses and studied the picture.

"Alex Mercer drew that of the suspect."

"The one he assaulted?"

"That would be the one."

"We have footage from the store. My partner's grabbing it as we speak."

"And I'm headed over to speak with the suspect now."

She arched a brow. "Shouldn't we send a detective for that?"

"I'm bringing one with me, but I want to lead this up."

"Your call. If you need anything, just say the word."

"Will do." Nick wandered the room until Anderson returned. "Let's head out."

They headed for Nick's black mustang with yellow racing stripes. No sense in showing up in a squad car, only to send the suspect running before they could talk to him.

"Do you wash it every morning?" Anderson asked.

Nick laughed. "Right, in all my spare time. No, I keep it in a garage."

"Thought you lived in an apartment."

"Condo," Nick corrected. "And I rent one of the fully enclosed garages. It was the only way I would live there." He patted the hood, remote unlocked the doors, climbed in, and started the engine.

"I'm surprised Corrine didn't get your car, too." Anderson shut the door and buckled himself.

"She knew better than to try, especially after taking the kids across the country." Nick squeezed the steering wheel and took a deep breath. This wasn't the time to think about any of that. He had to focus on the case.

"So, where does this guy live?"

"If he's not driving a stolen car, over in the Highlands." Nick entered the address into to the GPS.

"Really? This ought to be interesting."

"Could be." The Highlands was one of the most expensive neighborhoods in town. They rarely found themselves in the gated community that tended to police itself with a neighborhood watch headed up by a large former NFL star.

"He probably has a fancy attorney sitting at his front door."

Nick pulled out of the parking spot. "We'll find out."

Anderson speculated what they would find for the entire drive over. Nick nodded along, half-listening.

When they pulled up to the gate, Nick showed the security guard his badge. He examined it and then opened the gate.

The GPS told him to go straight and then left.

"Must be nice to live here. Look at these houses."

Nick was more focused on the road, but he did have to admit he wouldn't turn down an offer to live in one. Despite their differences, each house was sprawling and flawless. Not one had chipped paint, too-long grass, or moss growing on the roof.

Finally, they reached the house. It was tucked away in a back corner with more trees in the front than the others. It also had thick woods behind it.

A silver Volvo sat in the driveway.

Nick parked in front of the curb. "The car is where it's registered."

"Not stolen."

They got out of the Mustang and though he probably didn't need to, Nick set the alarm out of habit. They walked up the driveway, slowing as they passed the sedan. It was as tidy inside as the rest of the neighborhood.

Nick rang the doorbell. Everything was so quiet inside, he thought maybe no one was home. But then the door opened. A lanky, balding man studied them. "Can I help you?"

Both Anderson and Nick showed him their badges.

"I'm Captain Fleshman and this is Head Detective Anderson. We'd like to ask you a few questions. Mind if we come inside?"

"Sure. I'm heading out to a meeting soon, though."

"We won't be long," Anderson said. "Can you confirm who you are?"

"Flynn Myer."

It matched the name on the vehicle registration.

"Would you like to see my ID?"

"That won't be necessary."

Flynn led them to a large living room and indicated for them to sit on a brown leather couch. He sat across from them in a matching recliner. "Can I get you anything? Water? Soda?"

Anderson shook his head. "In this jurisdiction, even water could be construed as bribery."

Flynn's eyes widened. "Really? Well, I assure you that was the furthest thing from my mind."

"It usually is," Nick said. It was usually wads of cash or expensive electronics that shouted *bribe*.

"I assume this is regarding the incident at the Giant Pear?" Flynn leaned back and crossed one leg over the other.

Anderson pulled out his tablet. "We just have a few questions."

"I'm sure you do, considering I was accused of kidnapping."

Nick studied Flynn. He didn't fidget, glance around, break out into a sweat, or do anything else he would expect a guilty man of doing.

"Do you plan to press charges?" Anderson asked.

"Like I said at the store, no. I hope the poor guy finds his daughter safe and sound. I can't imagine what he's going through."

"What were you doing at around eight-thirty last night?" Nick asked.

Flynn scratched his arm. "I was giving a presentation at work to fifty people."

Nick and Anderson exchanged a glance. That was a solid alibi if it turned out to be true.

"Where do you work?" Nick asked.

"In the corporate offices of Speedwell Electronics."

"Seems like an odd time for a presentation," Anderson noted.

"The deadline for our different teams on what we'd been researching all month was six o'clock that night. My team was last, and we were all there until well after nine. I was nowhere near the missing girl."

"Have you ever seen Alex Mercer before he confronted you at the grocery store?" Nick asked.

"You mean aside from the news?" Flynn shook his head. "I recognized him from the news, that's it."

Anderson and Nick continued questioning him, and Nick paid special attention to his body language. The man was either innocent or had been trained well in how to fake it. It wouldn't have been the first time someone had faked all the right moves during an interrogation. Nick also studied what he could see of the house. The only thing remotely suspicious was how clean it was, but everyone in the Highlands likely had a maid service, if not a live-in housekeeper.

Nick finally rose from the comfortable couch. "That's all the questions we have for you. Thank you for your cooperation."

Flynn rose and shook both of their hands. "My pleasure. If there's anything else I can do to help, just say the word. Though, I don't know what I could do."

"Thank you for your time." Anderson nodded.

Flynn showed them to the door and gave a friendly wave as they left.

They got into Nick's car and headed back to the station.

"At least we can check him off the list," Anderson said. "I've never seen a suspect so obviously innocent."

"He was almost too innocent."

"What's that supposed to mean?" Anderson asked.

"Mr. Myer knew all the right things to say and do. It was a little too perfect."

"Just be glad we can take him off our list and focus on finding the real perp."

Nick nodded, but he wasn't going to remove Flynn from his list just yet.

Waiting

~

ZOEY TURNED HER PHONE on silent. It had been blowing up with alerts all day, and she'd finally had enough. Didn't people know she had more important things to do than to answer half a trillion messages? Her daughter was missing and right at that very moment, her fiancé was being questioned by the FBI. The FBI!

She glanced around the police station waiting room. Two hookers sat across from her discussing business practices and just a few seats down from them, she swore a guy was setting up a drug deal over the phone.

"How much longer?" she muttered. Why was it taking so long? Kellen had done nothing wrong. Sure, he'd left her parents' house at the exact time of the abduction, but he'd returned with the garbage bags. There was no way he'd have had the time for a kidnapping—not that he'd ever do anything like that.

Kellen was a stand-up guy with a good career that he'd never put at risk, not that he would ever think of hurting anyone, much less Ariana. He was always so sweet with her.

The door to the station opened, blowing in cold air and a few multi-colored leaves. Two men came in, both yelling over each other. A cop entering with them told them to shut up and directed them to the waiting room.

Zoey wrapped her fingers around the car keys. Surely, Kellen would understand if she went for a drive.

She sent him a quick message.

Text me when you're done.

Once locked inside the car, she felt better—at least as much as she could with Ariana missing and her fiancé being interrogated about it. Alex was the one they needed to question heavily, but he always seemed to get out of having to pay for any consequences. It had always been that way. Had his parents not been so willing to look the other way when they were young, they would have never ended up together.

Sneaking out of the house, smoking—they had always pretended not to see any of it. Heck, Zoey had gotten pregnant with Ariana under their roof. Maybe if they had been better parents, Ariana wouldn't be missing—or maybe she wouldn't even exist.

Zoey's stomach twisted. She didn't like that thought, either. She could blame people all day long, but that wouldn't bring back Ariana.

What would? Questioning Kellen? That was stupid. He had nothing to do with it.

She pulled out her phone and checked the news sites and social media—not that she expected any updates. She would be the first to know if anything changed. The news sites just reiterated the same information over and over, some with differing spins on theories. None of it brought them any closer.

On social media, the case was still a trending topic with people spouting so many opinions it made her head spin. She had nearly fifty unread messages, and scanning the list, it was just people expressing sympathy. Nothing urgent to answer.

Waiting was the worst. She wanted to get out there and *do* something. There were search teams in the various woods in the area, but Kellen's attorneys had advised them to stay close to home and to keep their phones on them at all times.

There had to be something she could *do*. There had been talk of a press conference, but nothing more. Maybe it was up to her to make that happen.

Her phone alerted her to a text.

I'm finished. Where are you?

In the parking lot. I'll come inside.

She climbed out.

"Are you Zoey Carter? Do you know what happened to Ariana?"

She spun around. A woman in a suit shoved a mic in Zoey's face. A cameraman stood behind her.

"I need to get in there."

"What happened to Ariana? Why did you give her up for adoption?"

Zoey shoved the mic away and glared at the woman. "It's none of your business. Move aside."

"How close were you to the missing girl?"

"We *are* quite close. Now leave me alone." She pushed the woman out of her way and ran inside.

Kellen stood in the waiting room, his arms folded. "Why did you leave?"

"Technically, I didn't. I just went to the car to get away from the crazies." She glanced over to see even more had come in while she was outside.

"Come on. Let's go."

"I need to talk to someone about setting up a press conference."

"You couldn't have done that while I was in there?"

"I didn't think of it then." She went over to the desk. "I need to speak with Captain Fleshman. He's in charge of my daughter's case."

"He's off duty. You can speak with Head Detective Anderson."

"Where is he?" Zoey asked, stepping toward the hall.

The clerk glared at her. "Have a seat."

"Why can't I go back there? My daughter is *missing.*"

"And our team is doing everything possible, including working around the clock."

"I need to talk with him so we can do more."

"Have a seat," the clerk snapped.

Zoey went back to Kellen. "What happened in there? Did they interrogate you, or just ask more questions? Did your lawyer leave already?"

He nodded, avoiding her gaze. "Let's go."

"What's wrong?" she asked.

Kellen sighed and looked conflicted. "This isn't what I signed up for."

"What does that mean?"

"Getting interrogated by the FBI for something I didn't do, that's what I mean."

"This isn't easy on anyone. I've never been more stressed out in my life—more scared. I might never see her again."

"And you act like you're the only one who cares. The only one who this is hard on. Wake up, Zoey. You're not!"

The druggies and hookers were starting to stare.

"Maybe we should have this conversation somewhere else."

"Great." Kellen stepped away from the wall. "Let's go."

"I'm waiting to talk to… what'd they say his name was?"

"Do whatever you want. I'll meet you in the car." Kellen stormed out the door, slamming it behind him.

Research

A LEX'S CHIN HIT his chest, and he snapped it up, awake. He stared at the laptop screen in front of him on the desk, trying to focus his vision. He'd taken a nap, but it hadn't been enough. He needed to find everything he could on the previous similar kidnappings.

He adjusted himself in the chair and clicked over to the images of the other girls. Chills ran down his back. They all looked so much like Ariana—and they'd all ended up dead on Halloween.

Knock, knock.

"Come in."

Macy came in, followed by the tabby. She gave him a sad smile. "How are you holding up?"

Alex groaned. "I don't know how Mom and Dad lived like this for so long."

She sat on his bed. "Ari's a fighter. I'm sure she's going to be back soon."

"I hope so." He rubbed his eyes. "Come look at this. These girls who went missing around the state every single year like clockwork—they look just like her."

Macy came over to the desk and studied the pictures. "Are the police looking into it?"

Clementine jumped onto Alex's lap and purred as he curled up. Alex scratched the cat's head and looked at Macy. "Maybe someone in the FBI is looking into it?"

"It seems pretty obvious to me." She glanced at him. "And you look exhausted. Do you want me to do this while you sleep?"

Alex opened his mouth to protest, but stopped himself. "You don't mind?"

"Not at all. I want my niece back as much as you do. I've been contacting reporters and news blogs all day, getting the word out."

"You have?"

Macy nodded. "They seem to like the angle that I was kidnapped, too. It sensationalizes it, so they want to interview me for the ratings."

"Of course they do." Alex clenched his fists. "Jerks."

She put her hand on his shoulder. "Whatever it takes to help find Ari. It's getting her story and picture out to more people."

"I guess. Doesn't mean I have to like it. They're so slimy."

"We'll use it to our advantage. Get some sleep." She shoved him out of the chair and sat.

"These are my notes." Alex clicked over to an open Word document that filled several pages already. "And these are the sites I'm looking at." He clicked over to the open browser that had about thirty tiny tabs at the top.

"You're nothing if not thorough." She clicked on a few of the tabs. "Let's see what a fresh set of eyes can find while you sleep."

"Oh, and this is what Fleshman gave me." He gestured to the unfolded paper, set Clementine on the floor, and climbed into bed, his eyes already closing. He barely had time to pull the blankets over him before falling asleep.

When he woke, he felt more rested than he had since Ariana had been taken. He stretched and sat up. Macy still sat at the computer. From the sounds of it, she was typing furiously.

"What's going on?" Alex asked, his voice groggy.

She turned around. "Zoey called. They're having a press conference a little later if you want to go."

His heart sank. "Right, because I'm so popular."

Macy frowned. "Then show them they're wrong."

He shook his head. "It's not worth it. I don't care what people think. My time is better spent trying to find the kidnapper."

"Oh, that reminds me." She held up his phone. "Your phone rang several times, and Fleshman called."

Alex threw the blankets off him and jumped out of the bed. "What did he say?"

"He wanted to talk to you, not me."

"Did he say anything?" Alex leaped across the room and grabbed the phone from his sister's hand.

"Just to let you sleep."

"This is more important." He called Fleshman back. "This is Alex. What did you find?"

"I interviewed the guy you punched and he has an airtight alibi, Alex. It wasn't him."

Alex swore. "Did you look into his story?"

"Yes. Many of his coworkers confirmed his story. He was nowhere near the Ball Palace at the time of the abduction. He was giving a presentation at that time in front of about fifty people."

"He's lying. Maybe he bribed them."

"We've got time-stamped pictures and video showing he was there. I'm sorry, Alex."

"It was him! I *saw* him. I'd bet my life on it."

"I believe you, but it had to have been someone who looked like him."

"Just like him?" Alex snapped.

"I've seen stranger things than that in this job."

"Did you go to his house?" Alex demanded.

"Yes. There was nothing suspicious. I can tell when people are lying, and he wasn't."

"Did you look for trap doors? People like that will hide a door underneath a rug, you know. You could have been interviewing him just feet away from Ari. She could've heard the whole thing."

"Look, Alex." Fleshman's voice lowered. "Everyone else has written him off, but I want to keep an eye on him."

"What does that mean?"

"Exactly what I said, but in the meantime, we need to focus on other leads."

"Like what? Why don't you want anyone to know?"

"I need you to focus on the other thing. Have you found anything yet?"

"They seem connected, but I don't know that's going to help us find Ari."

"Are you going to the press conference?"

"No."

"It would be a good chance to talk to the perpetrator. Chances are whoever did this will watch. You can appeal to his—"

"It's a media stunt. Let Zoey and her parents plead. If I make one wrong move, everyone's just going to jump all over it. People already blame me—why set myself up for more?"

Macy turned to him. "The press conference?"

Alex nodded.

"I'll go."

"Macy will do it."

"That's actually a good idea," Fleshman said. "Everyone will be thrilled to see her again, and she's the face of hope in these situations."

"And she's not me," Alex muttered.

"I wouldn't rule out some kind of statement. Does she know the information—time and place? Everyone needs to be there early."

"Hold on." He handed the phone to his sister, grabbed his laptop, and sat on his bed. He read over the new notes Macy had added to his list. The cases *had* to be related. How could they not? The girls all looked nearly the same, were taken around the same time every year, and found dead right after Halloween. It was entirely too much to be a coincidence.

The alert for a new social media notification sounded. Why hadn't he turned those off yet? He went over to the tab to fix that. Just as he did, he saw the preview of the message received.

His blood ran cold.

Threat

~

THE ALERT NOTIFICATION had shown the first line of the message: *Leave innocent people alone or you'll be sorry.*

Alex clicked it to read the entire thing. The message was sent by someone with a picture of a dog named John Doe. The full message read: *Leave innocent people alone or you'll be sorry. Don't hit and expect to not be hit back. Like your job? Then let the cops do their job and stay out of it! This is your only warning. And don't be stupid enough to show this to them. I'll know.*

Alex took several deep breaths and read it over three times, trying to believe someone had actually dared to threaten him.

Who knew about him hitting the kidnapper? As far as he knew, the story hadn't been told on social media. The cops knew, the people who had been at the store, and of course the abductor. No one else should've known.

He tried to study the profile, but everything was private. He could only see the nondescript, blurry profile photo.

Fury tore through him. How dare someone threaten him? And hiding behind a fake name, no less. What a coward.

Alex clicked reply and typed furiously, telling the loser off. Once finished, he read over the message that was so ugly it would've made the ex-marine he worked with blush.

"Are you okay?" Macy's voice broke through his thoughts.

He erased the message, closed the tab, and nodded at his sister. "As much as could be expected."

She squeezed his shoulder. "Sure you don't want to go to the press conference?"

Alex shook his head. In his mood, he'd only say something he was sure to later regret. "You'd have a better chance at getting through to the kidnapper. Is Fleshman right about the kidnapper? You think he'll be watching?"

"It wouldn't surprise me. If he's anything like Chester, he's so full of himself, he'll have a hard time not watching anything to do with him. Even if he doesn't watch live, he'll find replays."

"Thanks, Macy."

"Anything for you and Ari. I should get going, though. Fleshman says everyone needs to be there early to get briefed."

"Do you think we're going to find her?" Alex stared at a smiling photo of Ariana that popped up on his news feed.

"If I have anything to say about it, we will. Keep digging into those old abductions. It looks like you're onto something."

"I sure hope so."

She gave him a quick hug and left the room.

He closed out all the social media tabs. He didn't need the distraction—especially not messages from trolls. That had to be what it was. Just some idiot trying to get a reaction out of him. He wouldn't give in and respond.

Like Macy had said, his time would be better spent continuing to look at the other cases. But if the cops hadn't been able to find the guy, what made Alex think he could find anything useful?

He scanned over the notes and then read over several articles, hyper-focused on finding a clue that had been overlooked by everyone. He studied the maps surrounding each lake. There had to be *something*.

His eyes grew blurry, but then he saw it. He sat up straight and switched back and forth between the tabs.

That was it. He'd found the connection. *A* connection, at least.

Each of the lakes had a small island—if they could even be called that. A small chunk of land, each big enough to have some kind of plant life, sat on each lake where the Halloween girls had been drowned. That had to be more than a coincidence—and enough to get the FBI to pay attention to the cases.

Alex looked around for his phone. Macy had left it on his desk. He moved his laptop and scrambled over there, calling Fleshman as fast as he could.

"Change your mind, Alex?"

"No, I found something."

"What?"

"A connection between the other cases."

"What is it?"

Practically out of breath and stumbling over his words, Alex told him about the lakes.

"Hmm," was all Fleshman said.

"That's it?" Alex exclaimed. "This is huge. We can get the rest of your department on board with this. They'll—"

"It's not enough, Alex. We need a bigger connection—like someone who lived by each one at the time of the murders. Something like this is like saying they all happened on a cul-de-sac. It might be helpful, but we can't change the direction of the case because of it."

"This is something. It's a start. We have to tell them."

Fleshman didn't respond.

"I'm going to keep looking. I'll find more."

"Good idea. I'll give you a call after the press conference."

"Okay." Alex ended the call, deflated that Fleshman hadn't been nearly as excited about the new information as he was. They were definitely on to something. Maybe he just had to work a little harder to prove it to him.

His phone buzzed. Alex glanced at the screen—a text from his boss.

Just what he needed.

Call me.

Probably better to get it over with before he forgot all about it. He called.

"You coming in Monday?" Darren greeted him.

"Have you seen the news? My daughter was kidnapped."

"See, I thought that was someone else because in all the time you've worked here, you never mentioned a kid."

Alex bit back vehement retort. "I gave her up for adoption. Doesn't mean I don't care."

"Whatever. Just get back here Monday."

"I have two weeks of sick days built up, plus vacation time."

"You can't use the vacation time—not without a month's notice. And you don't sound sick to me. We have that big project next week, and you know how important that is. I need you for this job."

Alex swore. "My daughter is missing!"

"And we have a mansion to re-roof."

Was Darren for real? Or maybe Alex had been too much of a pushover, taking every opportunity for overtime given to him.

"You there?"

"Yes," Alex snapped.

"Will I see you Monday?"

"You can count on that." Alex ended the call. He'd either show up and have it out with Darren, or maybe bring Fleshman or a lawyer with him. Darren couldn't threaten to fire him for missing work because of this. It wasn't just heartless, it had to be illegal.

He hoped.

Hungry

~

ARIANA'S STOMACH RUMBLED. The house had been quiet since Lloyd had left. She'd had more than enough time to search every little part of the room. He'd sealed it tight. There wasn't even a piece of loose molding.

She went back to the window and stared at the woods. It was dark outside, but she hadn't turned on the light in the room. With no curtain or blind, she felt like someone could watch her from out there. There were so many places to hide out in those thick woods and she already felt so vulnerable.

The moon cast a light glow on everything and the branches rustled. Normally, she'd have loved the spookiness of everything, especially so close to Halloween, but all she wanted was to go home. To be safe and secure, able to hug all of her loved ones.

She couldn't help wondering what they were doing right then.

A noise startled her. It took Ariana a moment to realize it was the sounds of gravel crunching under tires.

Was Lloyd finally back? She was so hungry by now that she was actually excited for his arrival. If his mood had improved, maybe she could even talk him into a trip to the backyard.

Her stomach roared as she hoped for something to eat. He had been gone so long, maybe he was bringing takeout. She didn't think she could handle waiting as a meal cooked.

Maybe Jan had liked fast food. Lloyd really seemed to want to make her happy.

The thought of a greasy burger and fries made Ari's mouth water.

Lloyd pulled the sedan up to the house, but didn't get out right away. She strained to see what he was doing, but couldn't see into the car from her angle.

Didn't he know how hungry she was?

Ariana grew tired of waiting and went over to the bed. She stumbled over her own feet, feeling faint. Her stomach continued growling.

It had been so hard staying in the ugly room all day, knowing food was just on the other side of the door. So close, but so far away. She'd tried pulling and twisting on the doorknob, hoping to loosen the lock somehow, but had given up. The thought of breaking down the door had crossed her mind, too, but there was nothing in the room hard enough—just stuffed animals, dolls, posters, and paperback books.

She sighed and closed her eyes.

A car door slammed outside. Ariana didn't bother getting her hopes up. Not until Lloyd said the food was ready.

The house remained quiet for a while—it felt like days—until she finally heard something outside the room. It sounded like he was rummaging through something in the kitchen.

She moaned and then her stomach rumbled again.

More noises sounded from the kitchen. Pots and pans banged around. Water ran. A fan sounded. Dishes clanged against each other. Silverware rattled.

All familiar noises, but none of it brought any comfort.

Tears blurred her vision of what little she could see in the room from the moonlight. She tried to blink them back, but they spilled out and rolled down her face, pooling in her ears. Ariana sniffled and sobbed silently.

She thought about her parents—all of them—and her friends. Would she ever get to see them again? Or would Lloyd be the only person she saw anymore? What if he was the last person she ever saw?

Ariana rolled over and muffled her sobs into the pillow. She couldn't let that happen.

The lock clicked.

She sat up and wiped the tears from her face.

The door opened. The smell of garlic bread and spaghetti sauce filled the air.

"Are you sleeping?" Lloyd asked.

The light came on, blinding Ariana for a moment. She covered her eyes. When she lowered her arms, she met his gaze.

"You've been crying? What's the matter?" He rushed over to her, putting an arm around her and and pulling her close.

Ariana could hear his rapid heartbeat against his chest.

"Talk to your brother. Are you upset because I was gone so long?" He ran his palm over her hair, over and over again.

She needed to get into character. "Yeah. Where were you?"

He cleared his throat. "I had some business to take care of, but I'm back now. Are you hungry?"

"Starving."

"Let's get you cleaned up and eat."

Her stomach growled.

"Come on." He helped her off the bed and led her down the hall, into the bathroom.

Suddenly, she realized how badly she had to go. "Can I have some privacy?"

"Do you have to pee?"

Ariana glanced to the floor and nodded, silently pleading with him to let her go alone.

"I'll be right out here." He closed the door. "Don't lock it."

At least it was closed. "Okay." She opened the lid and sat. As she went, she studied the bathroom again, hoping to see something she'd missed. There wasn't even a vent. Only the door.

She flushed and then turned on the water to wash her hands. The door opened and Lloyd came in. "You'll feel better after we eat. I made spaghetti."

Ariana tried to force a smile, but her mouth wouldn't cooperate.

He opened a drawer and pulled out a hairbrush. While she washed her hands, he ran the brush through her hair.

"You're perfect, you know that?"

She washed her hands harder.

"Just like you always were."

What was she supposed to say to that?

He put away the brush and handed her a towel. "Let's eat. I think the meatballs are done sautéing."

Ariana followed him into the kitchen.

He pointed to a salad bowl. "Mix that while I check the meatballs."

Without a word, she did as she was told. It had strange purple leaves mixed in with the dark green ones. It also had radishes, celery, and other things she'd never seen in a salad.

He carried the hot food over to the table, so she brought over the salad.

"Have a seat."

Ariana sat in the one she had at breakfast. Lloyd dished them both food and poured her some milk. She ate so quickly, she could barely taste the food and she burned the roof of her mouth, but she didn't care. There was no telling when she would eat next and she was already so hungry.

She ate two full plates of food.

"Sorry about skipping lunch." Lloyd frowned. "Something came up, but I'll make sure that doesn't happen tomorrow." The look on his face seemed like he really was sorry.

"It's okay." Ariana hoped that was what Jan would've said. That's what Ari would have said to a loved one who felt bad about something.

He studied her. "You're upset about what I told you, aren't you? About Mom and Dad."

Ariana nodded. Jan would have been, and also she herself was really upset over not being able to see her own parents.

His expression darkened. "I shouldn't have said anything. Stupid!" He pounded his fist on the table.

"You're not stupid."

Lloyd smiled. "Thanks, Jan. I can always count on you to cheer me up. Can I make it up to you?"

Her breath caught. This was her chance to ask about going outside. Ari's heart felt like it would explode out of her chest. "Can we play in the backyard?"

Fenced

~

LOYD STARED AT ARIANA, unblinking and with his eyebrow twitching.

Maybe it had been too soon to ask about going outside.

She tried to think of something to say to make everything better. What would he want to hear?

"Well, we still have your favorite coat," he said. "I don't see how going out back for just a little bit will hurt anything. You're probably itching to run around, aren't you?"

Ariana's eyes lit up. "Yeah. I'm getting sore."

"That's my fault, too. We can't have you wasting away. Put the dishes away, and I'll find your jacket."

She jumped out of her seat and carried her plate to the sink. When she turned around, Lloyd had left the room. Her pulse drummed in her ears. As tempting as it was to run, she didn't know the setup of the rest of the house. It was too big of a risk. He'd agreed to take her outside, anyway. She only needed to wait a few more minutes.

There had to be a way out in the backyard. A loose fence board or maybe some way to get underneath. He hadn't been planning to take her out there, so maybe he didn't have it sealed tight.

Her mind raced as she put everything away. This nightmare could be close to over. Even if the yard was sealed as well as everything else, she could find a way to start digging a little at a time.

Noises sounded in the hallway, just outside of the kitchen. It sounded like things bumping into each other. Finally, Lloyd appeared, holding up an ugly brown and white striped jacket. At least it looked warm, and with the colors, it might help her hide as she searched for a way out.

"Remember this one?" he asked.

Jan probably did. Ariana nodded. "I can't believe you saved it."

He beamed. "Try it on. See if it still fits."

She set the bowl in her hands onto the counter, walked over, and slid into it. It was slightly snug, but would be fine. She sneezed.

"Sorry, it's been in the closet so long."

"It's okay. Can we go outside now?"

"Yeah. I'll finish the dishes later. Still love hide and seek?"

"Perfect." Things were really starting to go her way.

"Let's go out the back way." He opened a little door next to the kitchen that Ariana had thought went into a cabinet, instead it was a little staircase. Lloyd took her hand and led her down the tight, winding staircase. "The house has undergone some remodeling over the years, but this was never touched. I made sure some things would remain exactly the same for your return."

"Thanks."

"Just like the backyard. Some have called the old play set creepy, but it's not."

"I bet it's just like it was."

"It is. I've kept it all up just for you."

The stairs ended at a little entryway. The floor was tiled with white and gold flowered tiles. Pet dishes sat in a corner.

"Is there a dog?"

Lloyd squeezed her hand.

"Do you want me to get another one for you? I'm sure you're crushed about Barky."

Ari nodded. She'd begged for a puppy for years and years, but this wasn't how she wanted to get one.

"We'll think about it." Lloyd released her hand, opened a panel, and typed in a code next to a red, blinking light. He pressed enter and it turned off. Then he unlocked a chain and two deadbolts.

She swallowed. They were really locked in tight.

He opened the door and chilly, fresh night air blew in along with a few soggy leaves. One stuck to her sock.

"I don't have any shoes."

"Did you forget?"

She stared at him. "What?"

He gestured behind her.

Ari spun around. A shoe rack sat against the wall, holding a dozen pair of shoes. She grabbed a pair of sneakers that matched the coat.

"How do they fit?"

"Fine." They were slightly loose, so she tightened the laces.

"Everything's going to be just like it was." His face lit up, but then soured. "Well, mostly. It's just the two of us now, but I kind of think that's for the better, don't you?"

"It's nice." *Please let me outside.*

"Let's get out back before the rain starts again."

"Okay. You wanna be 'it'?" That would give her time to look around the yard.

"Don't you want to see the yard first? It's been so long."

"Sure. Then we'll play."

He threw his head back and laughed. "You really haven't changed a bit, Jan. Maybe this time we'll get it right."

"Huh?"

Lloyd shook his head. "Never mind. Forget I said anything."

Ariana had a feeling she really wanted to get out of there before she found out what he meant by getting it right.

He opened the door wider and she went outside. The sweet

autumn air had never smelled better. She glanced around the dark yard, not able to make much out.

Several lights overhead on the house came on and Lloyd stepped outside. "What do you think?"

It reminded her of a scary movie she and Emily had watched once when they were supposed to be sleeping. "Looks just the same."

"Oh, good. I've even been painting the swing set to keep it from rusting. You wouldn't believe how hard that is. Want to try it?"

"Then we'll play hide and seek?"

"Sure thing."

Ariana headed for the swings, forcing herself to put a bounce into her step. She had to stay in character.

The chains holding up the swings seemed iffy at best. She picked the lowest one just in case it didn't hold her weight and climbed on, clinging to the cold metal. Lloyd went behind her, grabbed the chain below her hands, and gave a hefty push. The chain pinched her palms.

"How's that?" he asked.

"Good."

"You're barely moving." He pushed again, harder this time.

Ariana clutched the chain, afraid the swing would give out at any moment.

"Pump your legs!"

She did, but wished she could just explore the yard. Her feet pumped, he pushed, and she kept going higher, higher, higher. Hair flew into her face and then off again. She almost felt free, but knew better. There was no way she could forget spending the entire day locked in that room.

Ariana wouldn't be free until she was home and in the arms of all four of her parents. She tried looking around the yard for a place to escape, but she was moving too fast to be able to concentrate.

Finally, he stopped pushing. The swing slowed and Ariana dragged her toes along the grass to bring herself to a full stop. Pulse racing, she asked, "You going to count?"

"What number do you want this time?"

"A hundred." She may as well aim high. The worst he could do was to say no.

"Why doesn't that surprise me?" He turned toward the fence. "I'm going to count fast, though."

"Okay."

He put his hands against a post and leaned his face against an arm. "One. Two…"

She spun around and studied the yard. Nothing was against the fence for her to climb and there were no boards for her to step on. On this side of the yard, the fence only had vertical slats.

Lloyd was already counting in the twenties. She ran near the house and walked along the fence line. There was no space underneath, either—not that she could see. She bent down and felt the ground, pushing on the bottom of the fencing. No space anywhere. Not even enough for a fingernail.

"Fifty-three. Fifty-four…"

She got up and jogged along the perimeter, studying the boards and the dirt underneath.

"Eighty-nine. Ninety."

Ariana had only made it about halfway around the yard, but she needed to find a place to hide so she appeared to be playing the game.

Conference

~

Zoey stared at the busy scene in front of her. The waiting room in the building behind the police station was filled with activity. Conversation out in the foyer grew louder by the moment as reporters waited, hoping they would get to sit in the theater for the press conference.

Kellen sat at the other end of the room, still upset with her. Macy and her parents sat, talking with Zoey's parents. Even Ariana's teacher and coach were there to speak.

Of course, Alex wasn't there. He, more than anyone should have been since he'd been the person who'd put everyone in this position to begin with. What a coward.

Captain Fleshman came over and sat next to her. "You know what you're going to say?"

"I'm going to tell everyone how much I miss her and how much she needs to be home with her family."

"You're going to tell *the abductor* those things."

"Right."

He held her gaze. "No, this is important. You're speaking to the kidnapper. We need to convince him to let her go."

"You really think that's going to happen?"

"He's human. We have to play on his emotions. Otherwise, what's the point of all this?"

"I thought it was to get the word out about her disappearance."

"Practically everyone in the country knows about this case. People like this tend to be full of themselves. The abductor is going to want to hear what everyone is saying about what he did. If you post something on social media, he probably won't see it. But if you speak to him here, I can almost guarantee he'll hear you."

"Okay. I'll plead my case to the lowlife."

"Just make it about how much she needs her family. Not the other way around."

"Got it."

"Sure?"

"Yes," she snapped.

He rose. "If you have any questions, just let me know. I'll start everything since I'm the head of the case. Then the teachers will share, Macy will speak, followed by you, and then finally, your parents."

She rubbed her temples. "Understood."

Fleshman went over and spoke with Macy.

Zoey glanced over at Kellen. He was speaking with another cop.

Why did they have to be fighting, now of all times? She needed his support. He was the one who always told her things were going to be okay when she was stressed out. He was still mad about being interrogated, but it wasn't like they'd taken him into custody.

She took a deep breath and glanced at her notes. She wouldn't use them when it was her turn to speak, but they had helped her get her jumbled thoughts organized. With any luck, she would remember most of what she'd written down.

Someone clapped in the middle of the room. It was Fleshman. "Are you all ready?"

A solemn chorus of yeses went around the room. Zoey tried to make eye contact with Kellen, but he didn't look her way. They all lined up and followed the captain and a couple other officers down a narrow, dark hallway that led to the backstage of the theater.

Macy took Zoey's hand and squeezed. She gave her a sad smile. "How are you holding up?"

A mixture of relief and overwhelming sadness rushed through Zoey. She'd really missed her childhood best friend. "Not well. It's like reliving what happened to you, only…" She struggled to find the right word.

"Worse?" Macy offered.

"Different. I was equally scared, but it's…" Worse. It was infinitely worse having her daughter missing. But she couldn't say that to Macy.

"I get it." She squeezed Zoey's hand again.

An officer with a tight bun lined everyone up in the order they were to speak. "Just wait quietly until I call you forward."

Kellen stood behind Zoey, but kept his distance.

Fleshman and Anderson went around the curtain, and a moment later, the noise from the audience quieted to a hush. The captain thanked everyone for being there and introduced himself and Anderson before going over some of the more important details of the case. He spoke of his own children, and said he couldn't bear to think of what the family was enduring. Anderson spoke about what the viewers could to do to help and then shared a little more about the case, particularly about the importance of the next day—the last half of the first forty-eight hours.

The lady cop directed Ari's teacher and coach onto the stage, where they shared about her being an excellent student and team player who always encouraged the other kids when they were down. They both broke down while speaking, which nearly sent Zoey over the edge.

Kellen stepped a little closer and put a hand on her shoulder. Macy went onto the stage as the teacher and coach returned.

Pushing back tears, Zoey inched closer to the curtain. Through a small crack next to the wall, she could see Macy standing at a podium in front of a packed crowd. She leaned closer to the mic and it squealed, sending a high pitched noise into the air. Gasps ran through the crowd.

Macy backed away from the mic a little. "Sorry. My nerves have gotten the best of me. The kidnapping of my niece brings back a lot of memories, as you can imagine." She cleared her throat. "Not only am I worried for her safety, but a lot of long-forgotten memories have been surfacing in the last twenty-four hours. Though I've healed, I'll never forget the fear I endured every day of my ordeal, wondering what that man would do to me—if that day would be my last." Her voice trembled. "Many times, I really thought it would be."

Zoey's heart shattered. Not only for what Macy went through, but for what Ariana must be going through right now.

"I'd like to take a moment to speak to the abductor," Macy continued. "You don't have to keep holding Ariana. Please do the right thing and return her to her family. Even if she isn't acting like it, that little girl is terrified out of her mind. She just wants to be home with her family—where she should be. Look deep within yourself and find another way to fill the hole in your life. This isn't it. Make a change in your life now. Start by releasing that sweet girl. Thank you."

As Macy walked away from the podium, reporters shouted questions from their seats. If she heard them, she didn't act like it.

The female officer turned to Zoey. "You're up."

Her throat closed up. Terror struck her. What was she supposed to say? Wasn't there something she *wasn't* supposed to say? What if she accidentally said that?

Kellen placed both hands on her shoulders and squeezed. "Come on. You've got this."

She struggled to breathe. He wrapped one arm around her back and guided her around the curtain as Macy came through. Her friend smiled at her through tears. Zoey couldn't even nod in response. She was going to suffocate right there on stage.

Reporters shouted louder questions as she and Kellen made their way to the podium. Bright lights from cameras flashed from every part of the auditorium. Her heart thundered in her chest, feeling like it would explode and kill her right there. She fought to breathe.

Kellen continued guiding her to the podium, leaving his arm around her. He kissed her cheek and whispered, "We'll get through this together. You're going to do great."

She shook her head. "I think I'm having a panic attack."

He swore and then pulled the mic closer to him. "I'm Kellen McKay, Zoey's fiancé. She's so distraught over Ariana's disappearance, she can't talk at the moment. I speak for the both of us when I tell you how worried we are for Ari's safety. We've hardly gotten any rest, nor will we until she's back home, safe and sound..."

Zoey finally managed a few shallow breaths as Kellen spoke about Ari's love for Halloween, telling them about the party she'd put on the other night. She still felt like her heart would kill her, but at least she was able to breathe. She managed a few normal breaths.

Kellen turned to her. "Are you ready to speak?"

She would regret it for life if she didn't. Zoey nodded and reached for the mic. Kellen brought it in front of her. She finally managed a full, deep breath and glanced across the crowd. Her heart rate returned to normal.

"Many of you have asked why I gave up Ariana for adoption, and I want to address that first. At no point have I ever *given up* on her, nor will I ever. I was young when she was born, and it only seemed fair for her to be raised by my parents who were at a more stable point in their lives and could offer her many things I couldn't." She took a deep breath. "While I finished high school, I lived one bedroom away from her and I was always very involved in her life. I never stopped, even after going to college and starting my own career. I hope that satisfies your curiosity."

Kellen whispered in her ear. "Don't forget to speak to the abductor."

Right. Her notes. What had she written?

She took another deep breath and focused on the crowd and the many cameras. Which one would send the video that Ariana's kidnapper would watch? She thought about him watching. Hopefully, he was choking as he waited.

"I'd like to take a moment to address the person who took Ariana. I can't even begin to imagine why you did this, but think about Ariana. This isn't fair to her. She doesn't want to be with you. She loves her family and she deserves to be with us. We all miss her as much a she misses us. You're tearing us apart." Tears blurred her vision and her voice wavered. "We're not going to be able to rest until she's back with us, where she belongs. She has not two but four parents who want her back. Friends that are worried about her. Think about what you're doing to them. You aren't just hurting her and us, it's the other kids, too. You can do something right—you can return her. Please."

The tears finally spilled from her eyes, and she couldn't speak another word.

Kellen pulled the mic closer to him. "Thank you so much for your time and help." He guided Zoey offstage.

Vigil

~

ALEX TURNED OFF the television and rubbed Clementine between the ears. He purred but didn't move. The conference had been good, and it was definitely better that he hadn't spoken. People in the audience would've yelled or thrown things. Zoey, Macy, and the teachers were clearly the best choices—they actually spent more than a couple days a year with Ariana. Even Kellen made more sense than Alex.

His phone buzzed. Clementine jumped, ran across the room, and licked his tail. Macy's number showed on the screen.

Could they have already gotten a good lead?

Alex answered the call. "Hey. You did great."

"Thanks. There's going to be a candlelight vigil at the big park by Ari's school."

"Yeah?" His stomach twisted.

"You should come."

"It's better if I don't." He gritted his teeth.

"No, it's not. You need to show your support."

"You've seen the comments. Everyone hates me."

"Show them they're wrong, Alex. Let them see that you care."

"If someone says something to me, I can't guarantee I won't punch their lights out."

Macy sighed. "Like I said, prove them wrong with your actions. Just being there will speak volumes. If you're peaceful and say something about how much you love Ari, people will see what

125

I do."

Clementine made eye contact with Alex. It was like they were both pushing him to go.

He took a deep breath. "Okay, let's say I go. What if people start saying the things they've been posting?"

"Then you tell them it's not true. All you want is Ari's safe return. That you love her very much."

Alex clenched a fist. "I'd be better off looking into the older kidnappings."

"Come to the vigil. For Ari." His sister knew how to hit where it hurt.

"What good will it do? Really?"

"It'll be good for *you*, Alex. It's all about everyone banding together for your daughter. It certainly wouldn't hurt your reputation."

Clementine pranced over and rubbed against Alex's legs, purring. He rubbed the cat's back.

"What do you say?" Macy asked.

"Fine, I'll go."

"You will? I'll be right over."

What had he just gotten himself into? "Maybe I should drive myself. That way if I have to leave early—"

"Nonsense. We'll go together. Everything will be just fine. You'll see."

"But I—"

"Nobody's going to do anything stupid in the middle of a candlelight vigil for a lost little girl."

Alex frowned. For someone who'd been through as much as Macy, she sure had an unrealistic view of the world. Or maybe it was because of all she'd been through that she *needed* to believe people were better than they were.

"I'll be there in ten minutes. Can you start a pot of coffee? It's going to be cold out there, and I don't know about you, but I want something warm to drink."

"Yeah, sure. See you then." He ended the call and rose before he could talk himself out of going. Clementine scampered away.

Alex went downstairs to the kitchen and got the coffee maker going. All was quiet in the house aside from the clacking of Dad's computer. He was probably updating his blog on the press conference. Alex headed back to his room to throw on some extra clothes. Macy was right about one thing—it would be freezing out there. It felt like it could snow.

Mom came out of her room. "You're going to the vigil?"

"I take it you talked to Macy."

She threw her arms around him. "I know this is hard on you, but it'll do you good."

He nodded, though he doubted she was right.

Fifteen minutes later, all four of them climbed into Macy's car, clinging to their mugs of hot coffee. Dad sat in the back next to Alex. "This brings back memories, doesn't it?"

Alex nodded. "Yeah. I remember going to our neighborhood park when Macy was gone."

They rode the rest of the way in silence. Alex's stomach twisted in knots. He didn't want to think back to Macy's kidnapping any more than he wanted to think about Ari's. Ten years later, his sister's disappearance still gave him nightmares.

The car slowed as they neared the park. Alex's breath hitched. A crowd gathered in a big, open field where kids often kicked balls, chased each other, and threw Frisbees. Macy drove around the parking lot three times.

Dad cleared his throat. "You guys get out. I'll park down the road."

"I'll go with you," Alex said.

"I'd feel better if you went with them. It's dark out."

Dad, the gentleman. It would be pointless to argue with him.

They all stepped out into the frigid night and Dad climbed

into the driver's seat. "I'll catch up with you in a few minutes." He drove away.

"I see Zoey and her parents," Macy said. "Let's join them."

Just who Alex wanted to see. Golden Boy was probably there, too, to make it even better. Alex walked silently with his mom and Macy. Staying quiet with them was good practice for the comments sure to be headed his way by all the online trolls now gathered in the park.

Alex should have had a couple beers rather than coffee before leaving. He didn't need to be jittery, he needed to be relaxed. Too late to worry about that now, though.

Valerie and Kenji were handing out skinny white candles with circular paper at the bottom. Valerie hugged both Macy and his mom, but ignored Alex. Kenji handed him a candle and gave him a sad nod. Alex nodded and braced himself. That would probably be the kindest greeting he received all evening.

His palms grew clammy and he felt too warm, despite the chilly air. He breathed heavily, white vapor exiting from his mouth each time like a puff of smoke. Great. Now he wanted a cigarette.

"Can I help hand those out?" his mom asked.

"Yes, please." Valerie gestured toward a box underneath a tree. "Grab a handful."

"I'll help, too." Macy turned to Alex. "Come on."

He shook his head. "I'm going to have to pass."

She pleaded with her eyes.

Alex crossed his arms. "You got me here. I draw the line at passing out candles."

Macy nodded and then caught up with their mom. Guilt stabbed at Alex, but he wasn't going to give in. He would make an appearance, but that was it. It wasn't like a bunch of people standing in a freezing park, holding candles was going to magically free Ariana. He was only here for his family.

He stood under a tree and watched everyone. Would Flynn

make an appearance? Alex would love nothing more than to question him. Press him for answers. He'd be under a lot more pressure with so many people around.

People gathered in a circle. Reluctantly, Alex left his spot against the tree and joined his sister and Luke, who had just arrived. Alex started to shake his hand, but Luke embraced him instead. "We'll find her. We will."

Alex returned the embrace. "Thanks."

A song started at the other end of the circle. It seemed vaguely familiar, reminding him of something he'd heard when his grandparents had taken him to church as a kid. Alex moved his mouth, pretending to sing. He hummed quietly to make it more convincing.

He couldn't wait to get back home and get back to his research—to do something that could actually help find Ari.

After a few songs, Valerie moved the to the middle of the circle and spoke about Ariana, sharing a few stories.

It sounded like a funeral.

Alex swallowed and forced himself to remain where he was. He wanted to run and quit participating. It wasn't a funeral. Ariana was alive, and they would find her.

Macy tapped his shoulders. "Do you want to say anything?"

He shook his head.

She nodded and turned back to the center, where one of Ariana's coaches shared about how she'd been a team player and leader.

Exactly the traits of a survivor. Alex took a deep breath and released it quietly. He glanced around, recognizing people from his childhood—neighbors, teachers, old friends, and other familiar faces. It was almost comforting, except for the fact he couldn't be sure who hated him and who didn't.

A few more from the community spoke, but no more family members did. People broke away from the circle and started to leave. Alex breathed a sigh of relief, glad for it to be over and eager to get back to his computer.

Macy and Luke spoke with some others near them.

"I'll meet you at the car," Alex said.

"Dad has the keys."

Right. "Okay. I'll find him." Alex stepped away from the crowd and scanned the faces. Everyone seemed to blend together. Between the dim park lighting and the visible breaths, it was hard to make out any faces.

Someone bumped into Alex. He ignored them and stepped aside. Someone else bumped into him—this time it was more like a slam. Another person rammed into him.

Alex clenched his fist and turned to a group of three guys a little younger than him. "What's your problem?"

"You are."

"How could you be so stupid?"

"What kind of jerk lets his kid get kidnapped?"

A fist grazed the side of Alex's face. He stumbled back and stared at them, not sure which one had struck him. He blew out his candle, dropped it, and ran at the three men.

Fingers wrapped around his arms and pulled him back.

"Come on, Alex," Luke said.

He struggled to get away. Luke tightened his grip.

More people joined the three hecklers.

"Let him go!"

"The cops won't give him what he deserves, we're gonna do it!"

"Selfish texting prick!"

Alex fought to get out of Luke's hold. "Let me go."

"We need to get back to the house."

Macy stepped between him and the growing crowd of jerks. "He didn't do anything wrong! Leave him alone."

"Oh, you need your sister to fight your battles now, loser?"

Alex broke free of Luke's grasp and ran at the men, fists swinging. He punched the nearest nose and kicked a shin. A fist hit him in the side, another in the back of his head.

"The cops need to leave Kellen alone and go after you."

The people shouted names at him, all the voices blending together.

Four hands grabbed Alex and dragged him away.

"Ignore them," Luke said.

"We need to get home," Macy added.

Alex pulled free of them. "I need to show them they can't mess with me that easily!"

"You can't take all of them on." Luke looked at him like he was crazy.

"Watch me."

"You want the crap beaten out of you?" Macy asked.

"I. Can. Take. Them!" Alex spun around and turned toward the haters.

"Hey, look at this!" a girl shouted. "A picture of Alex shoving someone into a van."

Terror squeezed Alex. "Liar!"

"No, look." She spun around in a slow circle, showing people her phone's screen.

"Turn yourself in!" someone shouted.

Alex clenched his fists. "I didn't do it!"

"Arrest him!" someone yelled.

"Yeah!" agreed others.

"Arrest Alex!"

"Arrest him!"

So many shouted it, it sounded like a chant. They repeated it, growing louder each time. The group—now at least twenty— walked slowly toward him, crying out for his arrest.

His stomach dropped. There was no way he could take on that many, and more were joining, making the protests louder each time they called for his arrest.

Luke grabbed Alex's arm and yanked. That time, Alex didn't fight him.

Collaborate

ALEX RUBBED HIS sore cheek and stared at the picture—it looked like him dragging a body into a black van next to the Ball Palace. It was either a photo that had been altered or it was of someone who could have been his twin.

If Fleshman didn't believe him, Alex was in trouble. He'd texted the picture to him, and Fleshman was supposed to have forwarded it to some photo experts, but the picture looked bad—really bad.

Alex studied the picture. He hadn't been wearing those clothes when Ariana had been taken. In fact, he didn't own any of those clothes—a faded, brown leather jacket, dark blue jeans, and a blue beanie with AF across the front. He'd never owned anything like that other than the jeans.

That had to count for something, right?

He paced the living room, staring at his phone. How long would it take for Nick to call him back?

"You're going to make yourself dizzy." Dad glanced up from behind his laptop.

"Is everyone else falling for it?" Alex asked. "Online?"

Dad frowned. "I'm not reading any of the comments."

"Well, tell them it's fake. That's not me!"

"I believe you, but it's hard for anyone who doesn't know you. It looks—"

"Just like me. I know."

"Tell them I was never there. Those aren't my clothes."

"Unfortunately, even if I said anything, nobody would believe me. I'm your dad, remember?"

Alex pulled his arm back, aiming to throw his phone across the room. He stopped. That wouldn't help anything, and he sure couldn't afford a new one.

His phone rang. It was Fleshman.

"Did your photo expert prove it wasn't me?" Alex demanded.

"They're both looking at it now. In the meantime, you should come here."

"What?" Alex exclaimed. "I'm not going down to your office."

"I'm not talking about the station."

"You're not going to arrest me, are you?"

"No. Come to my condo—totally off the record. Just two guys hanging out, talking about our kids over beer and chips."

Alex's mouth dropped. He struggled to find his voice. "Y-you'd do that?"

"Off the record—as in, it never happened. Got it?"

"What never happened?" Alex asked facetiously.

"Good. I'll text you my address. Parking's crap around here just to warn you. You'll have to walk a block or two."

"Sure, no problem. Thanks, Fleshman."

"I told you to call me Nick."

"Okay. See you soon, Nick." Alex ended the call and backed everything up on the cloud before powering down his laptop. Fleshman—Nick—was actually going to hear him out. It was strange to call him by his first name—it was like calling one of his old teachers by their name. But maybe if they were equals, he'd be able to convince Nick to take what they'd found out about the other kidnappings. Alex was growing more convinced they were all connected the longer he spent looking at the cold cases.

His phone buzzed with the text—Nick's address. Alex slid on his coat, put the phone in a pocket, and stuck his laptop in the case. He grabbed his keys from the desk and headed downstairs. His parents sat in the kitchen, drinking coffee, yet looking exhausted.

"Going somewhere?" Dad rubbed his eyes.

Meeting Fleshman never happened. He thought quickly for a cover story. "I'm meeting... a friend to look deeper into the cold cases."

"Didn't the cops say that was a dead end?" Mom clung to her coffee mug.

"They just don't think there's enough dots to connect yet. I know there are."

"Anything we can do?" Dad asked.

Alex shrugged. "I appreciate you posting about it on your blog."

He frowned. "It reminds me of the early days, posting about Macy's disappearance."

"It helped then," Alex said. "I'm sure it'll help now. I gotta run."

"Do you want to take my car?" Mom asked. "It's probably more reliable."

"Mine's fine." Alex hurried outside and plugged Nick's address into the ancient GPS unit. It wasn't too far away. He planned what he would say to convince the captain as he drove—he didn't want to forget a thing.

Alex had to park a block and a half away from the entrance to Nick's complex. He held the laptop case close and hurried to the condo, using the extra time to think more on what he would say to the captain.

Nick answered, wearing a black *Nirvana* t-shirt and blue track pants. His brows came together as he stared at Alex's face. "What happened to you?"

"Some people didn't want me at the candlelight vigil. I'm fine."

"Tell me you didn't hit back."

"I didn't. I hit *first*."

Nick swore. "We talked about this. You—"

"We talked about not hitting the kidnapper. These people came after me. I was peacefully attending my daughter's vigil."

"I hope so. Come on in." Nick took a deep breath and stood back, allowing Alex inside.

He stepped inside the mostly-bare entry. Everything was white—the walls, ceiling, the tile flooring. "Nice place."

"Wife got everything in the divorce." He led him to the equally sparse living room and gestured toward a faded brown leather couch with mismatched throw pillows on each end. "Beer or pop? I also have instant coffee and energy drinks."

A beer sounded so good, especially after everything he'd been through in the last day. "Beer."

"Exactly what I was thinking."

Alex sat, sinking deeper into the couch than expected, while Nick grabbed a couple bottles from the fridge—the one thing decorated in the place. It was full of children's drawings and paintings. Nick closed the door and pulled out a bag of chips from the pantry.

He tossed Alex a bottle and then opened the chips, setting it on the scratched glass coffee table. "Whatcha got?" Nick grabbed a handful of chips.

"First, what did those photo guys say?"

"It was altered." Nick twisted the cap off his beer. "Pretty obvious job. Nothing to worry about. Did you find anything new with the cold cases?"

Alex set his laptop up on the coffee table and turned it on. "There are a lot of small similarities between the cases. I—"

"Right. That's why I gave you what I had."

"But there's enough of them to make a difference."

"Yeah, but we need something *big*. The FBI looked into it, but they couldn't find anything convincing. Now they have their attention elsewhere. The hotline is getting hundreds of leads every day. We need to convince them this is worth looking into, and they have me so busy with other stuff, I don't have time."

Alex took a swig of his drink. "Not enough to look at Flynn or these cases?"

"Exactly."

"I thought you were the one in charge of the case—that they're only there to help you."

"True, but they're not going to waste any time or resources looking into anything they don't believe to be valuable. Especially not the ones they sent this time. If it's not airtight, they don't want to hear about it."

Alex groaned. "They're idiots."

"No comment."

Alex laughed, nearly snorting his beer out his nose. "So, you agree with me?"

"Of course I do. Like I said, show me what you've got."

"Gladly." He brought the laptop to his knees and opened up his notes file. "It's a lot more than just lakes with an island. They're all small and have a dock."

Nick arched a brow.

"They're not usually located all that close to where the girls were taken. And here's something interesting." Alex pulled up the map he'd been working on. "If you draw a line from each lake, they're all about equal distance from this town."

"Let me see that." Nick grabbed the laptop and zoomed in on the picture. It showed one of the richer parts of town. He swore.

"What?" Alex exclaimed.

"That's Flynn's neighborhood. Actually, that's almost right on top of his house."

They stared at each other, both wide-eyed.

"Is that enough to convince the FBI to look into it? I'm starting to run out of ideas, actually."

"I don't know, but it's enough for me to at least try. How did you think to try that?"

Alex shrugged. "I was measuring the distances between the lakes, and accidentally figured it out."

Nick swore again. "Show me everything. Don't leave out a detail."

They spent the next two hours going over everything Alex and Macy had found. Finally, neither one of them could keep their eyes open.

"Want to crash on the couch?"

Alex could feel the bottom of the couch through the cushion. "No, but thanks. I'll just head back to my parents' house."

"At least let me get you an energy drink. Email all that to me real quick."

"Sure." Alex send him everything as an attachment. As soon as he was done, Nick handed him a black and orange can.

"This'll keep you awake."

Alex glanced at the ingredient list. "Sure it won't give me a heart attack, too?"

"It's not supposed to."

"Great." Alex opened it and drank it down as fast as he could. His body started to vibrate almost immediately. "This stuff is crazy."

"Tell me about it. I'm going to the station with this first thing in the morning."

"Not now?"

Nick shook his head. "The FBI agents aren't there now, anyway, and this isn't something urgent enough that I can wake them."

"It's not? It gives more reason to suspect the kidnapper actually did it."

"Trust me. Get some sleep."

After the energy drink? Right. "Okay. See ya." Alex made his way back to his car and started it. At least Nick was now willing to show everything to the FBI. If they actually looked into it, they would probably put the guy behind bars and then find Ariana. At least there was still time before Halloween—the day he killed his victims.

Alex's blood ran cold.

Just as he was about to pull out of the spot, his phone buzzed.

Had he left something in the condo? Or had Nick figured something else out?

It was a text from a blocked number.

I told you to leave it alone. You didn't listen.

Stress

KELLEN HELPED ZOEY onto her couch and covered her with a blanket. She hadn't said a word since speaking at the conference. He'd ended up turning up the music just to distract himself as he drove.

"Can I get you something, Zoey?"

She barely shook her head and continued staring at a blank wall.

He sat next to her and pulled some of the blanket over himself. "You did really well tonight."

Zoey shook her head again.

"That was a really moving speech. I'll bet people will do more to help find Ariana."

She sighed, still staring ahead.

Sharp pains started at Kellen's temples and ran to the base of his skull. He took a deep breath and rubbed his neck.

"If I'm bothering you, you don't have to stay."

"It's not that. I have a headache."

"Isn't that supposed to be my line?" Her voice was flat, but she'd managed a joke. The Zoey he loved and adored was fighting to come out.

Kellen put his arm around her. "We're going to get through this."

"How do you know?"

"Because you're strong and so is Ari. She's going to fight, and you're going to make sure we find her."

Zoey leaned her head against his arm. "I hope you're right. I completely blew it out there."

"No, you were real. Everyone could feel your pain."

"I never have trouble talking in front of a crowd. I thought I was going to die up there."

"Give yourself a break. You're living every parent's worst nightmare."

She turned to him. "What if we don't find her?"

"We will."

"What if we *don't*?" Zoey repeated, starting at him with an intensity that made him want to back away.

"Keep looking. Never give up. Isn't that what you did when Macy was gone so long?"

"What if we find her, but she's dead or seriously maimed?"

"First of all, you can't think like that."

Zoey's brows came together. "You can't tell me what to *think*."

Kellen sucked in a deep breath and counted to ten. Then twenty. "Well, it won't do you any good."

"And thinking fluffy thoughts *will* if she's in a ditch somewhere?"

"You can't—it will make it hard for you to get through each day if that's what you're imagining."

"But if it's the truth, what does it matter?"

Kellen counted again. This was good practice in case he ever ended up on trial. "What do you think Ari would want you to be doing?"

She gave him a double-take. "What?"

"Ariana loves you. Do you think she wants you to be miserable and negative?"

"Do you think she wants me to throw a party?" Zoey snapped.

Kellen took another deep breath. He was running out of methods to calm himself. "That's not what I said, and you know it. She's a positive, upbeat kid. She'd want you to hold out hope."

"We're almost at the forty-eight hour mark."

"It's barely been twenty-four hours."

"And we're no closer to finding her than we were last night!"

"We don't know that," Kellen said. "You may have planted a seed of doubt in the kidnapper's mind. Maybe right now he's thinking about the possibility of returning her?"

Zoey opened her mouth, but then closed it.

"Maybe we should get some sleep."

"You think I'm going to be able to sleep?" she exclaimed.

"Yes. You're exhausted, and we'll be able to do more tomorrow if we're rested."

The corners of her mouth curved down. She seemed to be trying to figure out a good comeback. "Do you want her living with us after we get married?"

Kellen's headache intensified. "Why are you bringing this up now?"

"Do you want her to live with us?" Zoey sat up straight.

"Can we talk about this after she's back safe and sound?" Kellen removed his arm from around her shoulders.

"You said we need to think positively, right? When she comes back and we get married, do you want her living with us?"

"Why are you doing this, Zo?"

"Because you need to explain that expression on your face when I brought it up."

"I was surprised because it was the first I'd heard anything about it! You didn't give me the respect of even giving me a heads up, much less asking my opinion."

"So, you *don't* want her to live with us?" Zoey accused.

"Why the hell are you trying to trap me? I never said that."

"Then say you want her to live with us. It's not that hard."

"You could have at least given me a warning that you were *thinking* about it, you know? When we first got together, you told me you had a daughter, but that you'd given up all rights. It quickly became clear how much she means to you and that you two are close, and that's great. I'm sure you both need it. But never once have you mentioned even the possibility of splitting custody—which by the way, if you want to discuss shocked faces, your parents seemed just as taken aback as I was."

"So, you *don't* want her living with us."

Kellen jumped up from the couch. "Give me some time to let the idea sink in! It's common decency. You're changing everything and not giving me two seconds to digest the idea. You couldn't even give me the courtesy of talking to me privately first."

She folded her arms. "At least I know how you feel."

"You have no idea! *I* don't even know what I want. I'm sure I'd be excited by the idea if you'd have given me ten minutes to let it sink in first."

"You think you'd be excited?" Zoey arched a brow.

"At this point, I'd be thrilled just to have her back safely. I'd raise her all by myself if it came down to that. But, honestly, it's *our* relationship that I have to question."

Her mouth dropped.

"That's right. How can I trust you after pulling that stunt? What makes me think you won't blindside me with something else equally important? It's obvious how poorly you actually think of me."

"Now you're turning *me* into the bad guy?"

"Did I say that?" Kellen exclaimed.

"That's what it sounds like."

He threw his arms in the air. "I can't take this. I've been questioned by the FBI—interrogated, really—and I've always done everything to support your relationship with Ari. And now when everything hits the fan, this is the thanks I get?"

"Hold on." Zoey rose from the couch, too. "It's not like that."

"It's exactly like that. And another thing, I saw the way you were looking at Alex at the party. I tried to ignore it. Deny it, actually. But now I can't."

"What are you talking about?" she exclaimed. "I wasn't looking at Alex any way, besides irritated."

Kellen snorted. "Believe what you want, but for a moment it seemed like you were having second thoughts about him."

"Him? Never! I can't forgive him for what he did to me."

"Whatever. Just remember—*he's* the one who was too busy texting to watch Ariana. Now there's even evidence of him putting her in the van!"

Zoey shook her head. "Have you heard of Photoshop?"

"You said he was jealous when you showed him the engagement ring. Did you ever stop to think that he took Ariana to make sure he didn't lose you?"

"He wouldn't do that."

"Why not?" Kellen countered. "You've always said how all he thinks about is himself, right? Maybe he's scared he'll lose you or Ariana once we get married."

"That's ridiculous!"

"Is it?"

Her eyes shone with tears. "Yes!"

"Why?"

"Because he's had all this time to do something, but he hasn't."

"And yet suddenly, he wants a daddy-daughter date. Right after seeing your ring."

She shook her head. "It's not like that. He wouldn't kidnap Ariana."

"How can you defend him?" Kellen exploded.

"Because I know him! I've known the Mercers longer than I've known anyone."

"Really? You've hardly said two words to him since you graduated high school."

"Yeah, he's thrown his own life away, but he wouldn't do

anything to hurt Ari. Deep down, he's still the same person he always was."

Kellen wanted to punch the wall. He took a deep breath. "Even if Alex didn't put her in the van, he still wasn't watching her. Someone drove off with Ari."

"That place is huge. It could've happened to anyone."

He couldn't take any more. "Look, if you need me, I'll be at my place."

Her eyes widened. "You're going to leave me? Now?"

"*Leave* you?" he yelled. "No, Zoey. I'm giving you space. Clearly, you need it. I know I do. I have a lot to think about."

She shook her head. "Unbelievable."

He gritted his teeth. "My sentiments exactly."

Dismissed

~

N ICK HIT SNOOZE. He felt like he'd been hit by a bus, but then he remembered what Alex had shown him the night before. Although he had his doubts about the FBI taking him seriously, he was excited to show them what he had. He didn't know how Alex had managed to connect some of the dots he had—it was some decent detective work, especially from a civilian.

The alarm blared again. He stretched and turned it off before getting up. With any luck, between all the new calls to the hotline and these new clues from the cold cases, they would find the abductor. The all-important forty-eight hour deadline was rapidly approaching. After that, their chances of finding the girl alive would rapidly diminish with each passing hour.

Sure, there were cases like Alex's sister, but those were the rare ones. Definitely not anything they could count on.

Time was not on their side. But if they were right about this being connected to the other cases, at least they had a little more time—however Halloween was also approaching too quickly.

He got ready, his mind racing, and grabbed an energy drink on the way out. He made his way to the Mustang, safe in one of the few garage spots in the parking lot, and hurried to the station.

The entire place was buzzing when he got there. He put his coat in his office, recycled the can, and headed for the room. The white boards were filled with at least twice the notes, more papers lay scattered around the tables, and conversation was more lively.

Nick grabbed a donut from the box next to the door and stood by Williams, the head FBI agent, who was speaking with three others. She turned to him once she was done talking and pulled her light hair into a bun. "Did you get any sleep?"

"Some. Was there any good info from the hotline overnight?"

"Hard to say. There are a lot of leads to look into, but so far none of them are panning out. False sightings, mostly. Do you know how many eleven-year-old girls are out there with dark hair halfway down their backs?" She sighed and took a swig of her coffee.

"I'm sure thousands at least."

She nodded. "I've got teams checking out leads in other states. More AMBER Alerts are going out and I've got an entire social media team on it in Washington."

"This *is* Washington."

"Washington State. I'm talking about DC."

"Okay. I have something I want to go over with you. I found some new possibilities."

"It's not those cold cases again, is it?" A look of irritation crossed her face.

"I found some connections, and they're too similar to this case to keep ignoring." He stared her down.

"Fine. You've got five minutes."

That was five minutes more than Nick'd had last time he tried talking to her about the previous cases. "Come to my office."

She tapped another agent on the shoulder. "I'll be right back."

They went to his office and he turned on his computer and pulled up everything relevant from the cloud server.

"You do realize that hot leads are almost always better than the cold ones?"

"*Almost* always," Nick said. "Given the fact that there's a serial killer out there, we need to pay attention to these."

"We don't know the cases are related."

"Look at this." He showed her everything Alex had found, and for a change, she didn't cut him off and dismiss him. She listened, but didn't give any indication of what she thought. When he was done, he asked, "What do you think?"

"You could be on to something."

"Could be?"

"That map leading to Myer's house is a bit of a stretch though. Isn't that a new neighborhood?"

"It's been there for decades."

Williams looked deep in thought. "I'm not going to allocate any of my resources toward this, but if you feel strongly about it, keep looking into it. Take Anderson and question Myer again, but it's not a lead I'd put much stock into. If nothing comes of this, drop it."

At least this was better than nothing. "What would it take for you to take it seriously?"

"Something more convincing than this. Better leads. That's what we need to focus on."

"Like what?"

"The stepdad."

"She doesn't have—wait. You mean Zoey's fiancé?"

"Kellen McKay. He has no alibi for the time of the kidnapping."

"But Alex was there. He saw the abductor. If it was Kellen, he would've known."

"It was dark and he was upset. Distracted."

"Distracted? He'd already put his text away. He gave us a description of the man—and it looks just like Myer."

"Like I said, look into it if you want. I don't put much stock into what the bio dad says."

"Why on earth not?"

"He's only involved with the girl a few times a year and from what I've gathered, spends his free time drinking. We have a missing child, Fleshman. I can't spare a single resource for every off-the-wall idea that comes my way. Especially not from an unreliable witness."

It was a good thing he hadn't told her that Alex had helped him dig into the cold cases. "I realize this is about a missing girl. You think I don't know that? Why do you think I'm hardly sleeping? This is the niece of a missing girl I worked tirelessly on about twelve years ago."

A knowing expression covered her face. "I get it now."

"Get what?"

"You're personally invested."

"I—"

"You have to step back. You know that—you didn't get to be captain by accident. I can tell by the way your men respect you that you're a good cop. Everyone allows something to get personal once in a while, but you *have* to be impartial. That's how these cases are solved. Understand?"

He gritted his teeth. "Yes."

"If you look into Myer, let me know."

"Of course." There was no way he was going to drop this. In fact, her unwillingness to consider it a valid lead only made him more determined.

Frantic

~

ARIANA PICKED UP a book from the shelf, looked at the cover, and put it back. It had been hours since breakfast and she hadn't heard anything from Lloyd. Despite her fear of never seeing her family again, she was growing bored. She spent so much time in the bedroom. He pretty much only let her out to eat three times a day.

At breakfast, she'd tried talking him into another trip to the backyard, but he said he had an appointment. His eyes had darted back and forth, not paying much attention to her, like he was lost in thought.

She picked out another book. They all looked old and boring—and she usually liked reading. Maybe they would sound more interesting if she wasn't locked in someone else's bedroom. She shoved the book back and went to the window.

It was windy outside with a slight drizzle—the perfect fall day. It would be so much fun to run around in the grass, kicking up leaves. She and her friends loved piling up the leaves when they weren't too wet and throwing them at each other. It was also fun to hide in a pile and scare someone when they walked by.

Ariana giggled, thinking of a few days earlier when she'd scared Emily real bad. Then they'd teamed up and ambushed some of the boys, covering them in leaves.

What she wouldn't give to be able to go to school the next day. She'd even take two packs of homework if she could just show up and see her friends.

She leaned her forehead against the cold glass and sighed. What did Lloyd have planned? Just for her to continue her existence like this, pretending to be his sister?

Sadness washed through her at the thought of never returning to her old life. No, to her life. It wasn't old, it was where she belonged. Where she needed to be.

There had to be a way out. Maybe she hadn't looked hard enough before. Or in the right places.

Ariana walked around the perimeter of the room for what felt like the five-millionth time. Everything looked the same—sealed tight to keep her inside. She just had to look harder. Think more. Get creative.

She'd learned about how to get out of the trunk of a car— kicking the lights and stuff. The details were fuzzy, but the point was that there was always something she could do. Overpowering Lloyd was out of the question, but what if she could outsmart him? She could find a way out that he'd never thought of.

Sighing, she sat on the bed and glanced around, doing her best to think of something new. There had to be something she'd overlooked—that Lloyd had.

But what?

She studied the walls and the door. The lock was on the outside, but part of it was on this side. It was just a silver lump with a keyhole. Maybe she could find a way to unlock it. Sure, she didn't have the key, but that couldn't be the *only* way to get through. Everything in the room was ancient, and she'd seen old movies where people used bobby pins and paper clips to get through locks.

What if that worked?

Her mind raced, trying to figure out if she'd seen anything like that anywhere. Nothing came to mind, but she hadn't been looking, either. She would have to check the bathroom whenever Lloyd came back and let her go.

In the meantime, she needed to go through every drawer, nook, and cranny in the bedroom. Even if she didn't find anything useful, she might get an idea of something else to try. With as often as he left her alone in the house, she had plenty of time to find an escape.

Ariana opened the top drawer in the desk, but only saw blank stationary paper. Not even a pencil or a pen, much less paper clips. She moved to the top side drawer. Just erasers and some notepads. The next two drawers didn't hold anything useful, either.

She went over to the dresser, hoping that might be her answer. Perhaps Jan had left a paper clip in a pocket and Lloyd hadn't noticed when washing the laundry. Ariana rifled through the clothes, not finding anything. Even checking all the pockets didn't yield a single stray item.

The sound of gravel crunching under tires startled her. Lloyd was back and she had clothes strewn all over the room.

Panic-stricken, Ariana rushed around the room, grabbing clothes. She'd barely folded two shirts when a car door slammed outside. Her heart raced as she tried to fold everything neatly. Her hands shook, making it even more difficult.

The car alarm beeped outside.

"Please don't come in here," Ariana begged as she folded a powder blue hoodie.

Noises sounded downstairs, but it didn't sound like he was coming up. She breathed a sigh of relief and continued folding clothes as fast as she could.

Just as she was putting away the final pair of pants, the dead-bolt clicked.

Ariana slammed the drawer, grabbed a random book, and jumped onto the bed. She opened it to the middle and noticed it was upside down. She flipped it upright.

The door opened.

She looked up, trying to act natural.

Lloyd glanced around the room before landing his gaze on her. He played with the zipper on his coat, seeming to be in the same distracted mood as before. "You hungry?"

"Yeah, but I really have to use the bathroom."

"Sorry about being gone so long." He paused. "Something came up."

"It's okay. Can I go?"

He stepped aside, and Ariana ran past him, eager to see what she could find. She closed the bathroom door behind her and did her business. She turned on the water to make it sound like she was washing her hands, but she went through the drawers. She found a brush, a comb, some bars of soap, towels, her toothbrush, and toothpaste. Nothing useful.

"Are you okay in there?" Lloyd called.

She turned off the water and messed up the hand towel before opening the door. "Yep."

"Okay. Let's eat. I picked something up on the way." He took her hand and led her to the kitchen. A couple bags from a fried chicken place sat on the table. "Grab some plates. I'll get the cups and some juice."

Without a word, Ariana pulled a couple plates down. Then she opened the silverware drawer and put a couple forks on the plates. The butter knives caught her eye.

Could she use one of those to work loose the lock?

She glanced over at Lloyd. His face was blocked by the fridge door.

Heart thundering, she reached for a knife and slid it into the sleeve of her shirt.

Alone

ZOEY ROLLED OVER and woke up when her hand hit the empty pillow next to her. The fight with Kellen filled her mind and her stomach twisted in tight knots.

How could he do that to her in a time like this? When Ariana was missing? She needed him now more than ever.

She reached for her phone, hoping for news about Ari. Nothing besides the now-typical flood of sympathetic texts, many from complete strangers. How they'd managed to find her number was beyond her.

Zoey scrolled through them to make sure she hadn't missed anything important. It didn't look like it. She found her earlier texting conversation with her mom and sent her a text.

Have you heard anything?

No. Called the station earlier. Nothing new.

Not even after the conference?

They're going over leads.

OK. Thx.

She rolled over and closed her eyes. What was she supposed to do? It tore her apart that she couldn't do anything to help Ari. Nobody could until they found her.

There had to be something she could do. Maybe one of the leads would pan out, but in the meantime, she would go crazy in her apartment. But what could she do?

Fliers. They could hand those out—she could set up a big party like the one they'd had for Macy. It had seemed like the whole town had shown up. Their whole neighborhood had, plus a whole bunch of people she'd never seen. They'd canvassed the streets, getting the word out. It seemed like holding an actual paper made it more real for people than just seeing a picture on TV or the computer.

Tears welled up.

"I'm not going to be weak," she muttered and sat up. No, she would focus on setting up the flier party. She could order some of the police fliers to be printed at the nearest office supply store and then spread the word about the party. Thank God for social media. She could publish one post and tell all her friends to share it. Thousands would see it in minutes.

Zoey downloaded the flier to her phone and placed an order for five thousand copies, paying for a rush job. She posted the info about handing out fliers and meeting at the park next to Mom's house. She tagged as many people as she was allowed and then got into the shower.

Even if no one else showed, she would hand out every one of those papers herself. But given how everyone had rallied around them, the more likely scenario was that she should've ordered more copies.

Before getting in the shower, she called Kellen. After the second ring, it went to voicemail.

He was ignoring her call.

She tried again, but after the first ring, it went to voicemail.

More tears threatened. She shook her head, refusing to give in to them.

Instead, she sent Kellen a text.

We need to talk.

She gathered her clothes and checked her phone again. Kellen hadn't responded.

I don't want space. Talk to me.

Zoey got into the shower, her mind racing back and forth between Ariana, the fliers, and Kellen. When she got out, she still had no new texts or calls.

She decided to give Kellen one last text.

Everyone's gathering at the park to hand out fliers. Hope you'll be there.

Her stomach rumbled, despite her having no appetite. She grabbed some fruit on the way out and hoped that would be enough.

Setup

~

KNOCK, KNOCK.

Alex saved his file. "Come in."

Mom came in and gave him a sad smile. "Have you gotten any sleep?"

"Some. There's no time to worry about it now."

She rubbed his shoulders. "I know the feeling. I'm not getting enough myself. It feels like we're reliving Macy's disappearance all over again."

"I don't know how you did it." He blew out a series of short breaths to calm himself. "Especially for so long."

"You know, sometimes when I think back to it, I wonder how we did it, too." She paused. "It drove me to do some things I never thought I'd do."

Alex turned around. "What do you mean?"

Mom frowned. "The stress really gets to you. It affects the way you see everything. Just make sure you're taking care of yourself—sleeping enough, eating enough. It keeps your mind clear."

"Easier said than done."

"Don't I know it." She cleared her throat. "Anyway, I didn't come in to talk about that. I wanted to let you know that people are gathering down at the park again to hand out fliers."

"Again?"

"Sorry. I can't stop thinking back to Macy. I'm just as scared." Tears filled her eyes.

Pain gripped Alex. He jumped up and wrapped his arms around her. She leaned her head against his shoulder and sobbed. Alex rubbed her back, fighting his own tears. Mom's cries were too much for him. He thought of Ariana, and the floodgates opened. Together, he and his mom cried until she finally stepped back and wiped her eyes.

"W-we should get to the park." She wiped mascara from under her eyes.

Alex cleared his throat and nodded. "I'll be down there in a few minutes. I'm going to take a quick shower." He looked like crap.

Mom nodded. "Sure, hon. I'm going to have to wash my face. I don't know what I was thinking, wearing makeup."

"You're pretty without it."

She kissed his cheek and headed out the door.

Alex grabbed some clothes from the dresser—Mom had never gotten rid of his high school clothes. Luckily, they all fit. He'd put on some weight, but not much, apparently.

Just as he stepped out of the room, his phone buzzed on the desk. He almost ignored it—but what if it was news about Ariana?

He went over and dropped his clothes next to the phone. There was a text from his boss.

Get over here now.

Anger surged through Alex. How dare he? Not only was it Sunday—his one day off—but Darren knew Alex was dealing with Ariana's abduction.

Alex replied to the text.

Go to hell.

His thumb hovered over the send button before deleting it.

I'm about to go to a rally for my missing kid.

No, you're on your way here.

Why?!

Because of what we just found in your locker.

There was nothing in his locker besides extra clothes.

What are you talking about?

The thing you didn't want us to find.

Stop being vague.

The drugs, stupid!

He stared at the last text, trying to make sense of it.

Get down here now before I call the cops.

Alex swore. Had one of his idiot coworkers stuck something in his locker since he never locked it? There was nothing worth stealing, so he never bothered. He needed to get to the rally.

Are you coming? I don't *want* to call the cops.

But he couldn't help find Ariana if he was behind bars. He needed to sort this out right away, and then come back to the rally.

On my way now.

Good.

How could this be happening? Why now? Alex stormed around the room, looking for his keys. They'd fallen between his desk and dresser. He stuffed them in his pocket and stomped downstairs.

Mom and Dad were putting their shoes and coats on.

"What's wrong?" Dad asked.

"I have to go talk to my boss."

"Now?" he exclaimed. "Doesn't he know—?"

"He knows, but I could get fired if I don't go." Actually, Alex didn't care about getting canned. He would deal with the jerk later, but he didn't want to tell his parents Darren had all but threatened him with jail time. "I'll be back to hand out fliers, I swear." He might not be able to get back, but he would do his best.

"You want me to call him?" Mom asked.

"No," Alex said too quickly. "That would only make things worse. I'm an adult. I'll handle this."

"Well, if you need anything, you have our numbers."

Alex gave a quick nod and slid on his boots. "Thanks." He rushed out the door, got into his beater, and floored it.

As he drove, his mind raced with theories. He knew of more than a handful of coworkers who did various illegal drugs. Any one of them could've put them in accidentally if they were high. He couldn't think of one who had it out for him, though.

Then just as he turned off the freeway, it hit him.

What if Flynn had been behind it?

The mysterious message *had* promised Alex he would pay for interfering.

Alex studied him. His confident boss was uncharacteristically unsure. Alex took a deep breath. "It sure looks that way. How'd you find out about this, anyway?"

Darren licked his lips and kept his gaze low. "Doesn't matter."

Alex slammed his fists on the desk. "It matters!"

Darren jumped and finally looked at Alex. "A threat."

Fury tore through Alex. Probably the same person harassing him. "From who?"

"It was anonymous."

"They threatened you?"

"My family. Consider this a layoff. I don't want to do this, but..." His voice trailed off. He reached under his desk, pulled out a cardboard box, and handed it to Alex. "Let's clear out your things."

"Why'd you have me waste my time to come down here? You could've fired me over the phone!"

"It's part of the deal. You have to take your things home. I'm not going to turn you in. Just clear out your locker. I'll give you a good referral if you need one."

Alex stared at him, unable to find words. He shook his head, stormed to the lockers, and crammed his clothes and spare boots into the box. He stormed out of the building and threw the box in the back of his car. He couldn't think straight and didn't want to face the long drive back to his parents' place in the mood he was in. He peeled away, sending rocks spraying through the employee parking lot.

He went home to check on the apartment. The paint was still peeling and the floor still stained from previous renters. Everything was just as he'd left it. He grabbed a few clothes and took them out to his car, throwing them into the box.

Alex turned on the music and took a deep breath. He needed—wanted—to get to the park and hand out fliers, but in the mood he was in, he'd only reinforce everyone's preconceived notions of him. He'd likely punch someone. He should've hit Darren. The dill weed deserved it.

He went to the bar—he'd only have one drink to calm his nerves. Then he'd be able to drive, and he would at least feel a little better.

Inside, Cole greeted him with a surprised expression. "Didn't expect to see you here."

"Me, neither," Alex grumbled and sat on a stool. "Get me a beer, would you?"

"Sure thing." He grabbed one, removed the cap, and slid it over.

Alex drank most of it in one swig.

"Any news on your daughter?" Cole asked.

"Nope." Alex finished it off.

"Want another?"

Alex shook his head, dug out a bill from his pocket, and set it on the counter. "I just need to think."

"So you came all the way here?" Cole leaned on the counter.

"I was in the neighborhood. Boss made me come in to fire me in person."

"Fire you? For what?"

"Doesn't matter." Alex played with the empty bottle. "I didn't do it, but I'm still fired."

"That sucks. What are you gonna do?"

Alex shrugged. "Not much I can do. Not now. I have to get back to the search party."

"Here, have one on me." Cole slid him another beer.

"Thanks." Alex studied the bottle, trying to decide if he should or not. Why not? It wasn't like a second beer would get him plastered. He was still pissed off and wanted to punch a hole in something. He took a long, slow sip, hoping this one would help him feel better. Maybe it would help him figure out what to do about the threats. It was probably time to mention them to Nick—Flynn wasn't playing around, and he needed to be stopped.

Attempt

~

ARIANA GASPED FOR AIR as the deadbolt locked. She couldn't believe she'd managed to get the butter knife into the room. It was a miracle the thing hadn't slid out of her sleeve or showed much of a bulge while she ate. Lloyd had been distracted, though. In fact, he had to get back to something right after they ate.

At least that would give her some time to see what she could do with the lock now that she had the butter knife. He was now banging things around in the kitchen, so she'd have to wait. If she was lucky, he'd leave again.

She slid the knife out from her sleeve and stared at it, eager to test it out.

Knock, knock.

Ariana jumped, nearly dropping it. She shoved it behind some creepy dolls. "Y-yeah?"

He came inside. "Sorry to have to leave you in here again, Jan. I'm going to make it up to you. We'll have ice cream and watch a movie tonight, okay? Then tomorrow we'll get ready for Halloween."

"Okay."

"Do you need anything?"

Other than to go home? To her real home. "No."

"I'll be back soon. Sorry again."

"It's okay." What did he expect her to say?

The floor creaked under Lloyd's feet as he walked out and then locked the door.

She breathed a sigh of relief and went over to the window to make sure he was really leaving. A few minutes later, he appeared out by the car. He got in and drove away.

Ariana waited, holding her breath, just to make sure he didn't come back. Once she was sure he was really gone, she took the knife and stuck it in the keyhole. It didn't go very far, but she could wiggle it around. She tried several angles, waiting to hear the familiar click.

Nothing.

She pressed her shoulder against the wall, jiggling it and trying different angles.

Had stealing the knife been for nothing? No, it couldn't be. She wouldn't let it be.

Ariana kept trying and trying, until sweat dripped into her eyes. She wasn't ready to admit defeat, but she had to try something new.

Gravel crunched under tires outside.

He was back already?

She ran over to the window, and sure enough, the car was returning. Ariana looked around the room, desperate to find a hiding spot for the knife.

Where would Lloyd never think to look?

A car door slammed shut outside.

She jumped and breathed heavily, heart pounding. The knife shook in her hand. No, her hands were shaking.

The car alarm beeped outside.

Ariana ran over to the large, heavy dollhouse and lifted one side. Everything shifted down to the left in all the tiny rooms. She grimaced but shoved the knife underneath and set the house down, trying to keep it silent. Her middle finger got stuck underneath. She held back a cry as the pain shot through her finger.

She managed to lift the house again and pull her hand away.

As she shook it out, she noticed an indent in her skin. The finger grew hot and throbbed. She stuck it in her mouth, hoping that would somehow help.

The deadbolt clicked.

Ariana sat down and grabbed a couple dolls, careful to hold them so Lloyd wouldn't see her finger.

The door opened slowly. Lloyd appeared. "Are you all right? I thought I heard a thud." He walked over and looked at the messed up rooms in the dollhouse. "What happened?"

She swallowed. Time to think fast. "They had an earthquake—the dolls did. That's what you heard. Why the rooms are like that."

Lloyd nodded. "You had me worried, but I should've known better. You've always been so creative like that, Jan."

Ariana tried to smile.

"You ready for ice cream and a movie?" he asked.

"Yeah."

"Wanna skip dinner and go straight to dessert? Mom and Dad never let us do that, but I say we do what we want since they're not here."

Time to get into character. Ariana widened her eyes and forced a smile. "Really?"

He waved her toward the door. "Help me scoop the ice cream."

Ariana glanced at the dollhouse and back to Lloyd, but he didn't seem to know anything was wrong. She sighed in relief.

"Are you okay?"

Fear drummed through her. "Yeah, great."

Lloyd put an arm around her shoulders. "I can't tell you how glad I am to have you back. I hate that I keep having to leave, but some things came up that…" His voice trailed off. "Never mind. It doesn't matter. We're together now, and that's all that I care about."

"It's amazing."

They went to the kitchen, where three boxes of ice cream sat on the table next to five or six bottles of toppings.

Ariana's eyes widened, momentarily forgetting where she really was until Lloyd rubbed his hands together, his eyes equally lit up.

"I just knew you'd love it. You fill the bowls while I pop the popcorn." He went over to an old-fashioned popcorn maker and poured in a bunch of kernels. They made a lot of noise as they slid down. Popping filled the air, and soon the entire room smelled of popcorn. He turned on the stove and put a stick of butter in a pan. "You going to make the sundaes?"

"Right." Ariana turned around and scooped vanilla into each bowl, then chocolate, and finally almond fudge. There was still room for more, so she put extra chocolate into each before drizzling on toppings.

Lloyd drizzled the melted butter on top of the huge bowl of popcorn and then added salt. He picked it up with one hand and then grabbed a six pack of root beer with the other. "Are you ready to take all this into the rec room?"

She nodded and took the two bowls of ice cream, following him through a hallway she hadn't yet seen. He opened a door and nodded for her to go in first.

The room had two green flowered couches, a matching recliner, a huge brick fireplace, a pool table, and some brightly colored posters on each wall. Lloyd set the pop and popcorn on an intricately carved wooden table and turned on the TV. "Eat your ice cream before it melts."

Ariana sat on the nearest couch and dug in while he set up the movie.

He sat next to her and took the other sundae. "Mmm. You always make the best ones."

The movie started, and it was one she'd wanted to see for a long time, but her parents wouldn't let her. They said it would be too scary.

Lloyd turned to her and gave a friendly smile. "You're going to love this movie. I just know it." He put the bowl of popcorn between them.

She nodded and took a handful. Guilt stung at her for enjoying herself, but really, who could blame her? Ice cream sundaes, root beer, popcorn, and a scary movie.

Note

~

B Y THE TIME ALEX made it back, the flier-handing party had ended. A few kids played on the playground as their moms talked.

His heart sank. He'd really wanted to do something to help find Ariana. He popped a couple breath mints. Having beer breath wouldn't help anything. He sighed and parked in his parents' driveway.

He dragged his feet to the front door. Would he tell them their college dropout son who'd managed to let his daughter get kidnapped was now unemployed? It would take serious effort to sink lower than he already had.

Alex balanced the box while he dug out his keys and unlocked the door. Upstairs in the kitchen, he could hear conversation. It sounded like his parents, Macy, Luke, Zoey, and her parents. The whole gang.

No way was he going to talk about getting canned in front of all of them.

He slid off his coat and boots and walked upstairs, trying to be quiet enough to walk by unnoticed.

"Nice of you to stop by," Zoey said.

His stomach tightened into knots. "I had to talk to my boss. My job was on the line."

"Are you okay?" his mom asked.

"I'm fine. How did it go? I wanted to get back in time."

Macy smiled at him. "It went really well. So many people showed up that we ran out of fliers. But they're online so anyone can print them off. Sit down, you look tired."

Alex glanced at the full table and shook his head. "I'll head up to my room and print some off. I was serious about wanting to hand them out." He hurried up to his room before anyone could argue. Truth was, he didn't want to see Zoey right then. Not at his absolute lowest. He probably would end up hitting something.

He connected his laptop to his old printer and set it to print out fifty fliers while he brushed his teeth and took a shower. When he came back into his room, the pile waited for him and Macy sat on the bed.

Alex adjusted his towel around his waist, hiking it up. "What are you doing?"

"Just wanted to make sure you're okay. You seemed upset—I mean, more than before. Did something else happen?"

The concern in her eyes nearly broke him. "Can I get dressed first?"

She nodded and got up, glancing at his box. "Moving back in?"

He shook his head but shrugged. "Just seemed like I needed some more clothes. Hopefully, Ari will be back soon and I won't need them."

"So you can go back to your life?" There was no accusation in her tone, and that made the sting hurt all the worse.

"I don't know what's going on, Macy. I just need to focus on Ariana. Crap." He slapped his forehead. "I need to call Nick. I was supposed to call him earlier."

"Who's Nick?"

"Fleshman. Seriously, I need to get dressed. Scram or get a show."

"You're on a first name basis with the police captain?"

Alex reached for his towel.

"We're not done talking." She left, closing the door behind

her.

He sighed in relief and grabbed some clothes from his apartment. He brushed his hair and then picked up the fliers. Ariana's smiling face and big, innocent eyes felt like a punch in the gut. He sat on the bed, gasping for air as he read the flier with her age, size, coloring, and other information like where she'd been last seen and what she'd been wearing.

It was all so… He didn't know the word. Clinical? Impersonal? It should've said something about how fun and sweet she was, and how important it was to find her and punish the bastard who'd taken her.

Alex set the stack on the desk and shoved his clothes into the drawers. When he picked up one of his work shirts, a scrap of yellow paper floated down to the ground.

He picked it up, trying to figure out what it was from. There shouldn't have been any paper in his clean clothes. He unfolded it to find unfamiliar fancy handwriting in blue ballpoint ink.

I told you to stay out of it. You didn't listen. I hope you see now that I mean business. Drop your research, or your sister gets it.

Alex's hands shook as he read and re-read the note.

First, the weasel takes his daughter, then he plants drugs in Alex's locker and gets him fired. Now he dared to threaten his sister?

Blind fury tore through Alex. If he ever got his hands on the kidnapper, he would tear him to shreds. He would torture him slowly, making him pay for everything until he pleaded, begging for mercy.

Alex grabbed a stapler. He would make sure the fliers were on every pole in town. The kidnapper better hope the cops got to him before Alex did.

Longer

~

BY THE TIME ALEX got back home to his parents' house, he was exhausted. Hanging and handing out fliers was surprisingly tiring—maybe as much as roofing. Or maybe it was because of the mental exhaustion.

He'd been trying not to think about the kidnapper's threat against his sister, but how could he not? His anger toward that man went into every staple on every pole.

Alex was tempted to find the man and give him a piece of his own medicine. He had time now that Flynn had gotten him fired. Time was all he had.

The only question was whether or not to tell Macy there was now a threat against her. The first one had panned out—and Alex sure as hell wasn't going to give up the search for Ariana.

Macy deserved to know what was going on—but what if Alex could take care of Flynn first? He could outsmart the loser and find him before he made his next move. Then Macy would never have to deal with the stress of knowing he'd threatened her.

"Is that you, Alex?" called his mom from somewhere upstairs.

Alex closed the door. He'd been standing there with it open without realizing it. "Yeah, it's me."

He took his boots off and went upstairs, finding her in the kitchen. She was cleaning it, despite the fact that it was already spotless.

"I was out hanging fliers. Handed out some, too."

"Good. You never know which one might be the one that makes a difference."

He nodded and sat, doubting if they would actually matter. Everyone already knew she was gone from social media and the news.

"Are you hungry?"

Alex shrugged. He was, but he didn't feel like eating.

"You need some food, and we have plenty. Some neighbors brought over meals. Do you want lasagna or a casserole?"

"Surprise me." He rested his head on the table, trying to decide how to bring up the threats to Nick. One thing was sure—he needed to do it soon. Flynn had threatened Macy.

Clementine came into the room and rubbed against Alex's legs. He reached down and petted the tabby.

He realized his mom was talking to him, but he had no idea what about. Then the microwaved beeped, and she set a plate in front of him. He sat up and saw the steaming casserole piled high on the plate. "Thanks."

"Eat up. You need your energy." She poured some red wine into two glasses and sat next to him, giving him one.

"So do you. Have you eaten?"

"Plenty." She sipped the wine. "I hope we all get through this. A second kidnapping—that's two more than any family should have to endure."

"I'll drink to that." He downed the entire glass of wine.

Mom arched a brow, but didn't say anything.

Alex dug into the casserole, realizing just how hungry he actually was. He scarfed the whole thing down, burning his tongue in the process.

"How long are you planning on staying? You can stay as long as you want," Mom added quickly. "I'm just trying to plan."

"At least until we find Ariana."

"Your boss is okay with you missing more work?"

"He's not expecting me any time soon." Alex pushed his plate away, anger building just thinking about his interaction with Darren.

"Are you okay, hon? I mean with your job." She took his plate and glass, and carried them to the sink.

Part of him wanted to open up and spill everything. Mom had always been on his side. But he didn't know where to begin, and he felt like such a mess. "I just need to focus on finding Ariana."

She turned around and gave him a sad smile. "You're a good dad, I hope you know that. *She* knows that."

Alex looked away. "I'd like to be better. Speaking of, I need to make a call. Thanks again for the food."

As Alex went up the stairs to his room, he passed his dad.

"I've been blogging about Ariana like I did with Macy. I'm getting a lot of views and comments."

"That's great, Dad." He'd always been obsessed with his site's stats.

"It's really getting the word out about Ari. People are talking and searching—they're sharing possible sightings. I need to let the police know."

"I'm going to call Fleshman, so I can tell him if you want."

Dad put a hand on Alex's shoulder. "People don't blame you as much as you think."

Alex snorted.

"I'm serious."

"That's because they're commenting on your blog."

"It gets as many jerk comments as any other site. You should read some of the comments—you've got a whole Team Alex."

"Right." Alex rolled his eyes.

"You do."

"Obviously you haven't been on social media."

"You have to ignore the trolls. They're only there for the drama. At least until something more exciting comes along."

"Like I said, I'm going to call Fleshman. If I want things done, he's the one to talk to."

"I thought the FBI took the case over."

"They're helping. Hey, I'll check out your blog. I swear."

"It'll help to hear from people who believe in you. Ignore the trolls."

Alex nodded. "Thanks, Dad."

"We'll find Ari. We will."

"I know." Alex walked by him and into his room. His body begged him to crash on the bed and give into the food coma for a while.

Not until he spoke with Nick. The captain needed to know what was going on with the threats. He would know how to handle the latest one aimed at Macy.

Alex sat at the desk and called Nick's cell phone.

"Hey, Alex. I'm just heading home, and I found something you need to see."

"We have to talk."

"Meet me there."

Flynn had known the last time Alex went there. "Somewhere else."

"Why?" Nick asked.

"I'll explain when we get there."

"Do you think one of our phones are being tapped?"

Alex's stomach twisted in knots. He hadn't until Nick brought it up. What if Flynn had managed that? If he had, Alex couldn't say anything to Nick over the phone. "Ha, ha. That only happens in the movies. Let's just meet somewhere out of the way."

"There's a greasy hole-in-the-wall restaurant near the—"

"Hey, why don't you text me the address?"

"Sure." The call ended, and a minute later, the text came in.

Got it. Cu soon.

Alex stuck his laptop in the case, hurried to his car, and put the address in the GPS before punching the gas. It was definitely out of the way—the number of turns down obscure streets was ridiculous. He found a place to parallel park down a seedy side street. It was a good thing he didn't have a nice car. Someone stealing the Tercel would almost be a gift.

He secured the laptop case across his shoulders and kept a hand near his oversized pocket knife. A raindrop splashed on his cheek. He pulled up his hood and kept his gaze lowered as he walked. Several drug deals went down as he made his way down the road.

After turning down a few more streets, he finally reached the little dive. Bullet holes decorated the glass door between the chipped black bars. Nice. This place made his neighborhood seem like the Street of Dreams.

He reached for the door.

"Hey there," said a sultry feminine voice behind him.

Alex spun around. A woman old enough to be his mom stood there, wearing a torn red mini skirt and a tiny tube top.

"Lookin' for a good time?" She winked, making a large mole wiggle.

"Not really."

"I can make it worth your while. Discount for a super sexy hottie."

He hurried inside, looking for Nick, and found him at a table in the corner, sipping from a coffee cup and staring at his phone. Alex went over and sat, first wiping a pile of crumbs from the seat. Half of them stuck to his palm.

"You found it." Nick never looked up from the screen.

Alex tried wiping the crumbs from his hand. "Next time, I pick where we meet."

"You wanted something private. I doubt anyone we know will look for us here."

"Isn't that the truth? So, what did you find?" Alex scraped his palm along the edge of the table to dislodge the crud stuck to his hand.

"What did you want to tell me?"

Alex took a deep breath and told Nick about all the threats.

"Why didn't you tell me sooner?"

"I didn't think he was serious."

Nick shook his head. "You need to tell me stuff like this."

"Okay."

"Immediately. Forward me everything you have and I'll look into it."

Alex nodded, feeling stupid.

"In other news, I got an anonymous tip today."

"What did they say?"

Nick held Alex's gaze for a moment. "It would appear these cases have been going on for close to thirty years."

Pins

A RIANA WOKE TO the smell of bacon, feeling rested despite the stiff bed. After their movie night—Lloyd had picked out not just one but two scary movies, and he'd brought out bags of candy for the second movie—she'd been so tired, she had fallen right to sleep.

She sat up and stretched, taking in the delicious smell. Her stomach rumbled. She climbed out of bed and put on some clothes as the aroma of bacon grew stronger.

Just after she slid on the stiff green-and-blue striped sweater, her gaze landed on one of the dolls that had a fancy hairstyle.

Bobby pins.

Her heart pounded. That was exactly what she'd been looking for. Maybe the next time Lloyd went out, she'd be able to get through the lock. It would be a lot easier if she had her phone and could find a how-to video, but she'd seen enough TV that she was pretty sure two bobby pins would get it done.

She hoped.

The deadbolt clicked. Ariana reached for the hairbrush and ran it through her tangles.

Lloyd came in, smiling. "I made omelets. I hope you're hungry."

"I am. It smells delicious." She smiled back.

"Let me help you with that." He stepped behind her and took the brush, running it through her hair with care. He removed the knots without yanking. "Let's eat. Everything's ready."

He took her hand and led her to the kitchen, where the plates were already filled. A huge omelet sat at her place, filled with peppers and beef. Three juicy pieces of bacon sat next to it.

Ariana sat, and he poured her some orange juice.

"Dig in."

She did, and he talked about the two movies as they ate. When they were clearing the table, Lloyd turned to her. "Sorry to do this to you, but I have to go into work today. We're not kids any-more—well, I'm not, and bills have to be paid."

"Oh."

"I'll try to be back in time for lunch, but if not, I hope the big breakfast will hold you."

Her pulse drummed in her ears. This would be her chance if he was going to be gone all day.

Lloyd said something else, but she couldn't hear.

Ariana took a couple breaths to calm her nerves. "What?"

"I'll make it up to you if I can't get back for lunch, okay?"

She nodded. "I'm stuffed. It's okay. Last night was really fun, too. Thanks." She tried to give him a convincing smile. Hopefully, if he didn't feel bad about being at work all day, he'd stay there longer.

He patted her shoulder. "You've always been so sweet. Too sweet, actually. That's what got you—never mind. Let's not talk about that. Why don't you go to the bathroom while I get everything cleaned up in here?"

She stared at him. He was going to let her go back there with-out following her?

Lloyd gestured for her to go and turned to the dishes in the sink.

As tempting as it was to run down the hall and find a way out, she knew better. He was bigger and faster. She needed to wait until he was at work. Then she could get far away before he had any idea she'd even left.

Ariana went into the bathroom and took care of business and then dug around in the drawers, looking for anything else she could use to make her escape.

Knock, knock.

"Time to go to your room, Jan."

Disappointment washed through her. At least she had a chance of getting out this time.

She opened the door. Lloyd stood so that she only had room to walk into the bedroom. She went inside.

"I promise to make it up to you. And I'm going to try my best to work from home tomorrow."

"Okay."

"I'm really sorry. Come here."

Ariana walked over to him. He engulfed her in an embrace and then left without a word, locking the door between them. The woodsy smell of his cologne stuck to her.

She went over to the window to watch him leave. The alarm beeped after about a minute and then Lloyd opened the car door. He paused, looked up toward her, and waved.

Her heart nearly leaped into her throat. He knew she'd been watching him come and go? She forced herself to wave back. He climbed in the car and drove away.

Ariana leaned against the wall, trying to catch her breath. Maybe she wasn't as sneaky as she thought. If she didn't get out while he was at work, she'd have to be really careful with her escape attempts.

She waited a little while to make sure he didn't come back and then went over to the shelf where the larger dolls were. Ariana picked up a fancy one. Its hair was in a tight up-do. There was no way she could replicate that once she removed the pins. If she was lucky, the hairstyle would just stay in place. If not, then she'd have to think of something clever, like putting it in a hat or hiding the doll altogether—that was if she didn't get away. But she would, so it didn't matter.

Ariana slid the doll off the shelf and studied the hair. The pins looked like they would come out easily enough. They weren't glued in place. She sat on the unmade bed and held the doll at different angles. Her heart felt like it would explode out of her chest.

"Pull yourself together." This was her chance, and she needed to take it. Maybe she could be back home in time for dinner. That was what she had to focus on.

Hands shaking, she reached for the first bobby pin. The doll wobbled in her grasp and she missed the pin by a good two inches. She set it on her lap and held it with her arm instead. That time, she managed to not only touch it, but slide it out.

The pin fell onto the floor.

Well, it wasn't going anywhere. She reached for the second one and slid it out careful not to drop it. Once the end came out, the fancy hairstyle fell apart and covered the doll's face.

She would deal with that later. Ariana put the doll back on the shelf, tucking it behind the others. She had to rearrange them to hide it in the back.

Clinging to the second bobby pin, she got on her hands and knees and looked for the first one. She couldn't see it, but she finally noticed it under the bed.

Ariana couldn't stop shaking. What if she got caught? What if he had hidden cameras somewhere? But if he did, wouldn't he know she'd tried to escape already? He wouldn't have given her ice cream and popcorn.

No, this was her chance, and it was a good one. She only need-ed to pull herself together. Also, she had all day. It wasn't like he was coming back in an hour.

Holding one pin in each hand, she stared down the lock. The only thing standing between her and freedom.

She could do this.

Hopefully.

No, she could. She would.

Swallowing, she stepped closer to the door. One step. Another. Another.

She stopped a couple feet away.

Her mouth was dry, and suddenly, she had to go to the bathroom again.

Ariana rushed for the door and stuck both bobby pins in the lock. She wiggled and jiggled, hoping to hear a click or something. Who knew what would happen? Would the deadbolt click over? Was it even possible to unlock this kind of lock like this?

She'd find out soon enough. Gritting her teeth, she tried harder. Different angles, differing amounts of pressure. Nothing was off limits. She just had to get out of there.

Time seemed to slow down. Ariana fought and struggled with the pins and the deadbolt until sweat made the clothes stick to her skin. Her muscles ached and her head hurt even worse. She was out of breath.

Finally, she stopped. If she was going to do this, it would take more than just the pins. She would need the knife, too. But first, she needed to calm down and collect herself.

Ariana set the bobby pins on the desk and threw herself onto the bed. It creaked and groaned under her weight. She closed her eyes. Just a moment to rest.

When she opened her eyes, the sun shone in from a different angle.

She bolted upright. How long had she slept?

Ariana ran to the window. Lloyd's car was still gone.

There was no way to know what time it was without a clock. All she knew was that the sun was pretty high in the sky.

She needed to work on the deadbolt again. This time, though, she would use the knife. She went over to the dollhouse and lifted it, this time careful not to hurt herself.

Balancing the knife and the pins, she tried everything she could think of to get it unlocked. Nothing worked. She even tried sliding the knife between the door and the jam to make the deadbolt loosen from its place.

She held it there with her mouth and used her hands to put the bobby pins in the keyhole. She just had to make it work.

Sweat stuck to her clothes again. Doubt settled in. Maybe she wouldn't be able to get away.

Ariana pulled one of the bobby pins out. It stuck. She jiggled it.

Click.

Out

~

A RIANA STARED, JAW dropped, at the open door in front of her. She'd done it. Gotten through the lock.

Now she could make her escape. But first, she really had to go to the bathroom.

Ariana ran in and went, her mind racing the entire time. Once she was back out into the hall, everything was eerily quiet. She'd never been alone in a house before, and it wasn't nearly as exciting as she'd always thought.

Her heart wouldn't stop thundering. With the house so quiet, that was all she could hear. Well, that and her labored breathing.

She leaned against the wall. It was time to focus.

Where should she go? The stairs leading to the backyard? No, she couldn't get out of there. She'd have to find a different way out of the house.

Then she remembered the keypad. Lloyd had punched in a code to get them out. What if she couldn't get outside without the code? No, that was crazy. She'd be able to open a door without a code. An alarm would probably sound, but she could get out.

Ariana wandered down the hall, passing the rec room. This was the farthest she'd gone before. The only thing she could see were closed doors. She didn't want to know what Lloyd had hidden behind any of them.

She came to a different staircase. This one was wide and shiny, light-colored wood steps. No ugly carpeting.

Ariana took a deep breath and tiptoed onto the first step, half-expecting sirens to wail or for it to open up and send her falling to the ground below.

Nothing happened. She took another step and then another. Soon, she saw a bright and beautiful modern living room down below.

She stared in disbelief. How was it that the upstairs was like stepping into a time warp, but downstairs was so normal? Well, normal aside from how huge it was. It seemed big enough to be a mansion.

As she descended down the stairs, she could see an enormous kitchen off to the side and then a dining room. More rooms came into view as she got closer to the floor. The house seemed to go on forever.

The only thing she didn't see was a way out.

She felt out of place, and also expected someone to walk into the living room at any moment. How could such a place exist just below where she'd been staying?

Her throat went dry and she sat on the step behind her. Did she dare walk around? A place like that would surely have cameras. That explained the alarm going out to the backyard.

What if he already knew she'd gotten out?

That meant she needed to go outside right away.

Ariana jumped up and rushed to the bottom of the stairs. Nothing flashed or sounded. Everything was as quiet down here as it had been up there. She jaunted across the living room to the spacious, bright kitchen. There were no doors leading outside.

She spun around and went to the dining room. No way out. She ran back to the living room and opened a door. A closet full of board games and DVDs. Another door. A darkened office.

There had to be a way out. She followed a hall on the other side of the kitchen and came to an entryway.

Gravel crunched under tires outside.

Ariana's stomach dropped to the ground.

No.

A car door slammed and an alarm beeped.

Her throat closed up. She ran toward the stairs, running up.

A door opened and then slammed shut.

She skipped a step and stumbled.

Lloyd whistled a cheerful tune downstairs.

Ariana ran as fast as she could up the rest of the staircase and down the hall to the bedroom.

The whistling grew louder.

She made it to the room and closed the door as quietly as she could.

It was unlocked. She didn't know how to lock it.

Terror ran through her.

Footsteps sounded in the hall and the whistling continued.

She grabbed the pins and knife, stuffing them under the doll-house. Her mind raced with excuses. She'd had to go to the bathroom. That's why she unlocked the door. She didn't want to mess up the bedroom that meant so much to him. He could trust her—she was still in there.

The door opened.

Ariana flung herself to the ground and held up a couple dolls. She fought to breathe normally.

Lloyd came in carrying a bunch of colorful balloons. He smiled at her and held out the balloons. "We missed your birthday this year, so it's time to celebrate."

He hadn't even noticed the door was unlocked.

She tried to speak, but nothing came.

"I've left you speechless." His grin widened. "I hope you're ready for birthday cake."

Ariana managed a nod.

"Good. Why don't you put on a dress from the closet while I decorate the rec room?" He let out a giggle as he left, leaving the door unlocked.

She stared at the door, feeling light-headed. What had just happened? Ariana went over to the bed and fell onto it, trying to recover from the shock.

A few minutes later, she heard a commotion out in the kitchen. She jumped up and ran over to the closet. Half a dozen dresses hung in front of her. Did she want polka dots, flowers, or stripes? Like it mattered. She grabbed one. It had multi-colored polka dots. She slid out of what she was wearing and put on the scratchy dress.

Lloyd came in, grinning and clapping. "You remembered! That's my favorite one on you. Let me help you with your hair."

She followed him to the dresser, where he pulled her hair back into a ponytail and wrapped it in a pink bow.

"Perfect." He beamed.

Ariana forced another smile.

"Wait until you see this."

She nodded and followed him to the rec room. The walls were covered with pink streamers and balloons. A huge 'Happy Birthday' sign hung from the far wall. An enormous cake sat on the coffee table next to a stack of perfectly wrapped presents.

"Happy birthday!" Lloyd cried. He went over to a record player and fumbled with it. A chorus of the happy birthday song blared from the speakers. Lloyd sang along.

Ariana stared at the scene before her, having no idea how to react.

"What are you waiting for?" Lloyd asked. "Let's have some cake."

Realization

KELLEN KICKED HIS FEET onto his coffee table, opened a pop, and turned on the TV. A news reporter spoke about Ariana's abduction, speaking in circles as they always did. There was nothing new—she was still missing and they had no real suspects. They might if the FBI would quit looking at him.

If he could go back in time, he'd have never left for the stupid trash bags. But how could he have known the events that were about to unfold? He would've never dreamed that a simple act of trying to be helpful would make him look like a criminal.

He finished the soda, crushed the can on the arm of the couch, and tossed it onto the table next to his feet.

His phone rang. Probably Zoey again. Didn't she know what space meant?

Kellen almost didn't check, but did out of habit. It was one of his buddies from college. He accepted the call. "Hey, Trey. Long time."

"Yeah, long time. You're engaged and going to be a stepdad?"

"You saw the news?"

"Of course. Everyone's talking about it. Are you okay?"

"Define okay," Kellen said.

"Is it true they suspect you?" Trey asked.

"Half the stuff out there is pure crap, but yeah, I'm one of the people they've questioned." Kellen flipped through the channels and stopped on a cartoon and muted it.

"That sucks. They should look at the dad. He sounds like a real piece of work."

Kellen shrugged. What could he say that wouldn't make him look like a jerk? Of course he wished they would interrogate Alex instead of him. He had actually been there when the abduction took place.

"Okay. So, uh… what wouldn't be awkward to talk about? Sorry man, I don't really know what to say."

"It's all right. Thanks for calling. No one else has."

"Do you need anything?"

A supportive fiancée. To get the FBI off his case. His life back. "No, just have to get through this."

"It's been forty-eight hours, hasn't it?"

Kellen glanced at the clock, but then realized he wasn't sure what day it was. "Is it Sunday or Monday?"

"Monday."

Crap. He hadn't even called in to work. They had to know why. "Yeah, it's been over two days. She was taken Friday night."

"Well, if you need to get away for a while, I've got an extra ticket to the Seahawks game this week."

"I appreciate the thought, but it would look really bad if I went to a game while my fiancée's daughter is missing and I'm already a person of interest."

"Oh, I didn't even think about that. Well, I can round up a couple of the guys and we can come over."

"Maybe." Kellen would have to talk with his attorneys about something as simple as having friends over.

He hated his life.

"Call me," Trey said. "I'll do all the work."

"Sure. It's good to hear from you."

"You, too."

Kellen ended the call. If only he could go to the game or even just tell his friends to come over.

His phone rang again. He answered it without looking at the caller ID.

"You are alive," Zoey said.

Kellen swore under his breath. "I told you I needed space."

"We need to be together to get through this."

"Actually, we don't."

"Don't do this."

"I meant everything I said before."

"Can we talk?" Zoey asked.

He closed his eyes. "Talk."

"On the phone?"

"Unless you meant telepathically."

"You know what I meant. Come over here."

"Why do I always have to go to your place?" Kellen snapped.

"What do you mean?"

"You never come here."

"I thought you liked it here."

He took a deep breath. "This is exactly what I'm talking about. There's nothing wrong with my townhouse, yet—"

"Why are you arguing with me about this? Can't it wait until later? Ariana's missing. I need you."

"Exactly. It's all about you—all the time."

"My daughter's missing!"

"And now the *kid card* is more powerful than ever," Kellen muttered.

"What's that supposed to mean?"

Like she didn't know. "You bring up Ariana and automatically get what you want because if I say no, then I'm the kid-hating a-hole. You win again. Congratulations."

"It's not like that."

"Wrong. It's exactly like that. Welcome to my world of being the wicked stepdad no matter what I do."

"I can't believe this. My daughter's missing, and this is what I have to deal with. How dare you?"

Anger surged through him. "And I have to deal with your selfishness being masked by the *kid card.* How dare *you?*"

"That's really how you see it?"

"I call it as it is."

"Don't treat me like this if you want my support against the FBI."

"Support? You call anything you've done supportive?" Kellen laughed. "That's a good one."

"If you're trying to push me away, it's working."

"Great. Call Alex."

"Alex?" Zoey exclaimed. "What does he have to do with anything? And why would I call him? I loathe him."

Kellen's anger was joined by jealousy. How could she not see what was so obvious? "Stop trying to deny your feelings for him."

She gasped. "Excuse me? I can't stand that lowlife."

Kellen squeezed the couch cushion. "Love and hate are two sides of the same scale, Zo. You can't have one without the other. I've tried to look past your obvious feelings for him, but I can see clearly now. Especially after the way you were defending him last time we talked. It's not worth it. I'm *not* going to be your second choice."

"You're not—and especially not to Alex." She took a deep breath. "Obviously, we're both emotionally charged. Why don't we meet somewhere and discuss this over a meal? Have some wine and talk like civilized adults."

A wave of sadness washed through him. He hated the wild range of emotions that had been running through him the last couple days. He just wasn't himself—especially with all the rage and jealousy he'd been feeling. He was turning into a person he didn't recognize anymore. The last thing he wanted was to keep going down this path and turn into someone he didn't like.

"Did you hear me?" Zoey asked.

He took a deep breath and hated himself for what he had to say. "I'm sorry, Zo. I just can't take all this stress anymore. I'm not the person you need me to be."

"Wait. Are you saying we're over?"

"I wish everything could go back to the way it was, but it can't."

"You can't be serious."

"If we don't cut it off now, we're going to tear each other part. We're going to wind up hating each other, and I don't want that. We've had so many good times. Let's remember those times."

"But we—"

"I'm really sorry, Zo." His voice cracked. "Goodbye." He ended the call before she could talk him out of the breakup. It really was best for both of them, and that was all that mattered. For once, he didn't care what anyone else thought.

Crash

~

ALEX'S MIND SPUN as he researched the cold cases. The anonymous tipper had been onto something, and it did appear the older, out-of-state cases were the same. A girl around the age of twelve or thirteen disappears about a week before Halloween and then is found in a lake on or shortly after Halloween—and each time one is found after, it had been determined that she was drowned on or close to the holiday.

If only he and Nick could look at all this together, but there had been a string of robberies resulting in physical injury, so he had to focus on those and let the team focus on Ariana's case.

Alex wanted to wring the FBI agent's neck. How could she keep ignoring the fact that Flynn was the kidnapper? But Nick had been sure that if they could gather enough evidence pointing to the new cold cases, that would be enough for the woman. That was why Alex was taking meticulous notes, going over each case painfully slowly.

Knock, knock.

"Come in."

Mom entered with a steaming cup of coffee. "I thought you could use some more."

"Thanks, Mom."

She set it next to his mouse pad. "Do you have enough to take to the FBI agent?"

"I hope so. Nick wants me to email him everything at the end of his shift. If it *is* enough, he's going to show it to Williams and insist she put their resources into the lead."

"What do you have?" She pulled up a chair.

Alex sipped the hot drink. "There are eight cases, all exactly the same in Oregon. Before that, six in Idaho. There are even a few in Montana. Flynn must be moving around every time someone gets too close."

"And they all… end on Halloween?" Mom's expression tightened.

"Yeah. Every single one."

She closed her eyes. "That's just sick. What if the FBI still won't look at it?"

Alex clenched his fists. "Then that Williams bi—chick will have to deal with me."

"Don't do something to get yourself into trouble, Alex."

"If it'll get them to find Ariana, I don't care what happens to me. Halloween is getting closer too fast."

"I know." Her voice cracked. "When are you supposed to email Captain Fleshman?"

He glanced at the clock. "About an hour and a half."

"Do you need any help? I've got to do something other than clean. I'm going crazy, too."

"You can help me search for more cases online. You'd be surprised how much is out there—I was, at least."

"Okay. I'll—"

Alex's phone vibrated and Mom's phone played music. They exchanged a curious expression and both looked at their screens.

He had a text from Luke.

Call me now.

Mom gasped. "What's wrong?"

"I don't know. Call him."

She slid her finger around the screen and put the phone to her ear. "Busy."

"Let me try." Alex called his brother-in-law.

It rang.

"Alex?" Luke sounded out of breath.

"What's going on?" He put the phone on speaker. "Mom's here, too."

"Macy was in an accident."

Mom cried out. Alex put an arm around her shoulder.

"They're taking her to the hospital now," Luke continued.

"Is she okay?" Alex asked. "How bad is it?"

"I don't know yet. They called me at work. I'm leaving for the hospital now."

"You don't know anything?" Mom shook.

"They won't say. Meet me there. I gotta drive."

"Okay. We'll be right down."

The call ended.

Mom turned to Alex with tears in her eyes. "How much more heartache can I take?"

"I'm sure she's fine. Probably a sprained wrist or something. Let's just get down there and give her a hard time for worrying us." He helped her up and then went to the staircase. "Dad!"

He appeared below. "What's going on?"

"Macy was in an accident. We have to get to the hospital."

Color drained from his face. "Is she okay?"

"Nobody knows."

"I'll start the car."

Alex hurried into his room. Who knew when he'd get back? He needed to email Nick what he had now.

"I'll be right down," he told Mom.

She nodded, looking dazed, and went into her bedroom.

Alex uploaded everything he had into an email and sent it off to Nick, explaining what happened to Macy.

He grabbed his jacket from the bed. A yellow scrap of paper

floated to the floor.

The note from his locker.

It had warned Alex that Macy would be next.

Blind fury surged through him. Whatever injuries his sister had incurred, Alex would inflict on Flynn.

"Are you coming?" Mom asked from the doorway.

Alex took a deep breath. "Just a minute."

"Hurry, please."

"Okay." He picked up the scrap of paper, snapped a picture, and sent it to Nick.

Hospital

~

"**M**OM, SIT DOWN," Alex said. Her pacing made him dizzy. His mind already raced between Macy's accident and all the new info he'd found on the cold cases.

"What's taking so long?" Mom played with her hair. "The surgery was supposed to be done an hour ago."

Luke rose and helped her into a chair. "We have to stay optimistic for her sake."

Alex shook his head. Like that would help anything.

"I'll see if they can tell us something." Dad rose and headed for the nearest desk.

Luke spoke quietly with Mom in soothing tones.

Alex checked his phone to see if there were any updates from Nick. He was probably going over the information Alex had sent or he was talking to the agent. Or maybe she said no again, and Nick didn't want to bother Alex with the news while he was in the hospital with Macy.

It was a good thing Alex didn't have Flynn's address. If he did, he'd march over there and let him have it for what he'd put his family through.

Dad came back. "They can't tell us much, but the surgery is going longer than expected. A scan showed internal abdominal bleeding due to the rib fractures." He sat and took Mom's hand.

Alex got up. "I'm going to see if I can find out more about the crash. Sitting here isn't accomplishing squat. Text me when you hear something."

He made his way back to the parking lot, and leaned against his car. He didn't want to sit any more. It was so tempting to pull out a cigarette.

Why had he quit?

He needed *something*. If he had either a drink or a pack, he'd dig in right there on the hospital property. Instead, he texted Nick.

What's up?

Hopefully, he had some news on something.

Going over Macy's collision report.
And?

Alex's phone rang.

"What does it say?" Alex demanded.

"You really want to know everything?" Nick asked.

"Don't hold back. I need to know how bad it is."

"Her car was destroyed almost to the point of being unrecognizable," Nick said.

Alex took a deep breath. He'd been expecting that. "And?"

"They had to cut through the roof to get her out. She was pinned between the seat belt and airbag, hanging sideways. The medics on site reported multiple broken bones. Macy was lucky her spine and neck weren't injured. She'll recover. It won't be easy, but she was really lucky."

Alex took a deep breath. Now he wanted a smoke more than ever. "What about the guy who did this to her?"

"Some kid was delivering pizza in a tricked-out oversized truck."

"Let me guess," Alex said. "Walked away without a scratch." Probably paid off, too.

"Pretty close," Nick affirmed.

"Can I see the report?"

"How about you focus on your family? I'm going to talk to Williams about the stuff you sent over about those other cases."

"You think it's enough?"

"It better be. I don't see how she can turn a blind eye to thirty years of the same exact cases."

"Hey, did you get that picture I sent you?"

"Yeah, and I have one of my best guys on it. Look, I have a meeting in two minutes. Let's talk a little later."

They said their goodbyes and Alex wished he still kept beer and cigarettes in the trunk for emergencies. He took a deep breath and headed back inside, stopping at a little coffee stand outside the cafeteria. He carried a little tray of four espressos back to the waiting room. His parents and Luke were all in the same seats as before. He handed them all a cup and sat down with the last one.

"Thanks," Luke said.

"I talked to the police captain. He said Macy's car was pretty bad."

They all grimaced, not that anyone was surprised given how long Macy had been in surgery.

"She's got a lot of broken bones but was lucky it wasn't more serious."

"How could this have happened?" Mom exclaimed. Tears ran down her face.

Because a kidnapper thought he could control Alex with threats. Alex didn't see how saying anything would help.

A balding guy in scrubs came over to them. "Luke Walker?"

"That's me." Luke rose and shook the doctor's hand. "These are her parents and brother."

He introduced himself and shook hands with them all and then took a seat.

"Why did the surgery take so long?" Mom asked.

The doctor spoke in technical terms that made Alex's head

spin. He'd ask Mom or Dad for a translation later, but the gist was what Nick had said—that Macy was lucky based on the severity of the accident. Not that it was an accident.

Alex followed the conversation with his eyes, but his mind was far away.

He was trying to figure out how to get his hands on Flynn Myer.

Convincing

~

NICK LOOKED AROUND his office and rubbed his temples. He really needed to get some solid sleep tonight. But first, he needed to show the load of information to Williams and convince her that it was in the FBI's best interest to focus their resources in that direction. Hopefully she would be in an agreeable mood.

Mentally, he went over the major points. He had to be convincing—they needed to find Ariana and this had to be the same serial killer. There were simply too many similarities to be a coincidence. He'd seen people brought down with a lot less proof.

Knock, knock.

"Come in."

Williams entered, eating takeout. Nick's office filled with the smell of spiced chicken. "You wanted to see me?"

He motioned for her to sit. "I have some new information about the kidnapping case you need to see."

"What is it?" She sat and continued eating.

"It's the cold cases. They—"

"Why are you so hung up on them?"

"Just hear me out. This will help us find the girl."

"All right. You have my full attention for the next ten minutes."

Nick would have to talk fast. He glanced back down at the computer and then to her. "I believe this criminal has been getting away with these abductions and murders for the last thirty years in at least four states."

Williams froze, her fork midway between the container and her mouth. "Come again?"

"Thirty years, thirty girls, four states."

She put the fork down and set the food on the chair next to her. "All the same MO?"

"Let me show you." Nick spun the laptop toward her and went around. "It appears to have started in Montana, unless there are earlier cases I can't find." He brought the information he had on the first case. "Look, this girl bears a startling resemblance to Ariana Nakano, wouldn't you say?"

Williams narrowed her eyes and leaned closer to the screen. "A little older, but yes, there are similarities."

"Similarities?" he exclaimed. "These girls could all be related."

"Really?" Williams scrunched her face. "This one has fiery red hair. Look at those curls. And this other one—she's Hispanic. The only thing she has in common with the Ariana is brown hair and eyes. Did you notice they're all two years older than Ariana?"

Nick wasn't surprised she was clinging to those discrepancies. He'd seen it coming. "Ariana's tall for her age—that explains the age differences. Also, the redhead was wearing a brunette wig at the time of her abduction."

"And the Hispanic girl?"

"Brown eyes and hair! Same height!" Nick glared at her.

Williams studied the pictures again. "It's a stretch, Fleshman. Our resources are already tight. I can't allocate more resources on something this thin."

"They were all taken within eight days of Halloween! All found after Halloween, dead near lakes. Drowning victims. Taken from parks. There are too many similarities to ignore." Nick clicked from one case to the next, enlarging each photo. "Look at how much these girls look like Ariana!"

"And there are thirty of these cases?"

"Roughly, yes."

"Show me more."

Relief washed through Nick. He finally had her attention. If they had the FBI's support and resources, they stood a chance at actually finding the creep—and Ariana—before she ended up at the bottom of a lake. Next he went through each case, showing the pictures of each girl, their location, and how long they'd been taken before their untimely end on Halloween.

Once he was done, Williams leaned back in the chair and stared at the ceiling. "Unbelievable."

Nick arched a brow.

"I can't believe he has gone undetected all this time. How is that possible?"

She actually believed him? He nearly dropped the pen in his hand. "He's careful, and he's moved around. Also, not all of the bodies were found right away, making it harder for the local authorities to make the connection."

Williams looked deep in thought. "We need to figure out where he keeps the girls and what goes on while he has them."

"That's a good question. There has never been any sign of sexual trauma. It must be all about the kill. I'd like to run a search to see if Myer was near any of the other locations at the time."

"It's worth looking into. This guy needs to be stopped before he can kill again." Williams grabbed her food. "Email everything to me. I need to go over this and send some agents to look into the older cases. There has to be a clue to who this man is within all of those cases. He's been careful, but everyone slips up somewhere. We're going to find that out."

"What can I do?" Nick asked.

"Debrief the team. Get as many people as you can to come to the meeting. I need to call into headquarters and get more agents involved. We need them in each of the other three states. We don't have much time to save that little girl."

"Yes, we do." And they would've had more if she hadn't been so stubborn.

"We also have to figure out how to handle the media—if at all. Do we want the perpetrator knowing we're onto him?"

"It might push him to let her go. He obviously doesn't want to get caught. Otherwise, he wouldn't move around so much."

"He might also overreact and kill her early. We can't risk that." Nick shook his head. "He won't."

"You don't think so?"

"There's something special about Halloween. Maybe it's some kind of ritual sacrifice. I have no idea. But it's always done the night of Halloween."

"We'll worry about the media later. First, I need to find out what I can about all these other cases—and time isn't on our side."

Williams hurried out of the office. Nick sent a group text to everyone on the team. He gave them an hour to get to the conference room they'd set up for the case. Nick had to prepare a presentation to get the information to the officers as quickly as possible.

Renewed energy raced through him. Finally, they were on the right track *and* had the FBI's resources at their disposal. Maybe they could stop the murderer and put him away before he could kill Ariana or any other little girl ever again.

Reminisce

Z OEY SWALLOWED THE TYLENOL with a swig of black coffee. She'd woken with a splitting headache, and that was after hardly sleeping. Her mind wouldn't shut up. She couldn't stop worrying about Ari, and the more she thought about her argument with Kellen, the angrier she grew.

How dare he throw all that stuff at her, now of all times? And the *kid card*—what a bunch of crap. She didn't use Ariana to get her own way. Her daughter was important, and if he couldn't grasp that, maybe he was right about breaking off the engagement. As embarrassing as it would be to tell everyone they had split, everyone would be on her side. She couldn't marry someone who didn't support her as a mom.

She glanced at the calendar next to the fridge. Ariana's smiling face greeted her—a picture from last year's Halloween party. Zoey's heart ached as she stared at it until she couldn't take it any longer. She glanced down. How could it already be Tuesday? Tonight would make it twice as long as the critical forty-eight-hour time period.

Zoey leaned against the wall and slid to sitting, resting her head on her knees. Why couldn't they find her? Or at least a decent lead? Kellen may be a jerk—a first class one, even—but he was no kidnapper. She couldn't figure out why the FBI was so interested in him. They were wasting valuable time.

Her phone rang. She didn't want to get up, but it might be

news about Ariana.

Zoey pulled herself up and found the phone on the counter. It was her mom.

Heart thundering, she answered. "What is it?"

"Did you hear about Macy?"

"Macy? You mean Ariana?"

"No, Macy. She was in an accident."

The room spun around Zoey. She held onto the counter. "Is she okay?"

"She's in the hospital. Sounds like she might be there a while."

"I better get down there. There's no news on Ari?"

"Not that anyone's told me. Are they still questioning Kellen?"

"They released him, and his lawyer told them not to call him in unless they have real evidence against him."

"That's good. You guys visit Macy. I'll let you know if I hear anything."

"I'll visit her. Kellen and I broke up."

"What?"

"It's a long story, and I don't feel like talking about it now. I'll tell you about it later." Zoey ended the call before Mom could object, then got into the shower.

Could things get any worse? Zoey knew better than to think that, but really, it didn't seem like they could. Not unless Ariana—no. *That* was one thought she wouldn't allow herself to think.

She got ready as quickly as she could and headed over to the hospital, her mind swimming. Once inside, she found her way to the waiting room for the critical care unit. She shuddered, thinking of how bad a shape her childhood best friend must be in to be there.

Chad slept in a chair. She didn't see any of Macy's other family. They were probably in the room with Macy.

She sat next to Macy's dad. "How is she?"

Chad opened an eye and then sat up, rubbing both eyes. "Hi,

Zo. She's still intubated, on a ventilator, and sedated. Alyssa's in there now. Luke just went home to get some sleep."

Dread washed through Zoey. "She's going to be okay, though. Right?"

He nodded. "We're thinking positive."

"What about Alex?" Zoey asked, though she suspected he was suffering a hangover.

"Grabbing some more coffee. That kid can run off fumes longer than anyone I know. I'm not sure he's slept a wink."

"Can I see Macy?"

"You'll have to wait until Alyssa comes out. They're only allowing one visitor at a time. The room's really small, and it's crowded with equipment."

Zoey nodded. "There's nothing new on Ari."

"I hope today's the day we get some good news."

"We definitely need it."

Alex walked over, carrying a coffee in each hand. "I didn't know you were coming. I'd have grabbed you one."

"It's fine. I had some earlier."

Chad rose and stretched. "You can have mine. Once Alyssa comes out, we're going home for some shut-eye." He walked over to the nurses' station.

Alex handed her a cup.

She shook her head.

"It's not poisoned. I bought it for my dad—not that I'd do anything to your drink."

"Thanks." She took it and sipped the hot, minty drink. "You still like flavored mochas."

He nodded and drank from his.

"Have you seen Macy?"

"Yeah. I didn't know one person could have so many casts."

Zoey grimaced. "That bad?"

He nodded, his expression darkening.

She frowned and took another drink. They slipped into a comfortable silence—it had been so long since they'd been able to be in a room together without arguing.

Zoey watched him from the corner of her eye. He drank from his mocha, appearing deep in thought. She almost felt sorry for him—or maybe it was the younger version of him that she pitied. *That* guy didn't deserve any of this. Not after all he'd been through.

She did miss that Alex. It was too bad that he'd changed so much. He'd really had so much potential once.

Allies

~

ALEX WONDERED HOW long Zoey would watch him. He pretended not to notice, but it was growing increasingly difficult. On one hand, it was nice that she wasn't harping on him, but at the same time, he couldn't help but wonder if she was up to something.

Finally, he turned to her. "You want me to have my mom come out so you can see Macy?"

She shrugged. "It's okay. I don't mind waiting."

"Where's Kellen?"

Zoey stiffened. "He, uh, he's at home resting. The FBI's been giving him a hard time."

Alex clenched his jaw. "Don't get me started on them. I saw the kidnapper, but nobody will listen to me. They could just go to his house and arrest him—find Ariana—but no. They won't."

"You really think it was that nerd from the computer company?"

"I *saw* him."

"That guy doesn't seem like he could take down a puppy."

Alex held her gaze. "He has our daughter."

"Okay. Are they watching him? Nobody's told me anything about him."

"That's because nobody's watching him, or even thinking about him."

She played with a piece of fuzz on her jacket, looking deep in thought. "Maybe we need to take things into our own hands."

Alex chewed on his lower lip. Should he tell her what Nick had found? What if she turned around and somehow used it against him? They were hardly friends. Although, they both wanted the same thing—to bring Ariana back home safe and sound.

Maybe he could just tell her about the cold cases, but not bring Nick into it. What if he got in trouble somehow? The cops probably weren't supposed to talk about the cases with those who were involved.

"What are you thinking about?" Zoey asked.

"I kind of already have taken things into my own hands."

She arched a brow. "You mean by hitting that nerd?" The corners of her mouth twitched, reminding him of the old Zoey. The one he could tell anything to and talk to for hours on end about everything and nothing at the same time.

"No." He shook his head and quickly debated with himself about telling her. "I've been looking into some similar cold cases."

Zoey leaned closer. "How similar?"

"Girls that look like Ari abducted before Halloween."

Her mouth dropped. "No way. How many?"

"Maybe thirty."

Zoey's face paled. "They're cold cases, so they haven't been solved?"

Alex shook his head. "Not one of them. They've happened all over the Northwest, so he probably moves when someone gets too close."

"So the girls, they…?"

He nodded. "Died. On Halloween."

Zoey cried out. "That's her favorite holiday! And it's almost here. What are we going to do? You have to tell someone! You have, haven't you? We only have until Halloween? Are you sure?"

"Someone on the force is looking into it. Hopefully, the FBI will give this more credence than they have to Flynn."

"You really think that dork is capable of pulling off such an elaborate scheme?"

"I think he's the perfect type, actually. Think about it. Dude lives by himself, is the model guy at work, and nobody has a bad thing to say about him. Probably has severe mommy issues. He's living the perfect, docile existence. Who would suspect him? Clearly no one. Doesn't that fit almost every serial killer you've heard of?"

She stared at him. "You're right. How are we going to get Ariana away from him?"

"Hopefully, the FBI will be able to figure out it's him."

"What if they don't? What are *we* going to do?"

"I'll break into his house if I have to," Alex said. "Break everything in the house to find his hidden trap door."

"You think he has a secret room?" Her brows came together.

"How else would he hide the girls? The cops were over there, questioning him, and he didn't break a sweat. He knows what he's doing—he's been at it long enough."

Zoey leaned back. "That sounds... I don't know. A little far-fetched, don't you think? This isn't a movie."

"Real life is stranger than fiction. We both know that."

She didn't look convinced.

"Do you have any better ideas? If you do, I'd love to hear them."

"I wish. What can we do, though? I mean, really. It's not like we can break into his place."

"Why not? If he has Ariana, wouldn't it be worth it? I don't care if I go to jail if it means she'll be safe. Halloween's going to be here before we know it."

She wrapped her hair around a finger, making the skin turn white. "Can you show me what you've got? I'd like to see it myself."

"Yeah, of course." Alex reached for his laptop case, but realized he didn't bring it. "I don't have my laptop, but I can show you some of the stuff online." He pulled out his phone and went to the browser app. "Here, look."

Zoey took the phone and read the article. She turned to Alex. "That girl looks exactly like Ariana."

"Jerk has a type. Here, I'll show you another."

They spent the next ten minutes going over different cold cases until Alex's mom came out into the waiting room. "Oh, Zoey, I didn't know you were here."

Zoey turned to Alex. "Let me know as soon as you hear anything about those cases."

He nodded. "Okay."

Alex found his earlier texting conversation with Nick and continued it.

What did they say?

We found something. Come to the station.

Progress

I T TOOK ALL of Alex's self-control not to speed through town. How ironic would it be to get pulled over while driving to the station? Finally, he made it. He squealed into a spot and ran straight for Nick's office without stopping at the front desk.

The door was open, so Alex just went in. "What's going on?"

Nick looked up and waved him in. "Close the door."

"What'd you find?" Alex closed the door and sat down. "Did the FBI agree to help? You never let me know."

"Oh, that's right. I forgot after she said yes."

"She did?"

"Yeah, we've been on it, and everyone agrees it's the same guy."

"Of course it is. Are you closer to finding Ariana?" Alex asked.

"We should be. New details are popping up from the older cases—everyone involved is more than happy to help—finally."

Alex felt hopeful for the first time since Ariana had been shoved in the van. "You said you found something?"

Nick nodded. "Five years before the first missing girl, there was a similar case in Montana. Only this one was a little different."

"What do you mean?"

"The death was ruled accidental. A girl who looked just like all the others who'd died in a lake on Halloween. She was with a group of older kids, and due to them being minors, the records are sealed."

"I don't get it," Alex said. "What does that have to do with anything? She wasn't kidnapped and it was an accident?"

"Right. I can't get Williams to look at it because of that, but something about that case is screaming for my attention."

Alex leaned forward, trying to see where Nick was going with it. "It was like five years before the kidnappings started?"

He nodded. "But the girl looked just like Ariana and she died in a lake on Halloween."

"I'm trying to connect the dots. You gotta help me out."

Nick took a deep breath. "I admit it might be a long shot, but I think it's at least possible that these kidnappings are modeling that death."

Alex's mind spun. "You think Flynn is recreating that girl's death from like thirty-five years ago?"

"I think someone might be. Look at the picture of this girl." Nick spun his laptop around and showed Alex a scanned image of an old newspaper clipping. He could barely read the words, but the girl did look eerily like Ariana and the others.

"Why would he try to recreate an accidental drowning year after year?"

"Don't try to make sense of crazy. It'll send you down the same path."

"What if it wasn't an accident? Someone could be covering up for one of those teens. That has to be it!"

"Stay out of the killer's head. Let us do our job."

"Just as long as you guys catch the guy before Ariana gets hurt." Alex clenched his fists. "I don't suppose Flynn has anything to do with the case?"

"I don't know who the involved kids were. The only articles I can find are vague, and like I said, the police records are sealed. There also isn't an obituary that I can find matching the case."

"Seriously?" Alex exclaimed.

Nick nodded.

"Can't you get a court order?"

"We'd need enough to convince a judge to open them."

"A missing girl who is close to being killed isn't enough?"

"Not until we find a strong enough piece of evidence linking the cases."

Alex hit the chair.

"But with the FBI on this, that could happen." Nick leaned back and rubbed his temples. "At least we're on the right track finally. So, how's Macy?"

The question jolted Alex. "She's in pretty bad shape, but they say she'll be okay. That she's lucky. Lucky would be not being in the hospital. Not having her car totaled."

"Given the accident she endured, I'd have to agree that she's—"

"It wasn't an accident!"

"Given the threats, I'd have to agree. That reminds me, did you bring the note he left?"

Alex dug into a coat pocket and then another one until he finally found the little, yellow scrap of paper. "At this point, you'll probably only find my prints."

Nick nodded and held out a little plastic bag. "Put it in here."

Alex did and leaned back. "I'm sure I'll get another real soon."

"Let me know as soon as you do." He zipped the bag and read the note.

"Will do. What do you think?"

"I think you're too close. He's scared."

Alex bolted upright. "Do you agree that it's Flynn? I'm hot on his tail, and I'm the only one getting threats. Well, other than my boss, but that's because of me."

"I'm going to need your boss's contact information."

Alex snorted. "Good luck getting anything from him, but sure." He reached for his phone and texted Nick the information. "Why do you think Flynn hurt Macy instead of me?"

"Probably figured that would scare you more. I'm going to

give Darren a call."

Alex couldn't help but find a little humor in imagining his boss getting a call from a police captain about Alex.

He grabbed his phone from the desk and headed out to the parking lot. He sat in the car and ran through everything in his mind for close to ten minutes before heading home. As soon as he got out of the car, he received a new text.

If you did what I think you did, you're going to regret it.

Broken

ARIANA WATCHED AS the Volvo disappeared from sight. Finally. She was beginning to think Lloyd would never leave.

He had to go in to work, so he would be gone long enough for her to make her escape. She'd seen enough of the house to make her way to an exit quickly. Even if alarms blared, she would have plenty of time to get away. He would still have to drive back to the house, and by then, she'd be hiding in the woods.

She watched for another few minutes to make sure he didn't return. It wouldn't have surprised her if he knew something was up, and he was testing her. He hadn't seemed to notice the door was unlocked before, but that didn't mean anything. Ariana knew enough to be prepared for the worst—she was already kidnapped. She knew about things getting worse.

Finally, she was convinced Lloyd wasn't coming back soon. She went to the dollhouse and dug out the bobby pins and the knife. If only she knew exactly what she'd done to unlock the door last time. It had been more of an accident than anything. Either way, she would do it again.

Ariana jimmied the knife into the door jam near the lock. She was pretty sure it had been like that when she managed to unlock the door. She put a bobby pin in, aiming it low. Then she grabbed the second one, and stuck it in, aiming that one higher.

She wiggled and jiggled the top one, then the bottom, then both at the same time.

Nothing happened.

What had she done before?

Heart racing, she moved everything around without any particular method. *That* was what had worked last time. It would have to do the job now, too. Somehow.

After a few more minutes of playing around…

Snap.

She squealed and let go of everything. It had worked again!

Wait? It wasn't supposed to snap. It was supposed to click.

Ariana pulled the knife out. It was fine. She pulled out the top bobby pin. It was okay. Bent in a funny angle, maybe, but fine. She pulled on the other one, but it resisted. She tugged a little harder.

It came out, but not all of it. Part of the lower half had broken off.

She turned the knob and pulled. It didn't budge.

Maybe she could still get it unlocked. Ariana put the two pins back into place and moved them up and down, back and forth.

Nothing. Again.

Would she need to get the broken piece out for it to work?

Dread washed through her. Could she even do that? The piece was so tiny and she wouldn't know how to pull it out.

What if that piece kept the lock from turning on Lloyd's end? Then he'd know she'd done something to it.

Panic-stricken, she shoved one of the pins in, aiming it as low as she could, hoping to get under the broken piece. Then maybe she could bring it out. She had to.

What would Lloyd do if he knew she was trying to escape?

She couldn't let that happen—she didn't want to find out what he would do. It was already bad enough.

Ariana kept working on the bobby pin, growing more tired and frantic as time passed. The light coming in through the window started to fade.

Lloyd would be back soon.

Tears blurred her vision. She'd really hoped that she'd have been long gone by the time he came home. Now it looked like that wouldn't even happen. She tried to get the pin out again, but her hands shook, and she couldn't see through the tears.

She slumped to the ground and cried. Would she ever be able to get out? Was she stupid for trying? For hoping?

Gravel crunched under tires outside.

Careful

~

A LEX PARKED A BLOCK away from the library and walked, pretending to be involved in a texting conversation. In reality, he was glancing around for anyone who might be watching him—namely Flynn. But with as much as Flynn seemed to know, he couldn't be working alone. He had to have been getting help from someone. He certainly had enough money to hire a fleet of private investigators.

That was the only thing that explained how he knew Alex's every move.

He stopped in front of the library entrance and looked around, making a show of it. Nick's car was parked right in front. Good.

Either Flynn or one of his men had to be following Alex. He'd made it more than clear that he was meeting Nick. He'd not only texted but emailed him.

More than anything, Alex wanted to draw out the weasel. Unfortunately, he couldn't see anyone. As far as he could tell, all the vehicles in the parking lot were empty. A breeze blew by, the leaves rustling as they bumped across the parking lot.

Everything was all too normal for the quiet, boring suburb.

Alex waited a full minute before finally going inside. It was probably better that he speak with Nick first, anyway. He found the captain near the back, flipping through a stack of papers. Alex went over and sat next to him.

Nick glanced up. "What couldn't you tell me over the phone

that was so urgent it required a text *and* an email?"

Alex pulled out his phone and showed him the text.

"What did you do?" Nick asked.

"You can't figure it out?"

"He knows you told me?"

"Apparently he put two and two together when I went to the station."

Nick swore. A lady with two small kids at the next table glared at him.

"Sorry," Nick said and turned back to Alex. "Did he give you a specific threat?"

"Like saying he'd go after my sister? Nope. Just this one."

"We're obviously getting close."

"Not close enough," Alex muttered.

"Too much for his comfort. That's good. It tells me to keep going down the path we're on. Any update on Macy?"

Alex shook his head and sighed. It sickened him to think of her lying in the bed like a vegetable. "She's going to be there for a while."

Nick's phone beeped. He checked it. "I have to get back to the station. If you get anymore threats, forward them immediately. Don't meet me, just tell me."

"What should I—?"

"Doesn't matter. I'll know what you mean." He shoved a couple files over to Alex. "Look these over and get them back to me."

"What are they?"

"Something I think you'll find interesting."

Alex slid off his coat and slung it over the back of the chair. He stared at the faded tan file folder for a moment before opening it. Old, yellowing pages filled it.

Curious, he flipped through the pages. He stopped at an old, faded picture of a girl that looked like Ariana—not that it was much of a surprise, given the thirty other missing girls who resembled her so closely.

There was something different about this file, though.

It wasn't a missing child case. The file was dated thirty-five years ago and the thirteen-year-old girl had been found in a lake in Montana by her mother on the evening of Halloween. She'd left the house without telling her parents and had run around the neighborhood with some older teens. Her brother had found her body and ran home to tell his parents.

His name was blacked out, but hers wasn't: Janet Vassman.

Alex flipped through the pages, trying to make a connection to missing girls and Janet. Nothing made sense. Unless…

Could Nick be right about the other cases being copycats of this one?

His head spun as he tried to make sense of it all.

That had to be it. It was the only explanation. The missing girls had started five years later and continued for thirty years. Why else would Nick hand him the file?

He went through each page, reading every painful detail. Not much was known about who Janet had been with on her final night. Only that she'd defied her parents and wound up dead. Nobody had ever been charged with any wrongdoing.

Alex turned one more page and saw pictures of the bloated body. His stomach lurched. He turned and threw up on the library floor.

Leak

~

A LEX HELD ONTO the file, eager to give it back to Nick, but first he needed to see if he could find the spy. He went outside and glanced around. Just as before, he saw no one. Either Flynn or the investigator was good at hiding, or Flynn was busy plotting his next evil move.

Alex's stomach still felt weak. It was probably better he didn't have to confront a killer. He looked around again just to be sure and then headed down the street for his car. He expected the tires to be slashed or the windows broken, but it looked exactly as he'd left it.

That was almost worse. It made him wonder what was coming. He walked around the car using his cell phone's flashlight, looking all around. Once he was fairly certain everything was fine, he slowly opened the driver's side door. It opened as usual, even creaking where it normally did.

He climbed in and rubbed the back of his neck. It ached and radiated up to his head. He really wanted a drink, too, but that would have to wait. There was too much to do, and besides, once Ariana was back, he didn't want to be a drunk. Alex wanted to turn everything around in his life, including living here in town, even if that meant a higher rent or living with his parents for a while.

Just as he was about to start the car, his phone buzzed with a text. There it was. His new threat.

Actually, it was from Nick, telling him to get down to the station right away.

Alex started the car and wondered what the problem was—had Flynn moved to threatening the police captain? Or was it something else altogether? Nick might just want the file back.

He headed over, and as was becoming his custom, Alex walked by the desk straight to Nick's office.

"What's going on?"

Nick glanced up. His hair stuck out in different directions like he'd been pulling at it and his face was flushed.

Alex dropped the file on the desk. "It's all here."

"It's not that. Did you hear?"

"What?" Alex exclaimed.

Nick turned his laptop toward Alex. A livestream played with a reporter standing out in the wind outside the Ball Palace.

Alex grasped the edge of the desk. "What? Did they find her?"

Without a word, Nick turned up the volume.

"...possibly the worst serial killer the nation has ever seen. Thirty victims over thirty years, and he's continuing to get away with it. Now he has Ariana Nakano, and Halloween's only a few days away." Nick muted the volume and turned to Alex.

Alex's mouth dropped. "I thought we were going to keep this away from the media."

"That's what I thought, too. Any idea how this was leaked?" Nick narrowed his eyes.

"Wait a minute." Alex backed up. "You think I had anything to do with it?"

"The only people who know about this are you and those of us on the case."

"Macy was helping me look into it, but she wouldn't say anything. Neither would Zoey."

Nick pulled on his hair. "Anyone else know about this? Before the media circus, I mean."

"Just them."

"Every advantage we have is out the window." Nick jumped from his chair. "I want to find out who leaked this and wring their neck!"

"Well, it wasn't me. I was busy throwing up on the library floor."

Nick gave him a double take.

"I saw the picture of the first girl's body. It made me think of Ariana." Alex's stomach churned again. "I—" He grasped his middle.

"Don't puke in here."

Alex took a deep breath and focused on Nick. "I'll be okay. I just have to get that image out of my head."

"We'll get her back. Any more threats?"

"Nope."

Nick sat back down. "I really wanted to have the element of surprise on our side. It's going to be a lot harder now that the killer knows what we know."

"He doesn't necessarily know you know about the threats. We could use that."

"It's not the same." Nick stared at the screen. "Everyone's talking about this. It's everywhere."

"I'm sure it is," Alex muttered. That was also probably why Flynn didn't appear to have been following Alex when he met Nick.

"Go get some sleep. You look like you need it. I'll call you if anything changes."

Alex looked up and stared at him. "What's the plan now?"

"I need to talk with Williams and the rest of the crew. They want to know if you leaked it. I knew you didn't, but I had to ask."

"Was it a cop?"

"I sure hope not, but I can't rule it out." He got up. "Look, like I said, get some rest. You're going to need it as Halloween comes closer. I'll call you if anything important comes up. In the meantime, support your sister and let me know if you get another threat."

"Okay." Alex headed for the door.

"And do yourself a favor—stay away from the media."

"Why? Is there something you don't want me hearing?"

"Nothing new. You just don't need the distraction."

Nick gave a nod, closed the office door behind them, and went down the hall. Alex went in the other direction and headed for the parking lot. If Flynn wasn't glued to the news coverage, then he would know Alex had been talking with the cops.

Alex waved to anyone who might be watching and then climbed into his car.

Escape

~

ARIANA STARED AT the moon through the clouds. It seemed like every time the wind blew, it got covered up. She'd been standing by the window for what felt like hours. Her heart hadn't stopped racing since Lloyd got home. She thought for sure he would know she'd been playing with the lock.

He didn't notice.

When he unlocked the door, it worked just as it should. The broken bobby pin hadn't done anything. He'd also been harried from his job and hadn't noticed Ariana's stress. They'd had a quiet meal, and then he had her go back to the room.

The house had been quiet for hours. Ariana wanted to try to get out another time. She thought Lloyd must be asleep, but couldn't know for sure. What if he was awake downstairs, and she just couldn't hear him?

She watched the wind and the clouds for a little while longer, but couldn't relax. The woods seemed to call her, begging her to make her escape. She'd wanted to be long gone by now, but she was still locked in the room.

Ariana went to the door and pressed her ear to it. Everything was quiet out there. She squatted and pressed her ear against the fuzzy carpet. She couldn't hear anything.

Her heart raced. Maybe she should try one more time. She sat up and eyed the dollhouse that once more hid her escape tools.

Did she dare? Lloyd was home, but then again, who knew

when he would leave next? He'd mumbled something about working from home. She might not have another chance while he was out for some time.

Ariana took a deep breath to try and calm her racing heart. She needed to at least try. Maybe the other bobby pin would break. If it did, she would take that as her sign to stop trying—at least for now. She might need to find some new bobby pins later, but she wouldn't ever quit trying.

She tip-toed over to the dollhouse and lifted it, practically like an expert. Heart racing, she slid the items out and crept over to the door. She took another deep breath and got everything into position, extra-careful to be quiet. The pins seemed so loud next to her ear, but she knew Lloyd couldn't hear them from wherever he was.

The bobby pins slid in easily, and Ariana adjusted them so one was up and the other down. She jiggled them just so, holding her breath.

Click.

She froze in place. Had she heard that right?

Ariana set the knife and pins down and rested her hand on the doorknob. Her pulse drummed in her ears.

Was this it? Would it open?

The room seemed to spin around her. She struggled to breathe normally—she needed to. If Lloyd was awake, she had to be able to hear him, but right now, all she could hear was the sounds of her own heart thundering like a pack of wild horses running through a field.

Ariana forced a deep breath, then another and another until she could hear normally again. She pressed her ear against the door. Everything still sounded quiet. She listened to the floor, and couldn't hear a sound.

This was her chance.

She made sure the old sneakers were laced tightly and double-knotted the ties just to be sure. There would be no time for stumbling over those.

Ariana grabbed the doorknob and twisted. It creaked a little as it turned, but it did turn. She pulled the door open, half-expecting to find Lloyd standing there, staring at her.

The hall was empty and quiet. Dark, too, but at least her eyes were already adjusted.

She stepped out of the room and tip-toed down the hall, aware of every magnified sound. A wall clock clicked as the minute changed. The heaters rumbled, pressing air out of old heater units. But there were no footsteps, voices, or doors opening.

Ariana held her breath, reminding herself to breathe every so often. She came to the stairs leading down to the nice living areas.

This might be the hardest part. With as nice as everything was down there, there had to be an alarm on the doors. It wouldn't have even surprised her if there were red lasers shooting out from every direction on the floor—but that was probably her overactive imagination.

She crept to the top stair and glanced down. Everything was dark there, too. Hopefully, that meant Lloyd was sound asleep. She put her foot on the first step, testing it. It didn't creak, nor did sirens wail. She tried the next few just as carefully, finding them all to be safe.

By the fourth one, she was relatively sure the staircase was safe. She hurried down the rest and stopped at the last step, looking around. Nothing seemed dangerous—she didn't see any blinking lights or cameras or anything suspicious.

Ariana just needed to decide how she was going to get outside. The front door seemed like a bad idea—if anything would have an alarm, it would be that one. With a house this big—it seemed to go on forever—there had to be a back door somewhere.

She crept around toward where she'd seen the small office before and came to a hallway. She followed it, finding more rooms.

How big of a house did one guy need? It made her skin crawl, feeling like she might run into someone else. She shivered, but kept moving.

The rumbling of a clothes drier sounded from farther down the hall. Her eyes lit up. There was a back door from the laundry room at Emily's house. Maybe this house had one, too.

She whispered a quick prayer and hurried down the hall, not stopping until she came to the door from where the noise sounded. She turned the knob. A large laundry room greeted her, complete with a door to the outside.

Woods

~

ARIANA BRACED HERSELF and then ran for the door. If she couldn't get it open, she would break it down. She didn't care how. All she knew was that she needed to get out, and nothing was going to get in her way now. She'd come too far to let anything stop her.

She unlocked a deadbolt. It was so easy on this side without the stupid pins and knife. She twisted the knob and the door opened!

Several low beeps sounded and then an electronic female voice asked for a code.

Her heart nearly burst through her ribcage.

Ariana ran outside, slamming the door behind her. It would only be a matter of seconds before the system alerted Lloyd of her escape. She glanced around. The only thing she saw were the woods.

A wailing noise sounded inside. The alarm. Lloyd would be awake now.

She burst into a run, suddenly wishing she'd at least thought to put a hoodie over the thin, white nightgown. It was too late to worry about that. She ducked under some low-hanging branches and ran as fast as she could, darting around trees and thick bushes. She stumbled over a root sticking out of the ground.

Ariana grabbed onto a tree trunk to balance herself and kept going. An owl hooted from above. A wolf howled somewhere.

Maybe Lloyd wasn't the only thing she needed to worry about. It didn't matter. She *would* get out of the woods. The next bed she slept in would be her own.

She tripped over another exposed root, this time sailing through the air and landing with a thud on her stomach. It knocked some air out of her lungs. A branch dug into her side. She sat up, gasping for air.

A twig snapped somewhere.

Ariana jumped up and ran. She hadn't made it this far just to get caught.

"Jan!"

Her heart sank. Lloyd wasn't far away. She pushed her legs to run faster. Her mouth dried, and she gasped for air. Her ribs and side hurt. It didn't matter. The only thing that did matter was getting home.

Ariana used branches and trees to steady herself as she ran toward freedom. Something wet clung to her side. She wiped at it and glanced down at her hand. Blood. She'd bled straight through the nightgown.

She kept running until her breathing grew labored and her muscles all burned, begging her to stop.

"Jan," Lloyd called. "Where are you going?"

He sounded closer.

Ariana's body begged her to stop. The blood-soaked stain was growing bigger. Her muscles ached and burned more than before. There was no other choice but to keep going. Whether the woods went on for miles or she was almost to the other end, it didn't matter. She had to keep going until she reached a road.

Then she would probably have to keep going. She'd have to find a police station. Or at least someone with a phone.

She had to get out of the woods first.

"Jan! Why are you running from me?"

Tears stung Ariana's eyes. She hoped he didn't have that horrible-smelling towel he'd used back in the van to make her sleep. The thought of that only made her press on. She ran, continuing to dart around trees, now more careful of the roots. Her side hurt, but she did her best to ignore it.

She could hear leaves crunching and twigs snapping behind her as he followed. He had to have been able to hear the same from her. Her stomach tightened.

Ariana looked around for a bush to hide in. That was probably her best bet. She was tired and sore, and he could probably outrun her. Most of the shrubbery had sharp leaves and were small.

Maybe she could climb a tree instead. But then he would just have to look up to find her and the moonlight, though weak from the clouds, was shining down through the trees in places.

"Jan, come back! We need to talk." He sounded even closer than his footsteps made him seem.

A bush bigger than the rest came into view. It wasn't super big, either, but maybe it would do the job. She pressed on and then jumped in, scratching her arms and face on leaves and twigs. Ariana pulled her legs and pulled them close, wrapping her arms around them.

Her entire body shivered as she sat there. Even her teeth chattered. She tried to hold still. Once Lloyd left, she could come out and get away. She couldn't now. Not with him so close.

The sounds of his footsteps slowed not far away. "Jan?"

Ariana held her breath and tried to stop shaking. She could see a few leaves moving because of her.

His steps slowed even more. He walked around, staying close to the bush.

He stopped in front of it. "Jan."

Chase

ARIANA HELD PERFECTLY still. Not a single leaf on the bush moved. Her heart pounded and her pulse raced. She was covered in sweat, despite the cold air. Her side ached more than before.

"Jan, it's time to stop playing hide and seek. You need to come home. It's where you belong."

He paced around, never moving far from where Ariana waited.

"The game's over, Jan. You need to give up."

Never. She'd never give up until she was home, safe and sound.

Lloyd continued pacing near the bush. He had to know where she was, or at least that she was close.

"Come on out," he said, his voice even and smooth. "Before we have to discuss consequences."

Ariana swallowed.

He took two more steps and stopped directly in front of the bush. "You know how nice your brother is, but that can change in a heartbeat. You're walking the line now."

A cold breeze blew by. She shivered, determined to stay there in the shrub as long as she could. Her strength was already starting to rebuild. Another few minutes and she could probably run again. Although, it would be a lot easier if he would go somewhere else.

Raindrops plopped on nearby leaves. A few more and then they sounded all around, splashing on her.

"Come on out, Jan," Lloyd said, sounding annoyed. "It's starting to rain and—"

Thunder cracked in the distance.

"A storm is brewing. We'd best get inside."

Rain pounded down harder, making noise as it hit leaves and dirt. Despite being protected by the bush, Ariana was getting soaked.

Lloyd continued pacing, never moving far from the shrub. He was close enough that she could probably reach out and grab his ankles.

Her mouth went dry at the thought. Could she trip him and them run?

The entire area lit up with light.

He stopped, looking right at the shrub Ariana hid in. A loud crack of thunder sounded. She thought her eardrums would break.

Lloyd stepped closer to the bush. "I knew you were close."

Ariana screamed and then scrambled out of the other side of the shrub. Sharp branches poked and scratched. Rain came down even harder. Lightning lit everything up again.

She broke free of the bush and ran, covering her ears. Thunder boomed, making her entire body vibrate. The rain came down harder and faster. The ground was slippery as she ran.

Ariana glanced back. He wasn't far behind.

"Why are you running from me?" he called. "I thought you were happy to be back."

She turned back around and nearly ran into a low-hanging branch. Ariana ducked and kept running. Her feet kept sliding out.

The woods lit up again. She took advantage of the moment to take everything in. She covered her ears and ran faster, avoiding all the trees and roots. Thunder boomed, but this time it didn't feel so harsh. Maybe the storm was already moving away.

That had to be a good sign, right?

She ran as fast as she could, finding it hard for her eyes to adjust to the dark after the bright flashes of light. Her feet slid out, but she managed to catch her balance and keep running.

"Jan, stop! This is ridiculous."

He thought the chase was ridiculous? What about taking her from her home and making her live someone else's life? That was what was crazy.

Finally, her eyes readjusted to the dark. She picked up her pace and ran around a cluster of trees, hoping to finally lose him. Not that she really expected it to be that easy. He was obviously not going to give up unless she got away or—she wasn't going to think about the other option.

Bright light blinded her once again. She turned to the right to avoid a tree, but her foot caught on an exposed root. Her arms flew out as she tried to regain her balance. Her feet slid in a mud puddle, flying out from underneath her.

The ground was coming at her.

She landed with a hard thud. A rock dug into her arm. Her head hit the root. Ariana moaned and tried to pull herself up, but the wet ground fought against her.

Fingers wrapped around her shoulders. Lloyd helped her to stand. "All of this was so unnecessary."

Ariana struggled to get away, but he held onto her all the tighter.

"It's over, Jan. Come on." He sounded sad. His voice didn't hold a hint of anger. Even his grip, though strong, wasn't harsh.

He led her through the woods in silence as the rain continued to pour down. Lightning and thunder came one more time, but nowhere near as bright or loud.

Lloyd stopped just outside the woods. "I wish you hadn't done that."

He guided her back into the house. They came into the laundry room.

"Now you know about the other part of the house."

She gulped.

"I didn't want you to know about that. I didn't want to frighten you."

Ariana stared at him, unable to respond.

"Take off those ruined clothes."

Her eyes widened.

"I won't look. Just don't try to get away again. Okay?"

She continued staring at him.

"Okay?" His voice was harsher.

Ariana nodded.

"Good." He turned around. "Now hurry, and we'll get you upstairs."

Shaking, she slid off the wet, muddy shoes. She watched him, making sure he wouldn't turn around. He stood perfectly still. She pulled off the soaked, mud-covered, bloody nightgown. It stuck to the gash in her side. She managed not to cry out as it pulled away.

"Are you done yet?" Lloyd asked.

"Yes." Her voice had never sounded smaller.

"Follow me." He lifted a hand. "And don't try anything. You get your privacy as long as you do as you're told."

"Okay."

Lloyd led her through the bottom level and up the stairs to the time warp area. She followed him to the bathroom. He kept his word, not turning around. "Get cleaned up. I'll find you some clean clothes and will set them out here by the door."

She went into the bathroom and locked the door. Her emotions all exploded at once. She slid onto the floor and sobbed silently.

Changes

~

ARIANA SCRUBBED OFF the last of the mud, rinsed the soap, and turned off the shower. She grabbed the towel from the rack and wrapped it around herself, wishing she could stay there for the rest of time. Or at least until Lloyd had to leave—or maybe die—and then she could get away for real.

"Hurry up," he called from the other side of the door.

"I am." She dried off, cringing as the towel ran over her cuts, and put on the striped pajama set he'd picked out for her.

"Are you about done? We need to talk."

Her stomach twisted. "Almost." She ran the brush through her hair and stared at herself in the mirror. Her face was scratched, but it was nothing compared to the gash on her side or the scrapes on her arms.

"Come on, Jan."

Ariana took a deep breath and frowned. So much for staying in the bathroom forever. She opened the door.

"Let me see your cut."

She stared at him.

He gestured toward her side.

"It's fine."

"I need to make sure it isn't going to get infected. Let me see."

Sighing, she raised the side of her shirt. Hopefully, he would leave it alone after this.

Lloyd pressed a finger next to it. Pain shot through the gash.

Ariana winced.

"I'm going to have to put on some ointment. First, we need to disinfect it." He dug around the cabinet and pulled out a handful of items. He dabbed some yellow liquid onto a cotton ball and rubbed it on her wound. It made the cut hurt even worse than before.

It took all of her control not to cry out. The stuff stung worse than the actual fall and washing it with soap combined.

"Hold still," he muttered and finally pulled the cotton ball away. "Just let that dry."

She nodded, not even able to speak.

Lloyd fanned it and then applied some white cream and finally a Band Aid. "Anything else I should look at?"

Ariana shook her head.

"Okay. Follow me." He led her to the rec room and indicated for her to sit on the couch.

She hoped he would put on a movie, but knew that would never happen. Not after her escape.

Everything had changed, and she was about to find out how.

Lloyd sat next to her, but didn't say anything.

Her breathing grew labored. She wished he would just tell her.

Finally, he turned to her. "I'm really disappointed."

She swallowed.

"Everything was going so well. What did I do that made you so unhappy?"

Ariana's eyes widened.

"What?" He slammed his fist on the coffee table.

She jumped.

"I gave you a birthday party. Made your favorite foods. I've even been planning a Halloween party for you. But none of that was good enough for you?"

Ariana glanced away.

"Look at me when I'm talking to you!"

She turned back to him and held his gaze.

"It wasn't good enough?"

Ariana shrugged.

"What would it take?"

She blinked several times. Did he really not know?

He hit the coffee table again. "I did everything right, but it's still not good enough. Why is that?"

Ariana bit her lower lip. He would be mad no matter what she said.

"I really thought this was going to be it. That you were the one."

He glanced away and ran his fingers over the little hair he had and let out a long, slow breath.

Ariana shook, but tried to stop. She didn't want to give him any extra reason to be angry with her.

Lloyd turned to her, his eyes misty. "I was going to buy you a kitten."

"A kitten?" she exclaimed.

"You've always wanted one. Mom and Dad always said no. Remember what Dad used to say?"

Ariana shook her head.

"He would say, 'Stop flushing the toilets. There, now you have a cat—a house that smells like crap.' That's what he used to always say."

"Oh."

"Remember?"

Ariana nodded.

"But I wanted to give you a kitten."

"Wh-what's going to happen now?" she asked.

Lloyd frowned, but remained silent.

Ariana took a deep breath.

"The past is going to have to repeat itself." His tone told her that couldn't be good.

He leaned back and stared at the ceiling. "You don't remember, do you?"

"No."

"You never do."

Chills ran down her back. They sat in silence for what felt like forever. Finally, he sat up straight and looked at her.

Ariana played with a button on her shirt.

"Have you forgotten the first bad Halloween?"

She nodded.

"I can't blame you. It was traumatic for all of us. That's why Mom eventually killed herself and Dad turned to the drink. He became a mean, evil bastard. Worse even than you ever saw. They blamed me for Mom's death. But it wasn't my fault. It wasn't. I tried to stop you from dying. I did everything I could. That year, and every year since. I just can't change the past."

Ariana stared at him. What did he mean, and what did any of this have to do with her?

He twisted his shirtsleeve. "I really thought we'd be able to start over. Live our lives like we should have so many years ago. But now you've gone and run away from me. Instead of a Halloween party, we're forced to relive that night long ago." His voice cracked. "I really didn't want to do that."

"W-we don't have to."

Lloyd shook his head. "We do. I'll have to try again next year."

The room spun around her. "I'll be good. I promise."

He rubbed his eyes. "It's too late now."

"It's not."

Lloyd turned to her. "But it is. There'll be no party this year."

"What are you going to do?" She squeezed the cushion, not sure she could bear hearing the answer.

He held her gaze, not saying anything for a moment. "Same as every other year. We relive that night. I'll try to save you, but it won't work. You'll drown. Mom will fall into her depression and get sent to the sanatorium. She'll hang herself with her bedsheets. Dad will beat me and tell me what a waste of space I am. And then..." His voice trailed off and he shook. "Forget about that part. Then next year, I'll try to find you again. See if I can finally change the past. I can't keep reliving it. It won't go away. It needs to, but it won't."

Dread washed through Ariana.

Lloyd rose. "Come on. It's late. We both need our rest."

She got up, and he put his hand around her arm and led her to the bedroom, his head hanging. "I just wish it didn't have to be this way. I really thought you were the one. That this time would be different."

"I can be good."

He shook his head. "It's too late." He gestured for her to go into the room.

She stepped inside.

"Don't try to unlock it. I'm going to stick a chair under the knob. You're not going to be able to get away."

Intruder

~

THE PHONE RANG, waking Zoey from a deep sleep. She sat up and scrambled for it, fumbling and nearly dropping it. Could it be news about Ariana?

She stared at the screen. Blocked caller. Like she would answer that. They could unblock the number if they wanted to speak with her. She pressed ignore and lay back down.

The phone rang again.

Zoey reached over for it. Blocked caller again. She pressed ignore.

"Leave me alone," she muttered.

Something tapped on her window, just feet from her bed.

Zoey gasped and sat up, pulling the covers with her.

Tap, tap, tap. Scratch.

Fear pulsed through her. She shook so hard she dropped the phone on the mattress.

The silhouette of a man appeared in the window as it lit up from a car driving by.

She pressed herself back against the headboard, unable to breathe.

His form faded as the light disappeared, but he was still there.

Tap, tap. Knock.

Zoey cried out. "Go away! I'm calling the cops!"

She felt around for the phone, but couldn't find it.

Knock, knock, tap.

Her pulse drummed in her ears. She still couldn't find the phone. Hadn't she just had it right next to her? She pulled on the sheet and blankets.

The phone rang again, lighting up. It had gotten shoved under the pillow next to her. She grabbed it and threw it against the window.

The man pounded on the glass so hard, Zoey was sure it would break. And now her only communication with the outside world was underneath the window.

She climbed out of bed and pulled on a silky bathrobe that didn't cover much more than her nightie. She got down on all fours and felt around for the phone as the pounding continued.

Why had she insisted on a ground floor unit?

As she tried to find the phone, she came to a pile of dirty clothes on the floor. Kellen's stuff—she never left clothes on the floor. If only he was there. *He* had been the reason she thought she'd be safe on the first floor, but he hadn't spent as much time in the condo as she'd expected.

Zoey cursed him as she continued looking for her phone. The pounding grew harder. Then the glass cracked.

She froze. It would only be a matter of time before it shattered and the man could get inside.

"The cops are on their way!" Zoey threw Kellen's clothes all over, still unable to find her phone.

Why hadn't she thrown something else at the window?

The glass cracked again.

Then Zoey remembered something else. Her alarm system.

She scrambled to her feet and ran out of the bedroom into the living room to the little white box with barely-glowing buttons. She pressed the red one. The system screeched all around her.

A moment later, her phone rang in the bedroom. She ran back and saw the phone glowing under her nightstand.

"Hello?" She had to shout over the alarm and the pounding on the glass. The window cracked again.

"This is Mountainview Security Company," said a bored-sounding male. "Do you have an emergency?"

"Someone's trying to break into my condo," Zoey cried. "He's almost in!"

"I'll alert your local police. Please stay on the line while I put you on hold."

"Okay."

The window cracked again. This time, shards of glass fell onto the sill.

Zoey cried out. Clinging to the phone, she ran out to the living room again.

The pounding on the window continued. The glass cracked again. That time it did shatter.

He was going to get in before the cops arrived. She had to do something.

She glanced around. There was nothing that could be used as a weapon.

Zoey ran back to the bedroom. Arms reached in through the broken window. She slammed the door shut and pulled a shelf in front of the door. It wasn't too heavy, but at least it should keep him in there for a few minutes.

Something crashed inside her room. She screamed.

"Are you there, ma'am?" asked the man from the security company.

"Y-yes."

"The police are already on their way. A neighbor called just before me. Can you look outside and tell me if you see them?"

Zoey stumbled across the living room and lifted a blind. Flashing lights appeared across the street, but she heard no sirens. Maybe they were going to take him by surprise.

"They're here."

"Okay. I'm going to hang up now, unless you need something

else."

"No."

"Thank you for choosing Mountainview Security Company." The call ended.

Crashes and banging sounded from her bedroom. Her bedroom door opened inward. The shelf wouldn't stop him.

Zoey screamed at the top of her lungs.

Her doorbell rang and pounding sounded on the door. "Police!"

With tears stinging her eyes, Zoey ran to the door and opened it. "He's in my bedroom." She pointed to the open door behind the shelf.

They ran over, guns drawn, and one moved the shelf out of the way, knocking nearly everything over in the process. They all stormed into her bedroom.

Zoey fell onto her couch and shook.

One of the officers came out of the room and over to her. "The intruder escaped out the window."

"H-he's gone?"

"My two partners ran after him. I'm going to take a look around the apartment."

She nodded, too shaken to respond. Shouting sounded from outside. Something hit the outside of the building.

A man ran inside the open front door. Zoey screamed, afraid it was the intruder again.

"Zoey, it's me. Alex."

Comfort

~

ALEX RAN OVER to Zoey, who sat shivering on the couch. No wonder why—she was hardly wearing anything. He grabbed a blanket from the back of the couch and wrapped it around her.

"How did you know to come here?" She stared at him with wide eyes.

His heart softened seeing her so scared. He tightened the blanket around her. "Nick called me when he heard it was you."

"I was so scared."

He put his arm around her. "It's okay now."

"Did they catch him?"

"I don't know, but he's gone."

"Why's he going after me? Is it the same guy?" She shook harder.

Given the last threat, it was a good bet. "Let's not worry about it right now, Zo."

"Not worry?" she exclaimed. "How can I—?"

"I just mean we should focus on the fact that you're safe. Your window's broken?"

She nodded.

"Okay. I'll board that up for you until you can get it replaced. I—"

A cop came over to them. "No one's inside. I know you're upset, but I'm going to need to take your statement."

"Are you going to be okay?" Alex asked. "I'll try to fix the window while you talk to him."

The officer stared at him. "It's a crime scene. You can't touch it."

"It's her room. She needs to feel safe."

"I'll never feel safe here again," Zoey muttered.

"You can fix the window once we're done processing everything."

Another officer came inside and turned to the cop next to them. "He got away on foot."

"Would you process the bedroom?" Alex snapped. "I want to fix her window."

"You are?"

"A friend."

Zoey nodded.

"Were you here when this happened?"

"No," Alex said. "I came after Captain Fleshman called to let me know what was going on."

"You know the captain?"

"Yeah, Nick and I go way back." Alex stared the officer down, daring him to continue being a pain in the neck.

The second officer turned to the first "I'll process the room while you take her statement."

"How long's this going to take?" Alex asked.

"Maybe twenty minutes. Depends."

Alex rose. "My dad has the stuff to board up the window. If I'm not back when you're done, stay with her. I don't want her to be alone."

Zoey gave him a grateful look.

"Sure." The cop pulled out a tablet and turned to Zoey, asking her about the intrusion.

Alex glanced back over at Zoey as he headed out. Seeing her so scared made her look like she was much younger—like she was the girl he'd fallen in love with so long ago. Like she was the girl he'd let down.

He shook off that memory and headed home, grabbing what he needed from Dad's garage, and then returning to Zoey's condo.

The officer rose from the couch. "We're all done here. Do what you need to for the window."

Alex gave a slight nod. "Thanks."

They left. Alex locked the door and set the stuff down. "Are you okay?"

Zoey shook her head. "I can't ever stay here again."

He sat next to her. "Maybe you'll feel different in the morning."

"I won't! I'm not getting a ground floor unit ever again."

"Okay. Well, I'll get the window boarded up so your stuff will be safe at least." He got up, grabbed the stuff, and went into her room.

It was a disaster with glass and clothes all over the place. He stepped over everything and hammered the plywood over the window. Once it was done, he gathered up the pieces of glass, dumping them into a small, white trash bin with the Eiffel Tower painted on the side. A portrait of the landmark hung over the bed. Clearly, she still loved Paris.

He wondered if she had ever made it there. More than likely her golden boy had taken her. Mr. Perfect had probably flown her out for their first date.

Alex shook his head and shone his cell phone's flashlight around the room, looking for any remaining shards of glass. A tiny piece shone from the carpet near the molding. He picked it up and continued scanning the room. She would have to vacuum to be sure to get it all, but for the time being, he couldn't find anything else.

Peeking back out into the living room, he saw her sleeping. As tempting as it was to crash himself, he couldn't. Not here. He picked up some photos and knickknacks that had fallen on the ground.

The first picture was one of Ariana at the beach, laughing at the shore. Alex's heart constricted. How much of her life had he missed? And would he get the chance to make up for lost time? He set it on the nightstand and picked up another by the dresser. Zoey and Golden Boy both holding glasses of champagne and gazing at each other like they adored each other wholeheartedly. He put it face down on the dresser.

Another frame lay half-under the dresser. This one was of Zoey, Ariana, and Golden Boy in front of a Christmas tree. They looked so happy—like the perfect family.

He put that frame face down, also, and picked up the other random stuff lying around. Finally, only clothes remained. He threw some jeans into the laundry basket. Then a pair of boxers. His stomach twisted, but again, what did he expect? Alex gathered the rest of the clothes without paying attention to what they were and tossed them in the basket.

The room wasn't perfect, but at least it was better. Zoey wouldn't have to be reminded of the intrusion—at least not too much. If she wanted, he could help her replace the window. Unless of course, Golden Boy jumped in, which he probably would. The only reason he wasn't there instead of Alex was because Nick had called him.

Past

〜

ALEX WOKE IN a leather recliner, confused. He looked around the unfamiliar room, until his gaze landed on the empty white leather couch and the black knit blanket that had been wrapped around Zoey.

He lowered the chair, got up, and stretched. A shower sounded from somewhere in the condo.

His stomach rumbled. Zoey had to be hungry, too. He went to the fridge and found some eggs and bacon. There wasn't much he could cook, but frying things was simple enough.

By the time she stepped out of her bedroom, Alex was almost done with the breakfast—the coffee was even done brewing. He was pretty proud of himself. It was a lot better than the fast food he usually picked up on the way to work.

She gave him a double-take. "You made breakfast?"

"Thought you might be hungry after everything."

Zoey scrunched her damp hair. "I am. Hey, thanks for picking up my room. I assume it wasn't the cops."

"No, they probably made it worse than Flynn."

She arched a brow. "You're on a first-name basis with my attacker?"

"I got another threat yesterday. There's no way it's a coincidence." He slid the last egg onto a plate with several pieces of bacon and another egg, and he handed it to Zoey.

"You really think the same guy who took Ariana did this to me and also hit Macy?"

"We're getting close." Alex grabbed his plate and set it on the table across from Zoey and then filled two mugs with coffee. He gave her the one with the Eiffel Tower etched on the side. "Still into Paris."

She nodded and sipped the coffee.

Alex took a piece of bacon and sat. "Is it as magical in person as you always hoped?"

Zoey shrugged. "I wouldn't know."

"You haven't been there?"

She shook her head and cut an egg.

Maybe Golden Boy wasn't as perfect as he appeared. Speaking of the devil, why hadn't he come to check on her yet?

They ate in silence. He studied her from the corner of his eye. She seemed far more vulnerable than usual, reminding him of when she was younger. He longed to run his fingers through her hair, down her soft cheek, and to finally place his mouth over her soft lips.

He shoved his desires away.

Zoey set her fork on the empty plate. "Thanks for everything, Alex. I…" Her voice trailed off.

"It was nothing."

"No, it wasn't." She held his gaze. "You didn't have to, and I didn't want to be alone."

"I had to do something. At least now you feel safe again. You can keep living here."

She shook her head. "The only reason I could sleep is because… Never mind."

"What?"

"Because you were here."

His eyes widened. She looked away and slid her finger around her phone's screen.

She felt safe because he was there? Even after everything they'd been through?

The silence seemed to scream.

He squirmed in his seat. "Do you want me to take you shopping for windows?"

"I should call my insurance company. It might be covered."

"Okay."

She turned to him, her eyes wide and her expression even more vulnerable. "What happened that night?"

He twisted the hem of his shirt, not wanting to talk about the night he'd screwed everything up with her, and changed the subject. "Like I said, Fleshman called me about the break in. I came right over—"

"Not last night. When we broke up." Her expression held sadness rather than anger and bitterness.

Alex's shoulders slumped. "I was an idiot. Worse than that."

She sighed. "It was a long time ago. We both need to move past it, but I need to know why. Why did you do it?"

He felt like added weight had been placed on his shoulders, but this was his chance to apologize. "Zoey, I'm really sorry. I know that doesn't change anything, but I am. I've always regretted walking away from you."

She frowned, but didn't say anything.

Alex searched for the right words. If he was honest with himself, he couldn't even remember what they'd been fighting about that night. What he did remember were the harsh words that spewed from his drunk mouth. The things he'd said to her... they were things nobody deserved, much less her. There was no excuse for the things he'd said. "I wish I could take back all the things I said. That and abandoning you when you needed me most."

Her mouth dropped open. "What about cheating on me?"

Alex's eyes nearly bulged out of his head. "What?"

"Don't you regret cheating on me?" Pain filled her eyes.

The room spun around Alex. "I never cheated on you."

"But… but… yeah, you did."

He shook his head. "I swear on my life I'd never do that to you."

They stared at each other.

"What about Amanda Culbertson?"

"Amanda?" Alex exclaimed.

Zoey nodded. "Everyone said you slept with her."

"That explains why she slapped me in English class." Alex rubbed his face and held Zoey's gaze. "I was horrible to you. Those things I said to you…" He shuddered. "But no, there was no one else. Not before you dumped me, and not for a long time after that. I didn't *want* anyone else."

"You never cheated?" she whispered.

"Never. And I didn't mean any of the crap I said about you, either. You and Ariana are the best things to happen to me." And now it was too late. Ariana was gone and Zoey was engaged to Golden Boy. They would have the perfect wedding and then little angelic children, finally giving Ariana the siblings she'd always wanted when she returned. Alex would go back to his one-track existence building roofs and drinking his pain away.

Zoey opened her mouth and then closed it.

"What?"

She picked at a nail and then looked him in the eyes. "I'm sorry for how I've treated you. I always thought you had betrayed me in the worst way."

He found himself wanting to walk around the table and wrap his arms around her. To smell her sweet perfume and to taste her kisses. If only one of a thousand things had turned out differently.

Alex cleared his throat. "You should call Kellen. Does he know what happened?"

"Alex, he—"

Zoey's phone sounded and his buzzed. Alex's heart plummeted. If it was another threat, he was going to lose it. He whipped out his phone. It was from his dad.

Turn on the news.

Alex exchanged a worried expression with Zoey. They hurried over to the TV and she flipped it on. The newscaster spoke too fast to understand—or was it because Alex's mind was spinning?—but he managed to read the ticker at the bottom of the screen.

Someone had confessed to the kidnapping.

Confession

~

NICK STARED AT the full interrogation room from the other side of the mirrored glass. The young, slightly heavy-set Hispanic man looked nothing like the description Alex had given of the skinny, balding white guy who'd taken Ariana. The only way this made any sense was if he was the guy Alex had bumped into at the grocery store after confronting Myer, and that was a stretch. Sanchez was too young to have started killing thirty years earlier.

Williams threw question after question at the man. He remained in his seat, unflinching and with his heavily-tattooed arms folded across his chest. He answered everything perfectly, even giving details the media hadn't been privy to—which at this point wasn't much.

Anderson turned to Nick. "What do you make of this guy? Is Juan Sanchez our killer?"

"He has all the right answers."

"But he doesn't match the suspect." Anderson leaned against the table. "The dad has been consistent in his description of the abductor."

"Oh, I know." Alex was still convinced Flynn had Ariana. Nick wasn't ready to write the guy off yet, either, despite his airtight alibi.

"Williams seems pretty happy," Anderson said.

"Of course she is. She hasn't put an ounce of stock in Alex's description since day one."

"You think it's Myer, still?" Anderson sipped from a foam cup.

"Or someone who looks a hell of a lot like him."

Anderson nodded. "This guy doesn't strike me as a kidnapper, either."

"So, why's he confessing to a crime that could put him behind bars for life?" Nick studied the guy, who still sat in the same position he'd been in for the last half hour, answering the rapid-fire questions without breaking into a sweat.

"Maybe he's getting paid off or blackmailed. Who knows? If he's not our guy, we have to find a way to prove it—and fast. It's sickeningly close to Halloween."

"That it is." But how could they prove Juan Sanchez was just a distraction while the real kidnapper was preparing his kill?

Nick walked to the door.

"Where are you going?" Anderson asked.

"To find the real perpetrator."

"Let me know if you need anything."

"Will do." Nick left and let the door slam behind him. He really had his work cut out for him now. Williams and her partners were eating up everything Sanchez said in there. Nick wouldn't believe the man until he saw Ariana alive and well. He wasn't going to waste valuable time on a false confession when a real killer was out there.

Cheers sounded from the other end of the building. Did they really believe it was over now?

The girl was still missing.

He followed the noise and glared at the jovial officers. "There will be no celebrating until Ariana is back home with her family. Do you understand?"

Their faces all turned serious.

"I mean it. We don't slow down until she's found."

"But Sanchez—"

"But nothing," Nick corrected. "We don't have the girl. We don't know where she is or what she's enduring. Until we have those answers, we keep looking. Got it? Sanchez is a distraction, and nothing else. Now get to work."

They grumbled, but dispersed.

Nick's phone rang. He left the room and checked the caller ID. It was Alex. Clearly, he'd heard the news. Sanchez had announced his confession on social media before going to the station. Nick went into his office and closed the door. "Hi, Alex."

"What's going on?"

"You must mean Sanchez."

"Who else?" Alex exclaimed. "What part of old white guy don't you guys understand?"

Nick took a deep breath. "We have to follow every lead, no matter how ridiculous."

"Has he handed over Ariana?" Alex demanded.

"No. The FBI team is questioning him now."

"And they really think that joker is the kidnapper?"

"I won't know until they're done," Nick said. "How's Zoey?"

"Shaken, but more upset about this. What's it going to take for you guys to follow the right lead?"

"We still have people looking into everything else. Trust me, the investigation has not been put on hold."

"It better not be."

"The team and I are still looking for possible leads in the cold cases. We've narrowed down the lakes we think could be used this time. Looking into other clues, as well. We're going to keep pressing forward until we recover Ariana. But I need to get going. I'll let you know if anything comes up."

"Like you did with this?" Alex accused.

"First of all, this place is a circus right now, and second, we both know Sanchez isn't a real lead."

"Okay, but next time, let me know, anyway."

"Sure thing." Nick ended the call and opened his laptop. He found the file of cold cases and went to the case he was sure was the original—the one the others had imitated. Janet Vassman. The original lake girl.

How was she related to Flynn Myer? Nick had already done extensive searches, finding no links whatsoever. Flynn had lived a quiet, dull life without so much as a speeding ticket. He'd never even been to Montana as far as Nick could tell.

Nick closed the cold case folder and went over to look at Flynn's history again. The man had worked in the same company for years. Had lived in the same home for just as long. He'd gone through a long series of cars, apparently buying a new one every few years. He worked long hours, apparently so he could have the nice things.

He scanned the information again, hoping to find something useful. Just a boring guy, but the thing was, nobody was that dull. There had to be something. But no matter how many times he looked, nothing showed up—not even between the lines.

Nick went to close the window, but froze. He noticed something he hadn't before.

When Flynn was eighteen, he'd changed his name. That was certainly interesting. Most people didn't do that, even if they hated their given names. There was nothing on Flynn before the name change, aside from a driver's license. But then again, sometimes he had to dig a little deeper to find information on minors.

He spent the next half-hour looking into Flynn's—no, Gregory Myer's—childhood. Gregory had lived it up. He'd totaled three cars and had more than two dozen speeding tickets. He'd been busted for purchasing drugs, everything from weed to cocaine. Gregory had come close to flunking out of school.

Yet he was a star student in college? Went on to live a quiet life, mostly unnoticed but liked by all his neighbors and coworkers? That didn't add up. People didn't change like that, and Flynn had. He'd changed his name and practically turned into a new person.

Nick's head snapped up. A new person. Could he have...?

That was the only explanation. Nick went to the online search engine and tried some amateur digging on Gregory Myer, the flunky drug addict. There was his answer.

Gregory Myer had died a couple weeks after graduation. He'd overdosed on heroin in a closet and hadn't been discovered until the next evening. He'd had a small funeral, and his family moved away after that. Then two years later, Gregory had changed his name to Flynn and enrolled in college. The rest was a boring history—or more than likely, a cover up for a three-decade killing spree.

Waste

~

WILLIAMS ENTERED NICK'S office without knocking. "He's given us a location."

"Sanchez?"

"Of course. You coming?"

Nick shook his head. "I've got another lead. Take a look at this."

"We have a location, Fleshman. No other leads matter."

"This one does."

"I'm not going to waste valuable time arguing. If you don't want to be there when we find the girl, then it's your loss. The media is going to be all over this."

And ridiculing them, if Nick's suspicions were correct. "I'll take the risk. This is huge."

Williams shook her head. "I've met some ridiculous captains in my time—"

"Just go." Nick turned back to his laptop. He was determined to figure out who Flynn Myer had been before taking on a dead druggie's social security number.

The door slammed shut. His phone rang. Alex again.

"Alex, I told you I'd call if something came up."

"You didn't think a location was something big?"

"How did you hear about that already?" Nick exclaimed.

"Are you on my side or not?"

"I am. In fact, I've pissed off the FBI because I'm not going on that fool's errand."

"Huh?"

Nick scrolled through the screen, looking for something that would tell him who Flynn had been. "I'm digging through Myer's past. Found something interesting."

"What?"

"He appears to have been resurrected."

"Say what?"

"I'm going to have to explain it later, but suffice it to say I think you've been right about him this whole time."

"You do?"

"Yeah. I'll talk to you later."

Alex mumbled something Nick couldn't understand. "Okay. Talk to you later." The call ended.

Nick spent the next two hours trying to find Myer's past, but he appeared to have none. He'd covered his tracks well, but without more to go on, it would be difficult to figure out who he'd been, especially as a minor in days when that information had only been stored on paper and other non-electronic means.

A text came in from Alex.

You were right. Anything yet?
No. I'll let you know when I'm off duty.

Nick had searched everything he could think of between here and Montana, including near the locations of the other cold cases. Whatever Flynn had done, he'd covered his tracks well. Given that he'd managed an illegal identity and held onto it for so long showed he probably had connections. Ones who could cover up a paper trail.

Muffled conversation and heavy footsteps sounded in the hall. It sounded like the search team was back—and it didn't sound like they were celebrating a victory.

Despite his doubt of the lead, Nick's heart sank. He'd have loved to have been wrong and have Ariana back.

He went into the hallway. "Didn't find her?"

Williams shook her head. "It was just an abandoned shack. No one had been there for years."

"We tore the place apart," Anderson said. "Even the ground outside."

Nick nodded and then looked at Williams. "Care to hear what I've found now?"

"No, I'm going to let Sanchez have it. He's going to give us the real location." She stormed down the hall.

"What'd you find?" Anderson asked.

"It has to do with Myer."

Anderson shook his head. "Captain, why?"

"Because he's the only lead that makes any sense—and now more than ever."

"Anderson, come here," Williams called.

Anderson arched a brow.

"Go," Nick said. "I'll fill you in later. I'm still trying to connect some dots."

"Okay." Anderson headed down the hall.

Nick went back to his desk and opened the file on the original lake girl. If only he could find more about the kids Janet had spent her last hours with—they had to be the key to all of this. Not only that, but Flynn would've been a teenager. Perhaps the same age or a little older than the girl. It was hard to know for sure, now that Nick knew Flynn was lying about everything.

He opened a database and ran a search for Flynn Myer prior to his miraculous resurrection. Just as expected, Nick found nothing useful—and without knowing Flynn's true identity, he wouldn't be able to.

Nick's head hurt and his legs were sore. He got up and stretched, then headed down the hall to see what was going on with the FBI's investigation. Everyone in the room was either flipping through files or typing furiously in front of a screen. None of the FBI agents were in there.

"What's the latest?" Nick asked.

Reynolds glanced up from a stack of papers. "Williams is grilling Sanchez. That's all we know."

Nick nodded a thanks and headed over to the room behind the interrogation room. Two agents stood by the window while Williams yelled at Sanchez, who sat with his arms folded, looking bored.

"He's not speaking now," said one of the agents. "I've never seen Williams so pissed."

With any luck, she'd grow annoyed enough to actually hear what Nick had to say. He leaned against the back wall and watched the scene before him.

Williams paced in front of Sanchez, making empty threats. He probably knew it, too. He'd only confessed to cover something up. His job was done. He probably figured once the girl was found, he'd be free since he couldn't have done it if he was in custody.

"You guys willing to hear me out yet?" Nick asked.

"Still stuck on the computer programmer?"

"His physical description is an exact match to our eye witness's account."

"But his alibi—"

"Forget the alibi." Nick pounded his fist on the table. "Shoving that aside, he looks guilty. Much more so than this guy."

"He's an upstanding citizen without so much as a parking ticket. He pays his taxes on time and volunteers with the elderly twice a month."

"Myer also died when he was eighteen."

Both agents snapped their attention toward him.

"What?" exclaimed the one who'd been silent.

"Yeah, and his first name was Gregory at the time. Two years later, the troubled young dead man changed his name to Flynn and became the ideal citizen."

They both stepped closer to Nick. He filled them in on Gregory's life, death, and miraculous recovery two years later.

"That does give us reason to look closer at him, but that doesn't negate the fact that he couldn't have been there to kidnap the girl."

"I know." Nick's stomach tightened. That was the one thing that didn't make sense. How could he look exactly like the man who had put Ariana into the van when he was giving a speech?

Fury

~

A LEX JUMPED UP from the couch. "I can't keep watching this."
Clementine jumped from the couch and ran from the
room. Alex's parents both gave him startled expressions.

"They might be close," Mom said.

"Why doesn't anyone believe me?" he exclaimed. "I *saw* the
kidnapper. It wasn't that guy! He was a balding white guy, not a
tattooed Hispanic. Flynn is probably watching this, smug as
anything."

"What if the guy you saw was working for this Sanchez guy?
Or the other way around?" Dad asked. "It could be a group job.
Someone else has to be with Ariana."

"Because a criminal wouldn't leave an eleven-year-old alone,
right?" Alex snapped.

"Alex," Mom exclaimed. "We're on your side."

He took a deep breath. "I know. This just pisses me off. It's
gotta be a distraction. I need to go for a walk and clear my head."
Alex headed outside, grabbing his coat.

The temperature seemed to have dropped five degrees. He
shivered and zipped up. The wind blew, making it feel even colder.

Alex stuffed his hands in his pockets and walked down the
street, fuming over the confession. Flynn could have easily paid
someone off. It would be the perfect distraction away from
himself, and given where the dill hole lived, he had no shortage of
funds.

Alex stormed down the streets of his old neighborhood, going over every detail of the kidnapping. Before he knew it, he was completely on the other side of the development and he didn't feel any better. He was still angry and nothing had changed.

He pulled out his phone and sent Nick a text.

Is now a good time?

No. I'm neck deep in this confession.

It's a fake.

And it's up to me to prove it. Gonna be a long day.

Great. Thx.

Alex shoved his hands back into his pockets and made his way back home. Zoey came out of her parents' house.

"What's going on?" she asked.

"It's a load of crap. The confession. Everything."

"Why would he confess, though?"

Alex clenched his jaw. "To get the attention off the real kidnapper. It's almost Halloween!" Terror gripped him. The police and FBI were so focused on the fake confession, it just gave Flynn the space he needed to plan his latest kill.

That meant only one thing. Alex needed to take matters into his own hands if Ariana was going to live to see next month.

Tears shone in Zoey's eyes. "We're going to get her back, right?"

Everything in Alex wanted to wrap his arms around her. Not when Golden Boy was probably inside, watching. "I'm going to do everything in my power."

"What do you mean?"

"I'm going to make sure she comes back home."

"Alex…" Zoey's eyes widened. "What are you talking about?"

"I don't care what it takes to get her back."

She tilted her head and her brows came together.

"Why don't you go back inside? I have some things I need to take care of."

"Do you need help?"

"Actually, yeah. Can you go to the hospital and stay with Macy for a few hours? Luke's there now, and we're all taking turns. I'm supposed to be there in—" he checked his phone "—twenty minutes."

She nodded. "I'll go."

"Thanks, Zo."

They held each other's gaze. It seemed like she was going to say something, but then she just nodded.

Alex nodded and headed up his driveway. "Say hi to Kellen," he muttered.

He went up the stairs and nearly ran into Mom. She gave him a double-take. "I thought you were going to the hospital."

"No, I ran into Zoey. She's going."

"It might do you some good to focus on Macy for a little bit. I can see how worked up you are over the confession."

"Everyone else should be, too! This isn't good news."

She took a deep breath. "Do you want me to make you something to eat?"

"I don't want food," he snapped. "Excuse me." Alex went around her up the stairs and into his room and slammed the door.

He was done waiting for the police and the FBI. The fact that they were giving any credence to the confession told Alex that he was on his own in this battle. Sure, Nick believed him, but that did him little good. The captain was bound by miles of sticky red tape. Alex wasn't.

In fact, as long as Ariana ended up safe in the end, Alex didn't care what happened to him. If he had to kill Flynn to get to Ariana before Halloween, then so be it. He'd spend the rest of his life behind bars. It wasn't like he had much to lose. Zoey had her fiancé. Luke and his parents had to take care of Macy.

This was on him.

If Flynn was going to go down, Alex would have to be the one to do it while the police were busy with a fake lead.

He flipped open his laptop and opened a picture of Ariana. "This is for you."

Alex closed the image and opened a new browser. He was going to learn everything he could about Flynn, find him alone, and beat him until he brought Alex to where he was hiding Ariana.

For the next several hours, Alex studied the layouts of the building where Flynn worked and of his house. He studied and studied until he was certain he could find his way around either one in the dark.

Next, it was a matter of figuring out the jerk-wad's schedule and when the best time to strike would be. Time was not on his side, and he needed a plan. He'd never come close to killing anyone, and it might just come down to threatening that if Flynn wouldn't cooperate.

Ring

KELLEN'S STEPS WERE heavy and his breathing tight as he trudged down the quiet hallway of the hospital. His footsteps echoed around him. Harried conversation sounded from somewhere. His pulse drummed in his ears.

He hated the conversation he needed to have with Zoey, and even worse that it was going to be in a hospital. But that's where she was, and he couldn't wait any longer.

Kellen slowed as the room numbers grew closer to the one he was looking for. Finally, he reached the right one.

Knock, knock.

"Come in," came Zoey's voice.

His breath caught at the sound. He loved her—more than anyone else, in fact. That's why this conversation felt like it would crush him, especially given the horrible ordeal she was going through. He was a first-class jerk for doing this now. No better than Alex, really. Maybe she did have a type.

Kellen sucked in a deep breath and opened the door.

Zoey's eyes widened when he came in.

"Your parents told me you were here."

"Oh."

"How's Macy?" He stared at the mess of casts, making Zoey's best friend look more like a mummy than a human.

"She finally fell asleep." Zoey patted a chair, indicating for him to sit. "She was really uncomfortable, so they had to give her a sedative."

Kellen grimaced. "And the guy who did this to her walked away?"

"Apparently. Have a seat." She kept her focus on Macy.

His muscles ached. He hated to do this. Almost enough to put it off. He changed the subject. "I heard about your break-in. I'm glad you're okay."

She shrugged. "I never liked that window, anyway."

The corner of Kellen's mouth twitched. "At least you have a good attitude about it."

"I'm not going back there, though."

He sat in the seat next to her. "You're not?"

She shook her head. "Not alone, and that's my only option at this point."

"I'm really sorry, Zoey. This isn't how I wanted things to end between us. I didn't want them to end at all, but I can't be your second choice." He wanted her to deny it. To say she'd thought it over and realized he was the one and that everything would change.

The silence between them spoke volumes—more than words ever could.

"Did you come here for the ring?" she finally asked.

He swallowed. "I need to return it before the next payment is due. Unless…"

More silence.

Zoey slid off the ring and held it out.

Shaking, he took it. This was it. They were officially over.

She glanced up at him, holding his gaze.

It felt like a dagger to his heart. "I'll do whatever I can to help find Ariana."

Zoey nodded and then turned to look at Macy. "You should go."

"Do you need anything?"

She shook her head.

"I love you, Zo. It's just that we want different things."

"I know."

"Are you going to be okay? Do you need help moving your things from the condo?"

"No. Just take your things and leave your key on the counter when you're done."

A heavy air of finality settled on him. "Okay."

"That reminds me." She dug into her purse, pulled out her keychain, and slid off the key to his place. "Here you go. I'm pretty sure I didn't leave anything there."

"If I find anything, I'll drop it off."

"Thanks."

Kellen held the key next to the ring. He was supposed to be planning a bachelor party. How had things turned south so fast? He cleared his throat and rose from the chair. "Like I said, if you need anything, just let me know."

"Thanks."

"So, this is it."

She turned and met his gaze. "This is it."

No parting kiss, no tearful goodbye. Just a key, a ring, and a see-you-later.

"Bye, Kellen."

Scared

~

ARIANA'S HEAD SNAPPED down toward her chest as she started to fall asleep. She sat up and looked around her new room—in a whole different house. There was no way she was getting out of this one. Lloyd had made sure of that.

This room had nothing in it other than carpeting, and she couldn't use that to escape. She scraped a nail along the white wall. It had been hours since she'd heard anything from Lloyd. Earlier, he'd slid a plate of breakfast in without any utensils. He'd given her a bucket to pee in. Ariana had put it in the opposite corner and placed the empty plate over it to keep the smell in.

Her stomach rumbled. She wanted to eat, but even more, she wanted to go home.

Ariana rubbed her sore side. Her ankles hurt, too. Everything seemed to remind her of her botched escape. That was probably exactly what Lloyd wanted.

Her eyes grew heavy. Finally, she couldn't fight the sleepiness. She curled into a ball and fell asleep.

It was dark when she woke up. A banging noise sounded from a nearby room. Maybe that was what had woken her.

The noise continued. Every so often, it stopped. Then she could hear Lloyd grumbling. Then the banging started again.

Ariana's stomach growled again, fiercer than before. She sat up and clutched her middle. When would he let her eat again? Would he even let her eat another meal?

She crawled over to the wall nearest the sound and pressed her ear against it. It was too muffled to be able to tell what he was doing. She shivered, sure she didn't want to find out.

Ariana banged on the wall. He didn't respond. She pounded harder.

"Shut up!"

"I'm hungry!"

An electric saw sounded.

She waited for it to stop and then hit the wall again.

"I said to stop!"

Ariana banged with both fists until her knuckles hurt.

The door flew open. "Did you not hear me?"

"I need to eat."

"Did you learn nothing from pounding on your bedroom door? I can make things far worse than this."

She swallowed and backed away from him.

"That's what I thought. Now shut up and leave me alone. I thought it was going to work out with you, so I didn't prepare for this. Now I'm going to have to work extra hard to get this done in time."

"In time for what?"

"Shut up!" He slammed the door, locked the three deadbolts, and scraped the chair underneath the doorknob. Ariana was now all too familiar with those sounds.

The noises of the saw and the banging alternated as Ariana's stomach begged for food. She felt light-headed.

If only she hadn't tried to escape.

Plans

SOMETHING SOUNDING LIKE a jackhammer woke Alex. He sat up, hitting his head on the desk lamp. His phone was buzzing next to his laptop on the desk. Clementine jumped from his lap, ran to a corner, and stared at Alex.

He grabbed his phone and checked the text. It was from a blocked number.

You just couldn't leave it alone, could you?

"No, Flynn, I couldn't! Not when you have my daughter, you no good piece of horse—"

The door flew open. His mom came in. "What's going on? Who are you yelling at?"

Alex held up his phone. "I have to go."

"Where?"

"Out. I'll be back."

Her eyes widened. "I don't like the sound of that. Where are you going?"

"Don't worry about me."

"How can I not?"

"Then trust me." He grabbed his jacket from the end of his bed and slid it on. "I should be back soon."

"Should be?"

Unless he ended up dead or in jail. "Yeah. I love you, Mom." He gave her a quick hug and kissed her forehead.

"Alex…"

"Bye, Mom." He ran past her and headed outside, sliding on his boots as he went. He'd tie them in the car.

His phone buzzed in his pocket. He swore out loud before climbing into the Tercel. After he started the car and tied his laces, he checked the message. Another blocked number. No surprise there.

You're really testing my patience.

"And you're testing mine." Alex started the car and squealed away. He drove to Flynn's work first. It was pretty late, and chances were slim he'd be there, but it would also be the easier building to get inside.

Flynn's car wasn't in the parking lot.

Time to head to his house. It was going to be challenging to get inside a gated community, but he was determined to find a way.

Alex's phone buzzed again, but he didn't bother looking at it. The kidnapper could wait and say everything to his face.

He made his way across town and slowed as he approached the expensive neighborhood. A security guard sat in a little booth in front of a wrought iron gate. If this was the movies, Alex would just take him out and go inside. But he didn't want to kill anyone, not even Flynn unless it ended up turning into a life or death situation.

Alex needed to use some charm, first to get through the gate, and then to get inside Flynn's house. He'd often been able to get out of bad grades or a grounding when he was growing up. His skills were rusty, but he could tap into them. He needed them now more than ever.

He ran his hands through his hair and practiced his best smile. It was a start. He sat taller and drove up to the gate as though he belonged there.

The guard turned to him and opened his door. Alex waved. The guard motioned for him to roll down his window.

Alex did. "Can you open the gate, kind sir?" Maybe that was overkill. He grinned.

"What's your business?"

Other than to deal with a kidnapper? "I'm here to speak with Flynn Myer. He's expecting me." That was probably the truth, based on the threats.

"Hold on." The guard stepped inside for a minute.

Alex's mind raced with different responses. He just had to get in there.

The guard stepped back out. "Myer hasn't left any notes about a guest. You'll have to come back later."

"Can you call him?" Alex asked.

His expression looked put out. "Who shall I say is here?"

"Alex. He'll know who I am." It wasn't likely that Flynn would allow him in, but it was all he had. If nothing else, it would show the bully that Alex Mercer wasn't one to be pushed around.

"Give me a minute." The guard stepped inside again.

"Sure."

What would he do if Myer let him in? That would clearly give Flynn the advantage, but at least he would know where the man lived, and more importantly, where he was probably keeping Ariana. From what he could see through the gate, the houses lived up to their reputation, but that didn't mean anything. He looked like the type who kept a hidden torture room.

The guard stepped back out. "He says that unfortunately he's too busy for company now."

Alex nearly snorted. "Tell him I'll meet him at work. His office." Alex backed up and turned around.

It was his turn to strike some fear into Flynn's heart.

Office

~

ALEX PARKED NEAR the back of the nearly empty parking lot. He had no front plate and he had backed into the spot, hiding the back plate against a shrub.

Darkness had settled and the wind was beginning to pick up again. He kept his attention on the entrance and also on the building itself. Only a few lights shone from inside. Most everything was black. Empty.

It might actually be the perfect time to check out Flynn's place of work—with no one there to ask questions. If Flynn didn't take the bait to meet, that was what Alex would do. He had to be able to find something. Perhaps a stray note in his desk or something on his computer.

Flynn kept his house well protected, but maybe he let his guard down at work. It could be his safety zone—that was his alibi, after all.

Alex glanced back over to the parking lot entrance. Part of him hoped Flynn would drive in so he could beat the information out of him, but he also hoped he could go through his things inside the building.

He checked his phone. Just a text from Mom. Nothing from Flynn.

Had Alex actually rattled him for a change?

Alex watched the entrance, but it was dead.

He'd waited long enough. It was time for action. Alex reached into the back seat and felt around for a hat. He found a Mariners cap. That would have to do. He slid it on and shaped the bill so it would best hide his face. He'd have to be sure to keep looking down, because a place like that building was sure to have tons of cameras all over.

One last quick glance toward the parking lot entrance. Still nothing.

Alex stuffed his keys into his pocket and stepped out. He left it unlocked in case he needed to run out and make a getaway. There wasn't anything worth stealing, anyway.

He hurried across the lot to the building, keeping his gaze averted from any possible—probable—cameras. He pulled his hoodie out from underneath his coat and covered the cap, hoping for a little more shadowing of his features.

Someone wearing a fancy suit came out of the main entrance. Alex quickly grabbed his phone and pretended to be in the middle of an important conversation. He threw in some geeky tech words as he passed the man, careful to look away from him.

The guy didn't seem to pay any attention to Alex. He was busy staring at his own phone. Busy enough to stumble over a curb. Any other time, Alex would have found that funny.

He rushed to the door and grabbed it just before it closed. It was a good thing, too, because there was a code box on the wall next to the handle. That could've been why Flynn hadn't shown up—he wasn't worried about Alex getting in.

"You underestimated me, sucker."

He glanced around the dimly lit entrance and went over to a directory, doing his best to keep from looking up too high. There were about a dozen companies, and all their names were obscure enough that Alex couldn't venture a guess which one Flynn worked at.

Then he noticed an employee directory. It was a long list, taking up three columns, covering several businesses in the building. He scanned for Myer. There it was—Myer, F.

Bingo.

Flynn was on the top level. That would be just great if Alex needed a quick getaway. He sighed but wouldn't be put off. This was his only real chance to find out more about where he was keeping Ariana.

Alex passed the elevators and found some stairs. The chances of the stairwell having cameras were a lot lower than the elevators. He continued to keep his head low and hurried up the steps. His breathing grew labored and muscles started aching.

It was only the fourth level. Flynn was on the fifteenth. He vowed to start working out after all this was done.

By the time he reached the top floor, he leaned against the wall and gasped for air. Once he caught his breath, he opened the door and entered another dimly lit area. The hallway had freshly polished hardwood floors and framed awards covering the walls. The air smelled heavily of pine and cleaners.

Alex wasn't sure which way to go. He decided on left. His boots squeaked on the floor. He cringed, hoping no one was around to hear them.

He came to some doors, slowing to peek in the first one. It had some copy machines and other similar equipment. The next one had a fridge, table, and five different coffee machines. Apparently nerds and serial killers were particular about their caffeine.

Finally, he came to some actual offices. He checked the nameplate on the outside of the first one. Not Flynn. Neither was the next one or the next. Alex picked up his pace until he came to F. Myer—at last.

He paused, taking in the sight. It was a boring office, no different from the rest, really. It was kind of disappointing, but what had he expected? Posters of all the girls he'd killed? Newspaper clippings plastered along the walls? There was a clean desk with a desktop computer, a couple knickknacks, and a small pile of papers. Next to that was a file cabinet and a shelf full of manuals and other books. A few framed awards decorated the walls.

The only pictures were of him accepting some of the awards. No friends, no family, no girlfriend, or vacations. Not even pets. It made him seem even more like serial killer material. Who else would be so blatantly boring? It was like he was trying to convince the world he was docile.

Alex knew that was a lie as much as Flynn himself knew it. It was just a matter of finding proof—and some clue as to where he had Ariana. Maybe if Alex was especially lucky, he might find a spare key to his house—or maybe a secret second home. A storage unit, perhaps. If Flynn had enough money to live in the gated community, he had enough for a second house.

Excitement ran through him as he thought about what he might find.

He poked his head out of the office and listened. The only sounds were the electronic hums of various devices.

Alex adjusted his cap and studied the room. The desk drawers seemed the obvious place to begin, but the bookshelf called to him. If Flynn had something to hide, that seemed the logical place to put it.

He went over and squatted in front of the books and manuals. They all had equally boring titles. It was hard to know where to start. He grabbed one at random and flipped through the pages. Nothing fell out. He feathered through them again, looking for handwritten notes.

Nothing.

Alex put it back and reached for another. Again, nothing. He tried several more, coming up with the same result.

Footsteps sounded down the hallway.

Retreat

~

ALEX FROZE, MIDWAY through replacing the book on the shelf. The steps grew louder—closer.

Had Flynn taken the bait?

The footsteps slowed as they neared the office.

Alex shoved the book back into place and scooted closer to the desk, hiding from view. He felt his pockets for weapons. If he'd have been thinking straight, he would have brought his pistol, but he kept it at the shooting range and hadn't thought to bring it. All he had was an oversized pocketknife. It would do the job if he needed to use it—assuming of course that the other guy didn't have a gun.

The footsteps stopped.

Alex's heart nearly did, too. He wrapped his fingers around the knife, ready to pull out the blade at a moment's notice.

"Someone in here?" asked a male voice with a southern accent.

Flynn didn't have an accent.

"Huh. Thought I heard something. Guess not." Footsteps sounded again, this time growing quieter.

Alex leaned against the wall and breathed a sigh of relief. He crept over to the door and poked his head out.

A janitor walked down the hall, sweeping as he went.

That had been close. But not enough to sway Alex. He went back to the shelf and feathered through each book and manual, finding nothing. Not even a stray pencil mark.

It was time to go through the desk. The top drawer was locked—that had to be where the good stuff was located. Alex didn't have anything on him to pick the lock. His only hope was that Flynn had been careless and left the key somewhere.

He opened the next drawer, finding only pens and pads of paper. The next one had basic office supplies—staples, paper clips, and a three-hole punch. The next one had mail. Alex went through it quickly, still finding nothing.

It would appear that Flynn was careful. But nobody was perfect. He had to have slipped up somewhere, and if it was in the office, Alex was determined to find it. He opened another and—

His cell phone buzzed in his pocket.

Alex swore under his breath and pulled it out.

Blocked number, of course.

You have exactly thirty seconds to get out of my office.

Dread washed through Alex, but then he smiled. He'd gotten a reaction from Flynn. He raised his hand high into the air and gave him the one-finger salute. He spun in a circle to make sure that no matter where the hidden camera was, it caught the gesture.

Alex then returned his phone to the pocket and dug through the drawer he'd just opened.

Something beeped behind him. It continued in a rhythmic pattern.

Slowly, he turned around. A small red light blinked in time with the beeping from inside a cabinet. The light shone through the crack in between the doors.

Flynn wouldn't have planted a bomb in his office? Or would he? He might just be crazy enough to do just that—especially if he had evidence of his crimes in there.

His phone buzzed again.

The beeping sped up.

Alex glanced back and forth between the red light and the

open drawer. He couldn't risk his life before finding Ariana.

He burst into a run, sliding on the hardwood floor. His hands flew out and he knocked a frame off the wall. It crashed to the floor and the glass broke.

"Who's there?" the janitor called.

Alex swore again and ran toward the stairs. He burst through the door and flew downstairs as fast as he could without stumbling again.

An alarm wailed somewhere.

All this trouble, and he hadn't found anything. The only proof he'd gotten was that Flynn Myer was possibly the most boring guy alive—which he knew was a cover-up. The man was crazy. Who set up a bomb in their office? Clearly, someone who had something to hide.

Alex made his way down the staircase to the bottom level. He ran back into the main entrance. The alarm grew louder. Alex ran for the entrance.

"You, stop!" someone called.

He sped up and ran out the door, not stopping until he came to his car. It was tempting to race away, but that would only gain him a speeding ticket. He forced himself to drive a normal pace through town that wouldn't gain him any extra attention.

Alex took deep breaths, trying to calm his racing heart. He squeezed the steering wheel. If only he'd gotten some kind of proof that Flynn had Ariana or had taken any of the other girls.

Sirens sounded behind him. Alex glanced in the rear-view mirror. A police cruiser wasn't far behind, lights flashing.

He swore and slowed, hoping it would pass him. It didn't.

Alex pulled over to the side. The cop car did, too.

His heart sunk. He'd been going slow enough, so this had to be about being in Flynn's office building. Excuses ran through his mind. He slid off his hat and flung it in the back.

The cop tapped on his door. Alex took a deep breath and rolled down the window. "Can I help you, officer?"

Arrest

~

NICK STARED AT ALEX with a disapproving glare from outside the car window. "Tell me you weren't just in Flynn Myer's office."

His friend wouldn't make eye contact. "I wasn't just in Flynn Myer's office," Alex parroted, his tone flat.

"Why?" Nick exclaimed.

Alex looked at him. "I had to do something!"

"You do realize that's breaking and entering."

"I didn't break in—I walked in!"

"To a secure building?"

"The door was open. I'm sure they have a video of that."

Nick frowned. "You realize I have to arrest you."

Alex's mouth formed a straight line. "How's that going to help us find Ariana?"

"It's not, but you don't leave me much of a choice. Especially not when a man matching your description tried to get into Flynn's gated neighborhood just a little while ago. What were you thinking?"

"Do I really need to explain that to you?"

"You have to stay within the bounds of the law! Harassing the suspect doesn't fall into that category. Did you find what you were looking for at least?"

"I didn't have enough time."

"You leave me no other choice, but I need you to step out of the car."

"You're going to arrest me?" Alex exclaimed.

Nick stepped back. "I was supposed to be doing something else—trying to help find your daughter—but I insisted on this."

Alex grumbled, but got out of his vehicle. "So, we're just going to leave my car here?"

"I'll make sure it's impounded to the lot closest to the station."

"Let me guess, that's on my dime."

"That's the way it goes." Nick sighed. "This is the part where I'm supposed to read you your rights. Turn around."

Alex glared at him and then did as he was told. Nick cuffed him, recited his rights, and leaned close. "I know a few good attorneys. Hopefully, we can get you released without much fuss. Will you work with them and me? I want you there when we find Ariana."

"Still waiting on Sanchez to give up her location?"

"You and I both know that's a distraction. In fact, when I heard about your stunt, I was in the middle of nailing a connection between him and Flynn."

"What?" Alex asked.

Nick led him to the cruiser. "I don't know, because I'm here and not back at the station. And we can't talk about it in the car."

"Is it tapped or something?"

"Cameras inside and out. I'm probably going to be questioned as to why this arrest is taking so long." He helped Alex into the back of the car.

They drove in silence for a while before Alex spoke up. "He did it, you know. Flynn—he's the kidnapper."

"Do you have evidence?" Nick asked.

"Other than having seen him take my daughter? It was him!"

Nick took a deep breath. Alex was speaking to the cameras, not that it would do him much good. Not until there was any solid evidence against the man who somehow had the ability to be in two places at once, or at least knew how to make it look like he'd been.

"I saw his face. Flynn Myer took Ariana. I don't care about his alibi. He did it!"

Nick focused on the road while Alex continued going on about Flynn. Just before they reached the station, he called in to have Alex's car brought in. Then he parked outside the jail and escorted Alex inside.

"I hope we can get these charges reversed," he whispered. "I'll do my best to get one of those lawyers I was talking about. Can you do your part and be an ideal inmate?"

"Inmate? You make it sound like I'm in prison."

"You're going to be in a holding cell. Just be on your best behavior. You can do that, right?"

"Sure."

"Don't try to convince anyone about Myer's guilt. I'm going to work on that while trying to get you out. Just sit quietly until your attorney arrives. Then you need to work *with* him. Got it?"

"Fine."

"Hey, I'm serious. I'm trying to help you."

"Okay. I'll be good. I swear."

Nick shook his head. It was like everyone was trying to make his job more difficult. He took Alex to one of the officers. "Book him and put him in his own cell if there's room. His attorney will be here shortly."

The officer nodded and took Alex by the arm.

Nick made eye contact with Alex. They exchanged a glance, both understanding that Nick would do his part, but Alex needed to do his. At least he hoped Alex understood. That would make life a lot easier for the both of them if he did.

History

~

*C*LICK. *C*LICK. *C*LICK.

Ariana woke up and pressed herself against the corner of the wall in the plain white room, sitting taller. The knob turned slowly after the quick unlocking of the three deadbolts. Her heart raced and her stomach roared. She felt dizzy and wasn't sure if she should be scared or hopeful. Was there any chance he'd changed his mind and decided to be nice again?

The door opened just as slowly and Lloyd finally appeared. "It won't be much longer."

"What won't be?"

He glared at her. "Do I really have to explain it to you?"

"I d-don't know what you're doing."

"How can you not know?" he demanded.

She jumped. "I just don't. You haven't told me."

"We've been through this enough times. You know what happens when you don't play by the rules. That's why we've moved to this wretched shack. It's why I have to spend all my time building. You know all of this!"

Shaking, Ariana shook her head. "I *don't* know."

He slammed the door, making her jump. "What are you trying to do?"

"I don't know why you're doing any of this."

Lloyd's eyes narrowed, and he paced, breathing heavily.

Ariana continued to shake. Her teeth chattered, but she kept them from touching and making any noise. "Please just tell me."

He stopped and stared at her. "I've already explained all this to you. Over and over again—for the last thirty years! You really don't get it yet?"

Eyes wide, she shook her head.

"It's no wonder we can't get this right." He paced quicker now and released a string of profanities. "Everything went horribly wrong that night. You shouldn't have died, but you did. I've spent every single Halloween since then trying to undo it. Every one! Something always goes wrong—each time. This time, I thought we'd nailed it." He paused and let his gaze rest on her. "But then you ran away."

She gulped.

"Now we're back to square one. We're going to have to relive the horrible night one more time, Jan. It's not going to go any better than any of the other times."

"Can't we try to make it better?"

"Try?" he bellowed. "I've done nothing other than try! Three decades, and we still can't get it right. It's not easy trying to undo history. Do you realize that? It's damn near impossible—maybe it is impossible. I don't know anymore. My hopes were up high this time. I thought I'd finally have you back and then we could get Mom after Halloween. I thought I'd even found her. Guess I was wrong. Again."

Ariana bit her lower lip. "What if I try harder? Can I promise not to run off like that again?"

Lloyd frowned. "It's too late."

"It doesn't have to be."

"It *is.*" His pacing grew more erratic.

Ariana shook uncontrollably. She didn't want to find out what he had planned, and she really didn't want to know what all the hammering and other noise was about. "Please."

"I have to try again next year."

"What's it going to take to make everything right?"

He stopped pacing again and stared at her. "For you not to drown, but just like that one fateful night, you already snuck out of the house. All these years, and you still haven't learned. We'll never have our family back. Not you, not Mom. Everything was so nice before, you know? Mom didn't blame me for your death before you died. She was at home, not institutionalized. Before she killed herself. Dad never liked me much before that, but after you and Mom died…" He glanced up and shook his head. "Do you know what it was like to live with him after that? With someone who hated you for ruining the family? Who blamed you for the deaths of his favorite family members? Someone who was drunk and mean like that?"

Ariana shook her head. "It sounds awful."

Lloyd broke into a pace again. "You have no idea. None! Be glad about that. The mental anguish—torture, really. Nothing I could do helped. I couldn't make anything right, and I couldn't make them care about me. After you died, I lost everything. My entire world crumbled, Jan. I need everything to go back to the way it was. To have you back, to have Mom back." He paused. "For Dad to stop looking at me like he wanted me dead instead of you guys. For… for… our *whole* family to be back together. No one dying, no one running away, no one hating anyone else."

She watched him pacing. "It sounds like it was really hard."

He stopped and turned to stare at her. "It was worse than hard! If only you hadn't snuck away and gotten yourself killed, then none of this would've happened. But it did, and I have to make it right."

"Maybe you should try something else."

"What?"

Ariana swallowed. "Well, you've tried the same thing for so long. Maybe it'll never work. You might have to do something different."

"Like what?" he demanded. "What else can I do to make it right?"

"What if you can't?"

"Now you're starting to sound like the doctors. I refuse to accept what they call the truth. Their truth is a lie! Once I get it right, everything will go back to the way it was, and then we can all have the life we were supposed to have. I just have to get it right. It was so close this time—so close! I'll bet next time, we'll nail it."

"It's not Halloween yet. We can try again. Start over. You can take me back to the—my bedroom. We can have more nice meals together. Another movie night. It'll all be just right again."

Lloyd paused, like he was considering it. "It won't work. You tried to run away again. You snuck out just like that night you got killed the first time. Why do you think I have to lock you up? It never seems to work, though. What did I do wrong?"

Her mouth gaped. What was she supposed to say? Was there anything that could convince him to let her go? Or at least get out of this horrible room?

"You got nothing? It doesn't matter. I have the boat rebuilt. It gets faster each time. I could almost do it in my sleep at this point. I'll try to get to the overturned boat in time. I'm going to try to save you, but it won't work. It never does."

A jingle sounded. Lloyd pulled his phone out from his pocket and looked at the screen. He swore and then turned to Ariana. "I've got to go."

Tour

⁓

NICK PULLED ANDERSON into his office.

"What's going on, Captain?"

"Myer has agreed to another interview." Nick pulled on his jacket.

"Even though he's accused Mercer of stalking and harassment?" Anderson arched a brow.

"He's eager to clear his name—again."

Anderson shrugged. "Okay. Gives me an excuse to put off the pile of papers on my desk, anyway."

Nick glanced at his own stack. "I hear ya."

"What exactly are we expecting to accomplish?"

"Hopefully more than Williams is getting from Sanchez."

Anderson raked his fingers through his hair. "I don't know if I can take another fake lead."

"Then come with me."

"Let me grab my things." Anderson left and came back a few minutes later. "I'm all set."

They went out into the parking lot, and Nick headed straight for his Mustang. Anderson complained about the focus on Sanchez.

"You know I agree," Nick said. "I planted a seed in some of the other agents about the serial killer I told you about."

"And you really think that's a possibility?" Anderson asked.

"Seems to be our most likely option at this point. Other than our girl being a little younger than the others, it's a perfect fit."

"We need to bring in the other departments," Anderson said. "How long did you say this has been going on?"

"Could be three decades."

Anderson swore. "And nobody has ever linked the cases before?"

"Not that I can tell. He moves around a lot and only does this once a year."

"What a sick bastard."

Nick nodded and slowed as they came to the gated community. "And we might be about to see the perpetrator."

"What are we looking for?" Anderson asked. "To link him to the other cases, I mean."

"Anything we can find." Nick pulled out his badge and showed the guard. "Here to see Flynn Myer."

"Popular guy. Yeah, he already told me. Go on in." The guard stepped inside his little building. A moment later, the gate slowly opened.

Nick waved, rolled up his window, and drove in.

"But we found nothing last time," Anderson said. "What do you think we'll discover now that he's had more time to hide evidence?"

"Just keep your eyes open." Nick didn't want to admit that he believed Alex's theory of a hidden room. It was something usually reserved for television, but someone crazy enough to kill girls every Halloween for thirty years had to have something like that—some way to keep everything hidden from the rest of the world. And a house as big as Flynn's had to have plenty of space for that, especially given that he lived alone in a home big enough for a dozen people.

Nick parked in front of the large house and paused, paying particular attention to the woods behind the house.

"What are you thinking?" Anderson asked.

"That we should check the woods, too."

"Tonight?"

"No, after Halloween. Yes, tonight."

"We should call in the K-9 unit for that."

Nick shook his head. "I just want to look around. We can bring in the dog later, if we find anything."

"If you say so."

"Let's go." Nick double-checked his gun as he got out of the car. He remotely locked it and they walked up the driveway in silence. Lights along the house lit up as they walked underneath.

Nick held his fist up to knock, but the door opened.

Flynn nodded. "Welcome back, officers."

"Thank you for your patience."

"Of course." Flynn moved aside, allowing them entrance.

The house seemed exactly the same as it had been before.

"Would you like to have a seat?" Flynn asked.

"No," Anderson said. "We'd just like to look around, if you don't mind."

"Anything to help the investigation." He extended his arms. "Would you like me to sit on the couch and wait?"

Nick nodded. Flynn took a seat and picked up a magazine about computer coding. Nick walked around, looking for anything out of place or unusual. He tapped a throw rug in front of the couch, hoping to find a loose board or handle. Nothing seemed out of place. He pulled a few books from various bookshelves, hoping to find a trap door.

What was this? Scooby-Doo? He was Fred and Anderson, Shaggy? Nick silently chastised himself walked around until he came to a hallway.

"Mind if I go down here?" he asked.

"Have at it," Flynn replied and flipped a page in his magazine.

Nick caught Anderson's gaze and motioned for him to come along. They walked down the hallway, coming to a bunch of closed doors. Nick opened one and found a laundry room. A door led outside. He went over and opened the door. It led into the woods.

He closed the door and glanced around the sparkling clean room. Anderson looked inside the washing machine and drier.

Nick peeked behind them and then underneath.

A tiny splotch of red. He pulled out his phone and shone the light on it. It appeared to be dried blood.

He caught Anderson's attention and gestured to it.

Anderson's eyes lit up. He stepped out of the room and called Flynn over.

Suspicious

~

FLYNN STEPPED INSIDE the laundry room. "Yes?"

"Can you explain this?" Nick shone his light on the red splotch.

"Oh, that." Flynn squatted, swiped his finger over it, and showed it to them. "I spilled some ketchup." He licked it off his finger. "Definitely ketchup."

"Thanks for explaining. We're going to keep looking around."

Flynn nodded. "Whatever you need." He left the room.

"That was weird," Anderson said.

"Try disgusting." Nick pulled out latex gloves from his inside pocket, opened a plastic bag, and removed a cotton swab. He kneeled down, wiped what remained of the red residue, put the swab into the bag, and sealed it. He marked it and put it back into his coat. This alone could make everything worth the effort—unless it really was just a condiment.

He and Anderson went over every inch of the laundry room twice, not finding anything else.

"Ready to check the rest of the house?" Nick asked.

"More than ever." Anderson glanced around the tiny room one last time.

They went through the other rooms—an office, a home theater, a couple guest bedrooms, and a storage room—without finding anything useful. Nick continued looking for trap doors, but saw nothing of that nature, either.

Finally, they came back out to the living room. Flynn set down his magazine. "All done?"

Nick glanced at the staircase behind him. "Actually, we'd like to see what's upstairs."

Flynn's eyes widened just slightly. "Oh, there's nothing up there."

"Then you won't mind showing us around, will you?" Anderson asked. "It should only take a few minutes, and then we'll be out of your hair shortly."

"Sure. No problem." He rose and led them up the staircase. At the top, he turned around. "This is where my mother-in-law stayed before she went onto a better place. Everything up here is hers."

That was convenient. Nick nodded, now more eager than ever to have a look.

Flynn's mouth curved down and then he moved aside.

The first thing Nick noticed was shag carpeting. Then, looking around, he felt like he'd stepped into another era. It almost could have been straight from his own grandparents' home. He walked across the hall into a retro kitchen. He could almost smell Grams' oatmeal raisin cookies.

"When did you say your mother-in-law lived here?" Anderson asked.

"I didn't," Flynn said. "It was maybe ten years ago."

Nick turned to him. "And what about your wife? This is the first mention of her you've made."

Flynn held his gaze for a moment. "It didn't work out. You know how it goes."

"Why don't you tell us?"

"Okay." Flynn smirked and turned toward the kitchen. "Irreconcilable differences. We wanted different things out of life. Both of us had changed too much after marrying. It happens, right?" He turned back to Nick.

"If you say so. Mind if we look around up here?"

"Not much to see." Flynn went over to the fridge and opened it, showing that it was empty inside. He walked over to the table and swiped his fingers across it, showing a thick layer of dust. "I've had the cleaning staff leave this part of the house alone. To be honest, it kind of creeps me out."

Anderson walked around the kitchen, studying everything but touching nothing. "Then why not get rid of everything? If it belonged to your ex-wife's mother, why preserve it?"

Flynn's nostrils flared. "It's easier to ignore than deal with. I have enough going on in my life with work that I don't care to bother with it. Would you like to see the other rooms?"

"Yes." Nick squared his shoulders. "Show us."

"Okay." Flynn led them out into another hallway. It led to a bathroom and a few bedrooms. He opened the bathroom and wiped his finger along the counter. "See? Just as much dust. This place hasn't been touched in years."

Nick went into the bedroom next to the bathroom. It was a girl's bedroom, full of pink as far as the eye could see. An elaborate dollhouse sat on the floor near the closet. He walked over the window and looked out over the woods.

"See?" Flynn said. "More dust. You're going to find that on everything up here."

"Was this your mother-in-law's room?" Nick asked, unable to keep the sarcasm out of his tone.

"No. She lost a daughter when she was young. Her way of hanging on was to keep all of her things just as it had been when she died."

"Do you remember when the girl died?" Nick asked.

"My wife was a teenager."

"Your ex-wife?" Nick arched a brow.

"Yeah. She was a kid."

"Did her sister die on Halloween?"

"I wouldn't know."

"You wouldn't know?" Anderson exclaimed.

"She wasn't *my* sister."

Nick exchanged a glance with Anderson.

"You want to see my mother-in-law's room?" Flynn asked.

"Go ahead." Nick nodded to Anderson. "I'm going to look around in here some more."

Flynn started to say something, but then closed his mouth.

Nick gave him a look that dared Flynn to cross him.

"Follow me." Flynn led Anderson out of the room.

Taking a deep breath, Nick glanced around the room. "This place is creepy as—"

His phone rang.

"What?" he snapped, answering the call.

"This is Weiss." The best attorney money could buy. Hopefully, he needed a pro bono case.

"Thanks for getting back to me so quickly. Are you up for the challenge?"

"It's a huge case."

"The kidnapping—not the breaking and entering. Can you get him off?"

"I'll see what I can do. He's at the station now?"

"Behind bars, yeah. Thank you, Weiss."

"Don't thank me yet. I'll be in touch."

"Great. I'll keep my phone on." Nick sighed in relief as he ended the call. With Weiss on it, Alex stood the best chance of getting out sooner rather than later, and hopefully without the media catching wind of the arrest.

Nick looked around the room again, not sure what he was expecting to see. He sneezed from the dust. There was no way Ariana had been in this room. No one had in a long time.

He opened the closet and pushed aside clothes, disturbing more dust. He sneezed again and looked around. After finding nothing, he went into the hall. Anderson and Flynn were in an old rec room, also covered with dust.

Anderson glanced at him. "There's nothing here."

"Like I said." Flynn crossed his arms. "I've been nothing other than accommodating, and yet you refuse to believe me." He sneezed. "Are we done here?"

Nick exchanged some expressions with Anderson.

Flynn cleared his throat. "Unless you have a warrant, I think we're done here. I have some work I need to do."

"No," Nick said. "No warrant. Thank you for your cooperation."

"My pleasure. Let me see you out."

News

ZOEY LEANED BACK in the chair and watched Macy sleep. Her friend slept so peacefully despite all the noise of the hospital and the casts. Hopefully, the nurses would leave her alone for a while so she could get some decent rest.

If only Zoey could get some rest. She was exhausted and had spent more time at the hospital than anywhere else. The thought of going home made her stomach twist in knots. Being at her parents' house was torturous—that was where Ariana was supposed to be. The house just felt wrong with her gone—knowing why she wasn't there.

She leaned back in the chair and out of habit went to play with her ring. The one that wasn't there. A fresh wave of regret ran through her. Kellen was no longer in her life. She was no longer the future Mrs. McKay.

She grabbed the TV remote and flipped it on, hoping to find a mindless movie to distract her from her thoughts for a while.

A blonde news reporter said something about Alex. What were they blaming on him now?

"Alex Mercer has been arrested for the…"

Zoey's mouth dropped open and she couldn't focus on anything else said. Alex had been *arrested*? Did they think he was involved? As angry as she had been at him for so long, she knew he would never be capable of such a thing. He would never do anything to hurt Ariana. Aside from almost never seeing her, but in his mind, he probably thought he was doing Ari a favor.

She sat up and turned up the volume. Her mind continued spinning, making it hard to follow what the newscaster said. It sounded like he'd had some kind of altercation with a person of interest in the case.

Macy mumbled something. Zoey turned off the TV, not only so her friend wouldn't wake, but so she wouldn't hear the news. Macy needed to focus on healing. It would only stress her out to hear about Alex being arrested. She adored her younger brother.

Zoey sat up and watched Macy. Her eyes were closed, but she was muttering. The poor thing had been talking in her sleep for years—since after her own kidnapping.

Footsteps sounded in the doorway. Zoey whipped around, ready to tell the nurse to leave Macy alone.

It was Luke. He gave Zoey a sad smile. "How is she?"

"Finally sleeping."

"Did you guys hear about Alex?"

"I just did, but she doesn't know."

He sat next to Zoey. "Let's keep it that way."

"Definitely."

"Why don't you get some rest?"

Where? At home, where she wasn't safe? Or at her parents' house, where she felt like she'd entered a black hole? "I don't mind staying. I'm sure you have things to do."

Luke patted her shoulder. "Go on, Zo. I'll take good care of her."

"I wasn't doubting—"

"Yeah, I know. I want to be here, and you need to take care of yourself. Maybe you could check on Chad and Alyssa."

Zoey closed her eyes. Alex's parents had to be freaking out— their granddaughter was abducted, their daughter nearly killed, and now their son in jail. She nodded. "I'll do that."

"Thanks. Let me know if they need anything."

"You just worry about Macy."

They said goodbye, and then Zoey headed for her car. The only thing going her way was that she had been able to park close since they had reserved parking for hybrid vehicles. She remote-unlocked the turquoise sports car and climbed in, noticing the start of another headache.

She started the car, popped a couple ibuprofen, and thought about how she would tell the Mercers about Alex's arrest. They'd always been like second parents to her, so she needed to be the one to tell them if they didn't already know.

Zoey put on some music and headed to the Mercers' house. She parked in between their house and her parents' and walked slowly up the driveway. Staring at the tree in their front yard, memories flooded of times spent climbing it as kids and teens with Macy and Alex. She paused on the porch, trying to hold onto happier times. Finally, she sat on the bench and succumbed to memories, seeing them as vividly as the tree itself.

Tears welled in her eyes as the memories with Ariana came into view. The first time she'd crawled had been under that tree. She and Alex had been there, and they'd both been thrilled. Then later, she'd toddled around, picking flowers and chasing butterflies.

The front door opened, pulling Zoey from her memories.

"Zoey, are you okay?" Alyssa stepped outside, pulling her sweater tighter to protect against the cold air.

"Yeah, sorry."

"No need to apologize." She sat down. "I know what you're going through."

Zoey nodded. She needed to tell her about Alex, but was losing courage by the moment.

Alyssa patted Zoey's left hand. "A missing kid can put a lot of strain on a relationship."

Zoey glanced at her naked ring finger and sighed.

"Did you know things got really rocky with Chad and me?"

"Is that why you were gone for a little while?"

Alyssa sighed and leaned back. "Yeah. I wasn't sure we'd make it, but somehow we did. We almost didn't. I…" Her voice trailed off and her expression glazed over. She seemed to be as lost in her own thoughts as Zoey.

She studied Alyssa and decided she couldn't know about Alex's arrest. Not with as calm as she was.

Zoey took a deep breath. "Did you hear about Alex?"

Alyssa's eyes widened. "What?"

"I should probably tell you and Chad together."

"What is it?" Alyssa covered her mouth. "Is he okay?"

"He's not injured—"

"Tell me what happened."

Zoey frowned. "He's in jail."

Alyssa's face paled, and her eyes filled with tears.

Warning

~

A LEX SAT IN the interrogation room with his back to the two-way mirror as much as possible. The handcuffs slid through a bar on the side of the table made it challenging, but he was pretty flexible.

At long last, the door opened. Nick came in, a stern expression on his face. "Need anything?"

"I could use some water."

"Maybe later."

"Why ask?"

He shrugged and sat across from Alex. "What the hell were you thinking?"

Alex gave him a double-take. "What—?"

Nick arched a brow and glanced over at the mirror. "Breaking and entering? You need to let us handle the case. Got it?" He looked at the mirror again.

Now it made sense. Nick was putting on a show for someone. "Yeah. Sure do. I'm not going to do anything like that again."

"Good. I hear you got an attorney."

"Yeah." The one Nick had called. "I'm waiting for him to come back and talk to me."

"I want to talk to him, too. Stay here."

Alex shook the cuffs against the table. "I don't have much of a choice, now do I?"

"Just stay put." Nick got up and left, slamming the door.

Clearly, someone was putting pressure on the captain.

The back of Alex's head itched. It had started as soon as they'd stuck him to the table, and it hadn't stopped since. He slid down in the chair and rubbed the back of his head against the chair, finally getting the itch.

Mid-scratch, the door opened. Alex bolted upright, jamming the cuffs against his wrist.

Ralph Weiss, his larger-than-life attorney, entered. "Got you out of here," the six-and-a-half foot tall, stocky redhead bellowed. "Let's go somewhere with more privacy to talk."

"Sounds good to me. What about these?" Alex nodded toward the cuffs.

"Someone's coming in to release you. Any personal items I should retrieve?"

"Other than my car?" Alex muttered.

"We'll take care of that." He opened the door and stuck his head into the hallway. "We need someone to unlock these cuffs."

Alex's head pounded like a jackhammer. "Got any aspirin?"

"No. Toughen up, kid."

Alex groaned and closed his eyes. When would the nightmare end? He just wanted Ariana back safe and sound, and everyone off his back. His own guilt was more than enough of a burden to bear.

"It's about time," Weiss said.

"Yeah, yeah." Keys rustled.

Alex opened his eyes. An officer he didn't recognize walked toward him and released him from the cuffs. Alex rose and stretched. He twisted his sore, aching back.

"Follow me." Weiss gestured toward the hall.

"Gladly." Alex twisted each wrist until it popped, then he cracked his knuckles.

"You have some paperwork to fill out," his attorney said. "Get that done, and then we'll get down to business."

They went to the front desk, where Weiss was given a clipboard with a stack of papers.

Alex took it and headed for the waiting area to fill them out.

"No, this way," Weiss said. Everything he said sounded like an order from a drill sergeant.

Alex spun around, and out of the corner of his eye, he saw someone he recognized. He did a double-take. "Mom?"

She ran over and wrapped her arms around him. "Oh, Alex. Did they finally let you go?"

"Yeah, they—how did you know I was here?"

"Don't worry about that. Do you need anything?"

Alex clenched his jaw. "It's all over social media, isn't it?"

"You just need to focus on—"

"This way," Weiss boomed.

"I gotta go," Alex said. "My lawyer kind of scares me."

"You don't need anything?" she asked.

He shook his head. "As long as I get my car, I'll be home soon." He hoped. "I'll be fine. You should go home."

She looked like she might shatter.

"Is Dad here?"

Mom nodded, blinking back tears. "He's in the bathroom."

"You guys go home. I'll be there before you know it."

"Mercer," Weiss called.

Alex gave her a quick kiss on the cheek and hurried down the hall. Weiss motioned toward a door. They entered a tiny room with no mirrors or windows.

"You can speak freely in here. Start filling that stuff out."

Alex sat without a word and wrote his name on the first form. "How'd you get me out?"

"I'll do the talking."

If this was how he treated his clients, Alex would have hated to be an opposing attorney or a client on a stand.

The silence in the room seemed to echo. The only sound was of the ball point pen as Alex wrote.

"Do you understand the severity of the situation?" Weiss asked.

"Yes." Alex had to stop himself from saying *yes, sir.*

"Breaking and entering is stupid."

"Okay."

"Did I say you could talk? Don't do it again. It's going to be a lot harder for the authorities to get a warrant if you pull this kind of drama. In fact, you should leave everything to the police and the FBI."

"Didn't Nick tell you—?"

"I'm not done speaking. You're doing more harm than good. If you want your daughter found in time, let the professionals handle this."

Alex slammed down the pen and glared at Weiss. "You mean the idiots who are running after the leads of a fake kidnapper? How long is it going to take them to figure out he's nothing more than a distraction?"

Weiss sat across from him. "I agree. So does Fleshman—but that doesn't give you permission to pull crap like you did. Got it?"

"What else am I supposed to do?" Alex demanded. "Just sit around and do nothing? Because I can't do that!"

"Lucky for you, Fleshman wants to talk with you once you're out of here. I'm going to be focused on cleaning up your mess. There are a few loopholes I can work with, so this should be taken off your record, but I'm serious. Screw up again, and I won't represent you."

Alex took a deep breath and nodded in agreement. How could he argue against someone who could get jail time off his record? He continued filling out the papers while Weiss rambled on about what Alex needed to do and not do to stay out of trouble. Basically, he wasn't supposed to break any laws. He could have just said that, but instead, he embellished on it for a full twenty minutes.

Finally, Weiss took a breath. "I'm going to speak with Fleshman real quick. Finish that up, and don't go anywhere."

"Sure." How far could he get with his car still impounded, anyway?

The door slammed shut behind the lawyer.

A few minutes later, Nick came in. He dropped Alex's coat on the table. "Your phone's in the pocket."

Alex didn't look up. "Thanks."

"Hey, about earlier—"

"Don't worry about it."

"They're coming down on me about how much time—"

"I get it." Alex signed his name on the last sheet of paper. "Am I a free man now?"

"If by free, you mean everyone is going to have their eyes on you, then yes. You're a free man."

"Nice."

"I'll be right back. Then we'll get your car out of impound. And by we, I mean you and Weiss. You can't come here to the station to speak with me anymore."

"What about—?"

Nick lowered his voice. "Not *here*."

Alex nodded.

"I'll take those." Nick took the clipboard and left without another word.

Alex grabbed his jacket and searched the pockets, hoping he had enough cash for some drinks. Maybe enough to make him forget this night ever happened.

He found his phone and turned it on. A new text from a blocked number.

Just what he needed.

May as well read it before getting to drinking the night away.

You've finally proven yourself.

Alex stared at the message. What did *that* mean?

Free

~

ALEX STARTED HIS CAR and drove away from the impound lot, never happier to be in his little beater. All he needed now was to get Ariana back, but that would be ten times more difficult since he had to stay away from Flynn.

He kept trying to figure out what the newest 'threat' meant. He'd proven himself? For what, and how? It didn't make any sense. Not unless someone was messing with him. Maybe it wasn't Flynn. Had word gotten out about the threatening messages?

His head hurt and the pain squeezed down to the base of his skull to his neck. He stopped at a light and rubbed his neck.

A bar across the street caught his attention. That was exactly what he needed after everything he'd been through. Just a little something to help him chill—especially since he would probably have to explain his arrest to his parents. His headache squeezed harder.

After the light turned, Alex changed lanes, and made his way to the bar. He felt himself relax, just knowing he was going to have something to drink. A cigarette sounded good, too—but could he handle just one? Quitting had been hell, and he didn't want to go through that again. On the other hand, his daughter was missing, he just got out of jail, and his sister was in the hospital. If there was ever a time he deserved one, it was now.

He could just bum one off somebody and then have no more. He wouldn't give himself the chance to turn it into a habit. Just one to help him feel better. Oh, how much better it would make him feel.

Alex pulled into the lot, craving the alcohol more as each moment passed. He parked and headed inside. The place had the same feel as Cole's back home, except that he didn't know anyone. And today, that was a good thing.

He went up to the bar and ordered a beer.

"Cash or card?" The gorgeous bartender with big blue eyes held out her hand. Some of her long, brown hair fell into her face.

Alex grumbled, reaching into his pocket. That was one thing he liked about Cole's—trust. "Here." He handed her his card.

"Thanks." She smiled and handed him the beer. "You seem familiar. Do I know you?"

His heart sank. Of course she recognized him. He shook his head. "I don't think so. I grew up here in town, we probably saw each other as kids."

"That must be it. Are you visiting or do you live here?" She leaned against the counter and looked him over slowly, appearing to like what she saw.

Alex took a swig and held onto the taste a moment before swallowing. "Visiting my parents for a while."

"How long?"

What was this, twenty questions? "We have some family stuff going on, so I'm not sure."

"You just seem so familiar."

He shrugged. "That's how it is, growing up around here."

"True. What's your name?"

His stomach twisted. Once he told her that, she would know exactly who he was—the jerk who'd let his daughter get kidnapped.

The door dinged, announcing a new customer. Saved by the bell.

She glanced at his card. "Alex Mercer. Why does that sound

familiar?" She tapped Alex's credit card on the counter and stuck it in a pocket. "We'll finish this conversation in a minute." She turned to the other customer and Alex took a deep breath.

He was practically a celebrity these days, and it sucked in the worst way possible. He just wanted to forget about his problems, and not talk about them with the beautiful brunette who had probably been a cheerleader when he'd been smoking and drinking himself silly. She could've even been one of the girls who'd bullied Macy, sending her straight into the hands of an online predator.

Alex took a deep breath, finished off the beer, and looked around the nearly-empty bar. There were a few other customers scattered around, but it was pretty dead. He glanced at a calendar on the wall and realized he didn't know what day it was. It was probably a weekday—he was fairly sure about that much.

A different bartender came over—a dude several years older and full of piercings. "Another beer?"

Alex relaxed, hoping this one wouldn't ask so many questions. "Yeah."

He handed him the beer and leaned over the counter. "Leave Bella alone."

"Excuse me?" Alex exclaimed.

"I saw you talking to her."

"It was the other way around, actually. I'm just here for the drinks."

The guy arched a twice-pierced brow. "Just stay away from her."

"Don't worry. I got enough to worry about."

His eyes narrowed. "Good. How'd you get out of jail so fast?"

Alex gave him a double-take. "What's your problem?"

The dude leaned closer to Alex. "Bella runs the place, so if she doesn't kick you out, there's nothin' I can do about it. But the one thing I can do is tell you she's too good for you, so don't even think about it."

"I wasn't." Alex grabbed his beer and sat at a booth, hoping the bartender got the drift before Alex had to punch him.

A few minutes later, the brunette—presumably Bella—came over to him. "Don't let Scott bother you. He's my protective older brother."

Alex gave a slight nod. "He's fine." And probably right about his sister being better off staying far away from him. "Could I get another beer? And maybe some shots of something."

"Sure. Shots of what?"

"Surprise me."

"Okay." She laughed, took his empty bottle, and walked away.

He looked out the window and watched the wind blow multicolored leaves across the parking lot.

"Here we are." Bella stood next to him with a tray full of shot glasses. There had to be ten of them.

"I didn't mean that many."

She winked and sat across from him. "I'll only charge you for the ones you actually drink."

He grabbed the glass nearest to him and drank it. Vodka with a hint of something sweet.

"You said to surprise you, so I did. My turn."

Alex arched a brow.

"My bar, my rules, sweetie. I'm on break." She picked a glass in the middle, threw her head back, and drank it. "Tequila with salt. Your turn."

He picked one in front of her and swallowed it, not recognizing the taste. "Not often I find alcohol I can't recognize."

Bella laughed and pulled some hair behind her ear. Her one ear had more piercings than Scott had all over his face and both ears. "That one's from Iceland. I forget what it's called, but a sexy blond thing introduced me and I brought back an entire case."

"You run a bar and you don't know what it's called?"

She pulled all of her hair around one shoulder and laughed

again. "I can't pronounce it, and their alphabet is different from ours."

"If you say so." He grabbed another glass and drank.

"Hey, it's my turn."

"You distracted me."

Bella took two and poured them both in her mouth.

"Hey, Bella," Scott called from behind the bar. "I think your break's over."

"You the boss, now? I think you can handle the bar, bro."

Scott glared at Alex and cracked his knuckles.

Alex grabbed another glass and swallowed its contents. It was the Icelandic stuff again.

Bella laughed. "This is fun. Wanna go somewhere else?"

"Don't you have to work or something?" Alex grabbed another glass and drank its contents. It was too sweet. He cringed.

She snickered and then glanced around. "There's what? Like three customers. Scott's got this."

Alex looked over at her brother again. He shot Alex a deadly glare. "Maybe I should just go home."

"You planning to drive?"

"I'm sure not gonna walk."

"Can I see your keys?"

"Why?" Alex asked.

"I just wanna see them."

He knew where this was going. Cole never let him drive away drunk, either. Alex handed them to her. "Now what?"

"I live in the loft upstairs. Sleep it off." She held his gaze.

Scott came over. "I'll call him a taxi." He turned to Alex. "Don't worry. We won't have your car towed. It would suck to have that happen twice in one day, right? You can come get it later."

"Go away before I fire you," Bella said.

"Do you know who he is?" Scott exclaimed.

She looked him over. "He's so hot, I don't really care. Go away."

"He's Alex Mercer."

Her eyes widened. "Wait. Macy's little brother? Why didn't I make the connection before?"

Alex felt about two inches tall. "I should get going."

Bella shook her head. "No, you shouldn't."

Scott's nostrils flared. "Yeah, you should."

"That girl in the miniskirt is waving you over," Bella said, nodding toward a girl who was busy texting.

Alex's phone rang. It was Zoey.

Scott grabbed the phone out of his hand and accepted the call. "Hey, Zoey. Alex needs you to pick him up at Bar Bella over by Fifth and Forest Drive." He paused and laughed. "Yep, he sure is. Just come get him." He ended the call and handed the phone back to Alex.

Alex glared at him and put his phone back.

Bella got up and picked up the tray. "Stop being a jerk and do your job."

"I am doing my job—protecting my kid sister."

"Well, I wish you'd stop."

"He's a criminal!"

"Why? Because his kid's missing?"

"Because he was involved."

Alex slammed his fist on the table. "I was not!"

Scott stepped closer. "Then why does everyone say you were?"

"Because they're stupid." Alex raised his fist.

Bella grabbed Scott's arm and dragged him away while balancing the tray of empty shot glasses. She turned to Alex and mouthed, "He's off tomorrow."

Furious

ZOEY SLAMMED THE car door shut and stared at the bar, shaking her head. Sure enough, Alex's car was near the front. He gets released from jail, and that's where he goes?

A cold breeze blew by, giving her the chills. Zoey zipped her coat as far as it would go and headed inside. A guy with shoulder-length hair and piercings everywhere made eye contact and then flicked a nod toward the other end of the bar.

Zoey glanced over to see Alex sitting with Bella Martin, who had been the lead in every school play in middle school and high school. She was just as pretty as always, and she appeared to be quite happy talking with Alex.

Jealousy ran through Zoey. She tried shoving it aside—why should she care? She was supposed to be mourning her broken engagement, not worrying about her ex-boyfriend. Yet she wanted to smack the smile right off Bella's face.

She took a deep breath and walked over to their table. "Let's go, Alex."

He looked up at her, his eyes bloodshot and with dark circles underneath. He looked like crap, but then again, she probably didn't look any better than he did.

"Want to join us?" he asked.

"No, it's time to get you home."

Alex turned to Bella. "She's no fun, either."

Anger tore through Zoey. "Fine. Get yourself home. Hope you

don't hurt yourself." She spun around, hoping he would chase after her, but also hating that she wanted him to.

"Wait, Zo."

She spun around.

He stumbled out of the booth. "Don't go."

"We have more important things to do. If you'd rather stay here and get more plastered, be my guest."

"You're right." He turned back to Bella. "It's okay if I leave my car here?"

"As long as you need to."

Zoey held out her hand. "Why don't you give me the keys?"

Alex gestured toward Bella. "She has them."

"I'll take them." She extended her palm toward the brunette.

Bella shrugged and dropped the keys onto Zoey's hand. "Let me just run his tab, and then you guys can get going."

"Whatever. Come on, Alex." They followed Bella to the counter, and then a few minutes later, climbed into Zoey's car.

"Nice wheels." Alex closed the door.

"What were you thinking?" she exploded.

"I just meant I like your car." His words slurred horribly.

She rolled her eyes. "I mean in there. The bar. Getting yourself drunk."

"Just wanted a drink."

"*A* drink?"

"Fine. A few. Then Bella offered me some shots. That girl can hold her liquor."

Zoey bit back a rude comment. "We have to focus on getting Ariana back, and you go and get yourself drunk and arrested."

"You mean arrested and then drunk."

"Alex, what's wrong with you?"

He stared at her. "You're pretty when you're mad. Always have been."

She clenched her jaw, but part of her enjoyed the compliment from him. "Would you focus?"

"You're prettier than Bella, you know."

"Don't try to distract me."

"I'm not."

"Tell me what's going on, or I'm going to drive you to your parents and have you tell them."

"You think I'm worried what Mommy and Daddy think of me?"

"Isn't that why you moved away?"

"That was because I didn't want *you* thinking I was a loser." His face paled. "Forget I said that. I didn't say it."

Zoey stared at him. "You moved away because of me?"

"It's more complicated than that."

"You were worried what I thought about you?" Both her anger and defensiveness were melting faster than she cared to admit.

"Can we just go? I don't want to talk about anything right now."

"Well, we need to."

"Actually, we don't."

They stared each other down until Alex looked away. "I was close to finding something on Flynn."

"What do you mean?"

"The FBI is so focused on that Sanchez fake, they won't look into the dude who actually took Ari. If they're going to take him seriously, it's up to me to find the evidence."

"And getting drunk is supposed to help how, exactly?"

He folded his arms. "It's not, but I can't go near Flynn or his work or his house without going to jail again. That's why I went in for a drink."

"Why didn't you just call me?"

Alex shrugged.

"Talk to me."

"About what?"

"Us."

"Didn't we talk about that over breakfast? And besides, what 'us' is there? We haven't been together in years, and you're engaged. I blew it." He looked down and played with a scab on his finger.

She felt bad for him, but wasn't going to let him off the hook. "You blew it long before I got engaged."

"I *know*. I should've been there when you left for college, but I couldn't go back in time and change that."

"No, but you could've called me. You had plenty of chances to do that. Same phone number."

"You deserve better, anyway." That felt like a punch in the gut.

"I don't, Alex."

He turned and stared at her. "What?"

"You're the only one I ever wanted." She frowned. "I waited for a long time, hoping you'd call."

"So, I screwed that up, too."

"Yep."

"It doesn't matter now. You've got Kellen, and he'll give you everything I can't."

Zoey held up her ringless hand. "We called it off."

His mouth fell open. "Why?"

Because he could see what she couldn't. "It's complicated."

Alex tilted his head and his brows came closer together, the way they always did when he was deep in thought. He was as adorable now as he always had been. It brought her back to happier times. How many times had that one look led to toe-curling, passionate kisses?

Her breath hitched. She swallowed—the sound seemed to echo all around the small car.

"How complicated?" Alex whispered.

He's drunk, Zoey reminded herself. *He lost Ariana.*

But his big, almost-gray eyes seemed to scream how sorry he

was for everything—that it had all been a big mistake that he would take back in a heartbeat if he could.

Or was that just what she wanted him to say?

The air was so thick, Zoey felt like she could swim in it.

"I should get you back home."

Disappointment covered his face. "I can't face my parents like this, Zo."

"You want to go with me and face *my* parents?"

He put his face in his palms. "I just keep screwing up. I can't seem to stop. Worst of all, you're here to see. What am I going to do?"

"You should probably go home and sleep this off."

He sighed. "Yeah, you're right. Take me home. What's the worst my parents can do to me?"

Picture

~

A LEX WOKE WITH a splitting headache. Clementine purred next to him. It had never sounded louder. Moaning, he rolled over and pulled a blanket over his face to block the filtered sunlight and the loud purring.

Memories of the previous night flooded his mind—getting arrested and then drunk. Everything after going to some random bar was a blur. Something about Zoey. Oh, no… What had he done? Did she have his keys? Or did he have them?

He rolled over again, this time with his stomach lurching. How had he gotten home? A turquoise car?

Zoey's car. *She'd* seen him plastered. What had he said? He had a tendency to let his mouth run when he drank too much, and given how he felt right then, he'd drank too much and then kept going.

Knock, knock. It sounded like a jackhammer next to his head.

"Alex, are you awake?" called his mom from behind the door.

"Stop being so loud," he muttered.

The door creaked open. "How are you feeling?"

"That depends."

"On what?"

On whatever happened the night before. "Any updates on Ari?"

"Not that I'm aware of. The same news is being recycled everywhere I've looked. I was hoping you'd heard something from the captain."

"How close are we to Halloween?"

"It's today, honey."

Alex sat bolt-upright. "Today?" The light was like tiny daggers to his eyeballs.

She frowned and nodded.

He swore. "How did I not know?"

"You had a busy day yesterday."

"Can you blame me?"

Mom put her hand on his. "No, I can't, and I'd be a hypocrite to judge."

He arched a brow. "You?"

"I'll tell you about it later. Why don't you give the captain a call?"

"Can you get me some coffee and aspirin?"

She patted his hand. "Sure." She sniffed the air. "A shower might not be a bad idea, either."

"Thanks, Mom." He untwisted himself from his blankets and threw them to the side as she left the room. He stared at some bruises on his wrists. Must have been from the handcuffs.

His phone lay on the floor next to his desk. The screen flashed. He must've missed a call or text.

Each step he took made his head hurt more, but he made his way to the phone. There were missed calls and texts from the lawyer, Nick, Zoey, and Bella.

He pulled on a shirt and returned Nick's call.

"Where have you been?" Nick exclaimed. "I thought we were going to talk after you were released."

"We were?"

"Did you talk with Ralph?"

"Who?"

"Weiss, your attorney."

"Not yet."

"He got all your charges dropped. The arrest is going to be taken off your record—I hope you appreciate how huge that is."

Alex was sure he would when the pounding in his head stopped and his stomach settled down. "I do. Thanks for finding him, Nick."

"I have more good news. We released Sanchez a couple hours ago. Everyone is focused on finding lakes that match the cold cases in the area."

"Oh, good. Found any yet?"

"There are a few. Probably more with as much water as we have around here. We're excluding ones he's already used."

"Why?"

"Because it doesn't appear he's used any more than once."

"Doesn't mean he won't. What should I do?"

"Lay low. Our entire team is working on this, finally in the right direction. There are other forces helping us, too."

"Okay. If you find something, can you let me know?"

"Are you going to try to interfere?"

Alex scowled. "I want to help."

"I'll keep you in the loop. Stay near your phone." The call ended.

Knock, knock.

Alex covered his head. "Just come in."

Mom came in with a steaming mug, a bottle of painkillers, and a plate of toast. "Hopefully, this helps. I'm going over to the hospital for a while. Dad's in his office, updating his blog with the latest on Ariana."

"Okay." He sipped the coffee. "Thanks for all this."

She squeezed his arm. "I just wish I could do more. I love you, Alex."

He wrapped his arms around her, and she squeezed him. They held the embrace for a few moments before she stepped back. She gave him a sad smile before leaving the room.

Alex swallowed a couple pills with the coffee and then ate the toast, finding that it helped with his stomach. He emptied the mug and then headed for the shower. His mind raced and his heart felt like it would shatter.

Would they find Ariana in time? Halloween had come too soon, and the FBI had taken entirely too long to focus in the right direction. It better not be too late, or someone would pay. Alex would see to that personally.

His phone went off. He groaned, but rinsed off and got out of the shower.

A missed text from a blocked caller.

Alex's pulse pounded. Was Flynn taunting him or giving him a clue?

He wiped his hands on the towel and grabbed his phone.

Flynn had sent a photo. If it was a picture of Ariana hurt, Alex would lose it. Part of him didn't want to look. But he had to.

His hand shook as he slid his finger around the screen to see the image. He accidentally clicked on another app. Alex closed it and went over to his texts.

There was the picture.

Of a lake.

His heart crashed to the ground.

A thousand responses ran through his head, but he couldn't text any of them back to Flynn. Not to a blocked number.

He stared at the image. It looked familiar, but then again, he'd seen hundreds of lakes.

Alex forwarded the picture to Nick. It was the right thing to do. The professionals knew what they were doing.

Thwart

~

N ICK STARED AT the picture Alex had just texted him. Had Alex found it online? Why hadn't he texted any information along with the picture?

He called Alex.

"What's this picture?" he asked.

"It's from a blocked number again. Flynn's back at it."

"But why would he give you a picture of where he's taking Ari?"

"Who cares?" Alex exclaimed. "We just need to find it and get there."

"You don't know anything else?"

"No. I got it and forwarded it to you."

"Okay, good. If you get anything else, do the same."

"I will."

"I'm going to let the team know about this. In the meantime, see if you can find it online. The more people we have on this, the better."

"Are you going to put it on social media? Someone might recognize it. It might be faster, but given my 'popularity,' I shouldn't be the one to post it."

"I don't want the kidnapper to know we have the information yet. I'll see what Williams thinks. Talk to you soon." Nick ended the call and emailed the image to the computer, where he printed it onto paper and brought it to the main room.

Everyone went to work immediately, trying to find the location of the lake. Unfortunately, nobody recognized it from the picture.

Nick went back to his office to do his own research. They didn't have much time. This time tomorrow would be too late. They'd be searching for a body. His chest constricted at the thought, and his mind immediately went to his kids. If anything ever happened to them, he didn't know what he would do. It was hard enough with them living so far away now, but at least he knew they were healthy and happy.

He checked the time. It was early enough that if he called now, he could talk to them before they left for school. Nick closed his office door behind him and called their new landline number, hoping to avoid speaking with Corrine, his ex-wife.

"Hello?" asked a chipper female too old to be a kid, but younger than Corrine. Then it hit him—it was the kids' new nanny. The one Nick was paying heavily for. He couldn't remember her name.

"This is Nick. Are my kids there?"

"Oh, hi, Nick. This is Riley. The kids say you're on that famous kidnapping case. Is it true?"

"Yeah. Are they there?"

"Ava already left, but the other two are here. Hold on." Shuffling noises sounded on the other end.

"Daddy!" came Hanna's voice. "Guess what? We get to wear our costumes to school."

Nick's heart warmed, hearing his youngest's voice. "That's great, honey."

"They just can't be scary. Parker's mad about that, but I'm a good fairy, so I get to wear it all day and then tonight, too! And we're going to have a party in our class. We even get to exchange candy and eat cupcakes."

"Wow, it sounds like you're going to have a great time."

"Best day ever!" she squealed. "I just wish you could be here."

"Me, too, baby. As soon as daddy's big case is over, I'm going to make sure we have a weekend together."

"Yes! Will it be a long one? Will we get to miss school? Please say we can miss school."

Nick laughed. "I'll see what I can do. Is Parker there? I'd like to say hi before you guys leave for school."

"Yeah. Parker!" Hanna yelled into the phone. "Dad's on the phone. Get over here!"

He held the phone out until he heard his son's voice.

"Hey, Dad."

"What's wrong?" Nick asked.

"I can't wear my costume. They say devils are too scary for the little kids. How stupid is that?"

"Don't you have anything else you can wear?"

"Nothing cool. Mom said I could wear my Mickey ears, but that's so lame unless you're actually at Disney World, you know? Everyone has them there. I said I'd be a bloody Mickey, but then we're back to scary."

"What about your karate uniform?"

"The bus is almost here. Gotta go." The line went dead without so much as a goodbye.

Nick sat in the chair, his heart heavy. He was missing out on so much. The only way he'd see any of their costumes was in a picture, and that would be after pestering them. He cursed Corrine under his breath for moving the kids so far away.

He went to his computer to try to find the lake. That reminded him of why he'd called in the first place. At least they were safe and sound, with their biggest worry being about costumes.

Nick did a quick online search for local lakes. A travel planning site had a list of lakes with pictures, but none of them looked like the one Alex had sent. It appeared to have been taken from inside woods, given the tree branches along the edges, and probably not from a place most people would take a picture. That was going to make it harder to locate.

Wait. What if the image had the location embedded in the data? He should have thought of that sooner. Nick right-clicked the image, but found no data. The sender probably knew how to turn that off. It was always the first thing Nick did when he got a new phone.

He went to his phone and scrolled through his contacts. He knew a couple guys who were experts with photos. They would know how to find any information. He was about to press the call button when a call came in.

It was from Alex.

Nick accepted the call. "Did you find something?"

"You'd better look online. I've been framed again."

"What is it now?" Nick wanted to bang his head on the desk.

"It's a fake picture of me digging what looks like a grave."

Nick released a string of profanities and threw a pad of paper across the office. "Get down here *now*."

Disbelief

~

Z OEY HELD HER ringing phone, trying to decide whether to answer it. It was Kellen, and she really didn't feel like talking to him. She was a mess of conflicting emotions after talking with Alex the night before. Knowing that it was Halloween only compounded everything.

Finally, she decided just to answer it. She accepted the call and sat on Ariana's bed. "Hello?"

"Have you been online?" Kellen asked.

"I'm still trying to avoid it." *And you.* But that wasn't working. "Why? What's going on?"

"It doesn't look good for Alex."

She froze. "What do you mean?"

"There's a picture of him pulling a body into a white van. I assume it's fake, but people are saying there's no signs of it being altered."

Zoey's mouth dropped. She grabbed Ariana's stuffed elephant and held it close.

"And people are saying he's been seen at the police station. I think he's under arrest again."

She felt like she'd been punched in the gut.

Through the silence hanging between them, Zoey could hear Kellen's silent question—Do you really choose him over me?

"Thanks for letting me know," she said, feeling in a daze.

"I just thought you'd like to know. Do they still think today's the day?"

"Yeah," she whispered.

"Are you okay, Zo?"

"Okay?" she exclaimed. "How could I be okay? Ariana might be killed today!" The reality of it crushed her. Tears blurred her vision and she crumpled on the bed. The air crushed her.

"I'm coming over."

Zoey couldn't respond.

"You're at your parents' still, right?" Kellen asked.

She muttered something resembling a word.

"I'll be right there."

Zoey shuddered and then gave into the sobs. She curled into a ball, clinging to the stuffed animal, and wailed. No one had even come close to finding Ariana, and now the countdown was a matter of hours until that sick piece of trash took her life.

How dare he? He had no right. He hadn't given her life—he'd had nothing to do with that precious little girl until snatching her from everyone who loved her. Rage ran through her, equal in strength to the overwhelming depression.

She screamed at the unfairness of it all. The rest of the world was going on like nothing was wrong, and it could be Ari's last.

How would she survive? What would she do?

Hands rested on her back. Zoey turned to see Kenji sitting next to her, his eyes red and his skin tear-stained.

"We're all feeling it," he said.

Zoey threw herself against him, wrapping her arms around him. "Oh, Dad."

He squeezed her. "I know."

"How are we going to get her back?"

"The search team has a new clue they're looking into."

"New?" She sniffled. "Since when?"

"This morning. I don't know much, but apparently it's pretty big."

"Who told you?" Zoey sat back and pulled some hair from her eyes.

"Chad called. Alex is… in a predicament, though."

"You mean he's in jail."

"He's being held for questioning. No charges have been filed."

She gasped for air. "But they think the new clue will help them find Ari?"

"That's what they say. I sure hope so."

"What if they don't?"

He shook his head. "We can't let ourselves think about that, kiddo."

Zoey jumped up. "I have to get out of here. Call me if there's any news."

"Okay. Where are you going?"

"Out." She ran from the room, down the stairs, and grabbed her purse on the way outside. Her mind raced. She never knew life could be so crushing. It killed her that she didn't know what tomorrow would bring. It would either be the happiest day of her life—with Ariana returned home—or the worst day.

Zoey climbed into her car and started it. She didn't know where she was going. She didn't want to be anywhere. If only she could crawl somewhere and cease to exist.

Since she couldn't do that, she needed to do something that would matter. The only thing she could think of was going to the station. That was where they were working to find Ariana. Surely, they would take volunteers. They had to. A little girl's life was on the line.

She pulled onto the road and headed for the station. The worst they could do was tell her no. And then she would tell them off. She wanted to be part of the rescue efforts.

Zoey pulled into the station, realizing she couldn't remember how she'd gotten there. She'd been so lost in her thoughts.

Inside, it was loud and busy. People filled the waiting room and the buzz of conversation was overwhelming. She went over to the desk. "I want to help with the rescue efforts."

The lady waved toward the busy waiting room. "Join the club."

"No! I'm Ariana's mom."

The woman studied Zoey. "We told your family to wait at home. Someone will call you as soon as—"

"I'm not going to sit around. It's Halloween. We all know what that means."

"Well, have a seat. I'll let Special Agent Williams know you're here."

Zoey glowered at the woman. "That's not good enough."

"Look, we're doing everything we can. All you're doing right now is distracting me from what I need to do."

"Fine. Where's Alex?"

She gave Zoey an exasperated look. "I don't know. You'll have to speak with the captain about him."

"And where would I find him?"

"That way." She pointed down the hall. "Can't miss his office. It's the biggest in the building."

Zoey stormed down the hall, still not sure what she was going to do. She froze mid-step when she heard Alex's voice. It was coming from behind a closed door. She turned and stared.

A super-tall man in a suit stopped in front of the door and gave her a questioning glance. "Can I help you?"

"I'm looking for Alex."

"He can't see anyone."

"Who are you?" Zoey asked.

"His attorney. Excuse me."

"I'm his... uh... I'm Ariana's mom."

The attorney's eyes widened. "Well, come on in. Maybe you can help us out."

Held

~

Alex prepared himself for another long discussion with Ralph, the large lawyer who now wanted to be called by his first name. His eyes nearly popped out of his head when Zoey came in.

"What are you doing here?" he asked.

Her eyes were red, puffy, and tear-stained.

"Are you okay?"

She shook her head. "It's Halloween."

"I know, and I'm stuck in here." He clenched his fists. "But why are you here?"

Ralph came in and closed the door behind them.

"What's going on?" Alex demanded. "Why is Zoey here?"

"I found her in the hall."

Alex turned back to Zoey. "Why?"

"I need to do something."

"So, you came *here*?"

"This is where everyone is looking for her."

"Yeah, I guess."

"What's the deal with that picture going around?"

Alex covered his face with his palms and took a deep breath. "I've been framed again."

"Again?"

"It's a long story, and we don't have time for it."

Zoey turned to Ralph. "So, Alex is just going to stay here while Ariana's life hangs in the balance?"

"Until the photo experts can prove it's a fake. They say it's a really good one if it is fake."

"It *is*." Alex slammed his fists on the table. "I'm innocent." He turned and glared at the two-way mirror. "When are you guys finally going to start looking at the guy who actually took her? Flynn Myer is your guy! Not me. Him!"

"Take it easy," Ralph said. "I don't even think anyone's in there."

Alex clenched his jaw. "I'll take it easy after Ariana's back safe and sound."

Ralph nodded. "I'll be right back. I'm going to find Fleshman." He left, leaving the door open a crack.

"What are we going to do?" Zoey's voice cracked. "Time is flying by today."

Alex stared at the door. "Look."

"What?" Zoey turned to see. "I don't see anything."

"He left it open. It's my opportunity to get out of here and find Ariana."

"You can't leave."

"I'm not under arrest."

"You probably will be if you take off."

"This is a waste of time. Why do you think the picture was done? To keep me out of the way."

Zoey glanced between him and the door. "Still, I don't think it's a good idea. You were just in jail."

"But if I find Ari and save her, who cares if I go to jail?"

Her expression softened. "You'd really do that?"

"Of course I would," he snapped.

She frowned. "Sorry. I didn't mean—"

"I get it. I'm the absent jerk dad, and I know all too well how you feel about them."

Zoey flinched. "Alex, that's not what I meant."

"Yeah, it is and I deserve it. But first, I need to save our daughter."

She opened her mouth, but then closed it. "I'll tell them you're in the bathroom. Give you some more time."

He nodded a thanks and hurried for the door.

"Wait. I'm coming with you."

"You're my cover."

Zoey shook her head. "I'm going with you."

"It's going to get dangerous."

"I don't care. Ariana needs us."

Alex didn't want to see her get hurt, but she was so stubborn, she'd never back down. "Okay." He pulled the door open and peeked into the hall. The only cops out there were distracted, not paying him any attention. He gestured for Zoey to follow him, and he crept out.

No one turned around. He hurried down the hall, unnoticed.

"Hey!" called a deep male voice from behind.

Heart thundering, Alex spun around.

A cop spoke into a phone. "You need to tell me what you know, Cal."

Alex breathed a sigh of relief and continued his way. He passed the front desk, where the annoying clerk was busy arguing with a bald dude who had more gold in his teeth than around his neck—and that was saying something.

He and Zoey rushed out into the parking lot.

"My car's over there," she said.

Alex shook his head. "We'll take mine. I don't know what's going to happen, and I don't want yours getting scratched or dented. Mine's already crap."

"If you're sure."

"Where's that bar?"

"Follow me." They darted across the parking lot, down the

street, and finally crossed another road. A renovated pizza place now had a sign reading Bar Bella.

Alex dug into his pockets and found the keychain. He ran over to the passenger side, unlocked it, and ran to the driver's side. They both got inside and slammed the old doors.

"Where are we going?" Zoey asked.

"To this lake." He found the image on his phone and handed it to her.

She glanced down and up at him. "Ingalls Lake?"

"You know where that is?" he exclaimed.

"Yeah, I went there a few times with Summer Adman in high school. Her grandparents live there. I'd recognize it anywhere. It's tiny, but has this fun little island in the middle. Where'd you get the picture?"

"That's from a blocked number. Just like the other ones that have been threatening me."

"What are you waiting for? We're at least an hour away—if there's no traffic."

"You'd better call Nick and tell him that's where they are." Alex pulled out of the spot, tires squealing.

Boat

~

*C*LICK. *CLICK. CLICK.*

The door swung open.

Ariana tried to bury herself into the corner, not that it would do her any good. It wasn't like she could disappear into the walls and get away.

Lloyd stepped in, his eyes wild and his clothes disheveled. "Come on."

"What?"

"Get up. We're leaving."

"Where are we going?"

"Stop talking. Hurry up."

Ariana rose, trembling. Were they going back to the house with the bedroom, or maybe going somewhere worse? She didn't even want to think about the things he'd told her before.

He swaggered over to her and wrapped his hand around her arm, squeezing tight.

"Time to get this over with, Jan. Then we'll have to wait until next year."

She swallowed. It didn't sound like they were going back to the bedroom.

He yanked on her arm and pulled her through a small, one-story home with peeling paint and cobwebs everywhere. The rest of the house made the room she'd just left seem nice.

"Do you know what today is?" Lloyd asked. He stopped and

stared into her eyes.

Ariana shook her head, afraid to speak.

"Halloween."

A lump formed in her throat. Usually, her favorite day of the year. Not this time.

"Remember what happened the Halloween when you died?"

She shook her head.

"Answer me!"

Ariana gulped. "I snuck out of the house."

"You sure did. And what did that get you?"

"Killed," she whispered.

"And you snuck out again a few days ago, right?"

Tears stung her eyes. She nodded and sniffled.

"And what did that get you?" He pulled her outside. It was growing dark, but still pretty light. The air was freezing, especially with no jacket. Woods surrounded them and the tree branches swayed back and forth.

She opened her mouth, but only a squeak came out.

Lloyd yanked on her arm again. "Time to relive the past *again*. I'm so sick of this. Why can't we get it right? We almost had it this time!"

Ariana's shoulders slumped.

"Stand here." He shoved her toward the dirty house that looked like it had been white at one time, a very long time ago.

She stumbled to keep her balance and tried to watch him from the corner of her eye. He was doing something with his phone. It appeared he was texting. "What are you doing?"

"Did I say you could talk?"

"I just want to know."

Lloyd grumbled. "I'm arguing with someone, if you must know."

"Who?"

He pushed her closer to the house. "I need silence." He slid his finger around the screen faster and then put it in his coat. "Let's go."

Ariana stepped back.

"Did I say to move?"

"You said—"

Lloyd grabbed her arm and dragged her back. She managed to catch her footing and walk as he guided her, squeezing her flesh. They went around the house and came to a truck with a boat trailer attached. The boat was newly made, unpainted, and rough. It smelled like sawdust.

He pulled the green tarp off the top. "Get in."

She gave him a double take. "In there? While you drive the truck?"

"I'm sure not letting you ride in front with me."

"What about seat belts?"

Lloyd shoved her against the boat. Tiny splinters poked her face and arms. "Get in."

Ariana didn't see a way to climb inside. "How?"

"Do I have to do everything for you? Just get in!"

She reached her hands up to the top of the boat and stepped up on the edge of the trailer. Somehow, she managed to push herself up and throw one leg over the side, then the other. He gave her another shove, and she tumbled inside, rolling to the bottom, scratching herself on more tiny slivers.

Ariana pulled herself to standing. "Please don't."

He ignored her, focused on something outside the boat.

A small flash of light came from inside the woods. Inside them? She stared, curious how a light could come from the woods. It wasn't like the lightening the other night.

Lloyd pulled the tarp over her, forcing her down.

"No!" she cried.

"Shut up. I'm not happy about this, either."

Ariana's breathing grew labored. All she could smell was freshly cut wood and plastic from the tarp. Would she run out of air in there? It was already so hard to breathe. How long until they reached wherever they were going?

Gravel crunched under Lloyd's footsteps. The truck door opened and then shut. The engine roared to life. Gravel sprayed out as the tires moved underneath. Ariana jerked back, hitting her head on the boat. She crawled to the back and leaned against the little wall, hoping that would help to steady her.

She bounced around as Lloyd drove over what felt like every rock and branch in the woods. If whatever he had planned didn't kill her, then the ride might. She tried pulling out splinters, but each time she got one out, she would get slammed into the side of the boat and get at least five more.

After what felt like forever, the brakes squealed. They stopped moving. The truck door opened and shut.

"We're here."

Race

A LEX SQUINTED, LOOKING for the turnoff.

"It's almost there," Zoey said. "Just past the boulder on the right."

He saw the rock, but no road to turn down. He slowed, earning himself a honk from the impatient man behind him on the busy two-lane road. Finally, the gravel road came into view, hidden by the boulder. He slammed on his brakes and turned.

The man honked as he drove past, giving Alex obscene gestures.

"How far now?" Alex asked.

"I think a half an hour on this dirt road."

"A half an hour?" Alex exclaimed. The narrow, bumpy gravel road made it difficult for him to go faster than twenty miles an hour.

"There's a reason not many people know about Ingalls Lake."

"Apparently," he grumbled.

"Plus, I think it might be private."

"Have you heard back from Nick?"

She held up his phone and slid his finger around the screen. "Nope. Nothing since he confirmed sending people out this way."

"They're, what, twenty minutes behind us?"

"I'm not sure. Nick said he needed to debrief everyone. I have no idea how long that would take."

"Better not be long. I hope they don't arrive with sirens blaring."

"I'm sure they know what they're doing."

Alex glanced around for signs of Ariana or anything else that would indicate they were going in the right direction. What if the picture of the lake had only been to throw them off?

He couldn't let himself think like that. Not now.

"You've got a new text."

"What does it say?" he asked.

Zoey didn't respond.

"What?" he demanded.

"It's a picture of Ariana."

Alex slammed on the breaks. He grabbed the phone from Zoey's hand. The photo showed a rudimentary wooden boat with Ariana peeking over the top. Her hair was sticking out in all directions and she had on a torn t-shirt.

"Was that taken here?" he demanded.

"I don't know."

Another text came in. This time, it was a picture of the same boat, but showed a man covering it with tarp.

"What is it?" Zoey exclaimed.

Alex zoomed in on the picture. The man's profile—it was Flynn. There was no doubt about it. Hands shaking with both anger and trepidation, he showed her.

Zoey gasped. "Is Ariana in there?"

"That would be the assumption." He looked at the picture again, and then forwarded both images to Nick.

See? It's Flynn with Ariana.

The phone rang. It was Nick.

"Where did you get those? Did you find them?"

"They were sent from a blocked number."

"We're almost there," Nick said. "The local sheriff was out at the lake, but he didn't see anything. Where are you?"

"Just about to the lake."

"Don't do anything stupid, Alex."

"I'll do whatever it takes to save Ariana." He balanced the phone with his shoulder and hit the gas, sending both his and Zoey's heads against the seats.

"We're almost there," Nick repeated. "If you spook Flynn, he might do something rash. You're better off waiting for us. We know how to deal with these types."

"I've dealt with arrogant criminals myself." More than one had ended up in the hospital after threatening Alex's buddy.

"Just wait for us."

"Sure."

"Alex." Nick's tone held a warning.

"Gotta focus on driving." Alex ended the call.

"What was that about?" Zoey's face was pale.

"He doesn't want us to do anything. Probably has to say that to cover his butt." He drove over an exposed root, sending them up off the seats. "Stay buckled in."

"Don't worry. I'm familiar with your driving."

Alex ignored the jab and put more pressure on the gas pedal. "How much farther?"

"We're almost there, but if you don't slow down, all this noise is going to tip him off."

"Right." He eased off the gas, even though everything in him wanted to punch it.

"What's your plan?" Zoey asked, her voice quiet.

"Drown the bastard."

"And go back to jail?"

"Nobody would blame me. He's killed thirty girls, remember? If someone doesn't stop him, he'll probably kill another thirty."

They sat in silence the rest of the way. After about ten minutes, the road ended. A few empty parking spots sat off to either side and the dirt sloped down into the water.

"Is there someplace else he would've parked?" Alex asked.

"Sure. There are half a dozen houses with property around the lake. He could've easily used one of their driveways."

Alex turned the car off where he was and studied the lake. Adrenaline pulsed through his body. "There they are!"

Swim

~

ALEX STARED AT the little boat, mostly hidden behind the island. He wouldn't have seen it if he hadn't been looking so hard. He got out and inched toward the shore. Zoey approached him.

"I'm going to swim out there."

"Are you crazy?" She whispered as though that would keep Flynn from hearing them from their distance.

"Maybe."

"The water's freezing. You'll never make it."

"Thanks for the vote of confidence." He slid off his jacket and threw it on the wet ground.

"Summer's grandparents have a rowboat."

"That doesn't help us." Alex narrowed his eyes, trying to see if Ariana was still in the boat. He slid off his shoes and socks, throwing them on top of his coat.

"Their home isn't too far away. I know right where the boat is."

"Great, you get it. I'm going in." He pulled off his shirt, adding it to his pile, and shivered.

"Alex."

"Go." He unbuttoned his jeans.

"You're going skinny dipping?" she exclaimed. "You think you're going to fight off a serial in the nude?"

Alex unzipped and pulled off the pants, kicking them onto the pile. "No. I'm leaving my boxers on. I need to remove as much resistance as I can."

"Be careful."

He stepped closer to the water and braced himself before running into it. The biting cold went straight to his bones and almost stopped him in his tracks. Almost. He pressed on, running until the murky water reached his waist. He pressed his hands together and dove in, ignoring the utter chill on his skin.

Alex swam, feeling winded almost immediately. He kept going. There was no way he was going to stop until Ariana was safe and Flynn was either dead or in police custody, he didn't care which.

The cold made it hard to keep going. He could barely feel his legs. Alex stopped and treaded water for a minute, trying to catch his breath. In the woods, Zoey ran down a trail.

He glanced over toward the boat, but didn't see it. In a moment of panic, he looked around, nearly going under. The corner of the boat stuck out from the edge of the island. He was almost there.

"You can do it, Mercer." He gasped for air. "You have to."

A commotion sounded on the island. Two figures appeared, the smaller running from the other.

Ariana was still alive.

Blessed relief ran through Alex, followed by a renewed burst of energy. He took a deep breath and went under, swimming with all his might. The island was so close—Ari was so close.

He pushed forward. Water gushed into his nose, burning and stinging. He blew it out and kept going.

Finally, his fingers touched land. He'd made it.

He reached his feet down and felt the sand on the bottom. He stood and walked onto the land. The air was even colder than the frigid water. The cotton boxers did nothing for him.

Alex shivered and shook off what excess water he could. Ariana screamed from somewhere to the right.

Fury tore through him. He ran in the direction of her voice. Sharp rocks and twigs dug into the soles of his feet. He ignored the pain and pressed on.

Ariana was so close. He wouldn't let anything get in his way.

She screamed again, this time closer. He turned slightly, his heart nearly beating out of his chest. His lungs burned. Something dug into his right foot. He cried out in surprise.

"What was that?" Flynn asked.

Alex was closer than he thought. He raised his foot and pulled out a piece of broken glass. Blood gushed from the wound.

Sirens blared in the distance.

"They couldn't have found me," Flynn said.

A helicopter sounded from not far away.

"Ow!" Ariana cried. "That hurts!"

Struggle

B LIND RAGE RIPPED through Alex. He ran toward their voices, jumping over roots and rocks while getting dirt and mud in his cut.

They came into view, Flynn first. Alex wanted to tear him from limb to limb. The sirens and helicopters grew louder. They were too far away. Flynn could easily kill Ariana before they reached the island.

He ran over, pausing behind a tree. Ariana now wore a costume. She had on cat ears and wore all black. At least she had more clothes on than she'd had in the picture he'd received.

Flynn shoved Ariana against a tree. "Behave now."

Alex dashed toward them, no time to think or plan.

Ariana's eyes widened as she saw him. Flynn's back was to him. Alex put a finger to his mouth. She nodded.

Alex grabbed Flynn's shoulders and slammed into him. Flynn let go of Ariana and fell to the ground, taking Alex with him. Branches and pine cones dug into Alex's side.

"Run!" he told Ariana.

He punched Flynn in the side of the head. Ariana spun around and ran.

Flynn rolled over and grabbed his neck, digging into his flesh and squeezing. "You should've left it alone."

Alex gagged, unable to respond. He kneed Flynn in the crotch, and his hold on Alex's neck loosened. Alex scrambled to his feet and ran in the direction Ariana had gone, ignoring the pain in his feet.

The sirens and helicopter grew louder. A light shone down on the far side of the tiny island.

Something hard hit Alex in the back of his head. He stumbled and turned around, rubbing the knot that was already forming at the base of his skull.

Flynn ran at him. "You need to leave!"

"You need to give me back Ariana!"

"No, you need to leave Jan alone!"

Flynn threw a fist-sized rock at Alex. He ducked and flinched, barely missing getting struck in the forehead. Should he attack Flynn or look for Ariana? While he hesitated, Flynn took advantage of his delay and ran at him.

Alex balled his fist and punched him across the face. Flynn's head flew back, blood flew out from his nose. Alex spun around and ran. The whole island seemed lit up—police lights shone from where he'd left his clothes and the spotlight from above kept sweeping the area.

He glanced back to see Flynn running after him, covering more ground because he had shoes and clothes—and a knife.

Alex swore and sped up. "Ariana!"

"Stop!" Flynn yelled, sounding even closer.

Alex darted around trees, jumped over branches and oversized rocks. Something sounded in the water.

"Alex!"

His heart sank. It was Zoey. He spun around. She stood near the shore. He glanced back—Flynn was now running in her direction. He ran after him and kicked the back of his knee. Flynn stumbled, but didn't fall.

Alex grabbed the back of his shirt, pulled on the collar. Flynn gagged and flailed his arms.

"Zo, Ariana's that way." Alex nodded his head in the direction she'd gone.

Zoey burst into a run. "Ari!"

Alex slammed Flynn into a tree. "It's over."

"It's not. It never will be."

"Shut up."

Footsteps sounded from not too far away, followed by shouts and bouncing lights from flashlights.

"Over here!" Alex called.

Nick and two other cops appeared around some bushes.

"I've got him." Alex shoved him against the tree again for good measure. "Just like I said, he had Ariana."

One of the other cops cuffed Flynn while the other read him his rights. Nick turned to Alex. "Where's Ariana?"

"She went over there. Zoey went after her." Alex shivered.

"I'll find them. You get to our boat. There's some blankets in there."

Alex ran over to the shore and found the boat. He climbed in and wrapped one around him, continuing to shiver. The two cops returned with Flynn and climbed in. One held onto his arm and the other pushed the boat into the water and began rowing.

"What about Ariana and Zoey?" Alex exclaimed.

"They're taking the boat Zoey brought over. Don't worry. Your daughter is safe."

Shore

~

ALEX LET GO of the blanket and jumped out of the boat. He ran over to where he'd left his clothes and fought to slide them back on.

An ambulance barreled down the dirt road, stopping behind all the police cars.

The other boat arrived, carrying Ariana, Zoey, and Nick.

Alex ran over to the boat. Nick and the other cops were helping Zoey and Ariana out. Alex wrapped his arms around Ariana, squeezing her tight. She clung to him. He would never let go of her if he had anything to say about it.

Zoey wrapped her arms around both of them.

Tears stung Alex's eyes. He couldn't hold them in. With tears streaming down his face, he kissed the top of her head.

She looked up at him, tears shining in her own eyes. "You saved me, Dad."

"Did you doubt me?" he teased.

The corners of her mouth twitched, then her expression turned serious. "I was really scared."

"So were we," Zoey said. "I've never been more scared in my life."

"Me, neither," Alex said. "*You* really scared everyone."

Her eyes widened. "I'm so sorry. I never should've talked to him."

Alex kissed her cheek. "You're back now. That's all that matters."

"Just never do that again," Zoey said.

"I promise."

Nick came over and smiled. "I hate to break up this reunion, but the medics need to check you guys out." He nodded toward the ambulance. "Also, we're going to need some statements. Unfortunately, it's going to be a little while before everyone can return home."

Alex gave Ariana another kiss. "Go with Captain Fleshman. He's the best policeman there is." Alex let go of Ariana and threw his arms around Nick. "Thank you for believing me."

Nick returned the hug. "I'm just glad everything worked out— that she's safe." He stepped back. "Once this is done, I'm flying out to see my kids." He turned to Ariana. "I've got three kids. I bet you'd make good friends with Ava. Come with me. We're going to meet the medics so they can make sure you're still healthy."

She nodded and followed him, glancing back at Alex and Zoey. Then the two of them disappeared behind the ambulance.

Alex wiped his eyes and turned to Zoey. "We make a pretty good team."

Zoey nodded. "Surprisingly, we do."

Their gaze lingered. Alex wrapped his arms around her and pressed his lips against hers. Her eyes widened, but she returned the kiss and then rested her head against his shoulder. He held her close and rubbed her back. "Our nightmare is finally over."

Reversal

〜

A LEX OPENED THE restaurant door, allowing everyone else to go in first. Ariana went in followed by Zoey, her parents, Alex's parents, Luke, Nick, Kellen, and a handful of Ariana's friends and teachers. It warmed his heart to see so many people there for her welcome back celebration.

Once they were all inside, the manager led them to the private party room. Streamers hung from the ceiling and single roses rested at each spot on the table. Alex had told them it was for the newly returned Ariana Nakano, and they had gone all out.

He turned to the manager. "Thank you. This is perfect."

She smiled. "All of it—including the meals—is on us. It's our way of saying we're glad she's back, sir."

Alex's mouth dropped. "I don't know what to say."

"Just enjoy the party. Let us know if you need anything. Servers will be in shortly." She smiled again and left the room.

Everyone began taking their seats. Ariana waved Alex over. Zoey sat on one side of her, and she pointed furiously for Alex to sit on the other. He went over, gave her a hug—he'd been giving her a lot of them the past few days—and took his seat.

Dad sat next to him and pulled out his notebook. "Have you read any of the news articles?"

Alex shook his head. "After everything that was said before, I don't care. The only thing that matters is spending time with Ariana."

"It's a good thing she likes attention," he replied. "I don't think she's had two seconds to herself."

He frowned. "I don't think she's wanted it. From what she said about her time there, she was alone most of the time."

"I think everyone has done a great job of making up for that." Dad scrolled around the screen of his tablet and handed it to Alex. "Everyone's calling you a hero."

Alex gave him a double-take. No more death threats and name calling? He skimmed over the news article, which went over some of the details of the kidnapping and rescue. Sure enough, instead of being called a stupid idiot who deserved to die, he was now being lauded as a hero who had taken down a killer.

Zoey tapped his shoulder. "How are your stitches?"

He shrugged, stretching a few muscles. "Nothing that won't heal."

Ariana beamed. "You should've seen him. He fought Lloyd like in the movies."

Alex kissed the top of her head. "I just wanted to make sure you were safe."

Kellen came over and gave Ariana a hug. "I'm so glad you're safe. Everyone was so worried about you."

She returned the embrace. "Why aren't you sitting with Mom?"

Zoey and Kellen exchanged a glance. Kellen cleared his throat. "You'll probably see less of me, sweetie, but I still care about you just as much." He glanced back at Zoey. "We just decided that getting married isn't the best thing for us."

Ariana pouted. "I'm going to miss you."

"I'll come see you anytime you want, kiddo. Just send me a text, okay?"

Her face lit up. "Really?"

"Of course. Just because your mom and I aren't getting married doesn't mean we can't be friends." He gave her a hug and took his seat next to Emily's dad.

Maybe Golden Boy really wasn't so bad. Alex picked up the menu and glanced around. His appetite had doubled since Ariana's return. Probably because he'd hardly eaten while she was gone.

The door to the private room opened, and along with it came the smells of delicious food. Three servers came in, carrying trays of appetizers. They set them on the connected tables and took orders for drinks.

It was tempting to order a beer, but he ordered some sweetened tea instead. He wanted to live healthier for Ariana.

Alex's phone rang. It was Darren. Alex answered out of curiosity.

"Hey, boss. Am I late for work?"

"Funny. No, I'm calling to say I'm really happy your daughter's back."

"Thanks. So am I."

"I'm also calling to offer you your job back, and to apologize for the way I handled the threat. I shouldn't have fired you."

Of course he wanted Alex back. Now that Alex was a hero, at least according to the media. "No, thanks. I'm going to be staying here." He smiled at Ariana, who was pulling stringy cheese out of a cheese stick and giggling.

"Well, if you change your mind, it's always here."

"Maybe I'll stop in and say hi to everyone when I clear out my apartment. My rent's almost due, and I have to get my things."

"Give me a heads up, and I'll order some foot-long subs. We'll send you off properly."

A going away party after being fired for possession of pot? "Sure. How about Tuesday around noon?"

"Tuesday at noon?" Darren asked. "Got it on the calendar. Well, if you ever need a reference, I'll give you a glowing one. You've been one of my best guys for a long time."

"Thanks, but I'm working for family—at least for a while."

Dad claimed to need another assistant, so Alex agreed to help. He'd see if Dad really needed the help or if he was going to give him busy work to keep him home.

Alex said goodbye to Darren and reached for a cheese stick. He bit down and pulled, making the cheese stretch twice as long as Ariana's. She burst into laughter and tried to outdo him.

Zoey shook her head at them, but she had a grin on her face.

Luke came over, holding his phone. "Hey, Ariana. Macy wants to say hi from the hospital."

Ari put her cheese stick down and smiled at the screen for video chat. "Hi, Aunt Macy. I wish you could be here."

"So do I, but the good news is that I should be able to go home soon."

"Yay! Dad's moving over here, too. Did you know that?"

"That's what I heard. I can't wait to see you. Take care of Uncle Luke while he's there, okay?"

Ari giggled. "Sure."

Luke turned the screen back to himself and went back to his seat, still talking with Macy.

Alex leaned back in the chair and looked around the table. Everyone was so happy, but he was sure he was the happiest of them all.

Watching

~

THE MAN SAT in the back of the courtroom, shaking his head at the scene before him. His twin brother told the stories of their childhood, stories colored by his own grief and mental illness. He had been forever trapped in them, trying year after year to return everything to the way it had been before their younger sister had died and the family began the downward spiral from which they would never recover.

Their mom had killed herself in the nuthouse and their dad had sent himself to an early grave thanks to the alcohol. Not that Flynn minded—not after his father, his own flesh and blood, had kicked him out of the house before he was old enough to drive, just because he liked to have a good time. He should have sent Lloyd away, too, but he had always been the perfect one, the better one.

His goody-two-shoes twin was the one the who could've prevented Jan's death. He was the one who'd helped her sneak out that Halloween so many years ago. It wasn't Flynn's fault she had found him and his friends. They hadn't even known she'd hidden herself in that little boat.

Flynn and his friends had gotten drunk and high, then started a fistfight. The boat had flipped over. If Flynn would have known that Jan was in there, he'd have risked his own life to save her. But he didn't know until it was too late.

Lloyd stood at the edge of the lake, waving his arms like the ridiculous nerd he was, screaming something. Flynn had either been too high to understand or they were too far to hear. Flynn's friends started making fun of him for being related to the fool.

Flushed with humiliation, Flynn had stormed off into the little island, unaware of his sister fighting for her life only feet away.

It was a decision he would live to regret every single day of his life. Not only because sweet Jan didn't deserve to die like that—alone and scared—but also because of what Lloyd did with his own grief. The lunatic had relived the nightmare every year since, putting a new girl in Jan's place.

Finally, it had caught up with him. He probably would have continued getting away with it, but he'd dragged Flynn into it. Flynn had told Lloyd to stop killing girls as soon as he'd found out about his sick exploits years earlier, but Lloyd had threatened to turn Flynn in for his part in Jan's death. He doubted he'd be held responsible legally, but he never wanted to find out.

Then this last time, Lloyd had been careless. He'd been seen, and then the girl's dad had pegged Flynn. And why not? Despite Flynn's identity change, he and Lloyd were still mirror images of each other.

And now Lloyd had taken Flynn's long-standing identity. It was Flynn Myer on the stand for the murder of all those girls, not Lloyd Vassman. Not even Flynn Vassman, but the good name Flynn had worked so hard for. The rock solid alibi hadn't even helped—Lloyd had been caught with the girl and pretended to be Flynn. The fact that the cops couldn't explain the video didn't keep them from prosecuting him.

Luckily, Flynn was resourceful and smart. He already had a new identity and a new look. He surreptitiously checked his hair piece, making sure it was in place. His new brown, wavy hair was just right. His darkened skin was starting to fade, though. It was a good thing he had an appointment for another spray the next day. That reminded him, he needed to order more blue contacts.

The judge's gavel sounded, reminding Flynn why he was there. He made eye contact with Lloyd. Flynn narrowed his eyes, reminding his brother not to tell anyone about him. Flynn had long ago warned his brother that if his antics got too close, Flynn wouldn't hesitate to take him down. And it had finally happened.

The day Alex Mercer had confronted him in the grocery store, Flynn knew it was time he put a stop to his brother's sadistic hobby. He let Lloyd know what was going to happen, and then he started messing with Alex Mercer. Planting the pot had been a little tricky, but not too difficult. Sending the texts had actually been fun.

First, he'd found a file he and a friend had created so he could spy on his wife, who he was certain had been cheating. Flynn sent the file to Alex as a text attachment from a dummy email address. Alex had stupidly opened it, and it had given him full access to all of Alex's emails and texts.

Taking the picture of Lloyd and Ariana by the boat had been a nice added touch. It helped them to catch Lloyd, and even better, one girl's life had been saved.

The one thing he hadn't anticipated, though, was the cops coming to his house, not once, but twice. Flynn had nearly gotten himself in trouble when they'd seen the upstairs—one of Lloyd's many replications of their old house. Flynn had been stupid to allow Lloyd to use his attic one year. He'd been even more stupid not to get rid of the evidence, but part of him liked wandering the attic, remembering better times.

In the end, though, leaving it there had worked in his favor. It was covered in Lloyd's prints. Flynn had been careful never to touch anything, ever. He just kicked up some dust now and then as he walked over the shag carpeting.

Flynn's phone buzzed in his pocket. It was his new boss. He'd lied and said he was on jury duty so he could get out of work. Flynn ignored the call and listened to the prosecuting attorney question Lloyd.

It was fun to watch his twin squirm. He almost felt bad for the guy. Almost. It didn't matter what Lloyd said, with all the evidence against him—thirty years' worth—there was no doubt in his mind that his twin would never again taste freedom. The whole world wanted to see him pay.

Flynn pulled out his new driver's license. Hopefully, this would be his last name change. It would certainly be the last time anyone would ever be able to find a connection between him and his psycho brother Lloyd—unless the police decided to look deeper into the unexplained airtight alibi.

**If you enjoyed *Girl in Trouble*,
you'll love the Gone saga,
where it all began!**

The Gone Trilogy
A *USA Today* bestselling title

One poor decision will haunt her forever.

Macy Mercer only wants a little independence. Eager to prove herself grown up, she goes to a dark, secluded park. She's supposed to meet the boy of her dreams who she met online. But the cute fifteen year old was a fantasy, his pictures fake. She finds herself face to face with Chester Woodran, a man capable of murder.

Distraught over his own missing daughter, Chester insists that Macy replace his lost girl. He locks Macy up, withholds food, and roughs her up, demanding that she call him dad. Under duress from his constant threats and mind games, her hold on reality starts to slip. Clinging to her memories is the only way of holding onto her true identity, not believing that she is Chester's daughter. Otherwise she may never see her family again.

Dean's List

A *USA Today* bestselling title

Every marriage has secrets. Some are deadly.

Lydia Harris knows her marriage to Dean has problems, but when she finds a box of news clippings he took great pains to conceal, the problems go from disappointing to dangerous. Nation-wide murders... in cities where he has traveled. She doesn't want to believe him capable of such violence, so she searches for clues to explain the hidden clippings.

As the evidence begins to mount, Lydia is torn. Dean seems to be trying to rekindle their lost spark, and she yearns for what they'd once had. But can she look past her own feelings to uncover the truth, or will she be next on his list?

No Return

Family comes first. Until it kills you...

Rusty Caldwell is a lonely victim of tragedy. After losing his wife and kids to a drunk driver, he spends most nights towing drunks to keep them off the streets. His one-track existence takes a turn when he finds out his estranged sister Mandy has committed suicide.

After flying out to offer his support, Rusty learns there's much more to the story. It turns out his sister had been cheating on her husband Chris with Travis Calloway, the rich CEO of the biggest company in town. Before Mandy died, she claimed that Travis fathered one of her children and demanded that he pay up...

Rusty and Mandy's neighbor Laura look into Travis, only to receive death threats for their troubles. With Travis and Chris both looking guilty, Rusty better find out the truth before he's the next one to fall.

Other Story Worlds by Stacy Claflin

Stacy is a multi-genre author. If you enjoy romance—either paranormal or sweet contemporary—you're sure to find something you like!

Visit StacyClaflin.com for more details.

Author's Note

Thanks so much for reading *Girl in Trouble*. This story has been a long time in the making—I know many of you have been waiting! I appreciate your patience because I really wanted to make it as best as it could be. I've gotten advice from a police detective and this book has gone through more drafts than any other I've written to date!

As you may know, this book was born from my Gone Trilogy which takes place when Macy was kidnapped. Her kid brother Alex was always one of my favorite characters. He grew on me more and more with each passing book, and I always thought it would be fun to write a book with him front and center. Now he's getting his own series! That's right—keep your eyes open for more Alex Mercer books. Luke will be a prominent character in at least one—I've gotten a lot of requests for more of him.

Not all of the Alex Mercer books will involve kidnappings, but there will always be a perilous situation and some characters you've grown to love—along with some new ones. If you have any requests, feel free to drop me a note! Either reply to one of my newsletters or use the contact form on my website. I'd love to hear from you.

If you enjoyed *Girl in Trouble*, please consider leaving a review wherever you purchased it. Not only will your review help me to better understand what you like—so I can give you more of it!—but it will also help other readers find my work. Reviews can be short—just share your honest thoughts. That's it.

Want to know when I have a new release? Sign up here (stacyclaflin.com/newsletter) for new release updates. You'll even some free ebooks!

I've spent many hours writing, re-writing, and editing this work. I even put together a team who helped with the editing process. As it is impossible to find every single error, if you find any, please contact me through my website and let me know. Then I can fix them for future editions.

Thank you for your support!

~Stacy